PRAISE FOR
The Immortal Part

"Though some lies are unethical and destructive, others are an essential element of everyday diplomacy. But what if one lie leads to another, and one little accident to another, and soon enough the whole house of cards—your career, your personal life—comes tumbling down? Such a horrifying predicament is the engine that powers *The Immortal Part*. This is a thriller, all right. But one with a subplot that makes for intriguing psychological ambiguity. . . . Wakling's story manages to be both fast-paced and nuanced. A suspenseful, morally astute novel."   —*Newsday*

"[A] pulsing debut thriller about a single act of carelessness that begins the abrupt spiral of a bright young London lawyer. A nightmarish scenario unfolds. . . . Like the best espionage thrillers, Wakling's taut debut is a study of human foibles, with a vivid and all too fallible hero at its center."   —*Publishers Weekly*

"One of the year's key debuts. Subtle and intense—sucks you in like a dream and holds you like a nightmare."
—Lee Child, author of *The Killing Floor*

"An accomplished and page-turning thriller. A smart novel about identity, with a protagonist largely in flight from himself."
—*The Guardian*

"Cryptic e-mails, stolen files, car chases, shifty Ukranian metallurgists, disaffected lawyers, and mysterious sexual adventuresses . . . redeemed by Wakling's cinematic prose."   —*Radar*

"A genuinely disturbing psychological thriller."   —*FHM*

"Wakling knows how to turn a phrase. . . . This is a compulsively readable tale."   —*Booklist*

BENEATH THE DIAMOND SKY

CHRISTOPHER WAKLING

RIVERHEAD BOOKS

NEW YORK

THE BERKLEY PUBLISHING GROUP
Published by the Penguin Group
Penguin Group (USA) Inc.
375 Hudson Street, New York, New York 10014, USA
Penguin Group (Canada), 10 Alcorn Avenue, Toronto, Ontario M4V 3B2, Canada
(a division of Pearson Penguin Canada Inc.)
Penguin Books Ltd., 80 Strand, London WC2R 0RL, England
Penguin Group Ireland, 25 St. Stephen's Green, Dublin 2, Ireland (a division of Penguin Books Ltd.)
Penguin Group (Australia), 250 Camberwell Road, Camberwell, Victoria 3124, Australia
(a division of Pearson Australia Group Pty. Ltd.)
Penguin Books India Pvt. Ltd., 11 Community Centre, Panchsheel Park, New Delhi—110 017, India
Penguin Group (NZ), cnr Airborne and Rosedale Roads, Albany, Aukland 1310, New Zealand
(a division of Pearson New Zealand Ltd.)
Penguin Books (South Africa) (Pty.) Ltd., 24 Sturdee Avenue, Rosebank, Johannesburg 2196,
South Africa

Penguin Books Ltd., Registered Offices: 80 Strand, London WC2R 0RL, England

This is a work of fiction. Names, characters, places, and incidents either are the product of the author's imagination or are used fictitiously, and any resemblance to actual persons, living or dead, business establishments, events, or locales is entirely coincidental.

PRINTING HISTORY
First Riverhead trade paperback edition: August 2005

Library of Congress Cataloging-in-Publication Data

Wakling, Christopher, date.
    Beneath the diamond sky / Christopher Wakling—1st Riverhead trade pbk. ed.
        p. cm.
    ISBN 1-59448-104-0
        1. British—Himalaya Mountains—Fiction. 2. Islamic fundamentalism—Fiction.
    3. Himalaya Mountains—Fiction. 4. Kidnapping victims—Fiction. 5. Mountaineering—Fiction.
    6. Backpacking—Fiction. 7. Hostages—Fiction. I. Title

    PR6123.A38B46 2005
    813'.6—dc22   2004061479

PRINTED IN THE UNITED STATES OF AMERICA

10 9 8 7 6 5 4 3 2 1

For my father

PROLOGUE

"No turning back."

The wingtip bounced as Kate's instructor slammed the cockpit door. But his hand was steady, pressed against the window. Pink palm, white fingertips, spread across the glass. The hand left a print which faded slowly.

"Have fun."

He retreated to the clubhouse, framed in the side window. The space he'd left in the cockpit yawned wider with each step.

She checked her watch. This wasn't scheduled. The lesson had finished. One minute they were taxiing along the gravel strip to park up, a heaviness already setting into her arms and legs; the next he had told her to stop short.

"You're too dangerous to fly with, so I'm getting out. Practice on your own." He smiled and squeezed her shoulder. "I haven't touched the controls all morning. You're ready."

For a second, two, three, Kate hesitated. But he'd spelled it out:

no turning back. With the engine idling the propeller was still running. The longer she sat stationary on the gravel, the greater the risk a stone might fly up and chip the blade. She eased the plane forward, up onto the holding apron.

Once there, the routine took over. It was reassuring to run through the series of instrument checks and test the controls. The sequence had its own inevitability. Kate's voice, out loud, drowned her doubts with comforting jargon.

But when she glanced again through the cockpit side-window the truth stood in the shadow under her wing, cast by the low sun. The distorted shape of the little Cessna stretched across the blacktop and up onto the grass, a darkness cut out of the flaring dew. On the ground. This routine led elsewhere. She was test-ing magnetos, making a radio call, searching the massive, final-approach sky with automatic eyes. If she didn't stop now, that would be where she would end up.

Again Kate checked her watch—8:06. Ethan wouldn't yet be out of bed; Rachel would be in a tube carriage, on her way to work. She'd made the radio call now, spread her intentions across the sky. Her toes came away from the brakes, dropped to rest on the rudder pedals.

Without an instructor beside her the plane felt lighter. It bounced from the run-up bay to the head of the runway, a strip of ragged edged asphalt, and turned across the threshold in a mea-sured arc, onto the topmost tip of the centerline. The cockpit seemed suddenly hot. A decision was happening at a distance: obligation fighting dread. The runway stretched away before her, wire-tight to a dot. Above, cloudless, cerulean emptiness.

But that had nothing to do with anything, because one of the cardinal rules was not to loiter on the runway. Three seconds, two seconds, one last pause. She reached for the throttle and pushed it forward.

"One thousand, two thousand, three . . ." Her voice echoed in her headset over the whine of the engine. White lines sucked backward beneath the nose. Again the routine took over. She gave herself to the components of control, kept the rushing lines central with her feet, checked instruments in the green, watched the airspeed increasing from fifty to fifty-five, to sixty knots.

Takeoff speed.

There were precious seconds yet in which to stop. But her right hand collapsed all choice. It pulled back on the column, and the tarmac was no longer a sensation through her bucket seat. The feeling had gone because the white lines were dropping away, just as the nose was rising over the scrubby trees at the end of the runway, which was coming faster now: another irrelevance, since she was falling upward above it, flying.

The static in her headphones swelled to the sound of each breath. She leveled the wings and whispered the words.

"No turning back."

ONE

———✦———

ETHAN STARED OUT along the massive wing's trailing edge. It sliced a dawn cityscape as the jumbo banked, bisecting a road, a railway line, a perimeter fence, and finally a blur of scrub as the undercarriage thumped into concrete. The seat-back tray flopped into his lap. Then a roar of engines bit the air backward, leaving him pleasantly light in his seat. And finally the sag of slowing past terminal buildings and tail planes, fuel trucks, and a stumpy water tower.

"Check this out."

"What?"

Kate had given him the window seat. He leaned backward and pointed through the porthole.

"People squatting everywhere."

She craned forward beside him. Dirt-gray grass ran the length of the runway. It was studded with men, sitting on their haunches.

The plane was at walking pace now. A group of three figures rolled backward with the strip, thin arms thrust out across the tops of bony knees, counterbalanced. They didn't look up.

"Pretty relaxed," continued Ethan.

"What do you think they're doing?"

"How should I know?"

"Well, they've got to be there for a reason. Baggage handling. Grass cutters. Something."

He shrugged. "It looked to me like they were on for doing nothing at all."

Inside, the terminal was rush-hour full, and yet nobody appeared to be on their way anywhere. They waited. At his elbow in the queue, Kate took out a pad and began making notes. Ethan smiled. "Surely not, already."

She ignored him and finished her sentence. When he leaned over to see what she had written she angled the page away. He put on his Walkman and retreated behind its soundtrack. Eventually she swapped the pad for a guidebook and held it open. He waited for the song to finish before turning the volume down.

"Go on then."

"Don't you want to look?"

He ran a hand across the sharpness of his newly shorn head, then held it palm up.

"This is what it's all about." She smiled. "Planning routes, working out which way to go."

He allowed his pause to extend before breathing, "What are the choices?" Then, more kindly, "Show me. I bet you've got it all sewn up."

.   .   .

THEY STEPPED FORWARD into a flurry of taxi and auto-rickshaw drivers. Although it was still early, a stupefying heat pressed through the open doors of the terminal building. Ethan's back was instantly wet beneath his pack. The clamor of "Where to, sir?" was a wall.

"What's the address again then?" Ethan asked Kate. The drivers seemed to assume he'd be giving the order.

"I know where we're going."

"Well, tell one of them and let's get out of here."

"We're taking a bus."

The porters, horns, taxi touts, and fumes rose around them. "Why?"

"I don't want to be ripped off. We've only just landed."

An airport bus rolled past as they stood arguing on the pavement. Its open door was solid with backs. Kate strode after it. Ethan stayed put. He hefted his pack to the floor and sat down on it. Immediately, four prospective drivers were squatting beside him. "Where to? Delhi center? Paharganj? Going where? Sir?" One of them had a growth the size and color of a walnut on his upper lip. If he could have remembered the name of the place he would have struck a deal, just to get out of the heat, but Kate appeared over the nearest man's head.

"I know where to wait. The bus costs a *tenth* of what these guys will charge."

A collective outburst: "No way! Good price! I take you! How much?"

Rather than force the issue he stood into the straps of his rucksack and set off. A head taller than the rest of the population, he weaved to the bus stop, following Kate's freckled shoulders. This was backpacking, this was a holiday. No point in an argument. It wasn't as if it mattered.

THE BUS SET THEM down at the intersection of two alleyways. Black lines everywhere, a mesh across the sky. It would be impossible, Ethan decided, to trace any one of the wires, either back to its source or forward to its destination. He followed the nearest shopface down to street level, where it ended in a pile of shattered fruit crates. An elderly man lay across the heap, a hand flung out into the dirt, snoring.

Kate was struggling back to him, pink-faced, through the throng.

"The guidebook's shite!" She held it out. Touts fell away as she arrived.

"Face it, prices go up. Let's just choose somewhere, shall we?" He pulled a shirtsleeve across his wet forehead. "Come on. Where's near?"

She made the mistake of reading the words "Hotel Bright" out loud. The nearest tout exploded in Ethan's ear: "No good! Shut! No air-con. My hotel, short taxi! Come on, sir!"

"It's this way, back toward the railway station."

They set off back through the Main Bazaar, sidestepping carts, children, a fallen heap of bicycle wheels, an auto-rickshaw in reverse. Kate's fair shoulders had already come out in a rash. Sweat quickened from Ethan's temples, bloomed across the front of his shirt. The fifty yards they backtracked were a mile.

"Look, phone calls." She pointed into the darkness of a shopfront.

"You what?"

"The sign says international calls. I want to let them know we've arrived."

"We haven't got anywhere yet. The hotel will have a phone. Surely it can wait?"

The sense in this prevailed, but something else had caught Kate's eye.

"Fine, but I want to buy a newspaper."

A cow nosed between them, then swayed into the path of a cyclist, whose back wheel rose. The animal swung toward the nearest shade. Dropping her bag at Ethan's feet, Kate strode off again.

He shook his head and watched her go, felt the familiar attrition of affection and irritation with each purposeful flick of her heels. The cow was head down in among a pile of black vegetables. As he watched, it let loose a rope of piss. The place had a rotten, curdled smell. They should have gone to Nepal instead. The sooner out of here, the better.

"Nice room. Air-con. Breakfast inc."

Back at his side, Kate was saying, "They're out of English-language papers." The cow now looked over its shoulder, calmly chewing through a page of newsprint. The damp ground beneath it seemed to be steaming. Ethan began to laugh.

THEY FOUGHT THROUGH TOUTS to the guesthouse foyer. Once inside, the familiarity of backpacker-land was comforting. They waited in reception while the attendant argued with a tall figure in cotton trousers, whose head shook with the words, "No way. I'm checking out. I've paid. One night!"

"Eleven thirty sir. You arrived yesterday."

"Yes, exactly. *One* night. I'm gone, out of here. Now give me my passport!"

"It says on sign sir: eleven o'clock."

"What sign?"

The hotelier leaned forward across the counter and, without looking, pointed up above the hatch, repeating "Eleven o'clock."

"Well, fuck that. Thirty minutes! I am not paying." The man had an accent, but his English was fluent. "Give me my passport!"

The receptionist moved back from the counter, his head wobbling apologies. "Not up to me sir. Checkout by eleven."

Ethan, grinning, slumped on the top of his rucksack, waiting to see how this would play out. Kate tapped a foot.

The complainant tried another tack. "Tell you what. I'll pay for thirty minutes. One forty-eighth of the price of one night." He dug some coins from a pocket.

"No sir. Full price." The receptionist, taking a step forward, wagged a finger on a level with his thin mustache. "Read the sign."

He'd strayed within range. The tall figure suddenly had the receptionist by the collar, was dragging him up onto the counter, grabbing at the hand in which his passport was still tightly gripped. Once he had hold of that hand he twisted it sharply. The receptionist yelped. The passport flipped into the space between Ethan and Kate. Ethan leaned forward, picked it up, held it out.

"Thank you." With apparent calm the man turned back to the receptionist, picked up his bag, and flung the handful of coins at him. "Swindler," he said, on his way out the door.

Kate muttered something after him, then moved to the

counter, behind which the receptionist was straightening papers, tucking in his shirt. She paid for an en suite, air-conditioned room unseen. Ethan smiled at this, her apology on behalf of travelers worldwide.

Together they struggled to the top floor of the building, down a long corridor, into the windowless furnace of their room. From a ratty film poster a life-size Bollywood star grinned smugly at the rickety iron bed, the mattress stained with subcontinents.

Ethan collapsed onto it. Kate sat down beside him. The "air-conditioning unit"—a box full of damp straw with a fan embedded in one side—stood in one corner. In the other, the en suite bathroom was a sodden plaster cubicle with a hole in the floor and a rusty tap at head height. He watched Kate take these details in, reached to stroke the back of her neck as she fought the room into a positive light.

"Excellent." She paused, then: "We're here."

TWO

———◆———

KATE RECALLED TWO TRIANGLES, of sunlight and of shadow, locked in competition on a manicured lawn. The group standing in the brightness were a Brideshead pastiche. And on the other, purple side of the lawn, a knot of boys were kicking a ball to one another. There were blazers; one of the girls was wearing a hat. Not a picnic, but a garden party. Somebody flipped a switch and the sound of a string quartet threaded through the small talk.

Turning to go, she saw her sister, Rachel, before her in the passageway.

"Bo Peep! You made it!"

"I was on my way, in fact. Just off."

"What do you mean? I said be here for five and it's five now and that means you'll have just got here."

"Yeah, well. Not my scene really, is it?"

Rachel laughed. "Aren't journalists supposed to be investigative? Can't you just hang out and take notes?"

"I can pretty much guess."

"Now that's a cop-out!" Rachel was carrying a Fendi handbag, and wearing lipstick and a fake tan. Her eyes burned despite the makeup, already wired. "Besides. These are what pass for my friends. You might as well meet one or two."

Kate allowed herself to be steered toward the melee. Rachel's mouth was working as their footsteps became inaudible, moving from stone to grass, but Kate wasn't listening. Why she had fallen for the invitation was no longer important: now it was a matter of not being cowed. She steeled herself as Rachel propelled her into a group of boys, saying, "Guys, you've just got to meet my little sister."

Heads nodded; she registered a battlefield of acne, a wet-lipped grin, an outstretched hand. The quartet cut out; Kylie began to bounce off the stone walls. One face had not looked her way. Kate saw it come up from inspecting the ground to scan the space above the group indifferently. Calm blue eyes blinked once, slowly, then dropped to appraise Kate. She stood before their gaze, affronted yet flattered, coloring. Rachel was describing Kate to the others, an estate agent talking up a dud property, and one of them was handing her a beaker of warm Pimm's, but the figure had turned and begun to walk away. Before she could check herself the words fell out: "Who was that?"

Rachel breathed out smoke through a knife-cut smile. Deliberately, as if Kate were hard of hearing, she said, "Ethan Hughes. Not your type." Then, with forced jocularity, "Or so I should have thought."

The conversation ricocheted away. Kate felt leaden, a stone dropped into a stagnant pond. The walls of the courtyard seemed to grow about her. She looked up at the nearest: arches, ivy, battlements. In the middle of it, a sundial. She stared at the shape, trying to work out the time from the faded digits and single shadow, then checked her watch to see if the thing was accurate. Catching herself at it, she lifted her face to the sky, drank in the emptiness there, respite from the cloister.

"On me head."

Something cut the space above her. Kate followed its arc down to the upturned face of a boy in a sports jacket and jeans, a can of lager held out at his side. The ball punched into his grin, which vanished. People laughed. The ball bounced off a wall and came to rest at Ethan's feet. He put a foot on top of it, rolled it backward onto his toe, flicked it up to a waist height. Although he held a glass in each hand, he kneed the ball once upward, then punted it. The ball was still going up when it cleared the crenulations at the far side of the quad. By then, he had already turned his back on its course.

A voice groaned. Someone else was clapping slowly. Piano music overran Kylie. But Kate's immediate concern was that Ethan was walking straight at her, and she was on the edge of Rachel's group but not in it, unattended.

"Halftime."

"I'm sorry?"

"You've finished your fruit salad." He looked at Kate's plastic glass, in which a debris of rind and pith sat above the low-tide line. "And anyway, you shouldn't have to drink out of that, not if you're a guest."

"I was fine with it." All of a sudden the beaker's lack of sophistication appealed.

Ethan shrugged, withdrew the offered glass. His eyes dropped from Kate's face to her chest, waist, feet, then rose, looking her over unself-consciously again. She stood spot-welded, staring at the emblem on his T-shirt: the Coke logo in Cyrillic. The silence connecting them grew. She could snap its thread by walking away, but felt compelled not to. Rachel had riled her and, regardless, there was something captivating in the boy's gaze. It managed to be both intense and detached at the same time. Alternative sentences came to mind, each more idiotically bland than its predecessor. But the silence was over her defenses, eroding good sense, and before she could stop herself, "So, do you, like, play football, or something?" was out.

"No. Not really."

"Either you do or you don't, surely." He raised one of his eyebrows.

"I used to. I don't now."

"So, did you pick up an injury? What happened?" Did it matter to her?

"I just . . . stopped." He smiled, amused by the interrogation. "What about you? Football? Hockey? Darts?"

Kate allowed a smile back but said nothing. Over her shoulder, Rachel's voice in conversation: "I reckon on three years as a gimp, then whore out for an MBA, then *money*."

Both Ethan's eyebrows were raised now. He was staring from beneath them in Rachel's direction. Under his breath he whispered, to Kate, "Oh, for Christ's sake."

"What's that?"

"Listen to her."

"She's my sister." Kate felt her smile broaden.

"Makes no difference, I'm afraid." He drained the first glass and allowed it to flop forward, the stem slipping through one hundred and eighty degrees between his fingers, spilling fruit junk onto the lawn. Midway through raising the second, he thought better of it and extended the glass in Kate's direction again. Aping him casually, she emptied the detritus from her beaker onto the grass and handed it up to him. She watched as Ethan shared the contents between them, feeling oddly deferential. Their fingers touched as he gave the glass back.

Now Rachel was at Kate's side again, a hand upon her shoulder. "Making friends?" she snipped.

"Not friends, yet," said Ethan, turned still to Kate. "You've not told me who you are."

Kate's impulse was to say that he hadn't introduced himself either, but she found herself announcing her name, "Kate Cox," awkwardly, as if unused to its hard consonants.

"Good to meet you. A relief, in fact." He nodded now at Rachel, but did not pause to let her contribute, instead continuing to Kate: "What's your telephone number? We could meet up."

The ease with which he assumed her as his ally before her sister was exhilarating. While Rachel stood dumbstruck beside her, Kate took a pen from her pocket and began to write.

THREE

━━━◆◆◆━━━

BLARING HORNS AND SHOUTING. The death rattle of a thousand exhausts. Bicycle bells and jackhammers and motorbikes and more horns on top of horns.

Ethan held a flannel in one hand and a half-empty bottle of mineral water in the other. The flannel was wet through; his feet were damp in their boots. Kate's face was puce beneath a floppy hat, her eyes puffy, her back a prickly rash against the cotton of her shirt. Each patch of hard light they traversed was a quest for the next shade. The heat burned blisters in the asphalt, raised a stinging white dust, boiled the air.

An old man staggered past the doorway in which the pair were sheltering, weighing their next move. He dragged a pallet piled with bags of flour, or perhaps cement. It hurt to watch. Ethan brushed against a metal awning strut and flinched. He offered the water to Kate. She returned it after a single sip, and Ethan upended the bottle to drink the rest. Blood-warm. Tilting his head back, sweat ran into his eyes.

Kate's itinerary for the day—a trip to the tourist office on Janpath, and then out to the Red Fort—stretched ahead impossibly. Already they'd been driven into the air-conditioned foyers of two banks. Emerging from the second, a tout had scented them. He was still at their side now. Pressed shirt and trousers, smart polished loafers. His appearance irritated Ethan.

"Let me help sir."

"We don't need help, thanks," explained Kate.

"You are not understanding. It is easier with a guide." He took out a comb and rescored the sharpness of his part.

"Listen to her, will you? Piss off."

The guide's laughter was good-natured. "Very amusing, sir. But seriously, I am arranging this every day, it is my business. Where do you want to go?"

A second tout now circled. He, too, was well turned out. Apart from when he smiled, revealing the betel-nut disaster of his teeth. He edged closer. "Do not listen to him, my friend. Let me help you today. Connaught Place. Main Bazaar. Kashmir carpet."

"We're okay. Really."

Now an old lady was tugging at Ethan's free hand, holding one of hers out at chest level. Black fingers pea-rolling. A shawl, in this heat. Ethan shook her off.

"I have three stars. Am government approved."

"Quiet place to look at carpets."

"No, thanks. Go away."

"Just looking, no need for buying."

The woman had hold of Kate, pawing at her sleeve.

The first tout: "These people are a bother. Let me arrange it. I am taxi-guiding for ten years." As if to prove his worth he said something fast and incomprehensible to drive the woman back a few paces.

"Thanks, but no. No, thanks!" shouted Kate.

The woman was magicking something out of her shawl. Tout one was still smiling, shaking his head. "None of this is necessary. I am fixing it every day."

Tout two: "Tea. Or Coca-Cola. My brother makes lenga. Cotton pants. Much cooler on the legs."

The woman had her bundle out, was thrusting it past Ethan, into Kate's face. Kate slid against Ethan; he found himself holding her up. The shawl fell to the ground and the woman's bundle, which she now offered to Ethan, was moving. The second tout was laughing and Kate had doubled over Ethan's arm, wrenching him to one side.

"Baksheesh."

The baby's head, just inches from Ethan's, was entirely wrong. It had melted. One red eye stood above a single, open hole. Ethan couldn't tear his gaze away. Then his free hand grabbed the first tout's arm. "Where's this car? Show me, now!"

"Not a problem sir. This way."

The guide led them to a parked Hindustan Ambassador, rousing the fat man asleep at its wheel with a bang on the roof. He ushered them into the kiln of the passenger compartment and climbed in beside the driver.

"Starting at Red Fort today, I think, sir?"

"Whatever."

Kate, pulling herself together, said, "Yes." Ethan sensed she hadn't the energy to query the price of a guide *and* a driver.

"Can we stop to pick up a drink?" he asked. "My girlfriend isn't well." He offered the flannel to Kate, saying, "Horror show, eh?" Her rapid nod was childish and vulnerable and appealing again, their shared years plain in her upturned face. He reached an arm around her shoulders.

The car swung abruptly across the path of an auto-rickshaw, which in turn edged a cyclist to a juddering halt by the side of the street. Horns. The guide was leaning out of the open window, gesturing at a stallholder, who emptied the contents of a bottle of something orange, labeled GOLD SPOT, into a clear plastic bag. With a twist the vendor sealed the bag around a straw. He repeated the procedure. Then he put two samosas in the guide's outstretched hand, taking a note from between its fingers.

"No packaging," whispered Kate, approvingly. Ethan fought the impulse to withdraw his hand.

The samosas and drinks came at them between the seat-backs. "Here. Lunch. My name is Bulwan." The tout's part caught the sun. "Please feel free to call me Bully."

THE SANDSTONE WALLS on either side of Lahori Gate glowered, and despite the heat Ethan was impressed. Bulwan turned out to be a good guide. He steered them through the gift shops of Chatta Chowk, into Diwan-I-Aam and Diwan-I-Khas—the halls of public and private audience—describing the magnificent Peacock Throne ("having solid gold feathers") that once stood upon the pedestal there. They lingered in the shade, paused beside the fountain in the royal baths. Kate described the marble floors in her notebook. Ethan knelt to feel their coolness with a palm. Beyond the baths, Kate photographed the pearl mosque before Bulwan again propelled them into the calm of the Rang Mahal. They doubled back to view the river through the fine trellises of Khas Mahal and came to a halt there. Down by the river, kids were kicking a ball in the blinding light. Kate swayed. The sun moved in griddled lines upon her face.

"Very hot," observed Bulwan. To Ethan: "Forty degrees and up. Bad time for Delhi. Sir should be waiting for later. For the wet."

"Yeah. I agree."

"You should be going north. *Kashmir* is the place for July, not Delhi. Come back later. Agra, Varanasi, Rajasthan, Kerala. All too hot now for you. Go to the mountains."

"Different kind of heat there," said Kate. "The embassy says it's not safe."

At this Bulwan grew animated. "Propaganda! I am *from* there. My family is in tourist business for thirty years. Exactly like your Ireland. Always it is as safe as everywhere else. They say it is unsafe. Who? Travel companies from Europe who have never been. And bureaucrats. It is nonsense! Kashmir is best in July. It is *cool.* My family has a houseboat. . . ."

"Not now," said Kate.

"Soon then. Tomorrow or the day after. We have glaciers. You will see."

FOUR

ETHAN HAD SURPRISED HIMSELF by asking for Kate's number. He didn't know at first whether he had done so to gall Rachel, or because he liked Kate. Did it matter? No, a complicatedness between the two sisters pricked the skin of his indifference and that was enough. He'd see how far it went.

As they walked the canal path to the pub on their first date, though, he felt nervous. It made him slow down to look at her. Pearly skin, at odds with pale freckles. No makeup. She checked her watch with a quick, unmannered movement he found appealing; there was a firmness of purpose in the set of her jaw, undermined by the softness of her expression. Where Rachel was all poise and slenderness, her sister's beauty sat in her face. There was an arresting gravity about her, a forewarning of something larger than the combative tension between himself and Rachel. And the fact of their sisterhood was interesting. They had stopped beside an upturned pram on the towpath, with a black plastic bag tangled round its splayed wheels. He forced out the question despite this sordid backdrop.

"So how close are you to Rachel?"

"She's my sister."

"I know that, but what does it mean?"

Kate shrugged. "We don't exactly see eye to eye, if that's what you're asking."

Ethan took a breath. "Did she talk to you about me?"

Kate paused, a smile on her lips. "Should she have?"

He breathed out. "I don't suppose so, no."

"I know you're at the same college. But I didn't get the impression she knew much more than that."

"She doesn't know me, you're right. But what she thinks she knows, I don't think she much likes."

Kate's eyes stayed fixed on his. Her gaze was dauntless. He recalled her dogged allegiance to the plastic glass in the quadrangle; the way she'd copied him in emptying it on the lawn, and his throat felt dry. She looked away. The moment stretched, birdsong ringing in the pause.

"She didn't warn you off."

"No."

"You've not seen her since the garden thing? Not told her about today?"

"I have seen her."

"Well, what did she say?"

"She didn't say anything. Just wished me luck, that's all."

He ran a thumb along the line of his chin and smiled. "Well—"

Kate cut him off. "Whatever it is, forget about it. She obviously has."

"Yeah, well. All that careerist, materialistic bullshit. Curriculum vitae and Calvin Klein. Not my type of thing. She's not my type at all."

"Right. What is your type then?"

Her attempt to mock him was endearing. Had to hand it to Rachel, she showed admirable restraint. Probably expecting him to back off unbidden. She would not lower herself to interfere. Which amounted to . . . a challenge, of sorts, almost a dare. He looked down at Kate again and shrugged. "Someone more direct, I think. Less calculating."

That seemed to strike the right note. Her face rose; she smiled at him again. "I can deal with that."

"I just thought you should discount her . . . opinion, from the start."

Her smile widened, showing uneven white teeth. "The start of what?"

SHE STEERED THEM to the beer garden of a chain pub, besieged by wasps. He let her order the drinks. As she paused on the pub's doorstep he noticed that she was wearing flip-flops, and that she had delicate feet. She strode across the garden, paying no attention to the glances her way, if she was aware of them at all.

"We see most things differently, me and Rachel."

He nodded.

"It goes back to our dad, I think. He left, and she's never forgiven him."

"But you have?"

"He made one mistake. Rachel sided with our mum; I try to see both points of view."

"What kind of mistake?"

There was a pause. A wasp landed. He clipped it with his fingers and it wove angrily above their table, then returned to the rim of a spent glass and crawled inside.

"It's not important."

"No?"

"No. And neither is Rachel."

He smiled inwardly. The wasp had inched farther down the glass. In one movement he turned it over, trapping the insect. Kate stared at its buzzing. There was a natural soft line around her lips; unlike her sister, it was hard not to take her at face value. She brushed the tabletop with slender fingers. He recalled their cool touch in the garden. When she turned the glass back over to set the wasp free he had to hold himself back from reaching for her hand.

FIVE

THE MONKEY SUCKED EXPERTLY on its straw, drinking a Coke. Ethan and Kate watched it from beneath a striped awning, seated at a table on the roof of their hotel. There was a breeze this high up, but not enough to ruffle the monkey's fur. It paused from its sucking to look back at them. Ethan stared at its long tail; Kate noted the chain around its neck.

From beneath them, in the street, New Delhi clamored. But up here there was relative quiet. The city was at a comfortable distance. Other travelers at nearby tables were audible over the top of it. Kate tuned in to a particular conversation.

". . . Kashmir?"

"The guy in the room next to ours just got back from up there. Said it was the best."

"So, he . . . experienced . . . no trouble then."

"No. Had an unbelievable time. They treated him like royalty.

The two of them had a whole houseboat to themselves, just him and his girl."

"And they trekked?"

"Yeah, the works. Five days with a guide, a couple of pony guys, a cook. A hundred and fifty bucks a head. I mean, they're hurting for the business."

Kate glanced at the table. The American wore a cap with a bear's head on it. Next to him a slim girl was staring abstractedly across the rooftops. The other speaker, whose accent sounded Dutch, was young, blond, wispily goateed. He nodded in earnest at the American, who continued, "Which is why it makes sense to go now. I mean, the land of the free is the home of the handgun. Doesn't stop me from living there."

"Yes. Exactly. Last year I was in Guatemala," declared the goatee, blinking nervously. "Nobody suggests you go there either. Or Fiji."

The man in the bear cap nodded back, then looked out over the rooftops and began to whistle to himself.

Kate drummed her fingers on the tabletop. It was annoying to think of these travelers being so blasé, more irritating still to find herself caring. She allowed her nails to tap the plastic in time with the whistled tune. It wasn't a competition: she had her own reason for going, forged the previous night.

AT FOUR IN THE morning she had found herself half awake, tangled in the damp sheet with the word *trussed* hissing in her head. You couldn't trust the touts who told you where to go, because they all had their own agenda. Their brother had a . . . always. No, but at the Indian Tourist Board, the officials there were pretty straight. Proper air-conditioning. It was a municipal building, and yet it smelled of jasmine.

The hissing had become obvious: Ethan, taking another shower. The room seemed hotter at night than in the day: the sheet was oily against her skin. She joined him, picking her way through the fallout surrounding the bed. Her trainers had their tongues out, panting. Sunscreen, splayed guidebooks, flyers. The top one glowed: Kashmir's Dal Lake paradise, a real Indian treat.

Yes, but . . .

No buts. Her head had cleared as she stood beneath the tap. Kashmir wasn't the only alternative. Darjeeling would be out of the heat too, or they could go to the coast. Yet Rachel's voice echoed: *A journalist* . . . The British embassy advised against going just about everywhere. It was in their interests to do so. The local officials, however, the Indians, they knew better. And the Kashmiri touts on Paharganj were wide-eyed, desperate for business in the face of all the adverse publicity. It was about trust. The water made a veil of her hair. She leaned forward, allowing it to cool her neck. The decision made her happy, for deep down she felt obliged to go. *A journalist* . . . *investigates.*

ETHAN ROSE AND WENT to where the monkey was sitting. The animal was cross-eyed, fixated on its straw, but as he squatted before it the eyes refocused on his outstretched hand. He offered the monkey a slice of papaya, and saw the dilemma working in its face. Its pupils widened and then constricted decisively and a miniature clawed hand dropped the straw, flashed forward, scratched the papaya to the ground. The chain rippled on the ground as the monkey made off. Ethan saw a loop of it

about to close around a smart shoe, which stepped onto the roof
and away from the noose just before it shut.

"Sir!"

Looking up, Ethan saw Bulwan's flashing teeth and part. The
outstretched arms of an old friend. He appraised the guide's grin
from his haunches. Persistence personified. It was tiring just
looking at him.

"I have come to fulfill my promise to you!"

"Great." Ethan indicated their table and raised an eyebrow at
Kate as Bulwan took his seat, beaming at her.

"You have thought about it. Yes? I am arranging everything
in this trip for you, my friends. We are agreed?"

Kate knew that Ethan would follow her lead. Her watch said
8:30 exactly. The guide had promised to be here then, and it impressed her that he had turned up a minute ahead of time; it gave
her confidence in him. She was suddenly happy that the nearby
group were within earshot. They were talking about going—she
and Ethan would just go.

They haggled. Kate turned up a fresh page in her notebook and
said she wanted to go through the cost of each component of the
trip. From the auto-rickshaw to the bus to the houseboat, including meals and drinks on the way. Bulwan reeled off a price for each
and then waved a hand over Kate's scribble, addressing Ethan.

"I give you this pricing but there is no need. I am organizing a
big discount if you book everything with me. Including trekking."

Ethan shrugged, looked at Kate. But she shook her head. "You
can get us as far as Srinigar; I'll even take your houseboat rec-
ommendation, but I want to shop about for a trek, on the ground,
in Kashmir."

The monkey was sidling toward the table again now, pulling its chain into a line. The words *on the ground* rang in Ethan's head. They reminded him of his father. Pompous, pseudomilitaristic. Did she think she could fool this tout with travelspeak? He felt a fleeting urge to intervene, but looked up to see Kate smiling at the guide despite herself, and softened. In any case, Bulwan conceded the point with only minor head-wobbling. "Better price for the whole thing. All-inclusive. One fee. But my friend, if you are insisting . . ."

"Which I'm afraid I am," Kate cut in. The whistling had stopped. Glancing toward the American's table, she saw three faces looking her way.

"Then that isn't a problem. I can give you recommendations. Travel and houseboat with Bully is fine enough. I will need your passports and details for tickets."

"We'll get to that. First, the price. What sort of a deal can you do?"

Ethan fed the monkey another slice of papaya. This time the animal didn't run away, but sat beside his chair, hand-over-handing the fruit and nibbling quickly. When it bent forward Ethan noticed that a crescent of fur was missing from behind its neck, rubbed raw by the metal collar. As Kate argued over a few dollars Ethan considered the length of chain and what it would take to break it. The trouble was, it'd be hard to crack the shiny collar without snapping the monkey's neck. And if it ran off trailing the chain it would just be caught by someone else.

"Agreed?"

The change of tone was meant for him. He waited a second, still studying the problem of the chain, then nodded without looking up. "Sure."

"That is good, sir. All done." Bully took out a folded navy handkerchief and pressed it to his brow. Ethan noticed a dark triangle when he pulled it away, was pleased to see new lines in the man's ironed shirt, an imprint of the plastic chair as he stood up from it.

"Now, passports. I will make copies for ticket purposes and return with them in fifteen minutes."

Kate thought about objecting, about insisting she accompany Bulwan to the copier, but didn't. She'd just struck a deal with the man, wanted to appear trusting. Ethan pulled his passport from a back pocket, tossed it onto the table. Kate drew hers from a money belt. "Fifteen minutes."

He beamed at her. "Yes." And the smile stayed fixed as he about-turned toward the American's table, arms extended.

Kate followed the course of his crosshatched back, saw the nods of recognition, heard the "Sir! My friends!" She forced her gaze past the group, lifted it to the sky, felt the glare of the sun on her face as her hat brim rose.

"You have thought about it. You have your passports too, yes?"

The monkey, up on Bulwan's old seat, had a hand at the bottom of Ethan's bowl, but was keeping a wary eye on him all the same. Despite telling herself it made no difference, Kate found her fingernails biting the plastic again as, in the blurred periphery of her sky, the American and his two companions were handing over their documents, saying, "Sure we do . . . like we said . . . bring on the cool."

Then there was just Bulwan, striding past again, passports in one hand, swinging the other in a feint at the monkey, grinning at everyone in turn. "Shoo, shoo, shoo," he laughed at it. "Shoo!"

SIX

A CLOUD OF DUST boiled forward as the bus came to a halt, brakes shrieking. Ethan shifted uncomfortably in his vinyl seat beside her. Though now safely cradled in the lap of the valley, they were still on the outskirts of town. Kate levered her filthy window back farther, made out rooftops up ahead. Nearer by, two cars were drawn up at the side of the road, noses in the shade of a silver tree. Three men leaned on the hoods. One dropped his cigarette butt, ground it into the gravel beneath a sandal, and sprang lightly up the bus steps. He nodded at the driver, turned into the aisle, reached a stapled sheaf of papers from his back pocket, and cleared his throat.

"Some of you are getting off here. VIPs. For warm welcoming." He unfolded the pages, snapping them theatrically. "Mr. Clay, Mrs. Diane, Mr. Jan,"—he licked a finger, turned the page, continued—"Mr. Ethan and Mrs. Kate."

·   ·   ·

THE TWENTY-FOUR HOURS behind them had stretched in Kate's head to forty-eight. Her decision to take the front two seats (more leg room) won them the best view of each near miss, each rushing hairpin, each chasm unfolding bend after bend. During the night she'd watched the driver and codriver switch places at sixty miles an hour, clambering over one another, a hand each on the enormous wheel. Horns and indicators and flashing lights; the windscreen swaying with crucifixes and beads, ropes of bunting. A foot-tall brass elephant, planted on the dashboard, stared back at her throughout. Six frantic, waving arms. It was silhouetted by oncoming trucks as, plowing through the blackness, they in turn scattered ox-drawn carts, cyclists, rickshaws, and minibuses to the graveled shoulders of the road.

As soon as the bus picked up speed on the outskirts of Delhi, Kate had felt a sickening erosion of control. She sat acutely awake throughout the night, staring at the back of the driver's head, willing herself into it, straining to participate in each rushing decision. Had he been trained properly? How many hours could he safely drive without stopping? When was the bus last serviced? She imagined bald tires, shot suspension, a chassis buckling under this ridiculous load. How old was the bus? It had a snout, for Christ's sake. While Ethan somehow slept (on a pillow of rolled fleece wedged against Kate's shoulder) she counted the minute hand round her luminous watch dial, up off the great plain and into the mountains.

The trio of other Westerners troubled her. They were seated back in the middle of the bus, diluting her adventure. At two in the morning, during a rest stop, Kate found herself waiting in line for a long drop, immediately behind the slim girl. Both of them red-eyed, Kleenex in hand. Kate was annoyed by the automatic sense of allegiance she felt toward the girl. As she emerged from behind the cinder blocks the American threatened to make eye contact but Kate let her gaze wander above the corrugated roof, into the darkness.

Having prayed for the morning to come, its arrival only made matters worse. Now she could see how the road edge was unguarded for great stretches, often on the most dangerous corners. Eagles wheeled at eye level, a mile above the bottom of the canyon. They rounded a switchback, blared horns at an oncoming military convoy, swerved gamely out of its path. The edge of the bus leaned into nothingness, and Kate made out, next to the flashing river down below, the upturned wheels of another wrecked truck. It was tiny, as if seen from a banking cockpit, there for an instant and then gone as they lurched the other way.

There were signs at intervals along the roadside, many of them in English. Aphorisms: IT IS BETTER TO BE THIRTY MINUTES LATE IN THIS LIFE THAN THIRTY YEARS EARLY IN THE NEXT. Reminders: YOUR WIFE AND CHILDREN ARE AT HOME. Even rhymes, to make the point: IT IS NOT A RACE, NOR A RALLY, DRIVE SLOW, ENJOY THE VALLEY! Ethan was awake when this last sign sped past and laughed under his breath.

And then the road straightened, and the canyon and river came up to meet it, patchwork fields of yellow and green spread out on either side. In the distance, through the haze, a wall of enormous gray-blue mountains, dwarfing those they'd come through, ranged against the skyline. The bus ran toward them with the gaining sun, only to pull up here, just short of their destination.

"Mr. Clay, Mrs. Diane, Mr. Jan, Mr. Ethan, and Mrs. Kate. VIPs, yes!"

The guy had a flip-flop up on Ethan's seat, was leaning down between them. "Passports, please."

Ethan offered up his passport. Kate asked, "Who are you?"

"Representative of tour company B&K. You are all friends of my good brother Bulwan. My name is Sunil. Which of you are *you*?" He imitated Kate's tone, smiling at her.

The American and his group were making their way down the aisle. Kate felt another stab of *we are not alone in this*, equal parts security and annoyance. The man's toenails, flexing there on the plastic seat, were black. He checked off Ethan's passport against one of the photocopies.

"Mr. Ethan! Welcome to Kashmir!"

The girl's hand passed three more booklets forward. "I'm Diane, this is Clay, this is *Yan*."

It didn't feel right. The stop was unannounced. They were supposed to be met at the bus station. But the passports, the copies, looked like something organized. And the others, Ethan included, were up and off the bus, hitching day-bags onto shoulders and identifying rucksacks passed down from the roof. The American, Clay, was inspecting a battered guitar for damage, an ironic pose Ethan was apparently prepared to forgive, for they were shaking hands, Clay laughing at Ethan's deadpan "Smooth ride." The driver, as Kate stepped forward to the steps, appeared to wink at Sunil. She looked back down the bus, registered a mass of indifference—faces gazing out of open windows, or asleep, or staring at their laps. If there had been a way of saying something Kate would have done so, but there wasn't.

As soon as she was clear of the bus it ground forward in black fumes, leaving the five Westerners and three Kashmiris in a silence. Kate knelt beside her pack, spuriously checking its pockets. Playing cards, travel alarm, tiger balm. The man with the toenails, Sunil, was over by the cars, his back to the group, talking inaudibly to the other two Kashmiris. One of them pushed himself off the hood of his car, a child down a slide. He swaggered diminutively round to the driver's door, yanked it open, spat into the dirt. The other driver was older, bearded, opening the trunk of his Ambassador, motioning to Ethan to fill it with his rucksack. Sunil, smiling, explained.

"Two of you with me and Driver Ajay, three with Driver Natraj. We are not going far to houseboats. Express route, super quick!"

One of the drivers laughed.

Sunil clapped his hands, rounding the party up. Kate looked back down the empty road. The sky above it was invincibly blue, stamping hard shadows beneath the trees, but the air was breathable and the black nylon of her pack was no longer Delhi-hot to touch. She handed the bag to Ethan, who in turn swung it into the car. Sunil threw one of the others' packs in on top, clumped the boot shut. "In you get. Quick quick." Again he clapped his hands.

Kate found herself ushered into the sagging front seat of the car driven by Natraj, who climbed up onto a cushion beside her. Ethan and Diane slid into the back. As soon as they were in, Sunil slammed the door and hit the biscuit-tin roof twice. Kate twisted in her seat as the car doglegged into the road, looking for reassurance from Ethan. She caught his eye after it had worked its way over Diane, who was staring, unconcerned, at the rushing fence posts and brilliant green. Glossy pink lips. What was she doing in their car anyway? Through the plume of dust filling the rear window, Kate could see the other one jinking along behind them. But where were they being taken? Natraj could barely see over the hula-hoop steering wheel, despite the cushion, and yet they were ripping toward the outskirts of Srinigar at his mercy. Was nobody else concerned? Kate scrutinized the driver's little face. His eyes were an unblinking squint. And his miniature knuckles, a row of children's teeth on the wheel, looked anxious.

"Where are you taking us?"

No answer. Just a gradual tightening of the squint.

"I asked a question. Where are we going?"

"I'm not sure the guy speaks English," drawled Diane.

"Where, we, going?"

Eyes still slits against the glare of the road.

"We'll find out. Relax. Look at that view." Ethan pointed at the scimitar of lake between trees. In it dove-gray unwavering mountains bit down on the sky. A stone wall rubbed the sight out. The heavy old car picked up speed even as the road narrowed between buildings. Kate felt herself pressed against the door frame, then held back by her seat belt.

"Jesus. What's the rush?"

As if in response to this, Natraj hit the brakes and the horn simultaneously, slowing to negotiate a pile of spilled cinder blocks. Kate caught sight of a group of men in long white tunics, black beards, turning to watch their progress. A slung rifle. The second car beeped as it closed in from behind. Up to their left, through a gap in the gray-stone buildings, she glimpsed a wall made out of sandbags. Then, as the car again picked up speed, they passed a jeep full of soldiers parked by the road. Behind it, a military ambulance. For an age, pockmarked walls blurring past. She had a fleeting thought about her notebook: remember these real details. Another ambulance. More sandbags. And then they were down toward the pearl lake again, continuing to skirt through fringing green, the walls and roofs receding.

Natraj let out an audible breath, then said, "BK houseboats, number one." He nodded at the road ahead and then turned to Kate, a dent at each temple deepening with his smile. "Prime situations on Nagin Lake. Mr. Sunil is saying *every* visitor top VIP."

SEVEN

KATE STOOD IN HER sister's St. John's Wood microflat, staring at a photograph in a solid silver frame. In it, Ethan, shirtless, sat next to her on a rug in a park somewhere, amid the fallout from a picnic: hummus and pitted-olive containers, empty Cava bottles, heels of posh bread. She peered closer. Muscles laddered the lean curve of his side, like a boxer, with a tan. Staring at the camera with a look of disinterest while she, on the other hand, squinted off to one side, flushed beneath a cotton hat.

The frame was pure Rachel, overdone for this snap. Its contents intended as a signal of tacit approval, never mind that she still rubbished Ethan at every opportunity. Next to the photograph stood an Andersons binder, and a Perspex block carved with thanks for a great performance, from Boeing. A corporate tombstone. Kate looked at the sorry objects, then back at the photo. Examining it more closely, she made out a trace of amusement in Ethan's lips, despite the deadpan stare. Since Rachel had

started work he referred to her as "Spreadsheet Barbie." Kate returned the picture to the shelf and smiled in satisfaction.

She tapped a foot. Rachel was audible in the other room, on
her phone. She'd answered the door wrapped in a towel, her
breath wine-sharp, the phone pressed to her ear, giving the impression she'd been on it all day. No matter what she was doing,
her sister could never resist talking to somebody else at the same
time. It wasn't a pleasant thought, but Kate suffered it anyway:
Rachel pulling away from a boyfriend midway through the act,
in Pavlovian response to her mobile.

Kate sat on the white sofa to wait, calculating how many
pounds each square foot of the flat had set Rachel back. From the
couch to the plasma-screen TV, six feet of cream Wilton. One al-
cove of, well, stuff. Galley kitchen, matchbox bathroom, and a
hall filled with entry phone. Single bedroom dwarfed by Rachel's
stainless-steel-framed double bed, opposite three precious feet of
built-in wardrobe. When she and Ethan had missed the last tube
south a month beforehand, Kate's call asking for a night's floor
space had evinced an acidic "No." Given the size of the place, she
could almost see why.

Her sister was still speaking in her bedroom. Kate stepped into
the bathroom at eighteen minutes, widened her eyes at herself,
and flared her lips in the mirror. Crooked front teeth. Opening the
bathroom cabinet, she saw a tube of toothpaste and pack of fla-
vored condoms, a forest of designer lipsticks, eyeliners and jars of
foundation and bronzers. On the shelf beneath them, assorted
pill jars. Prescription or otherwise, Rachel ran on bent fuel. One
label said VALIUM in a scratchy little font. Another, PAROXETINE
HYDROCHLORIDE. Kate felt a pang of pity: her sister's success

somehow amounted to the contents of this cabinet set in this ridiculous, overpriced flat. She turned the bottles so that their labels faced the rear of the cabinet, and shut the bathroom door firmly behind herself. Back in the lounge she lifted the sash window and stuck her head out into the communal cavity, needing air.

"Don't jump."

Turning back into the room: "You're done then."

"I'm sorry. It's tricky cramming a whole social life into these occasional weekends."

"Must take it out of you."

"Better busy than not, though."

Kate pushed the point: "No, but really, I don't know how you keep going."

Rachel shrugged, tossed her hair back.

The hair had connotations. At school Rachel had gone from fiddling with it to pulling individual strands out. Strands became tiny clumps. During her exams, a thin patch began to show pale pink at her crown. She would sweep her fringe back to mask the imperfection. Her hair was back to being thicker than Kate's now, eye-catching strawberry as compared with black, and yet the gesture remained, a distracting veil to throw in any given situation.

Rachel moved into the galley kitchen, looked at Kate across the work surface. She turned on a tap and let it run. A hollow drumming softened as the water covered the bottom of the sink.

"How are you, anyway? How's the Glencore . . . health magazine . . . writing stuff?"

"Glen*care*," said Kate, regretting immediately that she felt it necessary to correct the mistake.

"Sure." The same gesture with the hair.

"They've offered me a promotion, I—"

"Well, that's a start," she interrupted. "I just think you've got to be sure to take it in the right . . . direction."

"Leading where, exactly?"

"Anywhere, so long as it provides you with the wherewithal."

Kate shook her head. "I don't remember sponging off you."

"I never said you did."

"What were you implying then?"

Rachel continued, determinedly nonchalant. "It just baffles me. I can't believe you accept the man's money. That you still see him at all is beyond me."

"And I can't believe that you *still* hold a grudge."

"My, my." A bored sigh. "So worthy!"

The two of them stared at one another. Kate dropped her gaze, saw her sister's fingers flexing on the marble. An image, of Ethan in the photograph, passed across her mind's eye: it made her feel unaccountably magnanimous.

"Dad's helped with the flying lessons. No more. And everything he's spent on that he's put aside for you, too."

Rachel looked around the room. "I can pretty much manage without his help."

"Can't you at least give him a ch—"

"One minute." Rachel cut her off. "Bear with me, will you? I'll be right back." She picked up her phone and strode from the kitchen to the bedroom, dialing as she went. Flirtatious laughter. She drew the door shut behind her, continuing inaudibly.

To smother her anger, Kate stared sixty seconds round the dial of her watch. She stood up from the sofa. In fact, looking carefully, it was a sofa bed, which cast Rachel's earlier lack of hospitality in a meaner light. The tap was still running. Washing-up froth rolled like lava onto the work surface. She forced herself to shut the tap off on her way out the door.

EIGHT

THE TWO HOUSEBOATS were moored back to back, their rear decks a step apart. Kate and Ethan had the smaller boat to themselves. Five-Star Deluxe. The other one, more than twice its size, was only Luxury Star C Class, but since the same cook and attendants serviced both boats, and since both were furnished in the same 1930s British style, Kate felt hard done by. Even the vaunted superprivacy was a joke: when they turned in to sleep the first evening Kate lay awake annoyed by a song Clay—a music teacher ("for which read 'failed songwriter,'" as he'd explained)—was playing on his guitar. Though he was barely singing, each word was clear above the whispering of the lake:

"Now, too much of nothing
Can make a man feel ill at ease
One man's temper might rise
While another man's temper might freeze.

In the day of confession
We cannot mock a soul
Oh when there's too much of nothing,
No one has control."

She woke to near silence, though, trod barefoot to the top deck, sat down with her notebook, and wrote: *The floorboards have been polished by thousands of feet. It's all dark wood furniture and beautiful threadbare rugs. I am in the before-dawn silence. A line of inky mountains is materializing beneath the sky. It goes gray, then silver, then pink. The lake is tight and flat as cellophane, stretched out from beneath me to the other shore.* She paused, then added: *The two of us are here together.*

She sensed a presence and turned to see Sunil standing behind her. His hair was wet and combed, his cuffs neatly folded back. Perhaps he was Bulwan's brother, after all. He bore a tray, draped with a lace cloth; a silver teapot, milk jug, and pair of china cups stood upon it. She shut the notebook.

"Lake morning paradise," he said, setting the tray down.

Kate nodded.

"Since you are an early bird, I am arranging a shikara for you and Mr. Ethan, for visiting our floating market. Now. This is a very nice morning. Lilies are on sale, with vegetables. You can buy a melon."

She considered the offer, which appealed to her. Up first, away before the rest awoke. Before she'd responded, the shikara in question was gliding into view at the bow of the houseboat. It was long and thin, a cushioned seat set in the middle beneath a canvas awning. At the back end an old man in a brimless cap wove silent ripples with a wooden oar.

"Ten minutes for tea, then go," said Sunil. "Mr. Ethan must get up now. He should not be feeling too much exhaustion."

It took Ethan a quarter of an hour to heave himself through sleep to the deck, but the valley was still in purple shadow when he surfaced. He drained his cup of tepid tea in one gulp, allowed himself to be shepherded by Sunil to the steps and down into the waiting shikara.

"Mr. Gollam is our chief oarsman. Motorboat arms!" said Sunil.

The old man raised his paddle and sang: "Floating market." He drew the boat in a circle with languid strokes. More practiced tourist patter: "All aboard."

THE MARKET WAS a long, glassy paddle away. Ethan stretched out on the embroidered cushions, his feet up on the boat's wooden edge. He watched a man on the bank, dexterous with a cutthroat razor and shard of mirror. Kate took a photograph of Gollam's oar as it stirred the black water without apparently breaking its surface. She took out her notebook and wrote, *Gollam, Hobbit! Oar, water like oil,* but it gave her little satisfaction: the point was what you couldn't see. Allegiances, alliances, tensions, betrayals, that was what she should find out about. She turned from the oar to Gollam himself.

"Is life difficult in Srinigar?"

He smiled, his gray head seeming to shake and nod at the same time.

"With the troubles? Do—you—find—difficulty?"

Again the subtle equivocation of his head. He fixed his gaze somewhere over Kate's.

"Violence? Conflict?"

"Floating market, up ahead. Beautiful photography in early morning. Buying lovely souvenirs."

They crisscrossed between punts piled with pale lily roots, marrows, marigolds, and long green reeds. Every now and then a shikara drew alongside and shawls, chess sets, carved salad bowls were thrust into their laps. Kate waved them off. There were floating trays of lotus flowers, pumpkins, tomatoes, and bulrushes. The morning air was fresh as cut cucumbers, suffused with chatter and the lapping of wavelets. Kate lay back against Ethan on the upholstery, felt the warmth of his chest as it rose and fell beneath her cheek, heard and felt the beat of his heart.

Soon the sun was up and the market vendors began to float away. Ethan saw how Gollam's ears, proud of his skullcap, glowed red as he pirouetted the boat through backlit glare. Their return route to Nagin Lake was different. He took them through dark canals, beneath a splayed wooden bridge, and past dilapidated stone buildings which appeared to be sliding into the waterways. Before one such house Gollam stopped paddling. He paused for a minute, bottom jaw chewing on nothing, then pointed with an oar at the shattered façade.

"At nighttime it is very dangerous here. New bullet holes. Look! Rocket damage too. Made by bad, dangerous men." He gripped Ethan's forearm. "Your wife asks is it safe? You and she must remain with Mr. Sunil and everything will be A-OK. It is not good for you otherwise."

Ethan patted Gollam's arm in return.

"My wife and I hear where you're coming from. Rupees to Mr. Sunil only. Loyal customers of BK Travel Associates."

Back at the houseboats, the morning bled into a soporific afternoon. There was a space on the top deck of each for lounge chairs. Kate noticed Ethan notice Diane stretched out in a bikini, and was doubly annoyed by the insults of his stare and her oblivious bare flesh.

That aside, the view of the lake was breathtaking. The line of inverted mountains was rock steady in the mirror. It seemed to waver more the right way up, white-tipped in the crystal air. They ate a lunch of vegetable curry and roti in the little dining room (the May 1978 edition of *Polo International* magazine next to a selection of Agatha Christie on the carved rosewood table in the corner) and then Kate spent an hour rowing a leaky canoe up and down the edge of the lake beneath overhanging willows. Dabchicks cut across her bow, scooting over lily pads on stunted wings. She shipped her paddle and lay back, watched an electric hummingbird quivering against the greenness overhead.

One minute the tiny bird was there, in the silence, and the next it had been sucked into a sky split open. Two jets tore across the water, chasing their reflected gunmetal bellies. Kate lurched sideways in the boat, turning to watch. Like a pair of skates the planes came apart and sliced sideways, seeming to accelerate into the curve, then disappeared from view, leaving a serrated rumbling in their wake. The quiet refolded itself as she sat in a circle of fading ripples.

Later she lashed the canoe to the back of the houseboat and climbed the steps to the top deck to find the entire party assembled, drinking cocktails. Sunil poured a glass of whatever it was from the pitcher in his hand and offered it to her, saying, "Sundowner tradition, very British. We have kept the good and given you back the bad!"

Kate hesitated a second and Sunil seemed to identify her concern. "On the house. All-inclusive."

"Thank you."

"Yes, we take the best care of you." He smiled at Clay, Diane, and Jan in turn, then at Kate and Ethan, saying, "Cheers." Everybody raised their glass, except Sunil, who raised both hands instead. In the silence that followed he continued: "Now, trekking."

Kate let him explain his proposal, but her mind was already made up. It didn't matter that Sunil was offering a discount for the group, claimed his guides were "absolutely the most trustworthy on the whole face of planet earth, further even," was prepared to add an extra day and upgrade the supplies to "Luxury A Class" at no extra cost. Neither did she care that the others were content to grin and nod and sip in front of him, or even that she liked Sunil's manner, thought the deal comprehensive, was prepared in principle to undertake the trip as part of a larger group. It was about making her own decision, choosing between alternatives. Since meeting Bulwan in Delhi she'd felt as if she were on a rail. The day-and-a-half's rest on the lake, in a climate that allowed her to think, had restored a sense of what this trip was supposed to be about.

Now Clay was saying, "Can't see the point in reinventing your wheel. We're in, yeah, honey?"

Diane nodded, smiling. Her row of perfect teeth looked naked in their whiteness.

Jan asked a question about a glacier, stroked his goatee, approved demonstratively of Sunil's answer. "Me too, I am in."

Ethan nodded too, but Kate could sense him tense up as the rest of the party turned her way. She glanced down to see him resolutely staring at the sun, which, impaled on a peak, was bleeding into the lake. She pressed on.

"It does sound good, but I'd like to shop around, to make some comparisons. No offense, Sunil, but tomorrow I'll go into town and see what else is available."

Sunil scrutinized the deck, head on one side. When he looked back up at her he appeared worried and offended in equal parts. "No need. I am organizing number one trek for you. BK quality. Three pony guides. New tents. Everything will be good. Two eggs for breakfast. Fresh fruit. *Safe.*"

"I understand that, but I still want to check."

She saw Ethan's toes flex on the deck, his gaze still out across the water. There was a pause.

"I think that is fair enough," said Jan. Kate let out an appreciative breath. "We'll make sure yours is the top deal, okay?" He raised a glass. "Then everyone will be happy."

Clay shrugged and said, "Delirious." Diane, smirking, sipped her drink. Something—a kingfisher perhaps—arrowed into Ethan's red lake.

Jan repeated the word "okay?" pleased to have become a diplomat.

Kate searched Sunil's face. It was reconfiguring, nodding reasonably, a decision made: "Fine then. I understand. Mr. Gollam will take you to town for researching other trekking opportunities. Morning-time is best."

"I can catch a cab, that's fine."

Now he shook his head emphatically. "No. We look after you. Mr. Gollam is taking you, no problem. Be ready at ten a.m."

NINE

S HE SAW WIND LINES score the lake, fanning toward the shikara. Treetops bent suddenly on the distant shore, willow branches slapping the water. Gollam was swinging the boat around with strokes that broke the water. His blade caught the surface, showering Jan.

"Big problem."

"No, it doesn't matter. It will dry."

Gollam shook his head. "No, big knockdown wind, problem."

Other shikaras on the lake were making for the lee shore, as they were. When the wind hit, Gollam's oar dug stationary holes. He tweaked the nose downwind and the canvas awning immediately swelled, threatening to tip them over. Kate and Jan instinctively counterbalanced the boat. Jan smiled, rolling his eyes at Kate. "Cool," he said.

But Gollam's face was full of apparent concern. His smile had hardened to a line. With the boat at this raked angle his oar worked as a rudder. They were being blown along, but not in the direction Kate needed to go. She struggled with a doubt—was this all part of the performance?

Jan had offered to come with her, which gave Ethan the excuse not to. Sunil made a great show of sending them off with Mr. Gollam. He would look after them door to door. It was a compromise. A chaperon would perhaps get in the way, make it harder to strike a separate deal, but Sunil's resolve proved insurmountable. "We must look after you," he explained. "You are our special guests."

Though she hadn't much felt like it, Jan insisted on a conversation as they trawled across the lake. At first, watching him pick at his goatee self-consciously, she wondered whether there was an ulterior motive behind his camaraderie, but the getting-to-know-you questions remained anodyne. He had a habit of blinking and looking to one side when he spoke, endearingly underconfident despite his bravado. For form's sake, Kate asked her own questions back. Jan was a student of international development (she nodded as if in recognition) from Rotterdam, midway through a four-month trip round India.

"I fried in Rajasthan," he explained, blinking over her shoulder. "But I wanted something more extreme. Kashmir, you know, it has this forbidden aura, an edge."

She found herself smiling to close the discussion down.

And now they were tucked into the bank, miles from town, and Gollam was tying the shikara to a tree trunk, explaining, "We must wait. Last week wind knock down seven boats. It is summer wind. People were drowning. Hot wind very dangerous for shikara." He patted the awning as he sat back down.

The three of them sat in silence to wait. It was impossible to know whether the danger was real or whether he was making it up. Should she assert herself and insist they go on, or trust Gollam and wait? Kate brooded, staring at the endless reconfiguration of reflections in the surface of the water, and suffering the memory of a worse disorientation.

HER FIRST PASSENGER FLIGHT. Ethan, a few paces ahead of her, slowing as they approached the airfield. She carried on walking, clicking her pen. It was important to project absolute confidence from the outset. She came to a halt on the grass in front of the row of little planes and checked her clipboard.

"We're in UGW."

"Right." Ethan paused. "What does that mean?"

"The blue one. With the yellow stripe."

They climbed into the cockpit. She took in the frayed seat with its shot springs, the sclerosis of peeling paint around the instruments. Repeating her instructor, she dismissed these cosmetic imperfections, explaining how each aircraft was subject to rigorous mechanical testing, but Ethan was busy figuring out the complication of his harness and seemed only to notice the flaws as they were pointed out. His single comment as, finally, he tightened up the straps was "My mum had a Fiat Panda once."

Despite the cramped configuration of seats and sticks and pedals, he managed to stretch out and look somehow relaxed. So at ease, in fact, that she began to feel self-conscious as she went through the regulation warnings, explaining how he must tell her if he felt uncomfortable at any point during the flight. She lowered her sunglasses and finished up by telling him he mustn't touch the dual controls, particularly the pedals: "It's an easy mistake if you've got long legs."

"No problem." He held his hands up, as if in surrender, and jiggled his knees.

She checked the sky while taxiing to the runway threshold, noted the bank of umber cloud moving away to the west, saw the wind sock by the clubhouse flick once and then flop flat. She squared the plane up on the centerline and, in the moment before shoving in the throttle lever, checked Ethan again: he was gazing at the end of the runway, eyes apparently unfocused, as if staring from the window of a traffic-jammed bus. The only indication that he was paying attention was the sound of his voice in her headset as she throttled up: "Chocks away!"

Once they were airborne, Ethan's obliviousness started to make *her* nervous. It felt like the wind was much stronger than the forecast had predicted. What was he thinking? The most interesting terrain was down where the river flushed out into the sea; hills crumpling into clifftops, sheer above intermittent strips of yellow and blue. She headed in that direction because he would be impressed by the sight whatever. But to hold her track over the ground she had to crab sideways, meaning the windspeed was definitely up, and although the river was slackening, opening its jaws beneath them, something made her execute a precautionary turn, one hundred and eighty degrees, to scan in the direction of the airfield. Her stomach lurched. The cloudbank had, impossibly, doubled back: it was clamping down on the airfield like a garage door.

Immediately she was on the radio, trying to keep her voice steady as she spoke. Glancing sideways she saw Ethan ease the headphones away from his right ear and scratch his cheek. The first drops of rain began to marble the cockpit glass. She wasn't qualified to fly in anything less than full visibility. Surely someone should have warned her if the weather was this unstable? Although the plane was descending rapidly, from four thousand through three, two-five, two, to a thousand feet, they were making slow progress. Inching into the strong wind, the fields scrolling beneath them laboriously. Up ahead, the railway line wasn't where it should have been and the river stopped short of the hills. The familiar horizon had been stolen, and the ground seemed to be rising in her chest. She watched the altimeter as it dropped further, through seven hundred feet, knowing that the airfield had to be just there, straining to make it out over the nose.

At five hundred feet she drew blood from the inside of her cheek and simultaneously saw the road at right angles to where it should have been, as impossible as the drumming of rain in her headset. She reached for the radio volume knob to shut the noise out, but turned it the wrong way and delivered a shriek of feedback into both headsets. Ethan flinched beside her. She said, "Sorry," loading the apology with much more than she meant. This wasn't happening. She couldn't be *lost* on her first passenger trip. And yet she was on the verge of making the humiliating radio call for help, struggling for the correct euphemism—*position uncertain, temporarily disorientated, location unknown*—when miraculously, over Ethan's shoulder, she saw the wind sock and clubhouse. She was bisecting the airfield illegally, at half the circuit height, and yet still melting with relief to be above the strip and banking harder left into an unauthorized base turn. She whispered, "Thank you," into the mouthpiece, the control column shaking like a drill in her right hand and, to steady herself for landing, began to tell Ethan how, another time, he'd see what she'd meant him to: on a clear day you were above it all, you could see for miles.

He patted her knee and smiled his best thank-you back.

THE PALE REFLECTION of her face, mouth set, was there in the water beside the shikara. She looked away. The memory tasted metallic. There were other boats on the lake and although Gollam's concern to stay put still felt real, Kate was suspicious.

"Can't we take the roof off?"

He wobbled his little head. Was it a no, or equivocation?

"It's just tied on, isn't it?"

"Not only the top." Now he tapped the wooden side of the boat. "The wind is pushing everywhere."

"But what about them?" Kate pointed into the distance. "They're carrying on."

Gollam shrugged.

"Can we perhaps walk round instead?" asked Jan.

Gollam said, "Too far," prompting Jan to reminisce about his trek up Mount Kilimanjaro. It seemed to Kate that the wind had dropped, anyway. Not just in the shelter of the bank, but across the lake too.

She interrupted Jan. "We'll be late back." She tapped her watch face. "Mr. Sunil will be worried. Take the roof off and we'll be okay."

Gollam's mouth bit nothing. Yet he was untying the awning

with slow fingers. Kate helped, as did Jan, who smiled and said, "We can always swim if we fall out."

With the roof stowed, Gollam reluctantly eased them back out onto the lake. The wind had dragged up little waves, which splashed against the shikara's stern. They skidded quickly before it. Gollam worked his oar in silence, the muscles in his neck and throat stiff with concentration. The veins in the man's hands made them look suddenly old. Kate felt momentarily guilty, then bolstered herself. Having come this far in the right direction she must not give up control.

But the jetty Gollam made for, when they reached the lily-strewn town waterways, belonged to what looked like another houseboat.

"How do we get into town from here?" asked Jan.

"This is the town. For trekking. Good trekking company based here. Mr. Sunil has made you an appointment."

Jan was climbing out of the boat, but Kate put a hand on his knee. Exasperated, she pleaded, "Can't you just take us to the town, Mr. Gollam? The ordinary town?"

Gollam again bit nothing. He looked genuinely worried. "This is good company. Main town is not safe for you. Talk with this man." He nodded at the jetty. A figure had materialized on it. He wore a white tunic and had an impressive ebony beard. Before she could object, strong hands were helping Kate to her feet.

She and Jan were ushered into the main room of the houseboat. Kate noted with dismay yet more rich carvings, the same sumptuous style. This wasn't an office. These people were impossible to deal with. They were cashing in on the purported danger.

Yet Jan, who, in his board shorts, looked particularly young and oblivious before this imposing man, was accepting the offer of a cup of tea, and making a start.

"We have a quotation for trekking from BK. Mr. Sunil." He nodded at Gollam, looked back at the beard, and continued, "But we want you to quote too. To compare prices."

"Yes. That I can happily do."

Kate drew breath, but the man continued.

"First though, tell me what price you have been given. What is the deal I am to compete with?"

Jan explained. The man was pouring tea. Handing a delicate china cup deferentially to Kate, not even listening to the detail of Jan's nervous gabbling. When it was over, he left a theatrical pause, looking at them both in turn, avuncular.

"Go with Mr. Sunil," he said, stroking his beard regretfully. "I am unable to compete with such a price."

Kate laughed out loud. "Oh, come on! This is India. You expect us to believe you're not working together, in cahoots?"

The man grew before them, thrust out a tanklike chest. His voice boomed in the little room: "This is *Kashmir*." He left a pause. "Mr. Sunil is a respected businessman. His is a different company. It is a good deal. You would do well to go with him."

Now it sounded almost like a threat. Jan was looking out of the window, scratching his schoolboy chin, regretting having offered to come, no doubt. But she would work this out.

"We appreciate your advice. We're grateful. But I want to make sure we're getting the best deal. You would feel the same way in my situation." Her teacup's reflection rose to meet itself in the polished wood. Jan let out a sigh. She gripped his skinny upper arm and led him out through the houseboat, Gollam and the beard in their wake. On the jetty, she turned back.

"We'll walk into town from here, and make our own way home."

The beard shook. Gollam looked up at it, confused, something like despair expressed by his upturned palms. Words were exchanged in another language, then the man turned back inside and Gollam was trotting behind them, over the rattling planks. "Mr. Sunil said to keep with you. Please, I must follow. It is my duty to help you to get back."

TEN

DIANE LIFTED HER FOOT up onto the wicker stool and stretched forward over a long brown leg to paint her nails. A cotton sarong parted over her thigh, revealing a shard of white bikini, stark against the tan. Though it was still midafternoon, the sky, in the aftermath of the wind, was cloud-shot purple. The same color as the nail varnish. Kate enjoyed the feeling of Ethan's hand on the back of her neck as she leaned against him, but was suspicious, at the same time, of where he might be looking.

Jan was midway through his account. If he wanted to take the credit, that was fine by Kate. Leaving aside the irritation of Diane's posing, she was content. Ethan's tenderness was as comforting as his evident relief on their return, hours late, from town.

After she and Jan had left, the wind had ripped the back end of their houseboat free of its moorings. As Ethan worked with Sunil and the cook to winch it back to the bank, two shikaras, making their frantic way back across the lake, had been knocked flat by a further gust. Sunil insisted on Gollam's unparalleled oarsmanship, but ran out of words in the final hour before their return. After helping her out of the boat, Ethan had kissed Kate's brow, cupping her face with (she was almost sure of it) trembling hands.

"So when we finally get to shore it's only another houseboat, with this bearded guy that tries to tell us we already have the best deal. He didn't even want to give us his own quote. It was that lame."

Clay, uncoiling the peel of an orange with his Swiss Army knife, was smiling to himself.

"But we said no way. And to be fair to Gollam, when he saw we were serious, he gave up with their scheme. He even pointed us in the right direction, toward town, and insisted on coming along for the ride."

Kate thought Jan could have dwelled a little more on Gollam's reluctance to show them to Tourist Reception Center mentioned in the guidebook; and his apparent unwillingness to interpret her map. As it was, they stumbled upon a street full of travel agencies before they reached Residency Road anyway, and were immediately swamped by the inevitable waterfall of touts.

"Of course, as soon as we're in the town properly there's hundreds of guys more than interested. I mean, how do you say?—they were . . . *persistent?* Like flies on a shit."

Clay laughed. Ethan's chest rose and fell behind Kate's back. Diane had her head to one side, admiring the finished article.

"They were literally fighting to speak to us. It was intense!"

Diane stood and stretched up onto her toes, pushing her shoulders back and lifting her long arms above her head. Even standing, her sarong revealed thigh. When she'd done she settled herself to paint the toes of her other foot.

"Anyway, one of them had cards and a brochure and we ended up going along with him. He seemed like the best for a bet."

Kate's diary contained more detail.

The man's fat hand is clamped around my wrist, reeling me into the shop. Bales of rolled rugs and shelves sag under dusty pottery. There are jars of beads and pickled eggs and one that looks like it contains teeth. And an outbuilding smell. The crowd following us stops short of the threshold, beaten back by hard words. Even agitated Gollam doesn't make it inside.

Once we're in the shop he leaves go, all courteous. He shows us through to a windowless office. There's a Formica-topped desk, a yellowed phone, and some plastic chairs. More tea appears from somewhere. These people are above all polite. The agent gestures at a big faded map on the wall behind his desk. His eyes jump from Jan to me as he explains "off beaten track" routes and "local" prices. Jan just blinks. The tout dismisses my account of the deal we've been offered as "second-rate, tourist price, tourist destination." (Tell us something we don't know.) There are concentric tree-stump rings beneath his pointing arm, and his fingers twitch. He's that eager for our business.

"It's always the same in these countries," Jan was continuing. "I remember this one time in Laos when I . . ." Kate let the tale dissolve as he told it, stared out across the calm-again green lake, waiting for him to get back to the point.

But when Jan paused, Diane took over, reminiscing about a swindle she and Clay had avoided in Honduras, involving out-of-date currency, bus tickets, and a boy with a plastic snake. Kate

could feel Ethan's annoyance building in response to such familiar one-upmanship. His chest tightened behind her, the rhythm of
its in and out slowing. Diane, mid story, was flicking between the
faces of her audience and becoming self-conscious: only Jan was
showing overt interest and Clay was focusing intently upon his
ribbon of orange peel, evidently embarrassed. Diane swung the
second finished foot down onto the deck and cropped the end of
her story, reddening. Clay helped her out: "Go on," he encouraged
Jan. "How'd your trip to town end? Any rubber reptile action?"

Before Jan could answer, there was a commotion in one of the
wood-framed houses set back from the shore where Sunil, the
cook, and the other houseboat attendants lived with their fami-
lies. Raised voices split one another. Everyone on the boat turned
to look at the noise, through the trees. A door banged open and a
figure stumbled backward out of it, knocking over a plastic
bucket. Kate made out a whiteness of milk turning black in the
dirt. More shouting. The figure, Gollam, was pulling on his skullcap, straightening his thin frame, and wagging his head and
raised hand vehemently. And Sunil was emerging from the
house now, his long shirt agape, waving Gollam away with a dismissive, imperial flicking of his fingers. Since Gollam didn't apparently want to go away, Sunil continued his advance, backing
the oarsman down the path toward the bow of the bigger houseboat, to which his shikara was moored.

Kate stood to keep the pair in view. Sunil pushed past Gollam
and stepped down to the edge of the lake. He was still talking fast
and gesturing, oblivious to a foot that had strayed into the water,
following it with the other, even, so that he was knee deep among
the mud and reeds, the cotton of his trouser bottoms clinging to

his calves. He bent to untie the shikara. While his fingers worked at the wet rope Gollam stayed rooted on the bank, his arms crossed, still shaking his head and gabbling. Eventually Sunil freed the boat and hauled it away from the steps, straining against the rope to drag the back end round through the shallows, a reluctant dog on a leash. Only when Sunil was obviously gathering himself to shove the shikara out into the lake did the old man move, and then too late—he was forced to wade after it, flailing for the rope end, chest deep and cursing. By the time he'd pulled it to the bank Sunil was a white shirt-back between the trees. Gollam's head-shaking became rueful as he climbed into his seat at the stern. With dignified strokes, he eased the shikara back into the lake. Throughout the altercation neither of the pair looked once at the group on top of the houseboat.

There was silence, before a riff of birdsong, over which Diane said, "Somebody's got a temper." She let the "r" stretch sarcastically.

"So you've got us another deal then," said Clay.

Jan was still blinking in the direction of Gollam as he minimized into the rippled distance, and in any case Kate couldn't resist continuing. She forced herself to nod nonchalantly. "If we want it. We've got six days instead of five, for twenty-five dollars a head less. Everything included, same catering, and a route that takes in some untrodden stuff round Sonamarg. Only if you guys are interested though."

"Twenty-five bucks," breathed Diane. "I mean, you spent a day of the trip hassling for—"

Ethan cut her off: "It's a saving of a hundred and twenty-five dollars between us. Here, that's a fortune. We get an extra day, in a less visited area. You can use your saving to buy more of those carved doilies, or whatever it is they keep selling you. I'd say Kate and Jan did us a favor. And anyway, they spent a day of *their* trip hassling, not yours. You got to . . . tan."

Kate saw Diane's throat color again, and felt a surge of gratitude. When Ethan wanted, he made his opinion count; it came reinforced by his indifference to what anyone thought of him as a result. Diane sat down and drew her sarong across her legs. Ethan squeezed Kate's side gently, settling something larger than this tension.

"We each get to make our own decision." Kate spoke kindly in Diane's direction. "There are two others already signed up for the trek. If you prefer to go from here instead, that's up to you."

"No," said Clay. He'd torn his coil of orange peel into a handful of chunks, and tossed them now into the darkness of the lake. "What'd be the point in paying more for less of an experience? I'm in."

"Me too." Diane's teeth caught the light. "You're right. Twenty-five dollars a head is, well, twenty-five bucks. You guys did well."

Kate smiled at Diane's feet. Toes smooth as pebbles in a streambed. "Good then. Because they're sending a guide round to pick up whoever wants to come. A little bloke called Nabbi; he's been mountain-guiding for years. We just have to be ready to set off tomorrow morning at nine."

ELEVEN

THEY HADN'T SPOKEN with Sunil since returning from town the previous afternoon, so Kate crossed to the bank in search of him before checking out. The plank drawbridge sagged as she trod in its middle, then bounced her onto the miniature path that led through the trees. Whitewashed tire halves ran beside the gravel track, pointing the way.

Needless to say, Ethan thought she was being oversensitive. It wasn't as if they owed Sunil anything. The tip they'd agreed on was generous enough, and he'd had the benefit of their custom this far. But Kate didn't want to leave without saying good-bye to his face; it would somehow be an admission of guilt if they just melted off the houseboats in silence.

The real houses were nothing like as well built as those floating on the lake. The biggest still only had a corrugated tin roof. An awning made from joined fertilizer sacks threw a shadow over the plastic chairs and child's tractor on the dirt front yard. An open fire pit smoldered nearby. Apart from that, there was just a water butt made out of an old oil drum, positioned to catch the run off, and some earthenware jars that, presumably, were used for storing rice. Kate took in these details and reminded herself to write them down when she next had time to make some notes: *poverty*.

A noise contradicted the impression. She knocked on the door, trying to work out what it was. When it opened, there was Sunil's outline saying hello, and some children were squatting behind him in a room devoid of furniture, as far as she could see. But the noise was louder and the contradiction obvious: Ethan's Tekken soundtrack. Although the room was bare it wasn't empty; the children were in fact clustered round a PlayStation, before a widescreen TV.

Kate stopped short, suddenly unsure of what to say. Sunil lowered a bowl of cereal to his side and drew himself up expectantly. The spoon in his other hand made tiny circles in the air. There was a pause; even the Tekken seemed to stop. Then one of the children squeaked.

"Die dead, mother."

Kate smiled, but Sunil remained impassive.

"Yes?"

"We wanted to thank you, for your hospitality."

Sunil inclined his head.

"Here." She held out an envelope containing the group's tip. Sunil lifted the flap to see what was inside. His lips came apart, showing clenched teeth. A muscle tightened in his jaw. He refolded the flap and tilted his head again in what looked like gratitude. But the envelope was coming back.

"I thank you, but cannot accept. We have not looked after you so well, or you would not be leaving with others."

Kate sighed. Her upturned palms said she would not take the envelope back.

"Keep it. We've enjoyed ourselves."

"I cannot."

"Well, give it to Mr. Gollam, then. He took care of us in the big wind yester—"

"No! We do not accept it!" Sunil's eyes had grown. The envelope was up in her face, trembling. It was absurd to have a tip refused in India. The Tekken had started up again; body blows and grunting invaded the standoff. An overwhelming desire that he stop this and take the money swamped Kate. She took a step backward, retreating into the yard, beginning to turn away with her smile still fixed. "Please."

But his hand was on her shoulder. She pulled away from it, stumbling sideways over the toy tractor. Sunil paused, momentarily deferential again while she righted herself and regained her composure. Then his resolve hardened.

"I *am not accepting* this baksheesh."

The dirt patch between them grew as she retreated. Sunil waved the envelope at her once more, then tossed it into the fire pit. For a second it rested flat and white on the coals, then a red eye appeared and the envelope twisted into smoke. She looked up to protest but Sunil was already walking back inside, pulling the door shut behind himself emphatically, cutting the high kicks and body slams dead.

Technically of course, she'd handed it over. What he'd decided to do with the money was none of their business. It wasn't a lot anyway. But there was something unnerving in Sunil's about-face that Kate decided she'd rather not share. Unless anybody asked, she wouldn't relay details of the encounter. The little path of stones wound her back to the houseboats. It was all part of the experience.

TWELVE

"I LIKE YOUR SHOES."

"Excuse me?"

The rest were with them on the forecourt, busily sorting gear into two piles as instructed, stuff for taking and stuff to leave.

"You have good shoes. Very nice for trekking."

Ethan looked down at his North Face boots, then at the guide's feet, in a tidy pair of Nikes. "Well, thanks." He shrugged.

"No, it is important. Best thing to have for walking is a strong set of shoes. I hope for a tremendous pair myself, one day."

Ethan stopped packing and scratched his head. The guide was standing too close, needlessly encroaching on his space. What was he talking about? He took a step back, nonplussed. "But yours aren't bad, either."

"Too old." Nabbi twisted a foot sideways, pointed to where a crease above the sole threatened to become a tear. "They were a present. From a good friend. We walked many miles in the mountains. He was my Japanese friend and client. At the end of trekking he gave them to me."

"Ah."

"A present," Nabbi repeated, smiling.

Ethan stood up straight, six inches taller than the guide. "My feet are a bit bigger than yours though. Bad luck."

"No. Not so much bigger."

Ethan glanced about. Nobody appeared to be listening to the conversation. He placed his foot beside Nabbi's to finish it.

But Nabbi wriggled his toes, looking down at the mismatch. "These are too small anyway," he said. "My Japanese friend had little feet, like children." More toe-wriggling, a salesman's winning smile. "I need extra room for thicker socks."

Ethan sighed, turned his back on the guide, and surveyed the scene. Jan was playing Hacky Sack in the sun, but didn't seem able to manage a sequence of more than five. The contents of Diane's rucksack could never have come out of it. Everybody else had completed the sorting exercise, but she was still staring down at an apparently insoluble problem. Her makeup bag was the size of Kate's bedroll. Clay offered to help and she cut him dead. He retreated, squealing, "Well, fuck you, Cleopatra," in mock affront.

Two figures emerged from the van, speaking with the fat man Kate had apparently dealt with in town. The first was familiar, with his close-cropped dark head and angular frame. The other was swarthy enough to pass for one of the guides. But the fat organizer was introducing both, to Clay and Diane first (she could, it seemed, turn both charm and frustration on or off at will), then to Jan and Kate, Nabbi next, and finally to Ethan, who made the link as he shook the first man's hand: day one, Delhi, the argument with the checkout clerk.

"This is Ethan. Ethan, meet your fellow trekkers, Rafi and George."

No recognition in Rafi's eyes, and George was new. New and *old*. Pushing forty, at least. He had a potbelly under his T-shirt, graying hair, weak eyes behind glasses, and a soft-palmed handshake, in contrast to Rafi's eager, military grip. Ethan accommodated both, gave a nod in each direction.

The fat tout's rings flashed as he clapped. "Off we go now. Make progress."

Nabbi had already taken his position in the driver's seat. He smiled out of the window, eyes bulging, waving at everyone to climb in behind him. Ethan took his seat. Kate, who waited to see that their packs were roped down securely on the roof rack, was the last to climb in. The tout waved them off with a fixed grin.

They swung through the town, Jan, Diane, and the newcomers immediately in an itinerary-swapping conversation which compelled Ethan to stare out of the window at rushing stalls and shopfronts. A tray of baking compact discs. Birds in a wicker cage. A film poster showing two swollen men with mustaches and handguns, on either side of a rearing horse. Nabbi squirreled the minibus through a maze of little streets, weaving through cars and bicycles. He turned some music on, providing a tinny soundtrack of sitars and synthesizers and nasal voices which seemed to swerve in time with the van, as if Nabbi were driving to the beat. Then the song was suddenly out of time; they came to an abrupt halt, the van rocking back on its springs, spent.

"Jesus, look at that!"

Ethan leaned across Kate, following the line of her finger as it jabbed against the window.

"Angry men," said Nabbi.

"Ohmigod!" yelped Diane.

Nabbi struggled for reverse, crashing the gears, an elbow over his headrest. Ethan stretched further to see what they were talking about. Kate began fumbling in her day-bag. Men in uniform were dragging something across the pavement. Ethan saw the form jerk but his view was, infuriatingly, blocked by Kate's arm as it came up with her camera.

"No, no, no!" sang Nabbi.

"What?"

"Yup. They're kicking the hell out of them," observed Rafi.

"Ouch." Diane's yelp again.

"Nice stock-work," Rafi continued, deliberately matter-of-fact.

"No! Put that away." Nabbi's hand flashed down, knocking the camera into Kate's lap.

"Oi! Why'd you do that?"

"What the fuck is going on?" muttered Ethan.

Nabbi sawed the van backward into a three-point turn, rotating Ethan farther away from the action. Now it was framed through the back windscreen, and Clay, Jan, and George had front seats.

"Christ, what did they do?"

"Fuck . . . Fucking *hell*."

Ethan stood up in the aisle and looked over the back of three heads. He caught a glimpse of soldiers bundling two figures around a wall of sandbags. A rifle barrel rose, two hands gripping it. There was a pause. Then the hands drove the gun down, butt first. The blow seemed to reboot the synthesized drumbeat, which flooded the van. Nabbi was nearly through with the turn. As the rifle came up again, this time in Ethan's side window, Nabbi accelerated hard, clouding the scene with white dust.

"What was that about?" asked Kate, inspecting her camera.

Nabbi shrugged his shoulders. The bald spot of his crown shook. "Wrong turning," he sang. "We take a different route."

THIRTEEN

THREE HUNDRED AND SIXTY degrees of sky, bent like a bubble above the peaks. Kate spun slowly on her heel in the snow, trying to fix the view in her head. There were clumps of dark-green firs in the depths, gray tongues of scree stretching to the snowline, then a brilliant glare reaching upward, overlain here and there with blue shadows, pocked with dents and boulders, the distant line of their progress fragmenting to individual tracks, then single footsteps, tracing the laborious hike all the way up, to here. Silver mountains at eye level in every direction, an endless disorientation of steepness. This was what they had come for; it was magnificent.

And yet if she shut her eyes the picture dissolved. The wind sung in her ears, overwhelmed the sun on her face, drew a cold veil over her bare knees and arms. Why hadn't Nabbi told them to bring something warm for the summit? There wasn't an answer, just a moaning drawn from the slope beneath her feet by a strong gust, and Kate's nose couldn't pick anything from the wind, just its sharpness. Nothing to work with except, perhaps, the faintest tang of sunscreen, reminding her that she should have brought the tube, that the cold was deceptive, that Nabbi could have helped out there too.

"How far do you reckon we can see?" George was asking Clay.

Kate opened her eyes again, managed only a squint at first. She pulled out her notebook, thought for a moment, and wrote *Himalayas* at the top of a page.

"I don't know. Ten, fifteen miles in that direction." Clay pointed back down the slope of their final ascent, coughed, bent forward to rest his hands upon his knees, and nodded. "That's one big hill."

"Young guy like you, no excuse to hack your guts up," replied George. Kate watched as he removed his glasses and inspected the lenses, then took a fold of his sweatshirt (SOLIHULL CHURCH YOUTH PROJECT in a happy font, beneath a cartoon cat, thumb raised) and buffed them methodically with the cat's puckered face. The detail somehow made it impossible to concentrate. She shut her notebook.

Clay, smiling, shook his head and said simply, "Killer view."

Diane, who'd brought a fitted sweater up the mountain, was stretching into it elegantly, then putting an arm around Clay's shoulder. She turned slowly, taking it all in, until her gaze crossed Kate's and softened into a smile.

THE PREVIOUS AFTERNOON Diane had gone up in Kate's estimation, when she'd done something about the chickens, which arrived with the bowlegged pony man. Approaching down the track, he at first appeared to have an enormous pom-pom hanging from each hand. Only as he drew nearer had Kate made out movement which was not the result of his swinging arms. Closer still, and she saw a fright of wings and necks and beaks. Each clump of orange legs was bound with twine. The man's smile remained as he looped the string up under one of the mule-packs and tied it off, leaving all ten chickens to jab and twist upside down. Kate stepped toward the pony, itself commuter-bored, then stopped: she was here to observe. Or was she frightened of insulting the pony man, or embarrassed to appear oversensitive in front of everyone?

There had been no need to answer these questions, because Diane's "Jesus, haven't you got a box or something?" pulled the pony man up short.

"Chicken, for dinner." He smiled.

"We don't have to torture them first though, do we?" Diane, with a hand on each hip, appeared accustomed to getting her own way.

"Dinner," the man repeated, "for later." He looked about in search of help.

"Yes, I get that." Diane approached the pony, her head to one side, a chicken's-eye view. "But I want you to stick them in a box, a bag even. Or else kill them now. You can't string them up like this, alive. We're going to be walking all afternoon."

"Fresh," said the pony man. He removed his cap and scratched a silver temple.

Exasperated, Diane strode off to find Nabbi, who fled before her to the minivan and retrieved from its roof a couple of cardboard boxes, recently emptied of bottled mineral water. Nabbi

stood back and shrugged while Diane jabbed the sides—
HIMALAYAN BLISS GANGAJAL—full of holes with a nail file.

NOW KATE, SHIVERING, smiled back. She could make
notes later. The landscape would draw everyone close. She turned
to search out Ethan. Perhaps if she fixed the picture in her head
with him they would be able to remember it better together in
the future.

He was with Rafi and Jan. Yet when she drew nearer it became
apparent that Ethan was there but not there; the talk, veering
from altitude sickness through Rafi's stint in the Israeli army to,
laughably, Jan's nearest equivalent, his personal best over ten
kilometers, was for Ethan's benefit, but he was not taking part in
it. Rafi put a foot next to Ethan's and began extolling the virtues
of his army-issue boots. Jan agreed wholeheartedly and went on,
blinking, "Punishing exercise is the one thing that helps me concentrate, though. Endurance is it. Otherwise there's just not the
time to get focus. . . ."

Ethan turned toward Kate as she broke into the circle, and Jan
gave up. After an embarrassed pause, he continued, "I'm going to
get that Nabbi to explain what is what." A hand gestured at the
endlessness. "There must be a famous Everest or something in
one direction. At least he could tell us." Rafi set off with him to
find out.

The silence they left was filled by the wind, which grew
around Ethan and Kate. Again she shivered. Ethan watched her
do so and then turned his gaze to the view, staring at it without
expression. Kate held her arms and did the same. After a while,
she saw from the corner of her eye that he was unbuttoning his

second layer and, having slipped it off, was extending it in her direction. The shirt flapped in the wind like a flag.

"Here."

The semaphore meant something, as did his arm around her shoulders once she'd put the shirt on. And the view, and the fact of Jan and Rafi retreating from them, and the staccato progress of two drab, miniscule, army lorries, way down below, obscured by trees and visible again now, throwing the shoulder of mountain into massive relief as they trickled around its base; they were part of it too. Kate tried to pin down the moment for them both. By pointing out the trucks, so far away, so small, whose course she felt sure Ethan had to be following too, the scale of the experience would become obvious, wouldn't it? She sensed his gaze snag as the vehicles disappeared from view, shared his relief when they emerged again. Now was the time to say something. She would seal the moment, there and then.

When she turned to speak, though, she could not. She suffered a brief memory of her first solo flight: just her, *alone*. Ethan's arm was still around her shoulders but he wasn't there. His face was lifted to the sun and his eyes were shut. Like a conductor in his separate spotlight, or a patient waiting in the dentist's chair.

FOURTEEN

⁘⸻⸺⸺⸺⸻⁘

THERE WAS SOMETHING the matter with the pony man. Ethan sat with the rest, faces glowing at the fire, absently watching the man's bandy-legged progress around their circle. He seemed unwilling to draw close, yet incapable of going away. A satellite stuck on its own trajectory. Not that it mattered because Clay had spared room in his pack for a bottle of whiskey, which was also now in orbit.

"So have you ever killed anyone?" Jan asked Rafi.

Diane put her hand to her mouth, anticipating Rafi's nod.

Jan approved: "Intense."

Clay rolled his eyes and breathed, "Vin Diesel, move over."

"It didn't bother you?" Diane's smile flared wide, excited by the prospect that it hadn't.

Rafi shrugged, took the bottle from Clay's outstretched hand, and lifted it to his lips, flame lurching in the glass.

"But was it necessary? Was it justifiable?" asked Kate. Shadows played across the planes of her face as she waited, unblinking, for an answer. Ethan was transfixed again by the contradiction of that soft mouth, so certain of its words, until distracted by a movement over her shoulder. At the edge of the clearing, by their separate campfire, Misbaah the cook sat with Nabbi, flourishing a blade. The steel edge flicked on and off in the firelight. On, and off, mouth and words. Eventually Misbaah chopped the knife still into a log and rose to pick up one of Diane's boxes.

Rafi was still considering the question. Eventually he shrugged. "Either way it wasn't up to me."

George left off scratching his gray stubble to ask, "What do you mean by that?"

"Means he didn't just go postal on his own," said Clay.

"Orders. I was a soldier. I did what I was told."

George pressed on. "But what did you make of those orders, yourself?"

"A macramé noose, a terra-cotta grenade." Clay again. "What do you think?"

The Israeli passed the bottle to Ethan, who drank. A hot fist formed in his stomach, turning a memory with it, of the last time he'd drunk scotch straight, from a bottle, with Rachel. He reached a hand out to stroke Kate's knee, allowing the smoothness of her fingers to close round his. Over her head he saw the cook put an arm into the box and pull a chicken free of the cardboard flaps by its wing. From behind, the fire made stained glass of the splayed feathers. Ethan looked away—before Kate caught up.

George continued, "I'm not saying you had any choice but to follow orders. I'm just curious what you thought about what your superiors asked of you."

"Nothing, really."

Jan nodded agreement, as if familiar with the problem.

"Because, if it was me, I'd find it difficult to bend that far, to somebody else's point of view." George passed the bottle without drinking. "Maybe it's because I'm older. If somebody told me to kill another man for whatever reason, that'd be at odds with what I believe. I couldn't do it."

"You're a cheek-turner," drawled Clay. "Me too."

"If you like." George's smile looked genuine. He turned back to Rafi. "Seriously, though."

"There are different circumstances."

"Not for me. It can't depend on the situation. For me, the rule is more fundamental. A line in the sand. Like the Bible says. Thou shalt not kill."

"Oh, please." Diane smiled.

Clay put a hand out to silence her.

"I respect that," Rafi said. "Just don't believe it, though. All depends on context. Seems strange to me what I did, now, thinking about it here. But back home it was just what happened." He cupped his chin in one hand and ground his teeth.

"How did you do it, though?" Jan pulled on the bottle, winced, and continued. "A gun? A knife? Hand to hand?"

"Give the guy a break," said Clay. "He's on vacation. Nobody's asking you to relive your last . . . semester."

Jan waved Clay down. "Of course not, but this is different. This is interesting."

"Sure it is." Clay lay back against Diane, pulled his guitar onto his lap, and began strumming one of his murder ballads. Ethan drank from the bottle again and drifted with it. Only the pony man's mothlike fluttering around the fire brought him round.

"What's that little guy up to?"

Rafi, glad of the diversion, looked over his shoulder and shrugged. "How should we know? Ask him."

"Do we owe him a tip or something?" Diane curled forward in an effortless sit-up.

"Not until the end, surely." Kate turned too, bringing the pony man to a halt.

Ethan stared at the big diamond pattern splayed across the man's wool sweater. Frayed cuffs flickered in the firelight. Was it the flames or his hands shaking? Two white eyes glanced furtively across to where Nabbi sat by the other fire. (Why'd Kate care that he kept his distance? One less evening fending off veiled shoe-compliments could only be a good thing.) Seeming to have come to a decision, the pony man sidestepped away. Ethan stood up and walked over to where the man had retreated.

"What's up?" asked Ethan. "Is there a problem?"

The pony man dropped to his haunches and gripped his head in both hands. He twisted his skullcap off and screwed it into a ball, as if to wring out an answer. His eyes, set in the dark folds of his face, gleamed. There was a fire in each.

"Yes, problem."

"Well, what is it? Money? Baksheesh?"

The folds knotted.

"No. Problem!"

Ethan sighed. There was no logic and you couldn't win: come out with it straight and they took offense. He bounced on his heels, waiting for the man to continue. Clay's song filled the silence.

"You said you wouldn't run, my friend,
You said you'd hold me close,
But when I fell you turned your back,
It's you you love the most . . ."

"Like chicken!" The pony man's cuffs gesticulated. "Chicken in a box!"

"Ah." What was he on about? Did he think they'd dock his tip because of the chickens? "Don't worry. Everybody's very happy. No problem with the chickens." Ethan bent his head lower in conspiracy: "Very tasty, I'm sure. . . ."

"No! Yes! Problem!"

The whiskey made it hard to concentrate, numbing the urgency in the man's words. Ethan heard *"But it's you, my friend, that's far away, Alone upon the treeless plain. So far from me, Far from me, Suspended in your bleak and fishless sea,"* and then the flames in the pony man's eyes disappeared, cut out by a shadow. Ethan turned to see Nabbi striding their way. He stepped straight past Ethan and shouted something down at the pony man, a string of jabbering that drove the skullcap back onto his little silver head. This Nabbi followed with a clumsy toe-punt, which sent the smaller man scrabbling away. Ethan rose, driven by an instinct to deliver a proper kick back.

"Stupid man," said Nabbi. "I am very sorry for him. He is bad in the head." The guide tapped the side of his own head. Ethan went to speak but Nabbi cut him off. "Tomorrow we will send him home. A new pony man is coming. I apologize."

The guide did not wait for a response, but retreated with a single nod.

FIFTEEN

Strung out in a line, they worked up toward the pass. Blinding white clouds boiled out of nothing near the left-hand peak. Down to Kate's right, the black stream cut a track through a luminous crust of snow. A goat stood knee deep, shaking its head at her.

Kate panted a question to herself: *Why the rush?* Nabbi was way off ahead, with Jan and Rafi competing just behind him. You could tell from the way Jan stopped now and then, hands on hips to recover his breath, that he was feeling the pace. Ethan had slowed from behind Diane to stroll just ahead of Kate. She couldn't decide whether that was pleasing or bad. The phrase "behind Diane" became "Diane's behind" as they walked. The unspoken accusation shamed Kate: Ethan dropped farther back until he was definitely accompanying her. In fact he was close enough to have overheard her whisper. He'd half-turned, stopped, was rolling his eyes.

"God knows. He's in a hurry though."

"First enthusiasm he's shown for a mountain all week."

Clay arrived, bringing up the rear, with George. Flushed with effort, he bent forward, hands on knees, shoulders heaving. "Maybe he's testing the Marines." He nodded up the track. "Seeing which one of them will drop back first."

"Hopefully Rafi'll catch up with him and break his neck," suggested George. He drew breath, then stepped forward again, prompting the rest to do the same.

Kate's thighs burned. She put her head down and pushed on up the path of scree and ice. Here and there it was dotted with abrupt tufts of grass; there was even an occasional, defiant yellow flower. She followed the measured flick of Ethan's heels. Again they drew away from George and Clay, following the climbing curve of the track.

Near the brow now. Clouds still spilling off the spike of a summit to their left, a draft of cold air dropping down from up there too. Relief from . . . was it the sun on her back, or the weight of her pack? The altitude. More than enough clothes today, and a hat. You couldn't trust him, you see. It was better to be safe than . . . *short walk, little stroll* . . . already two hours gone.

Yes, they were drawing to the lip; one last effort would do it. Nabbi had pulled up just short. Perhaps he was going to walk them the last yards together, for the view. That would be thoughtful. Jan flopped onto his back, levered himself up again, leaving a snow angel where he'd lain. Rafi sat doubled over, clutching his shins. Even Nabbi looked beaten, the closer they got: he was wild-eyed and panting. Kate drew some solace from the sight of a red-cheeked Diane. But, needless to say, Ethan was barely breathing; his eyes were fixed on the remaining stretch of scree.

The stragglers caught up. First George, then Clay, collapsing at the side of the path; one of them hawked yellow spit into the snow. Another flower. Kate's watch face was blinding at first, but read 10:21 angled away from the glare, and then she looked up from it and saw a silhouetted head appear above the ridge.

Another two followed.

Then another.

Four cutout figures now stood on the ridge. Three of them were carrying rifles. The fourth turned sideways and so was he. In unison they jogged down from the pass. Dirt-brown fatigues. One wore an olive balaclava. A second, in an incongruous denim jacket, was dropping to his knees, bringing his gun up to his shoulder. Kate tried to shake the sight out of her head, but he was still there pointing the rifle. She looked for Ethan but he hadn't seen: evidently the climb had tired him more than she'd first thought—he had settled on his hams and was inspecting a pinch of melting snow. Her hand reached out for his arm.

Meanwhile, Nabbi was stepping forward to meet the men. He held his arms away from his body, head back, like a welcoming host. Or was the gesture imploring? The man in the balaclava slung his rifle up behind him on its strap, casually, as if it were a guitar. Then, still talking to Nabbi, he stepped around him to survey the spent group. A *balaclava*.

Kate's mouth said, "What?"

Clay said, "Fantastic, the border. Can we go back downhill now?"

Simultaneously, Rafi whispered, "Shut up, sit very still," and Diane let out an indignant "Jesus!"

Ethan looked up.

There was a pause, in which Jan rolled onto his side. The snow

crust creaked as it gave beneath his weight. "Cool. Even the shep-
herds have guns," he said.

Diane stood, ignoring Rafi's repeated, "Sit still."

George, behind Kate, had risen too. "Nabbi?" he called.

Nabbi did not turn from his conversation. Its words ran back
down the hill to Kate, bubbling like a stream.

Very slowly, his voice blurred at the edges with the effort of
keeping his breath steady, Jan said, "Hold on. Is that man . . .
pointing his rifle . . . at *me*?"

George had taken a step forward and was now blocking part of
Kate's view. His hands were on his hips and his head was cocked, as
if scolding a child, saying *I've had enough of this* without words.

Nabbi was handing something over; or was he giving something up? Kate found that she was on her feet too. The moment
felt utterly wrong, but ahead of computation, like a slug of curdled milk before the misery of its taste hits. Perhaps there was still
time to spit it out. Like George before her, Kate said "Nabbi" into
the stillness. Both he and the man in the mask turned around.

"The holiday is over now. Trekking is finished," the balaclava
stated. His eyes were framed slits.

"This is a joke, yes?" Jan's voice was tight and high.

"No," breathed Clay, "this feels real."

George laughed. He took steps toward the guide and said,
"What's he talking about?" More steps in Nabbi's direction,
gathering pace.

As if to answer him, the balaclava shouted and one of the
others, the big one in the denim jacket, ran at George, rifle butt
raised. He aimed a blow at George's chest and delivered it without hesitating, sending George staggering backward to stumble

over Rafi, whose head was still bowed. George collapsed heavily and stayed down.

"Everybody sit," sang Nabbi. "These men are very serious."

Diane crouched down in front of her, but Kate's legs weren't responding; they wavered uncertainly beneath her. The terror simultaneously stopped everything dead and sped events up. Everything was shockingly real and, in the same breath, fake. She looked down and her feet were comically distant.

"You too." Nabbi pointed. George was groaning, clutching his chest. "Sit down, stay still," repeated Nabbi. His words were slaps with a flat hand. Kate felt Ethan pulling her wrist gently, and gave in. The denim guard had skirted the slope above the path and was squatting casually, his rifle leveled at them across a khaki knee. Now they were all huddling on the path like corralled sheep.

It was impossible to hold opposing thoughts and sensations apart. Kate crouched heavy as a sodden log but also hot-wired to run away. She'd never felt more inert or more alive. The path curved back down the mountain seductively, but in full view. There wasn't so much as a boulder to make for. And anyway, she was shocked to find, alongside her panic, a definite seam of excitement. Not only was she incapable of running, but a part of her seemed not to want to try. This was interesting. It would be something for the notebook, something important to relate. She focused on the purple shape of her shadow but saw, as if superimposed on the snow, a bizarre image of herself seated beneath the skylight in her old office, writing the story up. That was ridiculous; this scenario wouldn't fit between the covers of a Glencare publication. It would spring her into something much better. Yet what was she doing staring at the ground? She should be paying attention, making a mental note of the details.

The nearest of the four figures, the one in denim squatting on the bank, looked almost bored. He couldn't even be bothered to aim properly. With the fingers of his free hand he picked at strands in an impressive beard. But the one behind him, a boy of no more than eighteen, was apparently unable to stand still. He dropped down to the path, bouncing on the balls of his feet, cradling his rifle with twitching fingers.

Meanwhile Nabbi and the balaclava continued to talk. It didn't sound like English. Just indistinct words, murmuring on. Which was wrong. Kate asked herself why. The tone was the problem. Nabbi didn't sound like he was pleading, in any language. It was a conversation about the weather or a mutual friend. An unhurried shooting of the breeze. That, there, was definitely a smile. Which was baffling and yet made perfect sense. Nabbi would be negotiating. To do that effectively meant putting the fellow at ease.

Diane had begun to sob. No, it was Jan. The muscles in his jaw fought to end the noise. And Clay was whispering something. . . . "Don't panic. Stay calm. Stay calm. Don't panic." He sounded like an air hostess, his words undercut by the fragility of his voice.

Also in a whisper, someone else was more matter-of-fact. It was Rafi, saying, "We're fucked." Kate looked across at him, head still bowed, as if braced for impact. "Absolutely fucked," he repeated.

The words dropped through Kate like stones through water. They were obviously true. But she thought herself calm again: *I must remember this sensation; it is part of the experience.*

George had managed to sit up and was holding himself together, arms wrapped around his chest. His stricken face was the color of an avocado. As Kate watched, he drew breath and threw up into the snow. Diane, who was nearest to him, put a brown forearm across his shoulder. The arm was alive with goose bumps.

Now Nabbi was sitting down in the snow and the balaclava dropped to his side, head waggling: an extraordinary gesture here, made worse by the way he sat at ease on his heels. While Nabbi sat fiddling with something at his feet in the snow, the three unmasked accomplices closed in round the group.

The balaclava came forward. "I am announcing a change of plan. We are your tour guides now. Reasonable men. But, like Mr. Nabbi says, serious." His English was practiced. He bent over George, who seemed slowly to be regaining his composure, and continued, "You must do as we say at all times. Understand?"

George nodded. The balaclava twisted toward Kate, close enough for her to make out dark lashes and deep brown, expressionless eyes. She held his gaze; the moment stretched. She found herself mesmerized by the fact that the ski mask was knitted from rough wool. A sob rose in her throat and threatened to become audible, but was silenced by the banality of a trickle of sweat which, while she watched, ran from the man's brow into the corner of his right eye. He was hot from the climb too. A woolen balaclava. How *uncomfortable*. She began to cry.

"But what have we done wrong?" asked Diane. Her voice, snagging on "done," stiffened Kate's resolve.

The balaclava broke free of Kate and waggled again. "No questions. No objections. No problems." He paused. "If any one of you makes trouble, that means trouble for everyone." He stood up again, folded his arms. "Now you'll come with us."

Jan was saying something absurd about contact lenses, pointing fingers at his eyes. And George was adding to the idiocy by asking, "But what about our stuff, our stuff in camp?"

In answer the balaclava laughed. "In a war we must all learn to make do."

The youngest of the unmasked guards now leveled his gun at them from behind, while the other two stood on the uphill side. "Up," the bored beard said. His hand waved a little circle. "Let us go."

Tentatively, Kate stood. It was a surprise to feel that Ethan still had hold of her wrist. He did not let it go. As they began walking toward the pass she turned to look at him for the first time. His lips, a line in the bloodless surround of his face, managed the briefest smile.

Then he was being pulled away by Nabbi, who had trotted to his side. The group halted on the brink of the pass. Kate saw mountaintops overlain with mountaintops into the blue distance, a mouthful of needling teeth. Nabbi's raised voice turned her head. He was pushing something white into Ethan's stomach and dancing in the snow beside him.

"Shoes. Shoes."

The balaclava stood over Ethan as he took his boots off, at gunpoint. Nabbi stopped them steaming with his own sockless feet and stood happily watching Ethan cram himself into the exchanged pair.

"Very nice," Nabbi said. "Thank you."

He set off back down the mountain.

SIXTEEN

"Traveling?" Rachel bit down on the word as she repeated it.

Kate feigned interest in the contents of her bag, fishing a timetable from the clutter and setting it down on the steel tabletop, next to her dead cappuccino. The grid of frequencies was a comforting antidote to Rachel's incredulity, which extended while Kate worked out that the biggest gap between buses was sixteen minutes, on Sundays and bank holidays.

"Let me get this right. They're finally recognizing your talents at the magazine. They've told you you're next in line for promotion. But you're turning the opportunity down, to take a . . . a holiday?"

Two shrink-wrapped men in matching bomber jackets pressed past the picture window. One turned to check the Soho café for vacant seats, his yellow hair shining in the lamplight. Kate looked back down at the timetable, waited as Rachel took two long pulls on her cigarette. Ethan had bounced her into the decision, suddenly announcing that he wanted to go away. It was hard to imagine him organizing the trip himself, but, since he'd given up his pointless job there was nothing, in theory, to hold him back. Unsure whether or not he would wait, she had taken the first step to make sure. She briefly considered explaining this to her sister, but chose not to. The man was still scanning the café for a seat. Catching Kate's eye, he blew her a *cheer up* kiss. She smiled back at him, said nothing.

Rachel sighed. "Where then?" A pause. "When?"

"India."

"Right. Of course." Rachel stubbed out her cigarette. "Where's that beach bit? Goa?"

Despite herself, Kate explained, "I want to go all over. Some areas more than others . . . the north first, I think, the mountains . . . and then the desert. Wherever seems most interesting."

"How commendably thorough. Off the beaten track and all that, if anywhere still is." As Rachel spoke, her manicured fingers patted down her phone, interrogating it for any freak unmonitored calls. "Suitably hot and dusty in the desert anyway, I imagine. Lots of refreshing poverty to gawp at. I'm sure you'll have a lovely . . . challenging time."

Could it be more tiring? Every conversation creating a winner and a loser. The attrition was relentless: time spent with Rachel meant an endless circumnavigation of one trap after another. Barbed wire and land mines. Often you couldn't see what was coming for the mud and froth, but hit an issue direct, respond to it, and *bang,* you were maimed.

Like now: a lovely, challenging time. A meanness hidden in a throwaway comment, too innocuous to make an issue of. What would come next? Perhaps an omission, a deliberately avoided compliment, or congratulations withheld. Then the cut of a true insult, but delivered with laughter or a touch to the back of a hand, and followed so fast by a flattering remark that there wouldn't be a chance to respond. After that, perhaps, a truth told unflinchingly. Come on, we're sisters after all, we can talk straight, can't we!

Resentment surged. Why allow Rachel to make her feel like this? Why take any notice? To be so galled was itself galling. She should see it for what it was, nothing but a familiar assault course, of omissions, insults, compliments, truths. But they wore you down. Or rather, they mounted up, a cumulative onslaught, drip by needle-prick by knife-wound, finally becoming obvious, as if to say: okay, then, you dealt with that, now ignore this, keep rising above me, I dare you!

A white flag dropped between them to evacuate casualties. Kate bit back her resentment. She never aired her own misgivings about Rachel's vacuous existence, did she? It was to do with tolerance, and presumption and resp—

"What are you doing for . . . a . . . traveling companion?" There was an edge to Rachel's voice. Kate turned from the reflection in the window to look at her sister directly, saw that she was fiddling with strands of hair pulled forward from the top of her head, counting them from one thumb-and-finger to the other.

"Well, Ethan, of course."

"Of course." Rachel's fingers stopped. "What about his job, though? Surely he's not resigned too?"

"Yeah, he chucked it in." She continued staring at Rachel. The strands of hair started moving again but Kate felt sure her sister's gaze was focused beyond the blonde tips. She seemed gratifyingly blunted by this news.

"And when did you say you were going?"

"I didn't. But next week, since you're interested."

"As in, after this weekend?" Rachel's voice snagged.

Kate raised an eyebrow and drove the point home. "Yeah, Monday."

At that Rachel excused herself, heading for a ladies' room that didn't exist in this chain café. Kate watched the reflection in the window and the view through it: Rachel in a huff before the shrugging waiter, a cycle-rickshaw (PEDDLING TOWARDS A GREENER LONDON) limping self-consciously through the Old Compton Street drizzle. The conversation had taken a satisfying turn in her direction after all. Rachel couldn't help being impressed by the intrepid fact of their just going. She seemed to be pausing by the newspaper rack in the windowpane there, to collect herself, and the bedraggled passengers were climbing out of the cycle-rickshaw across the road, clearly regretting not having taken a proper taxi, and now Rachel was sitting back down with her studied coolness intact again.

"So the two of you are just dropping out and heading off?"

"I'm hoping there may be an article in it."

"Oh, please. You reckon people will want to read about your holiday?"

Kate looked away.

"Because unless you find yourself a convenient hot spot, a civil war perhaps . . ."

"I'll do my research."

Rachel laughed. "Of course. Well, you get out there. Off you go. Investigate."

Kate winced. When she searched her sister's face she found it deadpan, intent upon a cuticle. There was a pause.

Kate filled it: "Cheers. I'll do my best."

Neither of them seemed to know where the conversation should go from there. Both were mesmerized by the crescent of Rachel's nail, until she folded it into her fist. Kate watched Rachel's grip tighten. The hand was biting itself. She struggled to think of something to say, but her sister spoke first.

"Just go carefully. Mind you don't drink the water." The brittle tone lurched in vain toward lightheartedness as she continued, "And make sure that waster takes care of you."

SEVENTEEN

ETHAN KNELT, LACING the trainers. He could not feel his toes. Not because of the cramped shoes; he could not feel his fingers either, and there they were in front of him, lassoing one another. And not because of the cold. No, his toes were numb because all of him was numb, overtaken by an obliterating fear.

Now that he had finished doing Nabbi's shoes up, the youngest of the guards was prodding him tentatively, to join the back of the line. The others had already begun to falter away, opening a gap of snow in front of him on the path.

But Ethan continued kneeling over his front foot, reworking the lace into a better double-knot, ignoring another, more impatient pat on the back. The numbness meant that he was hovering above the path, a feeling heightened by the whiteness of both the shoe and the snow. It was like being a schoolboy again, bent double for the start of an important race. Set in a sprinter's starting crouch, floating above the track, ready to explode.

Even with his feet cramped like this he could run. The others, chaperoned by the three older guards, had drawn away some thirty yards, were all but at the crest. And this spindly kid was stamping impatiently at Ethan's shoulder, within arm's reach. He could knock the boy over and sprint back down the mountain.

The path they'd come up stretched away under Ethan's arm, with Nabbi bobbing jauntily along it, upside down. He would catch the guide and either use him as a shield or fell him on his way through. Nabbi didn't have a gun, wouldn't be able to stop him. And if Ethan upended this guard properly it'd take him five, ten seconds to scramble into a position to shoot. He might be able to put himself beyond range of all of them if he took this one chance, now.

But a confusion clouded his mind. The impulse to run didn't have a monopoly; it came accompanied.

For a start, this sequence of events simply could not be real. One minute there was the annoyance of a shifty tour guide and pointless mountain hike, set against the pleasure of watching Diane walking up ahead. If the problem then had been about subtly showing Kate that he wasn't paying that part of the view any attention, how could he now be facing this? Guns and balaclavas. Such a shift in scale made no sense.

Welded there, he stared down at Nabbi's bulging trainers, which underlined the indignity of having been robbed of his own shoes. How could that matter now? Because it meant something. A joke had gone wrong, and its implications were unthinkable. The guide was only visible from the waist up now, partly obscured by the fall of the slope. The theft of Ethan's boots heralded a terrible inversion.

He received a third, more insistent prod from the teenage guard. The boy was failing in his allotted task of bringing up the rear; panic showed in the way he delivered another poke at the shoulders bending before him. An exploitable weakness. Ethan felt something within him begin to give.

Still, he did not bolt, because of Kate. A pang of commitment gripped him. Or was it guilt? He could still feel the heat-echo of her wrist in his hand. There were betrayals, and betrayals; he could not abandon her here. If he tried to escape he'd be doing so alone, which would be unforgivable.

So he found himself starting forward instead, the urge to run fading with each step. Whatever *was* happening, it could not last. Following the rest did not feel like a conscious decision, merely the progression of inevitable footsteps. The initial shock of fear subsided; by the time they'd reached the crest a comforting heaviness had settled back into his legs. It would have been pointless trying to run. Better to stick it out. Why risk a bullet—the idea of such a phrase was laughable—when a little endurance would see them back to safety anyway?

They'd caught up with George now, the last in the line. On this side of the mountain the wind was blowing harder, dragging sheets of powder across the face of the slope at ankle height. Ethan put his head down against the sharpness, angling his face back up the mountain. Behind him on the path their footprints were already blurring.

EIGHTEEN

FINGERS WORKED BEHIND Kate's head, teasing apart the knot. She kept very still, kneeling as instructed, braced against the tugging. When the cloth finally gave it was like the miraculous end of a headache.

As soon as she opened her eyes, though, the brightness was too much and she had no choice but to screw them shut, migraine-tight again. A hand on her shoulder seemed to squeeze it reassuringly, prompting Kate, in the seconds before she was able to blink herself back into the scene, to suffer the fleeting and absurd hope that it had all been a terrifying stunt.

"Please, what's going on?" Clay's voice.

Instead of an answer, Kate heard a muffled slap. She forced her surroundings into watery focus despite the glare.

First, she sought out the others, saw that they were all kneeling, too. The guard with the beard was untying Jan's blindfold behind her. Beyond him the youngster was attending to Rafi. He looked like a reluctant child in the barber's seat, head obediently bent forward. Over her other shoulder, Ethan was shaking his neck loose, next to George and Clay. George's whole body was trembling, and he was talking to himself, or rather he was stuttering a prayer. At "Thy will be done," Diane, who was slumped beside him, twitched upright.

Kate tried to take in her surroundings. The courtyard was strewn with wood chips, which accounted for the relative softness beneath her knees and an oddly sanitary smell—pine resin. A block of shadow lay diagonally across the space, cast by a crude stone wall, prompting the memory of a quadrangle, which she fought with practical thoughts: that way was west, then. The deduction heartened her. She tried another: if the sun was so low they must have been traveling for six or seven hours. It had felt at once an eternity and no time at all.

THE COLD WALK DOWN to the truck, perversely easy after climbing to the summit, had seemed to pass in a flash. They'd been made to kneel like this, in the snow, facing the back of the vehicle, for blindfolding. Before they tied hers Kate had sat staring at the truck's garish rear axle. It was yellow, at odds with the green of the rest of the vehicle. The middle of the axle bulged into some sort of a sump, decorated with a painted face, eyebrows drawn upward in apparent surprise. Kate had stared back at the eyes, still too stunned to think, mesmerized by the stupidity of someone's having chosen to paint a face *there*.

Once they were all in the truck one of the guards had spoken. "Nobody must move. Nobody must touch eyes. Nobody must speak. Sit still and quiet for the journey." Then there was the metallic hitching sound of the tailgate being fastened shut, which became for Kate the definite cocking of a rifle, even before the gears crashed and the truck lurched away.

After that, time collapsed. She counted off seconds to steady herself, but the claustrophobia of the blindfold made concentration impossible and she kept losing her place. She tried to sense where Ethan was sitting, fancied the feet that occasionally brushed her own might be his, but could not be sure. Once, a hand was placed on her thigh. It did not feel like his touch and she shook it off, repulsed. Surely her other senses were supposed to compensate for this blankness. But her ears were useless, full of truck noise, which drowned out everything. Unless that, there, was an exchange between the guards? And the low resonance just after it, could that be someone moaning, or was it the sound of the engine straining? Diesel fumes overpowered all others, making her nose equally redundant. At one point a warmer smell—piss perhaps—bubbled up to the surface, but it could also have been sweat or tea or even some nuance in the fumes that she'd not previously noticed.

Fright and panic fused as the journey lengthened. She fought back waves of nausea. Why the blindfold? She had no idea where they'd started from anyway, could not even recall the name of the pass Nabbi had hauled them up. *Nabbi.* It was impossible to think about him. A blackness attached to his name. *Her* decision, a voice whispered, *her* responsibility. She concentrated on the engine noise again to shut the unthinkable out.

NOW ANOTHER GUARD was pushing backward through the wooden gate to one side of the little courtyard. Short and squat, he swayed toward them with their day-bags, carrying two or three in each hand, like shopping. As he passed Kate she caught sight of the *Trailfinders* tag on her own bag and saw herself scribbling her home address on the label in Earl's Court tube station. She'd done Ethan's for him too. A sob fell through her.

Arriving before the wall, in blue shadow, the guard released his grip on all of the bags at once, dropping them in a heap.

Jan started babbling in a child's voice behind Kate. She dared not turn round. Half his words were unclear. *Something something something*, "please say when," *something something*, "embassy details," *something something*. The young guard shouted "Shut up" over Kate's head, but Jan continued. The incomprehensible words were, she realized, Flemish.

"Easy, Jan, take it easy," pleaded Clay, his voice a gruff whisper.

Still he went on. The guard trotted around Kate and again she heard a slapping sound. In response Jan's hysterics just grew louder.

Then a deeper voice shouted. Kate heard a hollow thump. She couldn't stop herself turning to see what was going on, saw Jan on his side struggling to push himself back up, and the three guards grouped above him. The young one's eyes were wide. The fat guard raised a hand above Jan's head, but the young one caught his sleeve and held him back. An argument between the two flared. It was cut dead by the appearance of the balaclava in the entrance to the courtyard. He'd clearly just pulled the mask on again because the seam was showing. The mask was inside out. When he walked past Kate to the wall a little label wagged at her from the back of his head, like a mocking tongue.

Soon the contents of their bags were heaped before the wall.

All four men began picking through the jumble. At first Kate thought they were looking for something specific, but it became apparent they were dividing the spoils. Another argument threatened over someone's Gore-Tex jacket. Kate saw her torch pocketed by the beard, and it was easier to be outraged by this theft alone than to consider the fact of the courtyard and kneeling with hands bound in fear and silence. For a brief moment she even suffered a sliver of hope: was robbery the point? Then the balaclava faced them and began speaking.

"These things are valuable, and so are you. You are in the bank, in a manner of speaking. And I am the manager. No good manager loses his assets. No good manager lets them spoil. I will look after you. Unless"—he paused, clasped his hands before him—"you are becoming a problem." Another, longer pause, lips apart. They were shockingly red against the monotone mask. "But that will not happen."

"At least"—Clay's voice was hoarse, but warm, familiar— "tell us why you want us. What for? How long are you going—"

The balaclava cut him off. "Currency. You are part of the big cause now. Involved in the real Kashmiri experience."

"Jesus Christ," sobbed Diane.

The balaclava ignored her. "Khalid!" he exclaimed. The young guard trotted to his side and walked with him to the wooden courtyard door listening to orders issued in an unfamiliar tongue.

Now the denim jacket was squatting next to Kate, nodding. He smiled and reached out for her hand. Close enough for Kate to smell the man's peppermint breath. His full beard made the nodding gesture puppetlike, wiry blackness bouncing on his chest.

Everything inside Kate wanted to shout, or run away, but she couldn't move, caught in the headlights of his smile.

Very gently, he eased the sleeve of Kate's jacket back, as if helping a child make ready to wash hands. She felt him tap her wrist and looked down to see a hairy forefinger pointing at her watch.

"Give me," he said, "now."

Kate unclasped the strap. A cheap, waterproof Swatch, Rachel's present for going away. *Leave your good one at home.* It left a flat dent in her wrist. She inspected its face closely, as if she had never seen anything similar before. Then the guard clicked his fingers and she gave the watch up.

NINETEEN

THERE WERE TOO MANY voices. As Kate let Ethan in through the familiar frosted glass of her mother's back door the sound of overlapping conversations grew. Not the television she'd imagined, but a gathering: the little kitchen was a ring of figures backed up to the units and work surfaces. Kate saw her mother, Rachel, Grandpa, Gay and Robert from next door, and a dough-faced boy—presumably their son. Six heads turned toward them and the talking died. "There you are!" beamed her mum. "Both of you. What a surprise!"

Ethan stiffened beside her as everybody but Rachel took a step forward. Kate had told her mother she'd be dropping in alone, precisely to avoid a fuss. And she'd sold the idea to Ethan as a quiet drink, a chance for her to say good-bye before the trip. Now this huddle of faces. Rachel, for God's sake. Gay was looking Ethan up and down as if he were for sale and Grandpa was clutching at his hand, wheezing a *Welcome, what can I get you*, delighted to meet young Kate's man at last, after all this time.

They moved through into the lounge. It had shrunk; there weren't enough chairs. Ethan and Rachel remained upright while everyone else sat down, giving the room a lopsided feeling. The nest of tables had been unpacked; bowls of nuts and crisps stood on top of them, strategically positioned at intervals across the swirling carpet. The pattern was more prominent than Kate remembered. Gay saw that Jack, her son, had taken the big armchair, and she shooed him out of it onto the floor.

"So, India," Robert was saying.

Rachel left to fetch drinks. She nodded at Ethan, pink-cheeked, suggesting he take the vacated seat. She was blushing. Embarrassed by the humiliation of having Ethan scrutinize her humble beginnings, no doubt. Kate resolved to feel the opposite. The row of trinkets on the mantelpiece stared at her in silent cahoots.

"Never been there myself," conceded Grandpa.

"We have. Or rather, near it. Our cruise took us down the western edge. We saw Bombay at sunrise, you know, with that gate."

Kate watched Ethan settle back into the armchair, already apparently recomposed. He ran a hand across his newly cropped hair, let it drop to the velour armrest. With the other he took a carrot stick from the bowl Kate's mother was thrusting at him, and two more in response to the bowl's further insistent jiggling.

"Go on, take a handful."

Kate felt suddenly sorrowful at the thought of her mother peeling and slicing the carrots in preparation for this visit. The feeling intensified when she followed up with a tub of heartrending Marks & Spenser taramasalata. But Ethan's winning smile helped. One of his new orange fingers gouged an eye out of the tub and Kate's mother shone with appreciation as she turned to her other guests.

"We never docked, but half of the passengers still managed to catch something." Robert shook his head; his Milosovich hair wobbled. "Poor old Mr. Sanghvi; it was his fiftieth treat, you know."

"Quite," Grandpa acknowledged.

"You make sure to watch what you eat." Robert nodded wisely at Ethan.

"Oh, these youngsters can cope, I'm sure." Gay waved Robert down. "I bet you've got a stomach like an ox." The woman's lipstick clashed with the carrot it clamped down on. Was she fluttering her eyelashes?

"Anyway." Kate tried to draw their fire. "It'll be an experience—"

But Ethan, slapping his thigh, cut in gamely: "Absolutely, and once we've trawled through the obligatory cultural meccas, fried in the desert, frozen up a mountain, I may even persuade Kate to sample some of those beaches you must have sailed past." He flashed another charming smile.

"I'm not sure Mecca is in India," Grandpa queried.

"No, I—"

"He *knows* that," sang Kate's mum. "Don't mind the old man. He takes things a bit literarily."

"Literally," corrected Kate.

"Quite," agreed Grandpa, grinning.

Ethan raised his hands in surrender.

Rachel reversed into the room with a tray of drinks, pirouetting disdainfully amid the chintz. Kate caught a sugared watercress whiff of perfume. Odd that she'd not noticed it on Rachel's way out. The nonchalance with which she handed Ethan his glass of beer was obviously studied. Kate watched her sister's eyes, unable to stop themselves, flicking from the rim of the glass to Ethan's face at the last minute. Her red lips were a fraction beyond pursed. In fact, in the instant of eye contact, they were just about puckered.

How satisfying then, to see Ethan's blank response. A single nod of thanks and then his attention immediately refocused on Grandpa, over Rachel's shoulder.

"Cheers then."

"Good lad."

Ethan aped Grandpa's extravagantly raised glass. Toasting an absent queen. While both their arms were still aloft something hit the French window next to Grandpa's chair. Whump! A slop of ale landed in the old man's lap as he, along with everyone else, turned with a start toward the glass.

Jack, who had been sitting against the doors, said, "A pigeon." He swiveled back to face everybody and continued: "It looks pretty dead to me."

They made toward the door. Even Ethan stood up after Kate had gone past him to the window. She looked, haloing the glass, Grandpa's hand upon her shoulder. The bird lay on the paving stones outside with its head back and its legs akimbo, monumentally still.

"Yup," said Robert.

"It's a dove, not a pigeon," Grandpa corrected.

"How can you tell?"

"Well, . . ."

While he dredged for a plausible difference another bird settled on the patio. The same blue-gray as the dead dove-pigeon, it bobbed inquisitively at a safe distance.

"Do you think that's its mate?" Mum asked, still deferring to Grandpa.

"Well, . . ." he repeated, a red hand pressed against the creased map of his neck.

"I saw this program," Gay said, "about birds that pair for life."

"Discovery," Robert agreed.

"And I think doves do so," she said sadly.

"No," corrected Grandpa.

"I think so, like albatrosses. . . ."

Kate's mum, beneath her breath: "Good for them."

"No," Grandpa said again, his tone patient, or perhaps uncertain. Kate didn't find out because the dead bird twitched. Its leg kicked. The other bird rose away from it and settled on the freshly mown lawn, where it began pecking with a feigned lack of interest.

"Shall I go and kill it properly?" Jack asked, standing in their midst. The bird flapped weakly, still on its back. "We shouldn't let it suffer," he continued hopefully.

"Give it a second," Ethan said, above their heads. "Look."

Kate, meanwhile, flicked a stainless-steel catch and ground the door sideways on its runners. The bird flapped harder at the noise, managing to right itself jerkily, on limp legs. Its resolve strengthened at the sight of Kate's outstretched hands. In a panic it skittered into the flower bed.

Turning round, the group was framed in the window. Grandpa scratching his bald head. Robert with a *for life* arm around Gay. Kate's poor mum with her palms up: *what can you do?* Jack looking disappointed. Behind them, in the back row, Rachel was craning forward next to Ethan, pressed against his side, steadying herself with a hand on his shoulder. Four dark fingernails pressed into Ethan's unmoving yellow T-shirt.

"There you go," Ethan said. "Kate's healing hands. He's coming round."

The pigeon reemerged from the bed, joining the other one on the lawn. Between bobs, it shook its head at Kate. She stamped and both birds clapped themselves away. When Kate looked back at her audience, neither Rachel nor her paw print remained.

They retook their chairs, Robert and Gay already haranguing Ethan in tandem, with a port-by-port account of their historic cruise. His fixed grin looked natural. And Grandpa was saying something about the power of the dollar and slipping her a twenty under the tiny coffee table that separated their chairs. Kate took it, while saying no and stretching to steady the nut bowl with her other hand.

A dead bird, nests of nuts, a hand upon a shoulder. It meant nothing. Spreadsheet Barbie. When they came to leave, Ethan shook Grandpa's hand, and Robert's, even Jack's. Both Mum and Gay took a kiss on the cheek. Kate enjoyed a surge of gratitude: she'd never seen him this amenable, so prepared to charm.

Rachel only rejoined them in the confusion of kitchen goodbyes. Mouthing "new man" at Kate she rolled her eyes and tapped her phone. Better still, and enough to make Kate feel bad, Rachel was handing her a gift. Shop-wrapped, but . . . Kate's guilt burned harder when the paper came away to reveal a watch. Rachel put a hand over the mouthpiece and explained: "For the trip. Leave your good one at home." Ethan was already a shape on the other side of the kitchen door.

TWENTY

THE SPOKE OF LIGHT reached bricks, finally, and kinked. Now it illuminated the rough concrete floor, Kate's right leg, and a few inches of brick wall.

There were little peaks and valleys in her trouser leg. Shifting her position very gradually, Kate accelerated the passage of time in this mountain range, lengthening the shadows, drawing the leg-world toward her through its distinct day. By pulling her knee out of the beam entirely she could imagine the landscape into night.

But there was no way of speeding up the spoke. It turned at its own infinitesimal pace, sharp across the gray daylight hours, then dimming into unholy darkness. The day before, she had counted it across eleven bricks before the light began to fade. Now she whispered, "Eleven then," and resolved to repeat the observation again, to make sure.

On balance the sweep of light was a good thing. She had examined every inch of its arc, three times now. The spoke's attention to detail made the shed seem bigger than it was, during the day. But with the beam's passing at dusk the space shrank, leaving her to fight the timelessness and claustrophobia alone. Its countdown was a constant reminder of the impending horror of night.

Each morning, the light began at the bucket by the door, revealing khaki plastic. The bucket didn't have a handle, which meant the guard either carried it with a thumb inside the rim or, worse, hugged it to his chest. Next time he took it away, she would check.

She could not bring herself to use the bucket to begin with: it was an emblem of the balaclava, an opponent she tried not to give in to. When she first needed to go, she called until the boy Khalid came, with a handgun and twitching fingers. Showing the whites of his eyes through a chink of opened door, he made it clear she had no alternative. One toilet trip a day, the bucket at all other times. So far, it had not become an issue: she had passed nothing more than a trickle. But Kate feared that they may not be set free before the time came and then the bucket would be her only remaining option.

After the khaki enemy then, the beam spent hours trawling across a dusty swathe of floor, whose chief features were a ridge where the door scraped, and a broken section just short of the front wall. Kate had tried to sweep this surface clean with her hand, even flicking at it with a sock, but both methods drew flakes of dirt and rotten concrete unendingly.

At least she had the blanket to sit on. It was her only furniture. At daybreak, after the first night in the shed, she'd showed the cloth to the beam: it was a surprise to see brown and red tartan. Not very Kashmiri. There was a joke in this, to do with notions of authenticity, and knitting, and that ridiculous balaclava, and Clay would have made Ethan laugh at it, she was sure, but without an audience the joke was meaningless. Kate grimaced and decided, while she was thinking of it, to shake the blanket out. When she did so the spoke acquired a new dimension: a screen of motes swam above its line on the floor.

Yes, she'd have liked to talk about the tartan with the others, but they were not within earshot. The generator, if that's what it was, blotted out the detail of their noise. It groaned throughout the day and night, masking all other sounds in the courtyard. Kate tuned in to the generator again now and heard a new shape; it sounded, when she put her ear to the back wall, as if its bricks were growling.

After the initial stretch of kneeling in the wood chips, they'd been taken one by one to separate outbuildings. The men were led away first. Ethan whispered something at the ground on his way past. It sounded like "I'm sorry," but she could have been mistaken. This wasn't his doing. She retreated from the wall and focused instead on her illuminated slice of brick, fighting to suppress the guilt. She must not allow the notion of fault into the frame at all.

When it came to her turn, the young guard had shown Kate through a maze of stone walls to this cell, steering her through its open door with a surprisingly gentle hand. This sympathetic touch prompted a flurry of questions, but they came to her as the door shut, and remained unasked. She had to wait for his subsequent visits. But whether escorting her to the pit toilet or dropping off paper plates of rice and hard-boiled eggs, Khalid remained stony, refusing to answer her enquiries. Who was he? Where did Nabbi go? What did the balaclava want with them? When she asked, the boy shuffled from foot to foot and said nothing.

She would not give up. Brick by brick, the day wore on. When next the door rattled, and the spoke fanned into a wedge, she was determined to have another go. Khalid's extended arm offered a china jug and she took it. Water. The surface was black and silver crescents fighting. Before she lifted the jug to drink she caught his eye and smiled.

"Thank you."

He nodded in the pause.

"But please, can't you at least tell me how many days you're going to keep us like this?"

The nodding became an equivocal waggle, but he was still looking at her, and with calm eyes.

"Please," she repeated.

"Not long, I think."

She opened her mouth to ask what that meant, but he cut her off, gesturing at the jug.

"So drink."

Though tempted to press him further, she thought better of it on seeing his hand rise to take the water away.

Not long was a reassurance, however vague. Kate watched the spoke slide forward the entire length of another gray brick. Staring at the disintegrating join between the wall and the floor, she even surprised herself with the realization that, given the choice, she'd extend the period of captivity to about a week. It would make for a better story. Too short a confinement would not do justice to the fear she'd suffered in her very first hour. It was like a cut; after suffering the pain, she deserved a proper scar.

As soon as this rash idea registered, though, her sense of superstition demanded that she unthink it. The balaclava had to let them go *now*. Never mind that she hadn't managed to find out why they were being held, or who was doing the holding; never mind that the article would have gaping holes; she'd forfeit it all to be back in London, or even Delhi.

She stood up and put her eye to the crack between the door and the doorpost. In just these three days the view was already relentlessly familiar: a strip of dirt some fifteen yards wide, and then another wall. Once, she'd seen Clay pass by the gap, led by the denim jacket, and it was a flooding comfort to see what she had continually to force herself to believe, that she was not alone.

For the hours that she stared at the open space now, though, nobody crossed it. She rattled the door, trying to jar a wider view, again considering the flimsy construction of the hut. It wouldn't be hard to knock the door free of its hinges, dig up the shot concrete floor, or even pick apart a seam of bricks. But then what? Even if she managed to break out she didn't know where Ethan was, or whether she'd be able to free him and the others. Anyway, they were in the middle of who knew where. The Himalayas. Guarded by men with guns. And now the boy had said it would not be long. All she had to do was sit out the days and press through the nights and then, sooner rather than later, it would be over. Either they would be released or somebody would come to free them: it was unbearable to think of any other outcome, so she would not. Instead she refocused on practicalities, reasoning that she may even avoid the bucket, given enough hard-boiled eggs and a little luck.

Kate sat back down and saw with a shiver that the spoke had reached the last part of brick nine. She pulled the blanket out from beneath herself and refolded it around her shoulders neatly.

The light was failing. Claustrophobia pressed down again with the impending darkness, making each breath a conscious effort, each swallow of spit a deliberate act. Just to sit there required the constant exertion of will. She leaned away from the back wall, not wanting to touch anything other than the floor, staring at her knees, conspiring to conjure the illusion of physical space.

But the only likely escape was sleep, and even then there was the threat of unnavigable dreams. Ten bricks now. She watched the fading spoke until it reached the tip of brick eleven. It would be dark again soon: a cockpit at night, instruments dead. To beat the fear Kate made it her own. She curled into a ball and pulled the blanket over her head.

TWENTY-ONE

Ethan tiptoed the length of the storeroom, swiveled on his heel in front of the oil drum, trod minutely back to the other wall. Each step was a nibble; he could have bitten the room in two with a proper stride. He paused in front of the door and heard the noise again, a muffled scratching, coming from across the way.

Lying facedown, with his cheek pressed sideways into the cement, he scrutinized the familiar stretch of dirt and wood chips spread between his metal door and the one opposite. The gray paint on the door had peeled, leaving a negative shape: the outline of a royal head.

One of the others was behind that head. As with Ethan's cell, an inch or so of space stood between the bottom of the door and the concrete floor. In the last three days he'd seen feet moving in the gap. After his whistle that afternoon, he'd even made out the paleness of a face. Too far away to see clearly, but whoever it belonged to, the face wasn't Kate's.

When he shut his eyes to picture Kate, though, an image of Rachel swam before him instead. He saw her leaning forward, pulling an arm out of its shirtsleeve, lamplight catching the sharpness of her bare shoulder. Angles in place of her sister's soft curves. He let his face rest more heavily on the floor, until the pain of grit pressing into his cheek made it impossible to think of anything else.

The scratching sound happened again, higher pitched than the background droning. Ethan turned his ear to the gap and strained to pull the noises apart. Not scratching, perhaps, but gouging and chipping. The shapes in the slice of space beneath the queen's head had moved when he next looked. Somebody was close up to that door, he decided, and they were scraping at its base.

He wasn't sure what he thought about that.

Now that the fear had subsided, an inertia seemed to have taken its place. The uncertainty of those first hours, blindfolded, traveling who knew where, had not ended where Ethan suspected. Nobody had been killed. In fact, they'd treated him with something like respect, which had to be a good sign.

Still stretched out on the floor, Ethan kept his eye on the space under the door opposite, but his mind began working through the rest of the good signs, yet again.

A man in a balaclava was a good sign, because it meant that man wanted to protect his identity. He was a professional, unwilling to risk recognition. Who did he fear might recognize and identify him? Them, of course. And when? When they were set free.

Another good sign was that apart from George's altercation with the big bearded one, there had been no violence. Nothing unnecessary. If George had just sat still like the rest of them, the guard would not have hurt him either. All seven of them were assets—the balaclava had said so—and the plan was obviously to keep them in good condition.

Which made sense of the food and water and blankets: all good signs too.

Yes, if he concentrated on the positives, the brutal negative of being held here faded; Ethan almost managed to ignore it altogether. But the fearful truth re-formed around the shifting light and dark beneath that metal door. He considered another whistle. Yet even if he caught the face's attention, any communication with it would have to be too loud. He might draw the guards' attention and, above everything else, he did not want to risk that. Gray compliance was the tactic for this situation, the only way he could see of overcoming it, of emerging unscathed. Although he knew it was ridiculous, it seemed he did not want to disturb the guards for *their* sake, as much as *his*. The fear in his chest was held in check by a warm feeling, of protectiveness. Risible, yes, but he wasn't laughing.

Now the day was sliding into moonlit night. The space between Ethan and the other building had turned from brown to silver gray. Still he lay on his stomach, watching the darkness moving under the door and listening for the scratching. It seemed to have grown louder, and it now came in frantic bursts. Once, footsteps cut across the yard, and Ethan fancied that they paused just out of sight. Listening. He shook his head: the digger was an idiot; he should stop.

But he was still watching when the door opposite barked. Once, twice. Then silence. Surely everybody else must have heard. No, the silence continued. After long minutes, the queen's head, barely visible in the half-light, began, very gradually, to turn. A doorpost came with it, inching away from the rest of the frame.

Ethan did not dare to breathe. The ground he lay on ran out beneath his own door, across the space, right up to and under those silent feet. A figure, caped in a blanket, a comic-strip hero, paused in the doorway. Ethan felt a yell rise within him, but bit down on the sound before it came. His eyes shut in sympathy with his mouth. When he opened them again, Rafi's outline had gone.

TWENTY-TWO

Before the second tube rocked to a halt at Baker Street Rachel saw that it was as full as the one she'd skipped. Few people disembarked. She frowned. There was nothing for it; pressing forward with the crowd, she wedged herself into a gap between a suit-back and a sheet of warm plastic.

The trick now was to zone out, like the Dalai Lama. Later she wondered whether the newspaper triggered that link, Delhi to Dalai, or if it was a coincidence. Either way, her next thought was not about the printed page, wavering to the track-rhythm on the other side of the clear partition. Instead she found herself disapproving of the hand that held it: ragged nails, each one gnawed to its pink quick.

But the page snapped and moved toward her, flopping against the Perspex. Rachel blinked once and began reading.

FEARS GROW FOR BRITONS KIDNAPPED IN KASHMIR
By Paul Frost in New Delhi

Concern is growing over the fate of three Britons abducted by militants while on a hill-walking holiday in Kashmir. Ethan Hughes, 24, Kate Cox, 25, and George Arnott, 39, were seized along with an American couple and two others while trekking in the Himalayan foothills near Srinigar, the Kashmiri summer capital.

The militants initially abducted the group of seven along with their Kashmiri tour guide and cook, but later freed the Kashmiris, who raised the alarm. Last night British High Commission officials in Delhi were awaiting news of the hostages. The young couple, who have no children, had saved for two years to pay for the trip. Mr. Arnott is thought to have been traveling alone.

Officials have revealed . . .

The page concertinaed, severing the story. Rachel let out an involuntary "Wait." But her voice was lost in the wail of train brakes. Not braced to decelerate, she lurched backward into the suit. When she'd apologized herself upright, the paper was out of sight entirely, and the bitten hand was gone, lost in the crowd. Rachel steadied herself against a metal pole, too stunned to move before the train took off.

Mistakes in the story were her only hope. Kate wasn't twenty-five, and neither she nor Ethan had saved up for the trip. They just went. Which meant the journalist had the wrong names, there'd been a mix-up, a senseless error. She would buy the paper at the next station, and prove herself right.

But the train stopped in the tunnel. She stared at her reflection in the black window. It seemed to swim in newsprint. She shut her eyes, trying to blank the article out entirely, and succeeded; but relived a sickening childhood memory instead.

ARRIVING HOME FROM SCHOOL. Swinging her book bag onto the kitchen surface like normal, but the house all strange. Looking out back, the line was still strung with washing. Lots of her dad's shirts hanging upside down, waving for help. Their shadows waved back.

A noise came downstairs and her voice saying "Mum" went to greet it. There was no answer. Rachel walked with small steps into the hall. It was surprising that her feet wanted to go this way. Up each carpeted lip, onto the landing with its pictures of hills and sheep and the horse.

There was a mess in the entrance to her dad's room. She couldn't see in because one of his chutes had been taken out of its case. It was puffed to shoulder height and spilling from the doorway into the hall. Rachel stopped beside it and saw that the yellow silk of the canopy was full of ragged tears. The carpet beneath her tiptoes was a spaghetti of cut strings.

The noise was a sob, and it happened again, coming from the bathroom. There was something wrong. The first thing she saw through the crack were scissors on the floor. Orange plastic handles wide, steel blades mid can-can. Next, the naked soles of her mother's feet, curled and creased like the newborn puppies next door. Their wrinkles faded as her mum rocked forward, squeezed shut when she sat back on her heels. Something about her back rocking there made Rachel keep quiet. Instead of speaking she eased the door wider, hoping her mum would turn around.

There were newspapers everywhere. The bath was full of open pages; crumpled cuttings spread across the carpeted floor. The aftermath of Christmas in black and white. Beneath the sink, in fact, there were still some presents to go. Two unopened bales crossed with a ribbon of packing tape, a third on top of them, undone. Rachel's mother rocked forward again, took a folded newspaper from the top of the pile, spread it on the bath mat with one hand in a practiced movement. The Stanley knife she held in her other came forward and sliced out two-thirds of the open page. She paused with the cutting, then scrunched it and tossed the crumpled shape aside. The rest of the paper she flung on top of the others in the bath. Again the dry sob.

The bottom of the door snagged on a discarded page. Her mum slowly turned. It didn't look like crying. Her face was as blank as the tiles behind it.

"Oh, I see. You're back."

"What are you doing?"

"Nothing, sweetie." She stood up on stiff knees, pushed a hand through her perm, emerging from fog. "You must be hungry. Is Kate home yet?"

"No. I don't think so. Why are you putting all those newspapers into the bath?"

"She won't be long, though. She'll be back soon too. I ought to start on supper."

"Mum?"

"Those?" She pointed at the bath with the Stanley knife, then realized she was doing so and withdrew the blade with her thumb.

Down by her feet, the most recently discarded cutout was unfolding gradually, like a flower on television. "I'm not sure, honey." She paused.

"There's a lot of papers."

"Uh-huh."

"Why?"

"I'm not exactly—" Her face crinkled for an instant and then set again.

"And one of Dad's parachutes is all torn up on the landing."

"Right, darling." Her mum was nodding. Her funny, cartoonish smile turned from Rachel to the bath again. "Actually, that's not quite right. I *am* sure. I'm cleaning up. Someone's made an awful mess in those papers and I'm sorting it out. Because I tell you one thing, this is enough papers for a lifetime. I won't have another one in the house, ever. How about that then?"

"Okay." It didn't make much sense, but now wasn't a good time to say so. All that mattered was getting Mum out of the bathroom and downstairs, back to normality. "Shall I put the kettle on for a cup of tea?"

"That'd be nice." Rachel's mum took a step toward her and patted the top of her head stiffly. "I can finish up here later."

Rachel continued to look down. The flower had bloomed as far as it would ever do now. She was surprised to see, near its still crumpled center, her father's smiling face.

Now the train had finally reached Euston Square. She had already fought her way to the door: she must finish the article to make sure.

Yet she froze in front of the kiosk, not knowing which

broadsheet to buy. The words were black on white, so not the *FT*, but . . . she bought the lot and crouched with them on the platform, on a level with trouser legs and briefcases, coattails and skirt hems, searching for the only news.

> *Officials have revealed that they were contacted by a previously unknown group calling itself "F.N.R." which is demanding the release of fellow separatist activists imprisoned by the Indian authorities. Delhi has rejected all such demands in the past, calling on Pakistan to clamp down on militant groups, which it accuses of carrying out terrorist activity.*
>
> *Authorities in Kashmir have interviewed the tour guide, who was released by the militants shortly after the group's capture. Nabbi Alfan, 42, said, "Eight heavily armed men stopped us as we were returning to camp shortly before sunset. There was no violence and nobody was hurt, but I am fearful for my clients' safety if the militants' demands are not met. This is further terrible news for our tourist industry here. The government in Delhi must act to end the wider conflict without delay. I am praying for a peaceful outcome."*
>
> *The mountainous region of Kashmir is the subject of a fifty-year dispute between neighboring India and Pakistan. In the wake of recent violence, the Foreign Office had advised tourists not to go to the area.*

The story stood just above an advertisement for a hair-loss clinic. A hand running through a sequence of three increasingly hirsute heads. Or, the other way around, someone tearing their hair out. That Rachel should find out something so distressing as this in a

newspaper underlined the fact that it could not be true. She gathered a clump of her own fringe and wound it round a forefinger.
She'd goaded Kate into going to Kashmir: that much was plain.
Find yourself a hot spot. The finger tensed away from her head,
pulling tears into her eyes, each of the twenty or so strands
straining at its separate root. Guilt became anger and dissolved to
sadness, for Ethan, for Kate, for herself. The paper *must* be mistaken. She stared down at it, weeping. The first root gave. Then
the second, intensifying the needle-prick of pressure in each of
the other straining follicles until, with a hot crackle, the rest of
the clump came.

TWENTY-THREE

KATE SAT WITH HER eyes shut against the dark, willing sleep, which would not come. She was cold. She wrapped the blanket more tightly around her head and shoulders and sat shivering beneath it. Diamonds rushed her. Beautiful and individual and vicious and haranguing.

"Why did you come here?"

"Exactly, what a fucking mess."

"Think you could have avoided it?"

"Hungry? Cold? Dirty?"

"Well, think of the others."

"And it's all your fault."

"For twenty-five dollars."

"And a *story*."

"The buck—"

"Invest—"

"Any regrets?"

"How about another gray egg?"

"Your choice."

"Investigate!"

"It's either that or the buck—"

"All of it, your own doing."

"The bucket bucket bucket!"

"No!" A voice cut through the nonsense. She opened her eyes, shook herself free of the blanket.

"No-oh": the voice again.

The real darkness was worse than the diamonds. Bitumen black, ocean deep. She couldn't see the walls, roof, or floor. It felt like falling, tail first, at terminal velocity: an invisible tear in the night sky.

She forced herself to keep looking.

A spear of yellow light flicked across her floor. After a pause, it happened again, accompanied by a noise. Something heavy dragging itself across rough ground. Or being dragged.

"Why?"

It was a man's voice, at least the remnants of one. Next, a muffled thud like the sound of an ax stopping dead, in wet wood. And then the dragging started up again.

Kate sat up and felt her way to the door, helped by another flash of the yellow light. With an eye to the crack she searched the space in front of her makeshift cell. Two figures hauled themselves into view. Black shapes, occasionally jumping into full color at the command of a torch beam, coming from behind. Both leaned into their walk, as if hauling a boat ashore. Each of them pulling on his own rope. The torch cut from nowhere to a denim back, and there was a tight line slung over his shoulders, attached to . . . a pair of feet. For a second the feet were spotlit and Kate saw that one was bare. Then the beam jumped across the inert figure, briefly snagging on the shape of a shorn head.

"Ethan!" she screamed. "Eth—"

The beam cut back and it wasn't him. Black hair. Her eyes swam with tears, making it more difficult to see. And then she was completely blind. A voice behind the light spoke.

"He tried to run away but we have brought him back."

Already the front two figures were past the doorjamb, out of sight. Rafi's prone form moved to catch them up in brief bursts. The torch played over the scene once again. A bow-wave of dirt and wood chips spilling around his thighs. Kate saw a snapshot of arms, also tied together, flung back over the lolling head. Then it was just the dragging noise and shadows, sporadic on the far wall.

ETHAN WOKE TO HIS name. He lay listening, flat on his back, rigid with cold. Rolling up onto his elbow was prying a girder from frozen ground. For long seconds there was silence. He began to doubt that he'd heard the scream at all. But the memory of Rafi fleeing at nightfall came back to him and he found himself screwed tight to the gap under the door, staring out into the darkness, even before the first footsteps became audible. There was tramping, and a torch, and a body on its side. Rafi's head was hanging so far back Ethan thought he was dead. He stared, aghast at the inevitability of such a thing, absolutely unwilling to turn the corner it represented. And it worked. Rafi lunged sideways, definitely alive, grabbing, if somewhat pathetically, at the torchbearer's feet. As he did so, he called out. The noise was a plea beyond language, at once senseless and obvious.

The guard with the torch shone its yellow eye down at Rafi, and calmly kicked free of his feeble grip. Rafi twisted like a loose hose. Somebody spoke angrily, though Ethan could not work out who. The light skipped away and then returned. It dwelled on the denim jacket, apparently kneeling over Rafi now, at the head end. One of his hands worried at Rafi's collar. From so low an elevation, and in just the torchlight, Ethan couldn't work the picture out. Could-not became would-not: he looked away and shook his head, but was unable to dislodge the sight. They were dragging Rafi into the open door of his cell. The torch illuminated the smaller space from within, bouncing from its walls, a visible echo. Black figures multiplied around the heap in the doorway. Somebody was pointing upward and gesturing with the end of the rope. It took two goes to toss the knot over the rafter, and all three of them worked together to raise him, feet first, toward the roof.

Once satisfied that he was secure, the torch looked Rafi up and down lazily. A high diver the moment before impact, feet nicely together, arms extended. Ethan wished, with every fiber, for movement: a hand, even a finger. But the three figures pausing there in front of the open door seemed reverent before Rafi's inverted statue, and the same stillness took hold of Ethan as they drifted away.

TWENTY-FOUR

T HE GENERATOR STOPPED, unfolding a limitless calm. For a few seconds she tried not to open her eyes, as if by leaving them shut she could keep the fear and the dark at bay. In the end the urge to look overcame her, though, and it was a relief to see morning. No spoke yet, but four gray walls were better than nothing at all.

Kate's walking boots were paired to one side of the door, laces tucked into each open mouth. As a point of principle, she did not sleep in them. But now it was a new day and she put them on again, tying the laces slowly and deliberately, trying to rebuild a sense of normality by performing this mundane act with special care. The benefit did not last; the sight of her laced boots reminded her suddenly of Nabbi. In a snap of frustrated rage she kicked the bottom of the door.

The quiet that followed the bang was split by another sound. Kate left a pause and then kicked the door again, twice. Two distant knocks answered hers. She repeated the signal, smiled on hearing another response. It sounded as if the noise was coming from her left. Eyeing the crack again though, nothing had changed. It was impossible to know who was replying, yet enough to be sure that one of them was. To have overcome this isolation, even in so meaningless a way, felt like victory. It might be Ethan. Kate kept kicking.

The denim guard stopped her. He filled the door frame and Kate instinctively retreated to the back wall. It looked like he'd just woken up; one half of his hair was right-angled above a part. Bed hair.

"What?" he asked.

"Sorry?"

"What is it?"

"I don't understand. Nothing."

"Why this knocking and knocking? You have a difficulty?" He stuck his little finger in the ear beneath the part and jiggled it angrily. A ring on the finger flashed while Kate weighed the question and fought to contain her response.

"What have you done with Rafi?"

"Ra . . . fi." The guard experimented with the syllables.

"Where is he? What did you do to him?"

The finger stopped digging. The guard took a step further into the room, looking the walls up and down as if he hoped to find an answer to the question there.

"Well?" Kate put her hands on her hips, but the gesture just made her feel more ineffectual. She crossed her arms instead.

The denim guard watched her, unimpressed, stroking his beard thoughtfully. Eventually he shrugged. "He made trouble for everyone, so we have tied him up. You will see." The finger pointed at Kate. "In meantime, shhh!" He turned and left, slamming the door.

Kate sat in the gloom again. Rafi was a soldier. Perhaps he had managed to alert somebody before the guards recaptured him. By staring hard enough at the possibility she could make it seem real. There would be people looking for them by now. Special Forces, almost certainly. Faced with such a threat, the idiot balaclava would quickly give them up. Or there'd be a rescue operation and they'd be set free anyway. Although there wasn't much she could do to speed up their release, she could prepare for it by keeping vigilant. She moved away from the arc of the door and sat at the back of her cell, out of the way, listening hard.

LATER KHALID ESCORTED HER to perform. He did not meet her eye while they walked, stood intent upon his rifle strap as she shut the toilet-block door. The pit toilet again proved impossible, but Kate washed at the standpipe. It gurgled and spat icy water into a puddle on the floor, dirtying her boots and trousers, freezing her fingers from raw red to white.

The tap shrieked as she turned it off. Only the shriek was a muffled yell that continued for too long, nothing to do with the plumbing at all. Kate stood transfixed, her heart hammering in her ears. The mouth of the pit mocked her as she tried to convince herself otherwise, but the shouting came again, driven by an intermittent thwacking; the beating of wet washing against a wall. From close by, within the toilet block. They must be punishing Rafi. Kate found herself paralyzed by the noise, her throat dry with fear. She only started at the louder crack of a palm on the wooden door.

Outside the washroom the shouting stopped, or she could no longer hear it. Khalid fidgeted before her, ominously silent, prevaricating. Eventually, he steered her away with his gun barrel. But instead of turning left, back to her cell, Khalid led her round the other way. This was unprecedented and she found herself gulping air. The windowless room with its spoke was familiar and known and safe, but the farmstead was a confusing maze of low stone walls, sinister in the morning light. In one direction she saw mountains and was shocked to consider that just days ago they had been the point.

Then there were more outbuildings and a shape Kate understood ahead of recognition: Rafi hanging upside down in an empty doorway, his mouth sagging open below the bigger smile of his slit throat. The sight was at once real and fake, a pretend body and Rafi, joke-shop blood and death. She'd never seen a corpse before but was not surprised by this sight in the least, just kneeling down again and looking to Khalid for an explanation.

"My orders are that you must see. I am sorry, but this is what happens if you try to run away."

The boy gestured at the doorway, declining to look himself. Instead he pulled at his sleeve and moistened his lips, sucking both in turn. He appeared ashamed, or perhaps just sheepish. Which converted Kate's horror to anger; she found that she had dug two handfuls of wood chips and dirt, and was lifting one to throw in his face.

"Kate!"

Ethan's voice, nearby. The hand dropped as she swung about to find him. But there were only blank doors, and the guard was again steering her forward.

ETHAN'S EYES FOLLOWED HER out of view. He was shaking with fear and anger. That Kate had even risked raising a fist, there, in full view of Rafi's body, beggared belief. He had

watched the darkness through to dawn, seen the corpse material-
ize in its butcher-shop window. A sickening exclamation mark.
How could she put herself at such risk?

He fought to keep himself calm. An aberration. Kate wasn't
daft. She was calm in a crisis; she thought things through. That
trip in her little plane, for example, with the panic cloud and
forced landing. The cockpit thick with her fear. It had taken
everything he had to sit there silent, to appear unruffled for her
sake, yet her own self-control appeared effortless. She got them
down. That was capability, it would see Kate through. Better that
thought, than its opposite—the image of her petrified, alone in
her cell. A leadenness pressed him to the floor. How had he not
risen to the challenge of thanking her that day, of acknowledging
her . . . competence, at the very least?

Footsteps grew again. Ethan rolled back from the door when
its lock shot and was struggling to his feet as it opened. The
stumpy guard hustled him out into the courtyard, walked him
across it to the corpse, and stood next to it with his arms emphatically folded across the swell of his stomach.

"Run," he said. "Problem."

Ethan tried to keep all expression from his face. He barely
looked. But when he did it was impossible not to notice how the
roof of the mouth was purple behind crenulated front teeth. The
lips were swollen and cracked, the underside of the tongue black
in shadow. At least, upside down like that, the shapes had less to
do with Rafi. Khalid returned. The fat guard said something to
the youngster, prompting him to explain quietly, in English.

"We are to take you to Abu, who will teach you why this cannot happen."

The stumpy guard pushed him sideways. A stiff-armed palm-off, enough to make Ethan trip over his feet. Righting himself, he kept his eyes on the ground, allowed the guard to prod him further, past more stone outbuildings and in through another open door, which banged shut behind him.

This room was empty, but there was a window. Pale morning fell through the glass, giving the space a calm at odds with its stark contents, empty apart from a heap of sacks strewn in the back corner, and an upended plastic chair, on its side in the middle of the pile.

The sacks were a jumble of shadows at first, but as Ethan's eyes adjusted he saw that in fact part of the shadow was stain. He sat down on the floor, something inside of him giving in. A room full of stains, Rafi with his throat cut, hung from his beam, the life draining out of him drop by drop. Was this where he would end? Ethan stared down at his blackened fingernails and felt the blood pulsing beneath them and for the first time in his life feared that it would stop. What came afterward? He'd never really paused to consider that he would die. But now he felt a shivery otherness envelop him. Death was an ending, and an ending would make a frame. It meant perspective, judgment. He saw Kate walking toward him across a postcard Oxford quadrangle, each hyperreal blade of grass in place, the sunlight angling down over bombproof battlements. He saw Rachel raised on one elbow, blowing smoke at the ceiling. And then the pictures fell away and the room came crashing back into focus with its cold light and dirty sackcloth and single, fiendish chair.

The door swung open again and the denim guard, Abu, swaggered into the room. If the walk was a clue, the man's eyes gave him away entirely. They said: *Because I can.* Ethan had seen the same expression before, in playgrounds and dormitories, on sports fields and in front of nightclubs. Even, a long time ago, in the kitchen at home. The strong in their own thrall, securely differentiated.

"Your friend has done this," Abu stated. Behind him, the squat guard had also sidled into the room. He shut the door, wandered round to the chair, righted it: a teacher tidying a classroom.

"Sit."

"He was not my friend."

Abu, ignoring him, continued: "It was all explained. You are very valuable. Assets." The squat guard had pulled Ethan's unresisting hands together behind the chair and was tying them with a cord. Abu paced in front of the chair, working himself up. "But you are not valuable if you run away. Then you are worth nothing at all."

"I know that, I haven't—"

"See what happens if you try?" He waved a hand at the window. "You stop being important people." With the same hand Abu smoothed his black beard mechanically. Then he advanced and slapped Ethan on the shoulder—an incongruously comradely gesture. "Big man, eh. No difference."

Ethan saw that the hand was quivering.

"So we must make you think twice about running."

Now the blindfold. Ethan kept his head down, supplicant in every gesture. But, as his pulse quickened, his mouth couldn't resist a further plea: "I didn't—"

"For your own goodness. Yes?"

"I don't—"

The first blow was a relief. It jarred and bloomed, like the first tackle. From then on the next one was always coming; Ethan, blindfolded, was never and always ready for it. Better they beat him than Kate. He excised himself from the scene as far as possible, jerking unavoidably back to the present in the instant of being hit, but melting away in the gaps.

IT WAS IMPORTANT to be strong and brave, and not a coward. The walls at home said that. On plaques with insignia of beaks and arrows and red crosses and Latin, commemorating this Falkland Island skirmish and that honorable service in Ireland or Cyprus. In rows of shorn heads staring in lines, squared up in front of a field hospital, or hangar, or barracks. If you were brave and strong, and not cowardly, you'd get somewhere, the pictures said, you'd succeed, like Dad; there was hope that you'd make a true and successful young man. You could shut your eyes and hear him saying it, or something similar. Open them again and there he was, on the touchline in a deerstalker and sopping overcoat. "Come on you reds!" he cried.

When you went in, you should go in hard. That was all part of it. You went in hard because it was brave to do so and if you were brave you wouldn't get hurt. Like Mr. Phillips said, it was all about *committing*, whatever that word meant. The ball was coming out, streaked with brown from the cut-up field, plopping out of the back of the scrum like a special turd or maybe a baby being born into Doherty's hands. Now Ethan's legs had decided to start running.

Doherty was good, but Ethan was the captain and the star. Nobody disagreed with that. In a race, any race, Ethan won. The ball was looping out from Doherty, a slow bullet spinning through the rain, aimed a few paces in front of Ethan, which was right. He was already running on to it. He saw himself and the field from above and the gaps ahead were obvious. The squirt at inside center was one of them; he'd never stop Ethan, whose hands reached for the ball without looking and put it under his arm, gathering momentum in these first few strides, which was mass times something, applied force greater than its resistance. He'd look it up. Already the inside center was retreating, little red knees pumping in all sorts of wrong directions.

Maybe she was in the car because of the wet. Perhaps that was it. Dad was up by the opposition's touchline to watch Ethan running in the tries, as usual, but Mum was parked, because of the rain. Except that she never normally minded, and as Ethan aimed his next steps at the retreating little-un it was obvious really that it had to do with her eye, like her blue cheek after Christmas. The eye and the plaques and courage and cowardice and his mother and father: they didn't add up.

There was a funny look on the inside center's face. You could tell from it he knew he would be run down. Mashed. Ethan would go in hard, which you should do if you didn't want to get hurt, if you were brave and strong. He'd run the short-arse over. "Go on, then!" yelled Dad. "Go on!" The only other big kid on the entire field was their number eight, who had yet to pull his head out of the back of their collapsed scrum, and even then he was big and mean but ginger and pretty gormless, he couldn't have caught Ethan anyway, Ethan who was ten explosive paces into his angled run, bearing down on the inside center now, shoulder dipping. "Go on, then, go on!"

Which was funny because that was what Mum had cried after Christmas when she'd slipped in the kitchen on the floor wet from the leak that went away on its own. Upstairs Ethan had thought he was dreaming it but the Subbuteo green was in focus in the middle of his bedroom floor the second time he heard the words. You could see the players in the glow coming from beneath the bedroom door, casting stringy shadows. "Go on, then," she shrieked, her American accent twanging. "Go on!"

Ethan's knees pumped higher and he gathered himself for the impact, anticipating the delicious sense of continuation which, once he'd stomped through the tackle, was guaranteed. Marcus was outside him yelling "Pass," but what was the point in that? The object was to score points after all, and the scrum was breaking up to his right and this kid just here was a hole waiting to open; yes, their entire retreating three-quarter line was a field of bracken just asking to be trampled flat.

It was lucky Dad was an army doctor because he had all the gear. Ethan was padding downstairs in his pyjamas to find out about his mother, but only got as far as the hall before he met Dad coming the other way. His face was full of veins and the color of Christmas ham and he put a hand on Ethan's shoulder to steer him back upstairs, past the little shields with their mottoes and claws and gloved fists. "Back to bed now. Mum's fine, a little slip, an accident, damned dishwasher." His breath smelled sharp. "I'm just fetching supplies from the bathroom, witch hazel, to dress the bruise. You jump back into bed now. I'll kill that moron plumber. There's a good chap."

Ethan's feet had trodden obediently round the Subbuteo green and into bed then, like a good fellow, not a plumber, but now they seemed to have made an odd decision. Mum was in the car behind layers of perfume and misted windows and dark glasses. There with her red eye. Like last time, when it was the blue cheek, she didn't want to come out. As if sunlight might make the bruising spread. And Dad was yelling "Go on, son!" as if he had any sort of a right to comment or instruct. The field was minced mud flying from Ethan's heels, which were suddenly idiots, swerving away at this last minute, changing the angle of his attack, aiming him back at the heart of the opposition's pack.

Marcus was still outside yelling "Pass!" and Doherty thought Ethan was contriving some complicated reverse angle for him to bisect, but that wasn't the point at all. The little inside center's chapped knees were slowing, his eyes were wide in disbelief, and Ethan had caught up with himself, knew what his heels intended, ignored Doherty's clever tangent, plowed the remaining few yards straight at the number eight, whose first sight on looking up from the disentangling wreckage of the scrum brought an incredulous smile to his ox-face, a split of mouth guard there beneath that wire-wool hair, unable to believe his luck. The orange head dipped, arms agape. Ethan tilted lower too. Something to do with equal and opposite forces about to collide.

The jarring was like falling out of a tree. Then a black wave rolled over Ethan. He lay beneath it, oddly happy, with the words *brave* and *strong* and *coward* nipping at his fingers and eyelids and calves like tiny invisible fish.

AND HE WAS ODDLY relaxed when the wave rolled back. The beating was fists and open hands and Ethan hung on to a single idea: it could have been worse. Although he was not sure, the grunts that accompanied each punch and slap seemed to belong to one man. There was blood in his mouth, though it tasted like sweat. Or was that the smell of Abu, delivering the punishment alone? Ethan's own gasps became groans, but he suppressed the urge to yell in retaliation, struggled successfully not to struggle, tried to imagine Abu tiring quickly in the face of so immediate and complete a victory. There was silence.

(In her cell, Kate heard the pause in this further beating. To be under lock and key while it went on, powerless either to flee or help, was its own torture. The noise was indistinct, she couldn't tell who the cries belonged to. Eventually the urge overcame her and she delivered two further kicks to the bottom of her door, listened carefully for a reply. Bang, bang.)

The banging reverberated through Abu's silence, prompting him to turn back to Ethan and deliver two last blows. Then the beating stopped and the blindfold came off. Ethan felt himself scrutinized but kept from meeting Abu's gaze. His chest was wet and the view from one eye narrowed as he sat waiting for the guard to regain his composure. The hurt was a mesh, drawn tight around him, and oddly comforting. *I am here*, it said. Ethan noticed that at some point the guard had taken his denim jacket off. Keeping it clean. Wearing it before, but not now, because now it was folded neatly on the sill. Abu picked it up and draped it over his arm with a forced calmness, at odds with the sheen across his forehead and the studied indifference of his nod to the other guard.

Ethan stayed still as the squat one untied him and led him back to his cell. Such physical obsequy was an alien thing, yet his sense of outrage was dwarfed by the phrase that kept repeating: *It—could—have—been—much—worse.*

In the gloom, he broke the pain down into its component parts. The smarting eye, the swollen nose, bruised upper arms, a dull ache across his pummeled back and chest. At some point Abu had kicked his right shin. Running his hand over the lump, Ethan was cast back: this was a gross exaggeration of the familiar post-match stock-taking, his body reclaiming itself in the aftermath of adrenaline. Then, the pain had felt pointless, a punishment of success. Now, though, it was a hideous affirmation.

And there was something more. They hadn't taken him to where Rafi was. They could have done, but they hadn't. Despite their absolute power, the guards had refrained from taking the absolute step. Some sense of proportion had prevailed. Despite his anger, Ethan felt a spark of gratitude. In not taking his life the captors had given him a gift. Though it shamed him to think it, his tears were grateful, for generosity deserved thanks.

TWENTY-FIVE

THE HARDER SHE TRIED to hold on to where she was, the more she found herself thinking about where she was not. It even became difficult to concentrate on the turning spoke. One minute it was just that, a white line of sun counting down the bricks; the next she was staring along the leading edge of a wing into the patchwork of fields below.

"It's constant control," her instructor was saying, "minute adjustments ahead of the need for big corrections. Try again."

For a steep turn you banked the plane with ailerons and then pulled back on the stick to keep from losing height, tightening the curve with the elevators. Toeing in a touch of opposite rudder helped keep the plane balanced, and you throttled up going through thirty degrees, to maintain airspeed. It helped avoid that forbidden eyeballing of the altimeter if you picked a point on the nose cowl to stick on the horizon right the way round. And if you got it right, if you pulled through three hundred and sixty degrees without losing or gaining height, you'd feel it in the airframe, a satisfying jolt of turbulence as the plane hit its own slipstream.

Kate wrote the word *pen* in spit on the cement floor. Then she stared at her hand, allowing the line of sun to play across its palm. Flying was control, second by second: here time meant nothing and she had no control at all. There were shadows in the whorls of her dirty fingerprints. But the lines did not hold Kate's attention for their own sake. As soon as she focused on the intricate pattern she was hanging there in the sky, staring down at the lake through the cockpit side-window, at ripples spread by distant boats.

She shut out the image by putting both hands together and for a second that worked: she was alone, stuck with the reality of her cell. But then the sight of her wrists touching reminded her of how Rafi's had been bound, and the memory of them hanging beneath him in the doorway was vivid and unavoidable.

She was to blame. She had created this entire situation, and as such was responsible for everything that flowed from it. Yes. She was responsible for Rafi's death.

No. Rafi died because he tried to escape. If he'd just stayed put like the others he'd still be alive. But that begged the question, what might happen to the rest of them next?

Negotiations were undoubtedly under way. Embassy officials were surely in contact with the militants—perhaps even with the balaclava himself. Release terms would be agreed on. The hand-over was no doubt already in train. Journalists, local politicians, consulate staff; military personnel, special agents, crisis coun-selors: countless people would have come together to end the horror. Yet when she shut her eyes she could not bring a single face into focus, could not imagine where the officials might be gathered, what maps or charts would hang before them on the wall.

She veered from the unthinkable future back to the past. At what point had they been set up? Nabbi handed them over without even pretending to object. And yet she could not conceive of this being his plan. Everything about the man lacked initiative. Which pushed her further back, to the fat tout in Srinigar. *He* was to blame. But that just meant she was too. She had sold them all into the fat tout's hands, for twenty-five dollars a head.

Where was the proof though? She struggled further backward. Wasn't their fate sealed before they stepped off the bus? Wouldn't Sunil have delivered them into captivity as well? What was to say that *all* the touts weren't working together? If so—and for a moment such a blanket of deception seemed likely—each of their party was equally blameless. Or at least they were all equally at fault. But she now recalled the sight of Sunil throwing the envelope into the fire pit. She saw it twist and burn in the cell before her, pressed her palms to her eyes to block out the sight.

No, to avoid the guilt she had to go right back, to the start. They each decided to visit Kashmir, and ultimately their abduction was Kashmir's fault. Or theirs, for coming. All of them had risked traveling here, prepared to take the gamble either because they had discounted the danger, were willfully blind to it, or even because they were in its thrall. She wasn't to blame for that.

Why then did this reasoning leave her unconvinced? Because she suspected that not *all* of them had considered the risk. Kate felt the question—*Was Kashmir Ethan's conscious choice?*—but could not answer it.

Instead she said his name out loud—"Ethan"—trying to take heart in its familiarity. For although this room was absolutely familiar it managed, at the same time, to be the sum of everything foreign. She looked from the bucket to the bricks to the blanket folded in the corner, traced the join up to the rafters and the corrugated roof, seeing these things before her eye arrived at them and yet surprised by their nuances nevertheless: the crudity of that bolt, the burned blackness of the beam above the door.

Next to the word *pen* Kate traced out *paper* in the dust, but other words, spoken by her flying instructor, were ringing in her ears.

"Anticipation is the key," he explained. "Think ahead on every axis. Get it right, and you'll be spinning the horizon around the plane."

She had tried to think of herself as the still point, of the wings remaining fixed while she turned the sky smoothly about them and, gradually, she learned to master the maneuver. It was addictive; she honed her powers of prediction until she felt she could execute a steep turn with her eyes shut. Practicing alone, she would forget the horizon and look instead at the lowered wingtip, aiming it at overlapping fields, crosshaired sheep fences, a flashing edge of lake.

Remembering the brightness now, in the dark of her cell, was torture. She was not only her captors' prisoner, but subject to herself as well. She focused on the leg-landscape of her trousers and drew breath.

"Got to keep control," she said out loud. "Got to keep thinking under control."

The way to survive was to keep a record; she could tame the

past and make sense of the present by thinking of the account she'd write for the future. Already the words written in spit were evaporating. So that would be a project, wheedling a pen and paper from one of the guards. In the meantime, she must keep her observations fresh by repeating them over and again. She watched the letters until they had all but faded, whispering to herself.

TWENTY-SIX

"WE WERE JUST ABOUT to give up on you."

The taller of the two figures, who had risen to brush the creases from his suit as Rachel approached, stood now and held out both his hands, welcoming her home. In the streetlamp glow she made out two lamb-chop sideburns on either side of a pair of retro glasses. She stopped short of the stone pillar and shifted the briefcase to her left hand, freeing the right to reach inside her overcoat for her mobile phone.

"She's goin' for her gun," drawled the seated figure, from beneath the bill of a baseball cap.

"Look, we don't want to take up much of your time, but—"

Rachel tried to cut the man off. "I don't—" Yet he rode effortlessly over the interruption.

"I know, it's late, you've had a hard day and all that, and you made your position abundantly clear when we spoke earlier, but

I think you should reconsider. If you look at the big picture you'll see that this is a *positive* step; this is your chance to help."

THE CALL HE REFERRED to had been exquisitely timed. Earlier that day, shortly after Rachel had returned from a recuperative trip to the washroom at work, her boss slid across the floor on his chair. He squeezed her upper arm and spilled his suggestion: "Given the circumstances, I want to float the possibility of you taking some time off. Maybe a stretch of counseling. Just to help you climb back into the saddle."

"I wasn't aware that I'd fallen out of it." Her face overdid its smile.

"Maybe not; but you have to admit you've not been on top of your game these past weeks. Since—"

"I'm leaving all that at home. It's kind of you, but really. The last thing I need is time to dwell on it."

"But the work's suffering, Rachel. We missed last week's deadline and I just heard from BRS that they received a *draft* report this morning, full of blank pages. It's completely understandable. Your mind's elsewhere."

So were his eyes. Evading her own, they swept Rachel's desk, computer monitor, and cubicle partitions, stopping at her open desk drawer, in which her compact mirror sat in full view, BA club card lying across it. One of his hands worked at the other, cracking its knuckles in turn. Rachel swiveled toward him, nudging the drawer shut with her knee.

"We missed that deadline because the client wouldn't give us enough detail to report on in the first place, and I haven't sent *anything* to BRS—it must have been somebody else." She bit her bottom lip and allowed her foot to touch his calf.

"Still," he said, "the . . . pressure, is making you . . . erratic. I think you could do with some time to recoup." It wasn't working; he was staring at the drawer and he'd withdrawn his leg. "You've too much on your plate."

She shook her head and was about to reply when her phone rang. Her mother's voice, for the third time that morning. Rachel's boss cracked through the knuckles of his other hand while she spelled out again that she was fine, and gave more empty reassurances: they were bound to hear something soon. In the pause after she returned the handset to its cradle she could sense him searching for a way to say "See what I mean," but neither of them had the chance to speak as, again, the phone cut in. At least it wasn't her mother's number on the screen. Rachel punched the speaker button authoritatively.

"Rachel Cox?"

"Speaking."

"My name's David Turner. I'm calling from the *Sunday Telegraph Magazine*."

Rachel lifted the handset. Her boss rolled backward across the carpet tiles on his chair, waving *good-bye for now,* a look of triumphant sympathy on his face.

"What do you want?"

"We're keen to do a piece on your sister's story for this week's supplement. A human interest story. We'd like your comments."

"I'm not interested." She sniffed and wiped her nose. Human. Interest. Story.

"We just need some detail, some stuff on your sister's background. The kind of girl she was. Is, rather." He pressed on. "You know; like, did she give any indication of why she was going to a war zone for her holidays? And we're also after more information about the boyfriend. Edwin? The father's pretty much fleshed him out, but we'd appreciate it if you can add anything extra to that picture as well. You know . . ."

She'd read an article the week before, in which Ethan's father had spoken of the need to hold firm against the militants. He had every confidence that the Indian security forces, working with "our own boys," would secure the release of the hostages, either through negotiations or by other means. He knew Ethan would deplore the thought of causing any democratic government to set a dangerous precedent by acceding to the demands of a cowboy outfit like the F.R.N. Whatever transpired, his lad had backbone and wouldn't want to be the thin end of anybody's wedge. The thought of Ethan's take on this bluster would have been amusing, had it not reduced her to tears.

The reporter's disembodied voice was still buzzing at her down the phone line. Somebody's head appeared above the partition, mouthing a question. Rachel waved the person away. The rows and columns on the screen in front of her seemed to wobble and waver. The rush had passed now, leaving her nauseous and faint. Wiping her forehead with a palm, she raised her voice.

"No. Leave me alone. I don't want to speak to you or anybody else about what's happened, alright?"

"Sure, but—"

Rachel banged the phone down and sat back. Out of the corner of her eye she saw pale faces turn away.

NOW THE TALL MAN with sideburns was coming down her steps, arms still spread, jabbering like a politician. The seated figure stirred behind him, rummaging in a bag.

"Which part of "no" did you not understand?"

"The part that didn't mean it. Just think about the opportunity—"

Rachel thrust the phone forward, as if it were a talisman. She continued: "I'm going to call the police unless you leave me alone."

The baseball cap stood up now, laughed, and said, "Charming." A flashgun popped. It was as if a windscreen between Rachel and the pair had shattered. Glittering cobwebs remained. "One for my wall," the same voice said, "looker like you."

"He didn't mean that." The cracks melted and the man's sideburns came clear again. He was grinning amiably. "Look, we're prepared to pay for an interview. And the publicity can only be a good thing. I realize it must be difficult to talk in the circumstances, but don't you think your sister would want her story verified by someone close to her; by you?"

In the aftermath of the flash the reporter's face had appeared purple, his lips madder brown. His glasses winked orange. What would Kate want? The colors were helpful; they overshadowed the question, which was a good one, and yet obviously a trick. They would inevitably draw her to talk about Ethan, too. Over the reporter's shoulder she saw the polished glass of her apartment-block door swing open. She focused on the photographer, who rose to stand beside his colleague in the lamplight. Though pushing thirty, he wore different color Converse basketball boots; one was red and the other was sky blue. This detail offended Rachel. It spoke of a flippancy so at odds with what was at stake that for long seconds she could not bring herself to speak.

"Come on, love. We've waited here three hours. Be a sport." The photographer gave her a thumbs-up. The figure emerging from the block had stopped to watch, turning the confrontation into a performance.

"No. You've wasted your time." She started forward, spelling it out again as she did so: "You're wasting your time!"

The reporter stepped sideways and put a hand on the wrought-iron railing, cutting her off. The photographer closed ranks with him, so that the two of them barred her way.

"Look, we're going to write the piece anyway, with or without your help." The reporter dug his forefinger into a sideburn and scratched it abstractedly, underlining the fait accompli. "You might as well have your say."

Rachel pushed her hair back and met the man's eye. She left a pause, determined not to appear cowed in front of a neighbor. Shouldering between the two of them, her bag banged the photographer's slung camera, which clattered against the wall. She blotted out his "Whoa—" with a hissed "Piss off," and rounded on the reporter in retreat. "I'm not about to say anything at all."

TWENTY-SEVEN

THE FAT ONE was to blame. He delivered Kate's plate of food, and he spilled it. A crescent of rice slid onto the concrete and the peeled, hard-boiled egg followed it, picking up a gray stripe of dirt as it rolled across the floor.

"Breakfast." The guard nodded and slammed the door.

Khalid, who normally served the meals, did so with a waiter's attention to detail. He had a courteous manner which, Kate now saw, implied something like respect.

This stumpy guard's clumsiness felt like an insult by contrast. Something in Kate refused to let it pass. She gathered up the spillage, using the edge of the plate and her cupped hand, before dusting off the egg and setting it carefully beside the rice. Then she pushed the plate into the middle of her room, attaching a significance to it that it otherwise lacked. The meal was still there, untouched, when the guard returned for the plate. There were equal parts annoyance and concern in his face. He pointed at the food, then at his mouth, and made a question of his word for the day. "Breakfast?"

Kate shrugged.

Her ambivalence seemed to confuse the guard, who fingered his black stubble and paused with his mouth open to speak. He looked worried. Kate considered shoring up the gap by signing that she wasn't hungry, but something appealing about the guard's concern stopped her. Unable to proceed without words, he left to fetch the denim one, who took over.

"Mr. Sadiq says you are not eating. You are not I think hungry?"

Kate filed the name. Repeating the shrug, she said, "Of course I'm hungry. But today I've decided not to eat."

"Why? What is wrong?"

The question was suddenly funny. Kate's face lit up with a grin. The guards' concern vanished; she thought she saw a flash of fear in the squat one's eyes. Abu, however, was unimpressed. He shook his head, snatched up the plate, and shepherded Sadiq from the room.

She felt a perverse warmth after they left, not unlike the glow of having turned down the Glencare promotion. Immediate sacrifice for some unknown future gain. What, though? She stood and paced out the circumference of her cell, considering what she'd done, failing to understand herself or answer the more immediate question: was the lightness in her stomach hunger, or excitement?

Later, Khalid was back on duty. Kate heard his fingers at the padlock and looked up to see his young face thrust in at the door. He took a step forward and lowered another meal to the floor beside Kate's blanket, then stood back.

"Sadiq says you may be sick. That you would not eat. He says not eating would be a problem."

Kate's eyes adjusted to the brightness behind Khalid's head. She watched him suck both his lips in turn, and kept silent. His smooth brow broke out in uncharacteristic wrinkles. That such a simple act could create this level of interest, this quickly, was intoxicating. If she had been weighing whether to turn down the next meal—for the hunger was real now—Khalid's furrowed forehead made the decision much easier.

"I'm not sick."

"Good. Then you will eat now, please."

Kate smelled something new, coming from the plate. Instead of the plain boiled egg, a pool of what looked and smelled like vegetable curry swam in the middle of this helping of rice. And a red plastic fork stuck jauntily from beneath the steaming pile: the first cutlery she'd seen in three weeks, protruding from a *hot* meal. It was tempting to consider the plate a victory, but she held back from picking it up. The hot meal was just an attempt to check her revolution before it gained momentum. In refusing it she would amplify her protest tenfold. An exhilaration of influence pricked her skin, made her smile.

"No, thanks. You might as well give that to one of the others, before it gets cold."

Kate stared at her feet, hoping to see Khalid retrieve the plate. But he stayed put. "This choice meal is for you." His tone was imploring, not angry. "Please reconsider and eat." Out of the corner of her eye Kate saw Khalid drop to his hams in the doorway. When she turned he was squatting there, wringing his fingers at her, his head quivering expectantly. Was his concern mere self-preservation? Would he and the other guards somehow suffer for her refusal? Despite herself, Kate found herself reassuring Khalid.

"What are you meaning by this?" he asked.

"It's nothing personal." She held her palms up: *what can you do?*

"What will you hope to achieve?"

The hands bounced.

Khalid let out a loud sigh and retrieved the plate, his courtliness undercut by the vehemence with which he yanked the door shut.

KATE KEPT HER REBELLION up for seven days, during which time the hunger became a spellbinding discomfort. In flashes the sensation seemed its own victory, a demonstration of self-control that, she suspected, impressed the guards even as it annoyed them. On the surface they each had their own reaction: Sadiq met her resistance with disdain; denim Abu ranted; Khalid's wounded consternation deepened day by day. Kate knew that if her fasting engendered respect it did so against the guards' collective will; each response was calculated, above all, to make her change her mind and *eat*.

So she did not.

A welcome by-product of not caving in was the sidelining of the bucket. Unable to perform to order, Kate had been forced to use it. Now the bucket was largely obsolete again, and she felt she had won a minor battle. There was something funny about this triumph; the first time Kate went a full twenty-four hours without using it Khalid unwittingly added to the joke. He wore a

smile of pride on entering her cell. From behind his back he pro-
duced a plate of fragrant chicken, with a flourish that implied the
playing of a trump card. Only his hurt look when she declined
stopped her laughter.

Each hour of self-restraint increased her power, yet the opposite was also true; she feared the weakness in her limbs and suspected its numbing effect upon her mind. Did that matter?
They'd be out of here soon whatever. The authorities were already (it was impossible to think anything else) . . . on . . .
their . . . way. She should make a stand in the meantime, as an
apology to the others, a show of will.

Yet how the hunger unpicked her resolve! When the seventh
day passed it seemed significant, a valid place to draw a line in the
sand. She would have made her point. But a moral victory wasn't
quite enough. She needed evidence of a concession to mark her
resistance. The youngster Khalid offered the most hope. He, of all
the guards, had tried hardest to convince Kate to change her
mind, asking repeatedly what, other than making herself ill, she
hoped to achieve.

On the eighth morning she had an answer for him, but was
not hopeful that anything would come of her request. His flat
"That is not possible" confirmed her fear. Yet later in the day
Khalid's careful fingers undid the padlock once again.

"I am not really allowing this," he whispered, drawing the
door shut behind him.

"Allowing what?"

"But you have promised to eat again if I do, yes?"

"Depends what you're proposing," Kate repeated. "I'm not
sure."

"There is one condition, as well as the eating. You must not let anybody see that I gave this to you, okay?" Khalid took a small square package, wrapped in newspaper, from within his coat and laid it at Kate's feet. He looked almost excited, wide-eyed at the thought of his own initiative. "You must keep a secret. We are understanding each other?"

"I think so." She hadn't hoped to drive a wedge between her captors, and felt her blood course at the thought of such an outcome. Khalid's fingertips were playing at one another over the newspaper; she feared he might be having second thoughts, so reached out and took the package to cement the deal. Joy and relief fused in the young guard's face. For a moment his act seemed, to Kate, a transparent kindness. He had to struggle for authority again as he stood up to go.

"You will begin eating again with the next food," he ordered through the open door.

"Sure." She smiled. "Whatever you say."

Already the notebook was out of the newspaper wrapping and on Kate's lap, the single pencil squat and familiar between her fingers and thumb.

TWENTY-EIGHT

E<small>THAN TOOK A BREATH</small> of cold air, held it, and pushed up. His pulse thudded in his ears. He held himself rigid at the top of the movement until his stomach burned and the veins in his hands bulged. Then he lowered himself slowly back down between retreating forearms. At the bottom, when only his thumbs and forefingers were in view, he let the breath go.

The press-up threw him back. Now, his hands were splayed on concrete; then, his palms had sunk into sodden turf. Here, the movement, performed alone, had a meditative, monumental quality; there, pushing up in time with the rest of the squad, something had put him off.

"Come on, lads, put your backs into it. Give it some welly!" The coach's boots halted with a squelch in front of Ethan's head. "What's the matter with you? Why've you stopped?"

Ethan forced out a further press-up, in time with the rest. His arms complied automatically, a pair of pistons. But for some new reason his head was objecting, it was suddenly filled with a plain view of the row of identical backs jerking up and down in a line between the posts. Everybody else rose again, in time, but Ethan stayed down. The wet grass pressed through his rugby shirt.

"Are you alright?"

"Yes, Coach."

"Not pulled anything, I hope?" Everybody else dropped back down.

"No, Coach."

"Worn out then?" A sarcastic edge. Again the rest pushed up.

"No."

"Then what are you resting for?" Down again.

The damp had now seeped through Ethan's shorts. He pushed up once more to get away from it but, to the coach's consternation, followed through and stood up. In a quiet voice, he heard himself say, "I think I've had enough."

Somebody laughed, and collapsed onto the grass.

"Carry on, you lot. I didn't say to stop."

The coach removed his Welsh Dragon bobble hat and scratched the pinkness of his bald head. Everybody else was up-and-downing again. Steam rose from the man's scalp as Ethan stood before him.

"Look, lad. The whole team's got to train together. It's not just about scoring points, you know. Nobody's place is guaranteed."

Points were indeed pointless too. If the kamikaze swerve at his dad's "Go on!" five years beforehand had posed the question, this county coach was now answering it. Why bother going through the motions?

"I understand that."

"Well, then." The coach put his hands on his hips and cocked his head at the ground, then underlined the gesture by thumbing an imaginary lift. "Get back down and push."

The squad, in unison, rose. Ethan shook his head and said, "Sorry."

The coach's confusion barely had time to register; as the row of backs dropped again Ethan was already turning away.

Now though, this first press-up marked a new step. In the weeks after the beating his only aim was to recover. Enduring captivity, he saw, would take all his physical strength. The guards had determined a set of absolute parameters and Ethan, for once, saw the stark point in mastering the space those parameters defined. There were no longer any paralyzing gray areas breeding indifference: this new context was all about hardship, written in black and white. Questioning *why* the militants had taken them captive was as futile, Ethan saw, as questioning gravity: the only thing that mattered now was negotiating the consequences. Now the word *whatever* meant something new entirely.

His ambivalence evaporated. As the swelling went down and the bruises faded from black to yellow, he began a routine of stretching and pacing. The storeroom was not an easy space to exercise in, but that was part of the challenge. He calculated that the round trip from the wooden door to the rear wall and back was roughly twenty feet. Two hundred and fifty laps came to about a mile. He worked up to ten miles a day—a feat in his weakened state.

The monotonous diet of eggs and rice, he reasoned, was partly to blame for that. He suspected it would be more or less futile to ask for something else, but made the request anyway, and was surprised when, the following day, Khalid had brought a plate of vegetable curry. He made sure to express his thanks to the boy, which worked: a few days later a tepid helping of chicken had arrived with the evening meal. Khalid squatted in the doorway to watch Ethan eat, with something near contentment on his face. Given the circumstances, this gesture seemed a kindness. White generosity to the black of Abu's beating.

"You must eat to keep healthy," the guard had said.

"Yes."

"Without eating you would grow too weak."

Ethan paused between mouthfuls and flexed his biceps. Khalid returned the gesture straight, as if competing with a salute. Ethan lowered himself to the concrete once again, thinking that perhaps, for Khalid, there had been no joke. His next words, certainly, had been deadpan: "And it is important for keeping warm, at night. With no food blood turns to water and water to ice."

"Something like that." Ethan had nodded, keeping his smile in check.

He pushed up a third time, his thoughts dissolving with the astonishing effort this exercise seemed now to entail. The discomfort was intoxicating: it helped blank out his worst fears, which, he realized now, had to do with Kate. How could she possibly be coping with this? He paused at the top of his push-up, held square, and shut his eyes to meet the pain, as if it were possible to protect Kate from similar hurt by embracing it himself. A moment of transcendence.

THE OLD MAN'S EYE. Rippling in the bottom of his glass, then sharp into focus as the tumbler came down.

"Nice girl, that Kate of yours."

Ethan said nothing. The old man repeated the word *nice*, and ran a veined hand through the remnants of his hair. "Yes. Things seem to be going well for you." Taking another sip, he congratulated himself. "Very well." He scanned the room complacently, adjusted his striped tie. "I always thought you'd end up in finance."

"I haven't."

" 'Investment products' sounds pretty financial to me. Whatever it is, it's a step in the right direction."

Ethan shrugged. "Think Avon lady. Think car salesman. Down a phone line."

His father shook his head, pretending to be perplexed, then pulled at the wattle of his throat. " 'Investment products' is what it says on your card, son. You're just being modest."

Leaning back in his chair Ethan looked away from his father, let his gaze travel slowly around the restaurant. Bombastic portraits. The nearest of which depicted a man astride a huge brown horse, rearing on a rocky bluff. Sausage rolls of hair above his ears, indifference in his stare. Could he be bored by the prospect of falling off a cliff? Ethan slid forward in his jeans, stretched his trainers out into the aisle. The leather back of his chair creaked.

"And what about your sports, then? Looks like you're in fine shape." The old man reached out to slap his son's shoulder, but the table span was a fraction too much, and in any case, his hand seemed to have second thoughts. "Very healthy. Have you signed up with a club here in London? You should focus your efforts. Which are you going to keep with, the football or rugby?"

"I've not played either in years."

"Nonsense! You were in that team at college. An absolute bloody natural. I bet you can't wait to get started."

"You think what you want to think." Ethan held up his palms in surrender. "I'm not fussed."

His father reached for the tumbler again. "I will. It would have made your mother proud, to see you . . . making something of yourself."

Ethan ran a palm against the grain of his stubble, fixed his stare again on the heavy-framed horse. A rolling eye.

The old man's glass was empty. His wavering arm, thin now in its double-cuffed sleeve, offered it up into the path of a waiter, who somehow missed the cue, quickstepping away across the burgundy carpet. Ethan's tumbler (unordered, untouched) glowed there on the tabletop. It took the old man a visible effort not to reach for it.

"Yes, she'd find something to be proud about. She'd manage to see some merit in what you've done for yourself. What you're making of the opportunities provided."

A poodle was dimly visible in the blackened foreground of the painting. It, too, was prancing, gazing up at the lump of lard im-mobile on his horse. Ethan's stomach hardened with his fathers words, but still he did not reply.

The old man sat mesmerized by the tumbler, as if it were the hub of an axel driven into the dining room from the chandelier above, through the table, into the rock of Lancaster Gate. Every-thing revolving around it. Ethan imagined him reaching for the glass and ripping a hole in the lace cloth, the oak table, the car-peted flagstone floor. A tic had started up beneath the old man's left eye. He shut it, pressed a palm to his face. The whiskey burned in his voice.

"No, your mother would have been pleased. An All-American-style sports star, just like her. A whiz kid of finance. Bred of an

Englishman," he said as he raised his hands, "fulfilling your potential. She might have even made an exception for that little, wassername, Kate." He paused, the darkness beneath his eye jumping. "Despite her idiot sensibilities."

The spat words freed the glass, which the old man lifted to his lips. Ethan stood, loomed there above the table, a huge physical presence in the rarefied atmosphere of the restaurant. His father couldn't look up.

Anger gripped Ethan. He felt an urge to defend Kate, to speak up for her. But he held back. Forcing himself to breathe slowly, he gave in to the inevitable, resurging weariness, which permeated the entire room: even the waiter, heading back to the kitchen, seemed to be wading through water.

"If you could leave off from hypothesizing about Mum's feelings, which, let's face it, was a subject you never really nailed, that'd be good." He slid the near-empty tumbler six inches closer to his father as he edged around the table to leave. "Thanks for lunch. I'll leave you to finish up."

Still he held square. The concrete was sharp beneath his palms, his forearms burned, his shoulders strained as if lifting a person twice his weight. The blood churned in his ears. Only it wasn't the rhythm of himself that he heard because when he stopped and knelt back to rest the sound grew. The beat was mechanical, a low whup-whup-whup spliced together with a high-pitched whine. Ethan rolled over and put his ear to the crack under the door, his tiredness gone. Unmistakably, rotor blades.

The noise swamped forward in a rush and Ethan instinctively turned his eye to the crack, despite knowing that the view through it stopped well short of the sky. Nevertheless, as the whine grew into a roar and flared, he was sure that a shadow fled with it between the buildings: the stretch of wood chips in front of his door clicked from yellow to brown and back again.

Or maybe he had blinked. If so, he could hang on to the hope that this was a coincidence, that the chopper had sounded louder and lower than in fact it was, that it had not overflown the compound deliberately. Yes, the whup-whup-whup was fading now, softening into a monotone hum. In just seconds the fright would be gone.

Ethan sat up, overcome with confusion, and said, "What am I on?" out loud.

The helicopter's flyby was a good sign: he knew that.

It might mean that they—whoever they were—were out looking.

The guards would realize so and see the pointless risk of continuing with this hostage plan. Whatever they had set out to achieve, it was obviously failing. The helicopter would make the balaclava let them go, surely? If the thought of the chopper was intimidating to Ethan, think what Abu and the others must be feeling. The fact that he could still hear the distant drone was a good thing, wasn't it?

No! Despite himself, the words Ethan found he was whispering as the noise, unmistakably now, began to grow again, said just the opposite.

"Please, God. Turn the interfering bastards back."

For although the storeroom was unacceptable, it made sense. Four walls to outlast. The guards would give them up eventually. Think of Terry Waite and John McCarthy. But only if you played by the rules. Try changing the game entirely and *anything* might follow. Consider Rafi, hanging, upside down.

Footsteps scattered through the yard and Ethan lay back down to look. Somebody was yelling. Another set of feet ran the other way and halted, at the insistence of further loud words, out of view. Then a figure, Abu, wavered into frame. He shouted a response and stood listening to the sky. The droning rotor-beat expanded. At such a distance Ethan couldn't make out the guard's expression, but panic filled in the blank. The same current of alarm arced between captor and captive, so that for a second Ethan felt for the guard. Whatever the intentions of the pilot, this helicopter was simply making matters worse.

An engine turned over close by, temporarily blotting out the chopper. The sound became the tense whine of a vehicle reversing. Doors slammed. Ethan kept his eye to the crack, hoping for clues, but for elastic minutes there were none. When the engine juddered to a halt it seemed that the chopper, still audible, had receded, although Ethan now doubted his memory of how loud it had been beforehand.

Now Khalid came briskly into view, leading another stumbling figure, who had something wrong with his head. There was a bag over it. As Ethan watched, the person's feet caught and he fell forward in a heap.

"Up up up!" pleaded Khalid.

The figure levered up onto hands and knees, but could apparently rise no further. With the bag hanging down from his head he looked animal, like a dog or horse. Khalid leaned over and shouted "Get up" again, waving his hands in agitation, and again a spark of panic made Ethan angry. Why didn't whoever it was just do as he was told?

The bag ruffled forward over the dog's lowered head, revealing a twist of blond hair, which answered part of Ethan's question at least. Obstinate Diane. Across the ten or so yards separating them Ethan could see that she was shaking uncontrollably, as if the ground were alive beneath her, and the job of keeping square on all fours required a special skill. Khalid leaned down to pull the bag back into place and said something indistinct, more gently. Then he began helping Diane to her feet with a hand under each armpit, as if acknowledging her status as an invalid.

More banging, gunshot loud. Ethan rolled back from the crack as Abu reached the door and walloped it. Trouble with the lock slowed the guard down, but he overcame the obstacle quickly and kicked the metal door back with his heel, following through—so that he appeared to land in the room with a giant stride. In one hand he held a hessian sack, in the other a knife. Ethan's fear was momentarily shot through with a sense of the absurdity of such a sight: a pirate, boarding a ship. But that evaporated as Abu crammed the bag over his head and neck.

"What's happening?" Ethan pleaded.

No response. The sack smelled of leaf mulch, diesel, and mud. Ethan had time to realize that he was standing in his socks, but that was his own stupid fault, he should have crammed the shoes on when he first heard the helicopter. Had the chopper noise gone or was that it, there? A fading hum obscured Abu's panting. Ethan suddenly couldn't distinguish between his own ragged breathing and the guard's. They were joined again in their fright. He felt a jab of sickening complicity, and had to fight back an urge to retch into the sack. Nabbi's feet were too small anyway. Bravery and commitment were the thing. He did not complain as a hand gripped his shoulder and propelled him across the sharp ground.

TWENTY-NINE

KATE'S EARS SQUEAKED AGAIN, which meant they were descending. When she shifted position, to ease the discomfort of sitting cross-legged on the bouncing floor, the notebook bent reassuringly into the hollow of her stomach. The others, she sensed, were in the back of the truck too, rattling knee to knee. Somebody had cried out when bundled in after her, but since then nobody had dared to speak. How long had they been bouncing and jolting into one another now? Fifteen minutes? An hour and a half? The temptation overcame her.

"Ethan," she whispered.

There was a pause.

"Shhh!" breathed a voice. Kate was confused: she was certain it was him.

"You're okay?"

"No," whimpered Diane. "I'm not."

"Please, God." George's voice.

"Shhh!" Ethan whispered again.

"Diane, you're not hurt?" asked Clay tentatively.

"Me also. I am here," whimpered Jan.

"Diane?"

"Ethan?" Kate asked once more.

"All of you," he whispered, "we've been warned. Shut up."

But Kate sensed a gap. Gingerly, she lifted the edge of the sackcloth from her neck to her chin. Nobody objected. The cool that met her tilting face stung. She stared the dark interior into focus, counting five other figures in the gloom, all of them bagged. Clay, Diane, George, Jan, and Ethan. The truck hit a pothole and slewed against its brakes, shuffling those at the back forward. A floor, a ceiling, and four walls of clinkered boards. No windows, no seats. Some sort of an animal truck. And, Kate checked again, no guards. The relief of seeing Ethan and the others was as exhilarating as the clean air. She pulled the bag right off.

"We're on our own." Kate spoke over crashing gears.

Nobody moved.

"You can take the sacks off. They've locked us in here on our own."

The figure directly opposite unwrapped himself first. Clay's face was covered in grime, which became stubble, which he scratched, gasping.

Next George and Jan removed their hoods. George was newly gaunt, his face full of shadows, accentuated by the gray of his scraggy beard. He crossed himself and his shoulders shook. Jan was blinking back tears.

Clay leaned across Jan to lift the bag from Diane's bowed head.

Her hair fell forward in a second shroud as he did so. Kate saw the contradiction in this veil—whatever else happened, these people were now a part of her, and yet she had no real idea who any of them were. Diane did not look up, even after Clay had brushed the hair from her face.

"It's okay, honey. Okay?" He patted her knee.

Diane flinched at his touch. Then her head came up and her eyes, flashing from side to side, fixed on Kate. "No, no, no," she whined. "Not you. Bitch."

"What?"

While Clay tried to quieten her, Kate turned to Ethan, who was still sitting erect beneath his hessian sack. Like a Buddha, with a hand on each folded knee.

"Ethan. You can take the sack off."

"Shhh," he repeated.

"I've got you. You're okay, Diane. It'll be—"

Kate scrambled forward to help Ethan. She placed a hand against his shoulder, which was as rigid as a gate. "Ethan," she said again, "it's me."

THE HANDS FELT FAMILIAR but Ethan feared a trick. Why take the risk? Best to wait and see what happened next. Although the gentle touch had to be Kate, her fingers pulling his head from the earth in which Abu had buried it, he remained tensed and unsure until the bag came off and her face swam before him. Even then, the relief was tinged with difficulty, resentment even: might she have made a mistake? Any minute now the punishment for this disobedience would surely begin.

"That bitch!" Diane said again, this time more loudly.

"Did you see Rafi?" Jan asked, his eyes wild in his face.

"Calm down, calm down." Clay was still trying to soothe Diane.

"Beyond repentance, beyond forgiveness," George continued.

Jan: "Did anybody hear that helicopter? Did they land?"

Ethan, looking from one face to another, concluded that indeed they were alone. He slumped back against the side of the truck.

"And does anybody know who these guys are?" Jan asked.

George: "No. Nobody would tell me. No, no, no."

"*She* knows," Diane hissed. Her finger trembled up at Kate in the gloom. Then the truck hit another hole and Diane's pencil-thin arm waved madly, her dirty sleeve flapping beneath it. Clay clambered over Jan and tried to pull Diane to his chest, but she fought him away.

Everybody seemed to be missing the obvious point, which had nothing to do with blame or motive. Ethan stroked Kate's hand in reassurance. But while the feel of her skin beneath his fingers was a comfort it was dwarfed by the larger shock of society, which pressed in. The space was alive with opinion and conjecture and alternatives, threatening to clash like the gears. He found himself struggling against an urge to yell "Silence!" Only a sense of how strange it would sound held him back.

To have his new thoughts jar in this way hurt. He felt the awkwardness of a successful man reunited with failed schoolmates, a desire to play down his achievements, to conceal his insight. Kate's unbowed, adamant face was beautiful and impossible all at the same time. He would have to help her understand, but gradually, subtly. Not yet. She'd resist if he tried now. Though he kept stroking her arm something in Ethan withdrew for the time being, and twisted shut.

.   .   .

KATE SAW AT ONCE that she had to confront Diane. The pointing arm and finger were brittle, which meant they were ready to be snapped. "Don't be ridiculous," she told the truck at large. Glaring at Diane she continued: "We're all in this, all of us. Yes?" The hostility in her voice implied an admission; she wished that she had ignored the accusation. But, having started, she could not allow a pause. She pressed on more softly: "And the only way out is together."

"Exactly, Diane," Clay coaxed.

Diane's head dropped again, her puppet strings slack, and she allowed Clay to gather her in, a bundle of elbows and knees. Clay caught and held Kate's eye over the top of Diane's bowed shoulders, shaking his head apologetically.

"But, does nobody know? What do they want with us? Where are we going to now? What happened to that helicopter? Did Rafi get help? Who are these people, that have taken us? How long do they want us until? When, why"—the string of questions rushed from Jan like an anchor chain released, yanking to a stop with the repeated word—"Rafi?"

Nobody spoke.

The truck was gaining speed, plowing downhill into the resistance of its complaining engine, which masked the silence. The pause then exploded as the wheels hit another big rut, jarring everybody a foot from the boards.

"The heartless, murderous . . ." George shook his head. He had scrambled to the rear of the space and was intent upon the door. Ethan slid toward the back too.

"What are you looking for?"

"What do you think? A way out." George's fingers worked along the bottom of the doors, then up the join between them. Kate saw that his hands were shaking wildly.

"They'll have locked it."

George gave Ethan a stare.

Kate: "You never know."

Ethan turned back to her now. "They're professionals."

"In which case let's lobby their fucking regulator," muttered Clay.

"They're half-wit heathens," spat George. His eyes gleamed despite the murk.

"And Rafi?" countered Ethan. "A soldier. He managed to take advantage of these half-wits, did he? And what if they're about to release us anyway? You'll jump into—"

A further lurch of brakes crashed Ethan and George together, the physical contact cutting Ethan short. His anger remained visible behind a thin mask of self-restraint. As the truck slowed to shuffle through another turn, competing noises rose over its engine. A bell, a horn. Clay stood up and put his eye to a crack between the boards, prompting Kate to do the same. She saw a deep ravine running along her side of the road. The truck ground forward slowly, goats parting round it like water, and Kate glimpsed a brown river flashing down below. Up ahead, in the shoulder of a slow-moving curve of water, stood buildings. An overtaking car tore the town in half and then a screen of trees cut the scene into cine-film.

"Where are they taking us?" asked Jan.

Clay answered, "If it's a town, that means other people."

"Which means they're going to give us up, yes?" Jan's voice was thin.

"Sure, you're probably right." Clay didn't believe himself— Kate saw it as he looked away. She changed the subject.

"How long have we been going?"

"About forty minutes, I think," replied Jan.

"No way," contradicted Clay. "A couple of hours at least."

"Longer," George said emphatically. "More like three."

The futility of trying to guess which town they might be approaching quickly became clear, since nobody knew where the journey had begun. Each of Kate, George, Jan, and Clay kept their eyes to chinks in the plank side walls in the hope of glimpsing a signpost, but that proved pointless too; the truck turned away from the main road before arriving at the town and then somehow they were in among sliced gray buildings anyway and slewing to a halt.

"Sit down." Ethan's voice was oddly urgent. Kate turned to see him cross-legged again, hands twisting at one of the sacks.

Nobody took any notice. Through the chink Kate saw black exhaust fumes plume forward as they reversed. Something walloped the side of the truck.

"Sit down!" Ethan shouted. "What are you lot playing at?" The engine shuddered and died. Kate felt him grab at her wrist and pull her to the floor beside him. He shoveled a sack into her lap and hissed, "Everyone! Put the bags back on!"

The anger in his tone was unnerving. Kate saw Jan cave in to it, and noticed that George had gathered up one of the sacks too. Diane groaned as Clay steered her lowered head into the

darkness. Which was precisely the point. Since the sack meant indignity, Kate must find a way around it. She clung to the hope of
their imminent release, because all the alternatives were unthinkable. And if they were about to be released anyway . . . But
Ethan had opened the mouth of the bag in her lap and was hastily
trying to cram the thing over her head.

She resisted.

Ethan struggled with her comically from beneath his shroud.
His hands were shaking violently. Only when Clay, pulling on
his own hood, whispered, "He's right," did she give in.

THIRTY

—————◆◆◆—————

"New rules," said the balaclava, "but I am still um-
pire, understood?"

The rest seemed dumbfounded, slack-jawed around him. It fell
to Ethan to convey their consent.

The balaclava now turned sideways and ambled from left to
right before the cinder blocks of the front wall. Above his head
brightness fanned into the room through a small barred window,
illuminating fine strands of his woolen mask from behind: a halo.

"I hope you enjoy your new hotel. Like a Marriott!" He smiled
at this, expectant despite the mask. When nobody smiled back he
continued, gravely. "But in this hotel everyone stays together.
Men and women too, I am afraid. So we are erecting a partition to
keep your privacy. I am sorry but it is only cloth. No looking!" He
laughed again, then added, "Your very own line of control."

Now the balaclava strode through the seated hostages into the
middle of the room and pointed proudly at the ceiling. Somebody

had tacked a sheet along two-thirds of the length of one of the rafters, so that it hung like a curtain across the back part of the room. The improvisation was recent, Ethan reasoned, because the sheet was so white, unquestionably newly laundered. Its knife creases, which brought Bulwan fleetingly to mind, had yet to drop out; the grid on the sheet was as rigid as the room's four walls. In front of it, gesturing, the balaclava looked professorial, lecturing before the whiteboard. Or perhaps prophetic, silhouetted by a blinding sky. He was a bigger man than Ethan remembered.

"You men must sleep here." The balaclava indicated the larger part of the room. "And you ladies have the space behind."

Diane, kneeling between Ethan and Clay, began to laugh. Clay put a hand out to silence her but she shrank from it, toward Ethan. Somebody had to take control of the situation, Ethan saw, pulling her into his side. She crumpled like empty clothes in his grip; with no effort at all he squeezed the laugh shut. He looked down to make sure she understood, but quickly turned away from her upturned face because its gaunt pout was breathless and this prompted a sickening stab of desire. Carefully he withdrew his arm. Diane slumped without it, but stayed quiet.

Jan now diverted the balaclava's attention with his refrain, hopeful as a schoolboy: "Please, can you tell us why we are here? What is it you want from us?" He peered about shortsightedly, his voice wavering. "How much longer will—"

"It is not about you and it is not about us," the balaclava cut him off, shaking determinedly from side to side. "We are not wanting anything from you for ourselves. You cannot give it anyway. We are both in mercy of bigger forces, understand? How much longer is up to them. No time if possible, or for as long as they take."

Now Kate's voice made matters worse. "But who do you represent? Which organization? What does *it* hope to achieve by terrorizing *us?*"

There was a clamorous indignation in her tone. Though Ethan couldn't see Kate's face, he imagined its expression, her pale brow knitted above *no-nonsense* eyes, lips drawn into an adamant line. As if correcting a restaurant bill or disputing a taxi driver's preferred route. Endearingly direct in those contexts, appallingly misjudged now.

The balaclava walked around Ethan, whose eyes followed him to the end of the line, where Kate sat cross-legged on the concrete, as instructed. He squatted before her, bouncing on his heels like a backstop. "Believe me," he explained, "this is not terrorizing."

KATE LOOKED INTO EACH of the man's brown eyes, pools of hostility in the mask, and saw herself drowning there. A weakness within her made her want to look away, but she managed to return his stare. If he was in charge, he should be confronted, however meagerly. There was no point resisting Abu, Sadiq, and Khalid if the real battle was with this man. Her steady gaze back was a front of opposition.

Behind it, though, she was still reeling. When the truck doors opened, she had allowed herself too much hope. At that point anything was possible, good or bad, and her only means of keeping calm in the claustrophobia of her hood had been to ignore the unthinkable and envisage instead their release, which would

surely now come. Why else had they been brought down from
the mountains? Why else the secrecy of these terrible sacks?

A callused hand helped her to the ground and guided her, still
blind, into this room, where she was made to kneel along with the
others amid a blur of audible activity. A hammer striking nails
was bad, but the sweeping might have been good. Perhaps they
were smartening the room for somebody important. That was the
sound of a car pulling up, its doors slamming, which was surely
the diplomats arriving to take them away. She was even convinced
that Khalid had whispered, "Do not worry, he will be here to free
you soon," but had to concede now, still holding the balaclava's
stare, that it had sounded more like "to *see* you soon" instead.

By the time they'd been ordered to uncover their heads,
though, Kate had just about persuaded herself it was over. The
sight of the olive balaclava leaning against the wall was almost
too much. She dug her nails into her thighs and bit down on the
inside of her mouth in those first moments, and thought she'd
succeeded in holding firm, except that now her face was wet.

Abruptly the shape of the mask changed, woolen cheeks gathering beneath widening eyes, lifting the material across the
bridge of the man's nose. His pink lips stretched, then showed
pearly teeth. A kind smile.

"We are continuing to look after you best we are able," he said
lightly. "Food and blankets and soap for washing. And now you
have company for relieving boredom." He gestured from Kate to
the others, then looked back to her. The apparent smile had faded,
leaving empty, gun-barrel eyes. "Be patient and nobody need suffer hurt."

"Nobody *else!*"

The balaclava, still suspended there in front of Kate, absorbed her words without flinching, then shook in sympathy. "If you like. But Mr. Rafi hurt himself. If he did not try to run away he would not have paid price for failure." He stood to address them as a group, hands spread, a magnanimous host: "His punishment fitted crime. Nobody *else* will receive punishment without a reason."

Kate snorted derisively. The balaclava was just a man, waving his arms about in front of them, puffed up with his own power and vanity. The mask was frightening but also showed that its wearer needed to hide, which was a weakness.

THERE WAS A PAUSE. Ethan concentrated on the floor, following it to the man's feet as they stepped backward into a patch of sunlight. Shadows beneath his leather sandals underlined their incongruity. There was dirt between the man's toes. Far from revolting Ethan, this dust added to the picture's religious significance. He held his breath and willed Kate to join with him and keep silent. That prayer worked, but he hadn't considered George.

"What do you mean without reason? Tell that to Abu! I didn't try to escape, but he beat the shit out of me!"

"*With reason!*" Though Ethan tried to pin the sandals down with his gaze, the right one tapped out each syllable as the balaclava went on: "There must be punishment for everybody if one person gives a good reason!"

These words contradicted the man's last, and yet they didn't, because he wore a balaclava, which bypassed all logic. How could

George not see that? Why did he have to continue? But he did, spreading his retort out triumphantly, emphatic as a drunk.

"Well, make your mind up. Either you're going to beat us up for things beyond our control, or you're not. You're a joke."

The fool only had himself to blame. Ethan tensed up for the response to this disrespect, hoping against hope that by keeping his back straight and his eyes lowered the balaclava would register his dignified separation.

No response came. The balaclava allowed George's words to ripen and then wither. The man's power lay in his self-restraint, which stood in contrast to his prisoners' indiscipline. One after another his feet paced a circle around the kneeling hostages. Their course was inexorable as marching: left, right, left. Ethan saw in the man's orbit a self-belief which encompassed bravery and cowardice and going in hard, and yet transcended these qualities at the same time. He had a real purpose. The feet came back into view again, halting before the hostages. Ethan stared at them, planted squarely. For a heartbeat the dirt looked real and Ethan felt ridiculous, his sympathy for the balaclava obvious idiocy. But the moment passed and again the solution came clear. He must emulate this man's discipline. That would win respect, which in turn would break down his captors' resolve.

The sandals began their monastic pacing again. Blinking in time with each footfall, Ethan followed their course.

THIRTY-ONE

THE SCREEN, WHICH HAD been on all night, shed a filmic blue light in the living room. Rachel flipped the kettle switch as she passed but did not wait for it to boil, pressed straight on to jiggle the mouse instead. The seascape screensaver drained. She typed *Kashmir* into the search field and paused with her little finger hovering over the *enter* key, for long enough to think a prayer.

Headings fell down the results page. Rachel shut her eyes because the first entry was new and unreadable:

KASHMIR KIDNAP CRISIS ESCALATES
AS HOSTAGE IS EXECUTED
By Paul Frost in New Delhi and Samantha Hurst in London

The body of one of seven hostages taken captive by militants in Kashmir has been discovered by the Indian Security Forces.

Rachel's eyes clung to the full stop, unwilling to risk the next paragraphs. An air of inevitability descended. For long seconds she sat in a trance, staring at the square blur of the screen before her, until eventually the kettle boiled and clicked off, starting her forward again, word by reluctant word.

> The victim's body was found hanging in a derelict farmstead near the village of Anantang, 35 miles from Kashmir's summer capital, Srinigar. Reports suggest that the walls of the building in which the body was found had been daubed with the initials of the separatist militia group F.R.N.

Did they know, or not? The reporter's insensitivity seemed almost personal.

> The man's body is thought to be that of . . .

Rachel stood and turned from the screen. Not her. She had glimpsed the next words and dared not look at them directly, for fear that she was wrong. It wasn't him. She steadied herself, fighting back giddiness. Once composed, she returned to the kettle, reboiled it, and poured boiling water into a cafetiere. This she placed next to her cup on the stainless-steel tray which, returning to the computer, she set down: a sacrificial offering of thanks.

> . . . Mr. Rafi Kolatch (26), an Israeli national who disappeared over three weeks ago while on a trekking excursion in the region. The whereabouts and condition of Mr. Kolatch's six fellow

travelers, which included Britons Ethan Hughes (24), Kate Cox (22), and George Arnott (39), together with a Dutch student and an American couple in their late twenties, remains unknown.

Conflicting reports surround the circumstances in which Mr. Kolatch's body was found. Official sources say a local farmer reported the discovery to police, however there have been unconfirmed suggestions that the Indian military stumbled upon the body following a failed bid to rescue the hostages in the early hours of yesterday morning. It is not yet known when Mr. Kolatch was killed.

Now that Rachel was over the worst she read the rest of the article rapidly, searching in vain for a reason to hope, beset by a growing sense of indignation. Did the reporters have nothing concrete to say about the wider situation? Nothing new? No: they soon reverted to speculation and a rehearsal of background details.

The discovery is a setback to negotiations which, until yesterday, the Foreign Office had suggested were progressing. Mr. Hughes's father, a retired army doctor, reacted angrily to the news: "There simply can't be any truth to the suggestion that the Indians botched a rescue mission. I'm waiting for official news to the contrary." Ms. Cox's family have so far declined to comment.

Friends of Birmingham-based youth group worker Mr. Arnott have collected more than 2,200 signatures on a petition asking the Foreign Secretary to intervene personally in the negotiations to free the hostages. His wife, Michelle, said, "We are obviously extremely concerned for his safety. But he's a level-headed, intelligent guy and will stick this out. His faith will see him through. I wouldn't be surprised if he's befriended the men holding him."

Last week a spokesman for F.R.N. gave assurances that the hostages would not be harmed, provided the Indian government met the group's demands, which include the release of some forty-five named militants held in Indian prisons. The discovery of Mr. Kolatch's body will undermine the credibility of such statements.

According to Rajesh Rani, the Internal Security Minister, speaking three days ago, "The Indian government has created a working-party to consider ways to secure the hostages' release. In consultation with representatives from the embassies of the countries concerned, we have decided to restrain ourselves from taking any direct action."

Since 1989 some 40,000 Kashmiris have died in the separatist war. In 1995 a group of Western tourists were kidnapped by separatists while trekking in the area, but since then there have been few reported assaults on travelers. Local leaders have expressed dismay at the news of this killing, which represents a further setback for the crippled tourist industry, on which the region has historically relied. New Delhi dismisses the suggestion that official Indian tourist offices have been advising travelers that the area is a safe destination despite the conflict.

F.R.N. is a new addition to the many known militant organizations seeking Kashmiri independence. New Delhi claims that such groups receive funding and support from Pakistan. Islamabad has denied such accusations since before 9/11/01: claiming that in fact India itself creates groups like F.R.N. to

whip up anti-Muslim sentiment in the region and further
abroad. F.R.N. has so far claimed no religious affiliation.

Rachel poured the coffee. She tried to fill the cup to its brim, but stopped short and added a restorative inch of vodka to the mix instead. The drink helped, and for a time she was distracted. Eventually, though, there was no alternative but to give in to the screen again and, as she had done on each morning of her "compassionate" leave, trawl through all of the major news sites. By the time she reached the American and Indian versions of the story the sun had risen and the screen no longer glowed. She persisted. The quest was to uncover a more telling detail, anything to breathe life into the difficulty of the account so far. Yet each variation of the story simply cast the same bare facts in a different light, deepening a sense of strangeness. The repetition of reading familiar names, dates, and quotations was compounded by the encroaching numbness. She gave in to it. Not Kate, not Ethan, just words.

By midmorning, once she'd exhausted even the most provincial of accounts, the only remaining solace lay in the prospect of an update. Here was the chance to break the pattern that had overtaken her recent days.

She carried the tray back to the kitchenette, stared for a minute at the take-away cartons spilling from the silver bin.

Then she returned to the keyboard. For spinning through the sites in search of something new was part of the addiction. Pornography for the pious. And, very infrequently, the search bore fruit. Rachel's tired mental image of a shape called Rafi, suspended in an outbuilding, somersaulted into focus with the *Hindustan Times*'s jewel: *The body was found hanging, locals report, from the feet.*

THIRTY-TWO

KATE LOOKED DOWN and read the words again: ARMITAGE
SHANKS. She turned to the basin and ran the tap, then pulled the
notebook from her waistband and flicked through its pages, pausing on an entry titled *Marriott.*

Must have been some sort of public office. A courthouse even,
perhaps. Two of the three windows are bricked up. The one that's
left is a slit, above head height, no glass, but barred. Day one, we
all climb up to look out. There's a slope of boulders falling away
from the rear wall, down to the river below. Shines in the morn-
ing, glowers in shadow in the afternoons.

Our room had two doors, but one's covered now. Sheet metal
and bolts, encased in fists of cement. A buttress sticks out halfway
along one wall, next to the hanging sheet. There's a hole in the
plaster beside it, no wires, a mouth without a tongue. And a blind
ceiling rose up above. So no light at night. At the far end of the

room there's a single black radiator on the wall. Never on. Makes the cold worse.

They come each morning to escort us one after the other down the long corridor, past blank notice boards and more closed doors, to the bathroom, with its chipped basin and English toilet, where I sit to write.

Beneath this she'd drawn a map of the building, with their one window at its center, and an arrow indicating north. Her handwriting was tiny, more precise than before, regular as type, oddly pleasing. She'd not told any of the others about the diary, which remained a secret, even from Ethan. It had been her only companion during the stretch of solitary confinement, and now relieved the unending . . . company. Her own pilot's logbook. Although she'd found a hiding place near her blanket—where the floorboards subsided half an inch below the skirting board—she could only risk sliding the notebook in there when sure that nobody else was watching, which made it impossible some days. The front cover had rubbed gray against her skin. She opened another page at random.

Diane fares worst. Something's collapsed inside her, destroying all proportion. It's like cause no longer meets effect. Instead there's this schism of vitriol and softness. Blank fear of the guards runs parallel with a bizarre flirtatiousness. Yesterday Clay saw her stroke Khalid's arm as he took her to wash. Poor bloke. He sits head in hands till she returns, then snaps.

"What the fuck's that all about?"

Wide-eyed and innocent: "All what?"

"You can't risk . . . that . . . with them, Diane. Think it through."

"Same old paranoia, even here." Pouts. "Christ, I mean, why'd I bother coming?"

In a whisper: "Oh, please."

We're all staring at our feet. But she goes on. "This trip was always such a lame idea. We weren't working out anyway. You can't save a relationship by running away from it."

Clay's on his knees beside her now. She's got a look like she's going to tear his eyes out, but as he gathers her in it just . . . dissolves. Unreadable, at least to me. One minute she's telling me about her childhood pets, all "Come on, Kate, us girls together, we should start ourselves a sorority," and the next she just blanks me out entirely. She'll refuse to get up all day, even to wash or eat, and then start pacing the floorboards like they're a catwalk, deranged yet glamorous, all heroin chic.

Another page read:

Poor Jan is sick. First four days after we arrive he spends crouching over the communal bucket behind the hanging sheet. The noise bounces round the room. He's aghast at the indignity to begin with, then gets too low to care. All the macho marathon stuff right out the window, leaving him weak as water: his face wet with sweat, yellow as new-cut pine. Without contacts he can't see much beyond arm's length, which makes him all the more . . . helpless. His gums bleed, these white sores appear inside his mouth. Never mind the goatee, he's a skinny little boy now, and his nervous blinking is constant. He's all unrealistic hopes and fears. A car engine cuts out nearby and his face sparks up . . . he's sure it means we're about to be released. Then the fat guard brings us a load more blankets "to help with bigger cold" and he's inconsolable, convinced that means they're planning to keep us here right through the winter.

Outside the sky is all slashed grays and whites.

*White like the streaks in George's beard and hair. He sits
alone most of the time, whispering to himself. Scripture, I think.
Yesterday it was "A man shall not be established by wickedness:
but the root of the righteous shall not be moved." Over and over
again, all calm, like some feral monk. He's like that the whole
time until you disturb him, and then he rages—against Nabbi,
the guards, Kashmir, India, everyone. It's everybody's fault except his. I can see him fraying Ethan's nerves, but . . .*

Whenever Kate thought about Ethan she somehow couldn't
write much. What notes she did make were invariably painful.
The confusing part, when she managed to pin it down, was that
this version of him was the one she had craved: focused and mo-
tivated and taking control. And yet now she wanted the old
Ethan back. Today she paused to think and then wrote a single
word after his name: *blanket.*

Though Sadiq had left an extra blanket for each of them, Ethan
refused his. Instead he insisted on giving it to her, curled by his
side. This kindness hurt. It recalled their first night back together,
when he had suggested that they go along with the balaclava's
proposal and divide the sleeping quarters: men on one side of the
divide, women on the other. Diane, oblivious, said nothing. Kate
was too stunned to speak, leaving Clay to intervene: "Yeah, right,
tempting. But I'll sleep with Diane all the same."

"That goes against our orders."

"Orders?"

"We're to split either side, men and women. Why provoke
them by doing otherwise?"

"It was just a suggestion. What'll he care? If they insist, we'll
deal with that then."

Ethan stood in silence, head lowered, gazing at the foot of the suspended sheet. Clay looked imploringly at Kate.

"Ethan," she sobbed.

That broke through, but although Ethan had lain next to Kate and held her as she went to sleep, she woke to find their blankets disentangled and a floorboard, hand-span wide, between them. He had moved to her other side during the night, so that he lay nearer the sheet, as if straining toward his prescribed sector.

Since then she had found the same gap between them each morning. Not wanting to spell her fear out directly, she complained of the cold. Ethan's insistence now that she take his extra blanket therefore cut both ways.

There were a number of things she couldn't speak directly about with the others, the most obvious of these being Rafi. Kate said his name during their first evening back together, because nobody else did. The ensuing pause made her wish she had not.

"He won't have been butchered in vain," George said eventually.

Jan turned his face to the wall.

"What do you mean?" asked Ethan.

"I mean they'll pay for it," muttered George. "At the final reckoning, or before. One way or another, they'll pay."

Ethan now shook his head dismissively. George stiffened, but was diverted by the disturbance of Diane, who had broken free from beneath Clay's wing and was pulling at her own sides, hugging herself violently, mouth open, as if struggling for breath. When Clay tried to soothe her, Diane fought him off.

"If you ask me, it was an idiotic thing for a bloke like him, an ex-serviceman, to try," Ethan now continued. "You'd think he'd have known better."

Diane's breathing now became a noise.

"You can't say that. You have no idea what he was planning."
Jan turned back to the conversation. "He may have understood
what was coming next for him. Or he might have been hoping to
bring help. Who knows, he might have made the alarm before he
was caught. He might have alerted people, who are coming to
rescue us. He was definitely trying to bring help."

"Yeah, well, he did the opposite, didn't he," Ethan replied.

"What do you mean he did the opposite?" Jan's voice was a
whimper.

"They shifted us, crammed us all in here. No rescue. All that
happened is that Rafi made himself the first casualty."

"At least he had the bollocks to do *something*," George
growled. "Unlike the rest of us."

Diane's breathing sawed louder. In, a hollow pause, out.

"If you say so." Ethan shrugged.

"And I'm going to see that Abu, and the lot of them, stand before their—"

At this, Kate was sure of it, Ethan began to laugh. Everyone
but Kate missed his amusement, though, because Diane chose
that moment to hack out an incomprehensible syllable which cut
George off. In his place, Diane receded into a moan. Clay was at
last able to gather her up.

"Cheerleaders like you two," he said. "Real heartening."

Other topics were as hard. Jan was superstitious. Although he
craved reassurance that they'd be home soon, too much talk of
freedom or rescue made him fearful they'd jinx the chance of either. So they rarely discussed the practicalities of how their cap-

tivity would end, instead referring only to "afterwards," their voices heavy with conviction.

And if the future hurt to guess at, so did the immediate past. That way lay fault, and save for George's mutterings, blame was also off-limits by unspoken accord. Since Diane's outburst in the truck she had brought the subject up only once. Just after night-fall, she spoke into the darkness.

"I saw you, Kate."

"Shhh," Clay hushed her.

"No. I saw. I saw her with Sunil, plotting."

Kate, fearing protestation may backfire again, feigned sleep.

"Don't be ridiculous," said Clay.

"I did. Sunil threw our money on the fire. Kate let him. She must have known he was angry with us."

Kate shifted beneath her blanket, wringing her hands. The sliver of truth in what Diane was saying made her palms sticky.

"Shh," Clay repeated, though less forcefully.

"So what if he did throw the tip away?" Ethan spoke up.

"It shows something was wrong," said Diane. "She must have known."

"Well, if you saw it too, so must you."

Silence.

"And anyway, if there were signs of a problem, it was up to all of us to notice them."

Kate reached out for Ethan, grateful as he continued.

"Like the pony guy. The night before Nabbi took us up to the pass, I'm sure that he was trying to warn me. But I didn't pay any attention." He paused. "So I'm to blame too."

"He tried to tell me something, too," whispered Jan. "It wasn't just you."

In the pause that followed, George breathed in through his teeth.

"There's no point in this," said Clay quickly. "The only thing that's certain is that Nabbi betrayed us. Beyond that, we each made our own mistake. Right, Diane?"

Silence.

"Right." Ethan turned away. "Enough said."

Since then, all outward anger about the handover ran as far as the guide, and landed at his feet. "Admire the man's commitment at least," said Clay. "The ultimate sneaker-pimp. Seven hostages to upgrade his Nikes."

Kate, still perched now on the toilet, flicked through her note-book again. With thoughts of rescue and blame held back, conversation mostly focused on the minutiae of their day-to-day existence: the intolerably repetitive meals, the bone-deep cold at night, the sounds—a cowbell, the snap of distant gunfire (shocking at first, quickly mundane), children's high-pitched voices, a jet overhead—that occasionally split the quiet of their room.

Beyond this, they discussed the guards. Why did Sadiq take such childish pleasure in trying to steal in upon them without warning? What made Abu prod and goad the men on their trips to the washroom? Was Khalid suggestible?—might they hope that he would outgrow his zeal in time?

And every now and then somebody would steel themselves to talk about family. The previous day, for example, was the day of Jan's sister's wedding. They held a celebration in her honor and Clay made a dry toast.

Only occasionally did they speculate about the precise agenda behind their captivity, since none of the guards would be drawn further than the simple explanation "Kashmir" on the subject, and it hurt to sit staring at the unanswerable question. Kate saw that her notebook reflected this skewing of attention; the pages contained a journal, not journalism.

The entry she read now, for example.

Clay has a watch. An old windup model on an elasticized metal strap. He managed to slide it up his arm during our first, blindfolded ride in the back of the truck, and Abu missed it when he searched us in the yard. After Clay tells me about it I need to know the time, all the time. Knowing breaks the days down, which helps make sense of . . . everything. At first I try rationing myself, just asking when I absolutely have to know. But the question is persistent as rust. Even the act of predicting Clay's answer makes this confinement more bearable. Eventually, faking anger, he snaps.

"Come on! You'll have me wear the glass out if you make me look at the damn thing again."

"Sure. Sorry." I do my best to look unconcerned.

"Seriously; keep mentioning the time and sooner or later one of them will walk in on me checking. We'll lose the watch entirely."

I nod. "You're right."

Clay's sitting next to me before the pocked end wall. He draws his knees to his chest and folds his arms across them. I just can't help it . . . my eyes flick to his left wrist. Still looking at me, he reaches under that sleeve and pulls the watch forward, from its hiding place high on his forearm, up to his fingers. Once there, he

brandishes the face at me like it's brass knuckles, then slides it
from his fingers entirely. "Here, take it. Kind of makes more
sense if I ask you."

"I can't accept that," I tell him. "If they spot it—"

"Sure you can. If they take it then it's gone." He waggles the
watch at me, as if it were a trifle. I'm hypnotized. He's whistling
another of his damned I don't care tunes. So I take the watch,
stare at it till the song stops, then finally look up. He shrugs and
says, "You'll be as careful as I am, anyway." And that's that.

Kate felt the bump above her own elbow now, then folded the
notebook shut and tucked it into her waistband. Time was running out. She turned off the tap and angled the tip of her pencil
into the plughole. Working carefully, she scraped the lead on the
plughole's metal edge, shaving a new point. Once sharpened, the
pencil readied itself for writing again, secure between thumb and
fingertip. Kate stood back from the sink and inspected the lead
tip, mesmerized by its ordinariness, then switched her grip and
held the pencil up at arm's length, a conductor's baton. Where
had this pencil started out? H.P.P. LTD NATARAJ METALLIC HB. Did
that mean that the wood was Indian, and the lead? Which factory
made it, which workers, when? Of the countless pencils no doubt
turned out that day, could any other have acquired this significance? The pencil changed as Kate looked at it: suddenly it was no
longer mundane, but totemic. Six beveled yellow sides, a sharpened black tip trembling at the ceiling.

Footsteps expanded in the hall.

As alien and familiar as Armitage Shanks.

The door, behind the pencil, seemed to bounce in its frame.

Kate started. Then she ran the tap, making sure the water swirled the evidence from the basin, each shaving a stalled wing spiraling into the vortex.

"Finish!"

She tucked the pencil stub into her sock and pulled the chain.

THIRTY-THREE

STARS LIT THE SLAB of night sky, visible through the barred window. Ethan lay still for a long while, watching them rotate. He listened to the ensemble's breathing. Beside him, Kate's sigh extended into silence, which continued, and continued, until finally he turned to check, in time with her next drawn breath.

Lumps stood out of the floorboards, barely discernable in the darkness. The biggest shape was Clay and Diane in the far corner. George lay by the buttress just this side of the hanging sheet, which meant that was Jan against the other wall.

With everyone else fast asleep Ethan was more at ease. He turned back to watch Kate, her lips slightly apart, and felt a surge of tenderness. If only he could convince her it was in all their interests to be more patient with the guards, more understanding. But when, to cheer her up, he'd suggested they list the ways the Marriott was an improvement over the farmstead, she'd thought he was joking and her laughter was venomous. In sleep all anger relaxed from her face: the hope he felt looking at her became guilt, which made him turn away. In this new world of absolutes the old ambivalence rang hollow. It was easier to concentrate instead on the flat floor pressing up at his back, comfortingly forceful. Yes, if he lay for long enough without moving, the points of contact grew so numb he couldn't tell where his body ended and the wood began.

Turning back to the visible sector of sky, Ethan still couldn't identify any constellations; there was no recognizable pattern, no shapes, just stars. A shred of cloud moved across the gap, too thin to blot out the brightness behind, appearing to weave between the dots.

As he watched the cloud pass, a new noise joined the breathing. Metal on metal, the slow turning of a key in the door. He turned his head to face the sound, fear needling at him through the numbness of the floor.

A gray rectangle of door parted from its frame, and a figure moved through the crack. Ethan lay still as tree roots, yet his skin crawled. Leaving the door ajar, the figure trod noiselessly to the center of the room and paused, hands on hips. As Ethan watched, a burning sensation mounted in his chest. Witnessing this was wrong. The figure took more tentative steps across the room, drawing nearer to Ethan, apparently surveying the scene. Now he could make the man out. Heavy shoulders, a thickness through the trunk, fingers twitching at the ends of gorilla arms. The head turned in the starlight. A balaclava. But not *the* balaclava.

Ethan was sure of that. This man moved differently, less assuredly. Though he were forced to act this clandestine role, *the* balaclava would never skulk.

From in front of the sheet, George coughed out a blunt breath, rooting through his dream. The figure stiffened, seeming to blend into the darkness, until satisfied that George had settled. Then he walked over to Ethan and knelt down.

Ethan's eyes tried to shut, but couldn't. Squinting through a veil of lashes, he made out the man's square head, the blankness of his mask, the pale whites of his eyes. The hulked figure, bouncing minutely on his heels, seemed to grow in the obscurity, even as his identity became obvious. Complete power puffed the man up. He raised an arm above his head, closed his hand into a dog-head fist. The ring on his little finger caught the moonlight. Ethan dared not blink: waiting for the blow he smelled Abu's peppermint breath.

The fist didn't fall. For minutes nothing happened. Would he look more realistically asleep if he rolled over? No, Kate had not stirred next to him. Copy her, stay put. Abu's arm dropped. He scratched his head. The immediate fear receded, seeping between the floorboards. A crazed numbness remained. More minutes, another clashing memory: this was as wrong as his mum sitting on the end of his bed, before she left. The stalemate of watching and being watched. Ethan sighed as subtly as he could. She'd always said she could tell whether he was asleep or just pretending.

Menace made the time elastic, but Abu eventually moved away. He tracked around Kate and moved to the darker end of the room, where he sat observing Clay and Diane. Though heavy, he moved through the darkness noiselessly, as if under water. By the time he'd finished at the far end and had moved on to hover over Jan, Ethan's skin no longer merely crawled, but swam with imagined tics. He allowed himself to drag his hand an inch across the floor: the relief of a new sensation in that arm made the prickly rest of him almost unbearable.

Finally Abu stalked toward George. The granite square of sheet behind him meant that what followed was played out as if on the dimmest of screens. Abu bent forward over George's sleeping form, as he had done over Ethan. Again one long arm reached away from his hunched body, fist poised aloft, except that now to Ethan the hand had grown abstract; reaching for attention, or to pull a rope.

George rolled over and coughed again. Abu started sideways. Perhaps his heel caught on the boards; a big hand lunged out to steady his fall.

George's second wheeze became a startled "Huh!" He jerked upward as if beneath an opening parachute.

Already Abu was rising to his feet. Ethan, still nailed to the floorboards, saw the brutal outline of Abu's shoulders changing shape as the guard lashed out with a backhand swipe, through George, who slumped back, canopy strings cut. A wave of invective rolled upright with him, as he flailed to react. "Huugghhh?"

Woefully late. Abu was already through the door.

THIRTY-FOUR

THE FIRST "HUH!" was part of Kate's dream, an involuntary exclamation mark. She pretended not to hear it and instead pulled back harder on the control column. Rachel tensed beside her, but said nothing more. Kate, suppressing a smile, stared straight ahead. The nose-cowl came through the horizon and the little plane scooped upward, from shallow dive to steep climb, momentum slewing into a crisp September sky.

Stalling was simply exceeding the critical angle of attack. The smooth airflow over the wing broke into useless turbulence: an end to lift, the beginning of freefall. "When the plane stalls the nose will want to slide one way or the other," her instructor had explained, "and if you try to correct the turn with the stick you'll do the opposite. Imagine you're driving a car, and when you turn the steering wheel left to avoid an obstacle the car swerves right, into it. Unnerving, so—"

"So I'll stamp with the rudder to turn, and use the stick to shove the nose down."

"Right. Then, when the wings are flying again, you can use the elevators to bank and turn all you like."

As the nose aimed further skyward the engine pitch dropped, straining under the weight of so sheer a climb. No matter how many times she went through the routine, Kate's stomach tightened in anticipation of the plane dropping. With Rachel in the passenger seat beside her, no doubt a league of fear ahead, such anticipation was delicious. She decided to stretch the moment further and jerked level before the first squeak.

"Was that it?" Rachel's voice was scratchy in the headset.

"What?"

"Is that stalling, then?"

"No. That's climbing. You'll know when we stall. The plane falls out of the sky. You'll be hanging in your straps."

Headset silence. Rachel had only to ask and she'd stop. It wasn't as if she wanted to scare her for no reason. The obstinate pause extended, though, and Kate's resolve hardened. Puncturing that veneer of cool *was* a good reason. There was something deeply irritating about her sister's rigidity in the passenger seat, a self-containment that was really just self-satisfaction, a bubble of superiority cultivated for as long as Kate could remember, and just asking to be pricked.

"You okay?" Kate gave her another chance to call a halt. The plane was steady at three thousand feet now, on a ruled line through the still, morning air. Kate sensed Rachel fighting the temptation to say something, and losing. An intake of breath echoed in her headphones. Just say the word. Crack.

"So you've flown Ethan." Another deliberate breath. "What did he make of the . . . experience?"

Though she couldn't know, it felt like Rachel was jabbing at this nerve deliberately. Kate made a spurious radio call to avoid responding, and flicked the plane left-right to check the airspace beneath the nose. With a sidelong look to her left she saw that Rachel had blanched behind her designer sunglasses.

"Check your harness."

Rachel was fumbling for the correct strap. Kate leaned over and tugged on the frayed end for her; a gesture that felt intimate and sisterly and wrong. To compensate for it, she yanked out the carburetor heat control, cut the throttle, and pulled back on the stick. The little plane ballooned. Without power, it slowed much faster in the climb. She hauled harder on the stick, felt the seat compress beneath her as their trajectory bent further upward. She'd aimed them into the sun on purpose; a matter of seconds into the maneuver the canopy turned a searing white. Somebody underlined the moment with a garbled radio announcement, and then the stall-warning indicator overrode the noise with its brief harmonica shriek. The seat began to give Kate up to the harness. She dragged the controls back harder still, braced expectantly for the buffet of turbulence that would signify the stall itself. A guttural noise drowned the static in her headphones as the plane bucked once and began to drop. The nose, which had started to slide right, began dipping into the incipient turn. With automatic sureness, Kate stamped her left foot to check the slide.

The pedal didn't give. Her foot pushed down again, but met a bricklike resistance. The plane continued sliding further right, and somehow she was a beat behind the required response, unnerved by the panic which had swamped the cockpit. The thought caught up with her—*she's interfering with the dual controls*—

but too late to say anything; Kate had already begun wrestling her sister's knee-jerk reaction, her foot straining on the left-hand rudder pedal, and both hands pushing the control column forward against the equal and opposite force of Rachel's instinctive pulling back. The canopy blinked blind again.

"Off!" Kate yelled.

The plane fell faster, yawing sideways, beginning to rotate like a spun knife. Kate pushed, Rachel pulled. Their hands and feet and control and panic canceled one another out.

"Leave go!"

Out of the corner of her eye, Kate saw Rachel's hands jolt back from the column, fingers rigid.

"Feet!"

The pedal beneath Kate's left foot gave abruptly, as if a wire had snapped. As the nose dipped and steadied she throttled up, tilting into a powered dive. The engine whine fed back into her headset, reassuring as the next breath. She leveled the wings.

As glib as she could muster, she said, "That helped."

Silence.

The plane was chugging along smoothly again. Kate glanced right to see Rachel still shaking in the seat beside her.

"Huugghhh?"

The noise filled Kate's headset as her sister strained against her harness and was sick into cupped hands.

THIRTY-FIVE

SHE FOUGHT THE blanket and clutched at Ethan, fingers digging into his forearm. "Rachel!" she said.

George's bellow ended in words as he swam finally to his hands and knees: "What the—?"

"Poor Rachel."

In the pause Ethan heard, or imagined he could hear, Abu's footsteps receding. He breathed out.

"My face." George lurched upright, a gray shape.

Ethan risked movement himself now, first prying Kate's nails free. Their bite burned as she struggled beside him. "Shhhh," he said. "You're dreaming."

"It's not a fucking dream," George shouted back. He was stumbling toward the door. "He was just in here. Bastard hit me. I'm bleeding."

"I shouldn't have done that," Kate whispered. "Not to Rachel."

Clay had disentangled himself from Diane at the far end of

the room. He came forward into the half-light as George reached the door and yanked at its handle, then banged the drum of its flat surface with a balled hand.

"He cut me. I think he had a knife."

Clay caught George's wrist, halting the next thump before it landed. "Calm down, calm down," he urged. "What's the matter? What's going on?"

Ethan saw Kate's eyes open, bluish in the starlight, and told her again. "It was just a dream. You were only dreaming."

George continued yelling about a cut and a blade. Clay pulled him back from the door, saying "Let's have a look," and it was hard for Ethan not to explain that there hadn't been a knife, but doing so would mean revealing that he had seen Abu in the room, and he didn't want to do that.

Over by the barred window Clay angled George's face to the night sky. Ethan saw that the shadows above George's black beard were wrong even before Clay's sleeve smeared them. "Your eyebrow's split, but it doesn't look deep. Jesus, how'd you manage that?"

George recoiled, as if from an insult. "I didn't manage anything. I woke up and the one in the ski mask was just standing there waiting to attack me. He cut me and then he legged it. The fucker ran away. You must have heard the door slam?"

At that, a door shut down the hall.

"There! Someone's there. And a minute ago he was here." Now George rounded upon Ethan. "Look, mate, I'm bleeding." He jabbed at his forehead, as if accusing Ethan of idiocy. "It was no dream. The bastard had some sort of knife."

Now there were more misunderstandings to put right. Not a

knife. Not *the* ski mask. "I didn't mean you; I was talking to Kate." He nodded at her in the half-light, as if there was some doubt who he was referring to.

"What time is it?" Jan asked, his voice bleary. "What's with you guys?"

"Nothing," said Clay. "Go back to sleep."

"There fucking is! They're torturing us now, and I'm not going to let it lie." George bristled, his fists opening and shutting impotently at his sides.

Ethan looked back down at Kate, the boundaries of his own confusion blurring as Kate's face woke up properly. Her vulnerability in this half-state instilled an overwhelming sense of responsibility. He should tell them what he had seen, because *they* included Kate. He became conscious of a muscle flicking in his otherwise frozen face.

"What's wrong?" she asked.

The corridor light fanned into the room. Kate screwed her eyes shut against its brightness, then burrowed into Ethan's shoulder. There was silence; a stillness swamped the room with the shock of yellow that bounced from its peeling walls. Ethan felt Kate uncoiling from his side as George rushed toward the open door. He held on to her; she was a child whom he must keep safe. Clay rose to cut George off, steering him to one side of Jan, who had also risen to face the noise.

Abu filled the empty door frame. A slice of his black hair stood out from the side of his head at right angles, like a broken wing. Was that a deliberate touch, Ethan wondered, or just the result of having pulled off the balaclava?

"No drama, nothing to see." Clay grinned at Abu. "George

here sleepwalked himself into a wall. But everything's cool again. We're all back off to bed now."

Abu ignored him. "What is this? Why are you waking up to make noise?" He scratched his beard, staring blearily from face to face. The act was convincing.

"It's nothing"—Clay kept the smile up—"a misunder—"

"Bollocks, is it! Where the fuck's your boss? Where's the main man? The deviant in the mask? See what he's done to me?" George, tapping the side of his head, tried to approach Abu, but Clay held him back. Now that Kate had settled down, Ethan rose and clamped a hand on George's other shoulder, which trembled in his grip.

Abu now leaned against the door frame, staring down at Clay. He hid the beginning of his own smile, Ethan was sure of it, in a demonstrative frown and then, talking over the top of George's ragged breathing, tapped his own forehead, and said plainly, "He is a madman."

The words prompted a moment of clarity. Ethan saw that they were true. Madness meant inappropriate and unpredictable and George was definitely that; his shivering forewarned an explosion. The twitching below Ethan's left eye worsened as his own bottled panic grew. Somehow it was not Abu's fault, but George's. What might this man's lack of control provoke? Ethan's grip on George's shoulder tightened. Behind him, Kate spoke softly:

"George, best leave it be."

"No!" With a violent shrug George jerked free of Clay and Ethan, and stamped toward the open door. Abu drew himself up to meet his advance, stood unflinching as the smaller man stopped just short then continued looming over him impassively, as if daring further action. Toe to toe with the guard George swayed, panting up into his face.

"Tell the coward to come here himself," George shouted. "Instead of sending you."

"Coward?" Abu smiled.

"Hiding behind his fucking ski mask." He flapped his arms, a flightless bird.

Now Abu stifled a laugh. This was understandable, and yet provocative. George's arms stiffened mid wing-beat. If Ethan pulled him back now he'd run the risk of involving himself, yet George's posturing threatened a fragile balance. He could not bear to watch; instead he turned to the window, which was now black and sucked empty of stars by the electric light. He hadn't time to focus on the bars before Abu's laughter broke derisively and George snapped. Two thin hands gripped the guard's denim collar, pulling him a step into the room. Beard to beard the two figures pirouetted, momentarily off balance. Then Abu's arms drove up between George's and somehow George was on his back with Abu kneeling over him, the thumb of one hand pressed hard into the whiteness of George's throat. Though covered in gray bristles his neck was skinny as an old man's. His lips were purple and open, and the thin noise coming from behind them was pathetic.

Clay took a step forward, then halted when Abu looked up.

"This man is not making sense. He makes noise like a dog."

"Leave him al—"

Kate, too, was cut short by the glare.

"I do not think you should be putting up with such nonsense," Abu continued, rising to his feet. George clawed his way up with him, a contradiction of stiff limbs and loose joints, like a puppet. "He is a dog and will be better in the kennel," Abu explained, smiling. His teeth were luminous beneath his beard. "Yes?" The question was aimed at George, who did not respond as Abu pulled him from the room.

THIRTY-SIX

KATE'S BREATH WAS visible in the corridor. It lingered like the conversation coming through the open door to the guards' quarters. She halted to listen. Not a conversation; the tone was wrong. Radio, in English. The back end of an unbelievable news story. She waited for more detail, ignoring Khalid's gentle tap on the shoulder, but the announcer moved on to the sports report. More familiar names echoed in the hallway, entirely out of place, news from the Premier League. Khalid moved past her and shut the door, muffling the sense from the words. A further cloud of breath hung in front of her as she gave in to a more insistent prod and continued toward the bathroom.

In the little room a tremendous shiver overtook Kate. She steadied herself, gripping the dirty basin with both hands and staring at the discolored bruise of paint that remained in place of a mirror. Her throat felt raw and tight; she opened her mouth and whispered "Ahhh" at the spot where her reflection should have been. The noise was both amazement and sorrow.

This was the first she'd heard of the world beyond their captivity. The story hurt to recall, so she repeated the football result instead: Newcastle United 0–Aston Villa 2. Villa was Ethan's team—he'd taken her to a match once, on a biting January afternoon. Beneath a low sky she'd endured the boredom of a nil–nil draw, marooned in the middle of a jeering crowd. The sublimation of supporting baffled Kate. Yet Ethan seemed to draw a pleasure from precisely that. Following the fortunes of a team he'd picked at random as a schoolboy mattered. Watching him sing taunts at the opposition fans, she couldn't decide whether she found this aspect of his character endearing or an affront. The singing showed hidden fervor, but did it count?

She turned on the tap and listened to the water cough its way up the pipe. How far had the radio waves traveled? That depended: was it long-wave, medium-wave, or FM? The plane's radio was VHF, which was good for about ninety miles if you were up high, but only sixty if you were lower down. How high? Why, when she'd known the exact numbers by heart so recently, could she not remember them now? She stared at the water running into her cupped hands, but felt nothing. The faucet spat; she heard only the fractured static of a signal moving out of range. Her fingers went slack and water ran from between them in icy tendrils. Then she shut them again and, as the pool reformed, concentrated on recalling more detail. VHF only worked if the transmitter had a clear view of the receiver; a mountain in the way made communication impossible. Such obstacles would block the range of the other frequencies as well. She understood that there were ways around the problem—a signal could be bounced off a satellite relay station to reach down into a valley such as this. Yes, a satellite could increase the signal's range, but what were the limits of such trickery? She didn't know. Steeling herself, she stripped to the waist and prepared to wash herself methodically. Like taking off her shoes at night, the routine was vital protection against the threat of falling apart. The coldness Kate splashed into her face was hard as grit and made her gasp.

She would pass on the football result to Ethan. Perhaps he'd connect with that news. She felt a stab of longing. What would she now give to have the old Ethan back? In past weeks he seemed to have hardened. Nothing she said got through. The night before, she'd heard him muttering, and reached for his hand.

"Say again?" she whispered.

"Say what again?"

"I thought . . ."

"You must see, Kate."

"See what?"

"The importance of it. How crucial . . . not to react." He was hard to make out. "We have to work *with* them, together . . . survive."

"Together." She repeated the only important word. "Ethan, I . . ."

"Shh. Whisper."

She swallowed once, put her lips to his ear.

He squeezed her hand, but said nothing. You couldn't expect to continue the private language of a couple, without privacy. He was never much of a talker at the best of times—a fact Rachel enjoyed pointing out. His reticence now was just more of the same, surely. And in unspoken ways—this pressing of her hand in the middle of black night, the gentleness with which he passed her a helping of watery rice—he was if anything *more* attentive than normal. She finished washing and shut off the tap, found solace in the silence that replaced its sputtering.

THEY'D KEPT GEORGE in the kennel for over a week. When Sadiq returned him the previous day (again the fat guard played his tiresome joke of attempting to steal unannounced into their midst) he appeared to have shrunk. Everything about him was smaller; it was as if he was crouching within a compressed version of himself. Between his matted hair and beard a crust of scab straddled the concave bridge of his nose. His black eyes had sunk further into their shadowed sockets; the gray in his beard and hair was now echoed in the pallor of his skin. He sat clutching his shoulders, arms hooked over bony knees, terminally quiet: even his anger appeared to have eaten itself up.

Still, their relief at seeing him again had been a high point. Kate licked the tip of her pencil and recorded how Clay's pat on the back had turned into a full, if unreciprocated, hug. Jan rose to join in before coughing himself back into his mound of blankets. Even Diane had sensed an occasion, seen that George's suffering topped her own, and stepped beyond the perimeter of her self-pity to plant a kiss on his cheek: "Like, welcome back. Into the fold." She curtsied and gestured at the corners of the room with an upturned palm, part salesgirl, part lady-in-waiting. "Let me reacquaint you with the five-star facilities of our suite."

George did not smile. "We must get away from here," he said, his voice flat.

"Of course," said Clay. "We will. We just have to hold together and they're bound to let us go in time."

"No. If we don't escape they'll kill us."

Clay tried to laugh. "It's like the man said, we're valuable. They'll work out a trade eventually, and we'll—"

"I mean it. We have to get out," George continued deliberately. "We must prepare."

"Either they'll let us go or . . . somebody will come to get us," reasoned Clay.

George's silence was caustic.

"Maybe he is right, no?" continued Jan. "They've kept us like an animal for over two months now. Maybe we must make something happen."

Ethan was staring balefully at George.

"If the opportunity arises, then . . . perhaps. But think of the danger. Think of Rafi. Patience is what—" Clay's soothing voice was again cut off.

"There'll be a sign," George began muttering to himself again. "We must prepare through prayer, and then we'll be shown the way."

Clay squeezed the older man's shoulder again and said, "Sure thing, no harm in that, pray away."

George rolled over to face the wall.

Beside Kate, Ethan's fist had pumped the map of his forearm into definition; the cabling of his athlete's neck stood rigid, collarbone to ear, for a split second. Kate saw incredulity in his eyes harden to hostility, and watched him bite down, clamping his mouth shut. Finally he doused his anger with indifference and slumped back against the wall. The performance was a familiar echo of how he responded to his father's goading, by shutting it out. When she smoothed the knee of his trousers reassuringly he shook her hand off.

Now the guards' door opened and closed in the corridor, allowing the radio voice to swell and die again. Yesterday evening, picking her moment carefully, she'd asked Ethan: wasn't George's return a good sign?

A pause, in which her fingers worried at one another. Ethan's eyes wandered over the opposite wall. "The bloke's a liability, Kate. He's not all there. I'm just surprised. They know that; I can't see how they think they'll benefit from . . ."

"What's *their* benefit got to do with anything?"

His face said it was obvious, yet this only deepened her concern. Her fingers continued twisting, struggling to wring a drop of logic from his words. "You mean what's good for them is good for us, in the long run?"

More silence. His eyes stopped still, lapsed into an unfocused stare. "Something like that."

There was no way Ethan, or any of the others, could take more bad news. She'd keep it to herself. Kate's pencil wrote *News* and drew a box around the word. She should record the radio story she'd overheard here, even if she had decided to keep it from them. She checked her watch, then wrote, *At approx 0745 on 12 September I overheard a radio news story fearing us dead.*

THIRTY-SEVEN

"IT'S JUST A MATTER of time."

Rachel heard her mother's mantra over the grinding of the dishwasher, but the words had long since lost their meaning. Through the rain-spotted window she watched the clothesline whip at the sky.

"Sooner or later they'll see sense. We've enough names now."

Her mother continued scouring at the sink, the top of her head bobbing at Rachel across the breakfast bar. Rachel noted the new blond highlights cut into a recently tightened perm. She stayed put on her stool as her mother assembled another pot of tea, warming the pot, measuring out the tea leaves, stirring to infinity. Slow hands placed the ensemble of cups, milk jug, and sugar bowl on a tray with the precision of a theater nurse, and carried it through to the lounge as if leading a church procession.

The optimism was terrifying. The house smelled odd, too clean. Rachel found it suddenly hard to breathe. She took her usual seat in the lounge and sat staring at the sideboard. The familiarity of the group of objects displayed there made them collectively invisible at first, but while Rachel's mum continued with the ritual of the tea the lump of the thing broke into its constituent parts, and she found herself before a shrine.

Framed photographs, of Kate and herself for the most part, stood in clusters on shelves crammed full of figurines and vases and homemade ornaments. Either side of a pair of shell boats, painted with nail varnish, stood twin primary-school head shots. Kate wore an Alice band; her tentative smile beneath it was as much gap as teeth. Rachel was flawless by comparison, beaming at her sister like a weather girl, through lollypop-stick masts.

Those photographs predated the scandal, but the one on the shelf above, of the pair with their mother, astride New Forest ponies, came from just afterward. It brought the memory of that unfolding cutting back. His face beneath the indelible words: SCHOOLGIRL PREGNANT BY DEPUTY HEAD. Rachel shut her eyes, then opened them and fixed her stare on the photo again, saw the straining togetherness of the holiday displayed in her mother's stoical grin. How determined their mother had been to take part in the group lesson. Neither Rachel nor Kate had tried to stop her then, both awed by her brittle hopefulness, fearful, in the wake of their father's departure, of the consequences of its failure.

By the time the picture above that was taken, though, fifteen-year-old Kate had begun resisting on every front. No matter what their mum did or said, Kate found a hole in it and tore the thing apart, leaving Rachel to patch and mend. Kate even started seeing their dad again, indulging him in his failure, despite the prick's lack of contrition. The photo looked anodyne enough,

Christmas dinner, stupid hats, yet the battle lines were evident even there: Kate's nut roast obstinately opposing the lavish turkey at the top of the table.

"We've just short of five thousand names now and Michelle is planning to re-present the petition to the Foreign Office when we reach the magic number. She thinks that should be on Tuesday or Wednesday. Really, she's a brick. You've never seen someone work so hard. Five thousand! They'll have to intervene now, Rachel, you'll see."

"Sure." Carpet cleaner. That's what smelled so strong.

"All that pressure. It's marvelous." A gaunt smile at her lap. "You'll come with us to hand over the signatures, won't you?"

Rachel bit her lip. "Of course."

"Good girl. The public pressure is everything."

Her mother's teaspoon plinked around the cup. Outside, the garden was a silent frenzy: the apple tree, bare of fruit, shook its stunted limbs at the sky, while next door's willow thrashed at the top of the hedge. She'd even managed to normalize this. Reduced it to numbers and a new friend called Michelle; the two of them stiff-backed against the same wall. Ignoring entirely the ugly speculation in some of the more recent news stories. It was almost as if she enjoyed battling to stay unruffled. The teaspoon tapped its cup-lip twice before settling into the saucer. Not calm, becalmed. Stagnating behind her double-glazing in a mire of false optimism.

And in all of this, what about him? Rachel's gaze returned to the sideboard submerged beneath its memorabilia. Their father built the thing, after all. Or assembled the flat-pack, at least. A last stab at domesticity before he bailed out for good.

What right had he to crawl back now?

Her mother had been out fetching unnecessary groceries when he showed. Rachel, steadying herself against the door frame, refused to meet his eye. The pink shapes of his baldness and pleading hands were reflected in the frosted glass of the door, until she shut it. He stood in the driveway for twenty minutes. The thought of him waiting flooded Rachel with a bitterness she could not swallow.

On top of that, they'd received calls from Ethan's dad. Since the news about the Israeli had come through, his bullish front had apparently dissolved. The press ran a story intimating that he thought Ethan had been landed in this mess by his girlfriend. The irony of it. He was adamant that Ethan had "only gone with her out of a sense of duty—to keep her safe."

A day later he woke their mother in the middle of the night, ringing through a drunken message that made her, in turn, call Rachel for advice. Her "Ignore him" hadn't worked. She'd not yet returned to bed before the phone had gone off again, and she'd failed to follow her own advice.

"Piece of work, your sister, little Kate."

"Pardon?"

"Head full of BS, and planted right up her own backside. With her claws in my boy, too. Blind to it, he was . . . is. But I saw."

"I'm sorry?" She felt no anger; in fact the old man's slurring brought something like relief. Ethan lived in it. She forced herself to ask the unnecessary, "Who is this?"

"I'm the father. His dad. And we're thick as thieves. They have to send my boy back."

"Please, it's two in the morning. I appreciate what you're going through, believe me, but—"

"Two in the morning *here* maybe." A longer pause. "But"—his tone became triumphant—"not there, young lady, not there."

"Whatever you say. I'm hanging up." She placed a finger on the disconnect button, but held back.

"Such a sweet boy. Courageous, brave, and good-natured. Not one to desert her in the thick of it. She's used him." His voice was poured mud.

"She's not used anybody."

Despite herself Rachel began arguing with the old man. It had taken her ten minutes to draw the conversation to a close.

Outside, water lilies slapped at the fishpond full of fallen leaves; inside, perched on the edge of her floral armchair, Rachel's mother babbled on about lights at the end of the tunnel.

In vain. There'd been no proper news for weeks. Rachel's days before her computer screen—her compassionate leave had been ominously extended—were a seamless frustration. The only recent articles described the mainstream Kashmiri politicians' unanimous condemnation of F.R.N.'s tactics, one leader after another urging the militants to give up the hostages for the sake of the state. In this way hard news had become conjecture and opinion and was drying up entirely. All that was left was Ethan's father's slander, together with the repeated "Ms. Cox's family have so far declined to comment."

She watched her mother picking invisible specks of lint from her navy skirt. Scrubbing sinks, stirring tea, pecking at her lap: her fingers would not stay still. Behind the calm front she was all twisted nerves.

So was Rachel. Nothing could numb or divert the viciousness of what Rachel, at her darkest, truly felt. Kate and Ethan's stupidity *warranted* this punishment. Ethan should never have gone with her to Kashmir. And Kate shouldn't have risen to Rachel's idiot challenge in the first place. *Investigate.* Come on! She focused again on one of the photos of Kate, wanting both to tear it up and to hold it to her chest. Shame engulfed her. The punishment was rightly *hers* and Ethan's, not Kate's. Her eyes stung when she wiped them.

An immense silence, seeming to emanate from the fitted carpet, bounced back off the patio doors. A new smell of polish, sickly as custard, rose above the carpet cleaner. She stood and walked to the window and pressed her forehead against it. They had breathed up all the air.

THIRTY-EIGHT

ETHAN LEANED BACK against his patch of warm wall, pressing his shoulders flat to the cinder blocks, and looked about. Midafternoon. George lay curled opposite in his familiar stupor, a hip bone jutting at the beams above. Diane dozed on in her heap. One pink foot nosed out from under her blanket, then retreated. The only activity was in front of the big square of graying sheet, where, to the tune of one of Clay's unending songs, Kate knelt next to Jan, playing the stone game. Five pebbles thrown, caught, and shuffled in a Byzantine sequence that Ethan hadn't bothered to learn. When cajoled to play, he accepted instructions at each turn, and did his best not to win.

An engine died outside. Down the corridor, doors slammed. Nobody paid any attention. Unseen people came and went from the building once or twice a week, but it made no difference. For all Kate and Clay's speculation, what went on in headquarters couldn't be any of their business. Nevertheless, Ethan found it somehow reassuring to imagine the strategies planned and orders given on the guards' side, where the bigger picture was surely pinned to a corkboard or projected upon a whitewashed wall.

Now though, a set of feet halted before their door. Ethan leaned forward from the wall expectantly and said, "Guys." They oughtn't to be caught playing like children.

Inexpert fingers worked the key for seconds before the lock gave. The door creaked open and the balaclava stepped into their midst. He glided across the dirty floor and stood considering the scene. Kate, Jan, and Clay swiveled to face him in unison. Diane sat up and rubbed her eyes. When the man's gaze met Ethan's he nodded, barely perceptibly, but Ethan was sure of it all the same.

"Everything is satisfactory?"

Ethan, willing the pause to last, heard his heart in his throat. He dreaded that Kate would contradict the man, whose words were as much statement as question. When the eyeholes turned back to him he ventured his own minimal nod in return.

The balaclava continued forcefully: "Nobody is ill." A telltale head-wobble compounded the emphatic negative, but the mouth-hole kept moving, disputing itself. "You see, I am hearing the opposite. I am hearing there is trouble with sickness."

Jan replied with a gravelly cough. The balaclava turned to face the noise and quickstepped to the group in front of the hanging sheet. But he knelt next to Clay. An easy mistake, Ethan considered, for they all looked as ragged as each other. Even he had had to scale down his training to conserve energy in recent weeks. At least this visit showed that the twin chains—of command and intelligence—were working; the guards had taken note of Jan's condition and alerted their superiors.

"Are you needing medicine?" the balaclava asked gently.

Out of the corner of his eye Ethan registered the configuration of shapes directly opposite him move and settle, as George stirred.

"Not me." Clay mustered a charming smile. "Junior here. He needs a proper checkup. Antibiotics. The works." He turned the smile on Jan. "Don't you?"

"He's worst," Kate added. "But we all need to see a doctor. Everybody's been sick. What do you expect?"

Ethan bit harder on his lower lip. She meant well. But the balaclava only nodded, rising above the insult. "And you are eating good food. With enough blankets. There is enough warmth in the night."

Ethan nodded again. Of course the food was rank, repetitive slush, and the nights had grown achingly bitter, but what else could they expect? There were circumstances to consider. What they had was adequate.

"We freeze half to death and I wouldn't make my dog eat that shit." Diane rapped out the insult. The balaclava twisted to look at her. Ethan concentrated on the back of the man's neck, watched the woolen ribbing corkscrew slowly. Diane met the eyeholes with a peal of silly giggling and Ethan felt a part of himself shut down inside. Improbably, however, the man's shoulders shook with reciprocating laughter.

"Thank you. This is honest, which is good. I see what we can do, okay?"

Now Diane batted her eyelids. Ethan withered.

"But I am serious." The man's knees cracked as he bounced up from his heels and moved toward Diane. "My men are looking after you okay? They are treating you with due courtesy?" He paused in the center of the room with his hands on his hips, proprietarily. "No complaints?"

Silence.

Then a roar so loud it seemed to come from all directions at once. George flew up with the noise. Ethan turned to see him suspended mid lunge. There was no continuity; one minute he was a shape hanging in the air, the next he had crossed the gap and was on the balaclava's back. The balaclava staggered beneath the weight and Ethan found himself leaping into the fray. But the air seemed viscous—he had to heave through its resistance to reach the pair. George's face wheeled around on the balaclava's shoulder, mouth open, eyes two blank disks, its own mask. One stringy arm was pinned across the balaclava's upper chest, fingers digging into the man's fatigues. As the composite figure tipped off balance toward Ethan he saw George's other hand flashing up to the leader's throat.

The roar broke into syllables: "Spine-less-cow-ard-fuck."

Somehow Ethan managed to right the falling mass for a second. He reeled with them in a confusion of flailing limbs, his face pressing into George's hair, which smelled of earth. Looking down, he saw George's feet clear of the floor, pedaling air. Ethan grabbed at the sharpness of his shoulder to rip the two men apart but, when he pulled, both figures lurched off balance with him again. Together they fell in exaggerated strides, Ethan sliding round the knot of George's back until his nose was inches from the gray fingers still digging at the balaclava's hidden throat. Working blindly, he drove his own hand between George's chest and the balaclava's back, but still couldn't separate the two men. As they stumbled Ethan saw George's nails disappear into olive wool and yank it upward. He realized what was happening and began to fight properly.

They spun. Ethan's "No!" rose above the balaclava's yell for help. The room ran round them and he saw that the door was open and something was moving through it and then the view was just an arc of shaven chin growing as the mask slid upward. George's nails took lumps of the man's face with them as he hauled, leaving gouged lines yet to fill with blood.

A charge went through Ethan. Something fundamental and awful was happening and he was their only hope. The balaclava dug in vain at his waistband. Sadiq had a stick and was coming to the rescue, but not fast enough. George had already torn the edge of mask above a black mustache. Ethan's legs began pumping; both the smaller men were enveloped and overcome by his panic. He bundled them all toward the sheet, which flapped theatrically as Ethan drove straight beyond it, into touch. He took a trailing leg out with one of his, upending the lot of them into the dark rear of the room. Out of sight.

"Who the fuck?"

George's growled words were barely audible over Diane's screaming. He had the woolen hem rumpled up beyond the bridge of the leader's nose, revealing frightened brown eyes. The mask came off in a rush, like a peeled sock. Ethan felt a stripe of heat across his shoulders but was already rolling away so as not to see. Instead the view became Sadiq wielding his length of wood. George buckled as the pole broke across his lower back and immediately afterward Ethan saw his own fist connect with the side of George's face, which was surprising and yet made sense at the same time. George fell away. There was just the shape of him sprawled on the floor, and the balaclava was crouching in the corner scrabbling for the mask. Before Sadiq managed to drag him off, Ethan's bare foot stamped twice on George's head.

THIRTY-NINE

KATE COWERED AS ETHAN launched the balaclava and George past her and through the curtain. She tried to get up but the larger force of Diane's band-saw shriek pressed her down into a terrified huddle with Jan and Clay. One of the guards charged past, into the obscured end of the room. The saw hit a nail and died. Kate wobbled to her feet. From behind the curtain came the sound of blows and snorting breath, a horse panicking in its box. She took steps further forward, toward the edge of the sheet, but before she arrived the center of the square bulged and slid upward, giving birth to Sadiq. He dragged George into the bigger part of the room by one leg.

Ethan followed, his hands raised in a protestation of innocence, and the balaclava came last. Ethan said, "Please understand, I—" but the rest was drowned by Diane. Her wailing started again at the sight of the balaclava's extended hand, which held a pistol. The barrel waved wildly from Ethan's back to

George on the floor and then in the vague direction of the scream, which again stopped dead. In the silence that followed, the balaclava walked round George and aimed at his head. Blood ran down the side of George's face and blackened the dust.

"He's hurt," pleaded Jan, in a whisper.

The balaclava's shoulders heaved. His gun barrel shivered, tracing minute circles. With his spare hand he pulled the bottom of the ski mask straight on his head. The gesture looked childish, petulant. An open mouth appeared in the main hole and panted something foreign. Sadiq dropped George's foot and scratched his bearded chin and Kate's Swatch peeped at her over his cuff. Indignation gave her back her voice.

"He didn't mean it. He's unwell. Your damned kennel made him mad. Still currency, yes? You have to keep him healthy, help him, take him to a doctor."

A bubble of snot and blood appeared in George's open mouth. It grew, then popped.

"The punishment will fit," the balaclava panted. Then more foreign. Sadiq lifted George into a sitting position. His head lolled. With a hand beneath each armpit, Sadiq began dragging him toward the door. Meanwhile, the balaclava pointed the gun at each of them in turn, as if picking out faces with a torch beam. It lingered longest on Ethan, whose head was bowed. A statue. "You are next," the balaclava said.

AT FIRST THEY sat in silence, trying not to listen. The thread of time came apart in Kate's head. She hitched her sleeve to her elbow—above the simple face of Clay's watch—and sat staring at the second hand's measured sweep, trying to keep

calm. Nobody spoke, yet in each face Kate saw her own dread reflected. The quiet was intolerable, and seemed unending. When,
finally, George's voice first rang down the corridor, relief was immediately overtaken: his shout became a bellow, climbing in
pitch. What were they doing to him? Only Ethan moved. He
paced up and down, wide-eyed, his stare leaping from his hands
to the floor and ceiling, to her, and back again. He began to mutter to himself.

"How did I let this happen? What have I done?"

"It wasn't your fault. You tried to stop him. Of all of us, only
you had the guts to intervene."

"No. No. You don't understand. That's not true."

"It *is* true," Clay contradicted. "He went off so quick. You did
your best. You couldn't have done any more."

"I should have stopped him. I should have prevented it entirely. I let him attack the main man. My fault."

"Nonsense. Calm down."

Down the corridor the wave of George's wailing rose and
crashed, retreated in sobs, regathered and broke again. The noise
drew them in—each of their faces a study in shared pain.

Ethan was still muttering to himself. "Weak, weak, weak."

"They'll see you were meaning to help, that you tried to hold
George back," Kate urged. "They won't do anything to you."

"No, no, no," Ethan muttered, "you don't understand. I should
have finished the stupid bastard off myself."

"No way, no way," said Jan.

"You're better off having left the guy alone," Clay agreed.
Kate watched him scrape a handful of dirty hair back from his
forehead and continue in a measured, reassuring tone. "First up,

how were you to know he had that gun? Even if you'd managed to stop him using it there would still have been Sadiq and the others to get past. Trust your instincts—they told you to drag George off because it was the right thing to do."

Ethan's stare had fixed on his bare feet, a world apart. With these last words, Kate saw his face awaken; the change was as abrupt as if it had emerged from a shadow.

"Sure. You're right." His nod at Clay was an act, almost eager. Clay was smiling back, but she had caught a glimpse of something and knew better: a strange gap within Ethan was opening up. He continued: "I hope they leave him—"

The sound that stopped Ethan short was sudden and otherworldly. Kate started, looked involuntarily at the door, felt her insides twist. A deeper silence filled the room, quelling them all. Diane began to hum. Three notes, descending, again and again.

SADIQ AND ABU returned George at dusk. In the half-light Kate couldn't immediately interpret the strange whiteness of his face; as the two guards lowered him to the floor it became a crepe bandage, wound tightly, blanking out his eyes, nose, and ears. The dressing was clean and sterile and repellent in its contrast to everything else. His beard and hair and shirt were caked in blood and dirt. In their midst George sat cross-legged, shivering.

"What did they do?" asked Jan.

No response.

"You're alright now," he continued, his voice hollow. "You're back with us again. Think if they took you for longer. This is much more positive."

"Want us to take a look at you?" Clay asked. Though his voice was calm, Kate noticed his hands trembling. "What's going on under that bandage then?"

One by one they had drawn closer to George and were now, with the exception of Ethan, squatting in a ring around him. Diane reached out and touched his hair with electric fingers; he jolted from her and made them all flinch.

"George, this is me, Clay. Can you hear?"

The question was immediately pointless, since George's silence was enormous and impenetrable, underlined by the bated in and out of Jan's breathing. Kate found herself ahead of its rhythm, her heart racing. The bandage was mesmerizing. George's gray cheek bulged below its wire-hard edge, exaggerated by the swell of his beard. Kate felt the claustrophobia of the sacks, tenfold.

"Let me unwrap you. That thing looks way too tight. We can always do it back up again. Okay? I'm going to untie this knot above your ear here, alright?"

Still he did not respond.

"You think that's a good idea?" asked Ethan.

Kate turned to see him standing above them, hands on hips. Authoritative, impatient almost.

"Unless he says otherwise, yes, I do."

"Looks to me like they've done a pretty competent job." Ethan shrugged. Then, on seeing Kate's slack-jawed disbelief, he added, "They've no doubt bandaged him up for a good reason."

"Nevertheless, we should check." Clay agreed with Kate. "We can't trust them. Who knows what . . ."

Kate reached out for the knot. George flinched, then began to mouth a silent prayer to himself as she persisted. Clay tried to reassure him by patting his shoulder. Her fingers were gray against the whiteness of the bandage. Yet she had to free him from the darkness, had to unstop his ears. Pinpricks of blood became rosebuds, blossomed with each unraveling layer. The front of his face. Two. A tattered parachute unwinding, a tumble of spilled silk. Clay's hand shrank back. Kate knew in her heart what she'd uncover when the last round of cloth fell away.

FORTY

THEY CAME FOR ETHAN first thing the following morning, as he knew they would. He'd spent the night waiting, stretched flat on his planks, staring into the darkness in anticipation, his fear insistent as the drumming rain. Would they do to him what they'd done to George? He couldn't, or wouldn't, believe in that possibility. The balaclava wasn't an idiot. He knew Ethan had done his best to help. They'd been true to their word so far: a punishment to fit the crime. So . . . no crime, no punishment, surely.

He allowed Sadiq to lead him down the corridor and through an open door on the right. The guards' quarters. Ethan froze for a minute, startled by the fluorescent strip-light overhead. The same peeling walls, sticks of blackwood furniture, a battered couch, a thinning rug underfoot. In one corner was a table made from a tea chest. On top of it, still boxed, sat a Polaroid camera. The bright blue packaging caught Ethan's eye before he was distracted by movement. In the opposing corner, trailing wires to an ancient socket, stood a television and video. On screen Jean-Claude Van Damme knelt before a child, delivering what looked like a passionate plea, in silence. A photograph of a politician with a mustache hung in a frame on one wall; magazine pages depicting unknown cricketers and Michael Jordan and the old Arsenal squad were pasted onto another. The sight of them was as odd as the warmth of the room, which took a while to register. Ethan just had time to take in the fire burning in the grate before Sadiq steered him on past the posters toward a door in the far corner.

Now he found himself alone in a further cold room that smelled of piss, acrid and at odds with the wooden desk, upholstered chairs, and mantelpiece, which gave the room a formal air echoing the houseboat or his father's London club. Ethan stood still. Specific details of the old man's club came back—ancient leather chairs, a rack of magazines, the painting of that fat general smug on his horse—but not enough to make the memory whole: the old-world landmarks had rotated beyond his new horizon.

A mirror hung on the wall above the mantelpiece. His reflection wavered within its frame. He stared at himself. In place of his khaki combats and blue shirt was a uniform of stains. The crop had become a rough pelt, beneath which his face was gray. Drawing himself up, Ethan squared his shoulders at his reflection, tensed every muscle, heel to jaw. No use, still a shambles. Even the whites of his eyes looked dirty.

That Diane still wanted him, looking like this, confirmed she wasn't all there. The flirting had tailed off, for the most part. Yet not a week ago, while Kate had talked with Clay and Jan behind the buttress and sheet, he'd woken from dozing to find Diane's hand in his fly, a veil of fair hair descending with her face. Stiffening in her grip, he'd gaped into her eyes, unsure what was happening at first, then incredulous, and then not knowing how to stop her without risking a scene. Only when Diane's lips parted above his did he wrench her wrist free to roll away. "My, my," was her whispered, smiling response. As unpredictable and dangerous, in her way, as George.

The whites of his eyes. Ethan advanced to the mirror and stared at their bloodshot circuitry. He refused to blink, allowed the smarting sensation to build instead. Why, when the last of the bandage fell away into George's lap, had he *felt* so little? No real pity, no remorse, not even disgust. Just curiosity satisfied. Save for a smiling cut above the eyebrow, the left side of George's face was closed up entirely, swollen shut, but in the other there was still a hole. It looked like they'd smeared the wound with charcoal, which showed professionalism: hadn't he read somewhere that it worked as an antiseptic? As Ethan considered this, Clay broke the silence.

"What have they done to you?"

"George, tell me." Kate's ordinarily pale face was now translucent. "Is it both eyes? Can you see out of your left?"

But George just knelt there, calm as a stone prophet, quelled.

Ethan backed away from himself and sat down in the recess of a window casement, which should have been flat, but was not. Standing again, he checked, saw that he'd sat on the only other object in the room, a steel-shafted claw hammer.

The hammer brought Rafi and George and the four walls crashing together, and something in Ethan gave. But there were voices in the corridor and the hammer, in his hand, demanded attention. He had to make a decision about it *now*.

Surely it was an oversight? Left there, next to the glass. A voice reached him, as if from across the sea. The hammer was a *weapon*; an opportunity; think what damage he might do with it! But the voice was tiny and immediately drowned out by the yell of a much bigger fear. This had to be a deliberate trap. Pick it up! . . . Give us the excuse! Ethan put the tool down. And yet he couldn't just leave it there, in full view. A hammer, in this room of piss and stains. Two silver fangs curving away from the fist end, trembling in Ethan's grip as he turned to find somewhere, anywhere, that would do for a hiding place. The voices were closer. He stretched to where the pitched roof ran angled from the wall and slid the hammer, handle first, into a gap between beams, then stood back. The tip of its metal head poked out inquisitively, yet there wasn't time to find a better spot. The voices had stopped on the other side of the door, replaced by shuffling footsteps.

With his hands behind his back, in the middle of the rug, Ethan stood upright, waiting. The mirror opposite reflected a big square of the room, but the silver tongue in the rafters was all that he saw. Should he have left it where he found it? Was that the test? Each ten-second chance that slipped by was a wasted opportunity either to return the hammer to the windowsill or hide it properly. An eternity of indecision passed, in which he fought to avoid the worst of all possible outcomes, that of being caught red-handed. The gaps stretched like so many sprung traps. He stood firm. Eventually the door swung open, ending debate.

The balaclava walked into the room, followed by Abu. While the leader gestured for Ethan to take a seat at the desk, and did so

himself, Abu ambled to the window casement and sat down. Just
out of Ethan's view, but surely he was looking for it. A confession
welled; Ethan felt his hand ready to point.

"Very shameful, your Mister George," the balaclava said.

"Yes."

"And he is regretting so now, of course."

Ethan nodded. Behind him, Abu shifted and sighed.

"And you, a strong man, are throwing everybody around,
which is also bad."

"I—"

"Please do not interrupt. I am not a stupid man. None of us
wish to cause this hurt, but we are in charge and if it is necessary
must use all means. Everyone is realizing this now, I hope?"

Again Ethan nodded. Which way was the man going? His tone
was unreadable, equal parts threat and reassurance.

"You people understand an eye for the eye, yes? If you are
striking me I must strike you back."

"I didn't mean to hit *you*. I swear. I was trying to help."

"Yes, yes, yes, but that is not the point now, is it?"

"I don't understand."

"You do. If I ask you why I wear this"—a finger pulled the
neck of the ski mask away from the man's Adam's apple and let it
snap back—"I am betting you do understand."

"Of course. It's a precaution."

"A caution. Yes." The balaclava smiled. "In my position I must
be a careful man." He drew a palm the length of his face, like a
mimic. "No looking."

"No."

"No. But, my friend, you saw."

"No!" The thing crystallized.

Quietly, the pink mouth said, "Yes."

"I didn't look. I stopped the others from seeing."

The balaclava shook.

A hopelessness descended. Ethan tried to sit up straight beneath its weight, imagined his spine a brave stake driven into the seat, but felt himself wavering. His voice sounded childlike. "I didn't see anything, I promise."

A pause. Abu shifted again with impatience in the space behind him.

"You are not telling the truth."

Ethan looked at his cupped hands, in which the imprint of his only lie—the cold hammerhead—burned. If he came clean about that, would they see then that he was telling the whole truth?

"But I can make things plain beyond a doubt," the leader continued. He ran a thumb around the neck of his collarless shirt, twisting his head sideways. The thumb scooped upward and began to drag the back of the mask with it. Ethan saw a woolen edge snag on the bottom of a skin-tone plaster and screwed his eyes shut tight. He bent his head further forward, and clasped his hands beneath the table, pious. A longer pause.

"Look at me."

"I can't."

"Yes, you can. Look at me."

"I must not."

Out of nowhere Abu planted an open hand on the top of Ethan's skull and gripped it like a basketball. Five points of pressure, edging toward pain, before which Ethan's straining neck disobeyed and allowed his face to be tilted upward.

"Look."

No words. Eyelids fused shut. Patterns of purplish brightness, encompassing every fearful possibility, swimming pink inside his head, and then reverberating to the laughter, which wasn't a fabrication, but real, coming at him across the desk. Ethan felt numb with fear, which welled in his chest and threatened to break. Nails dug into his scalp, pressing a thought home. He *deserved* this punishment. It was the price of his betrayal, just retribution for the lies he'd told Kate.

The fingers relaxed their hold and became a palm, cuffing the back of Ethan's head, gentle as a parent. Turning his face down to his lap, Ethan allowed his eyes to open, but kept his focus fixed on the seam of his fly. The leader was moving across the table, standing up, still laughing. Next the figure was squatting beside the desk and from the corner of his eye Ethan registered the olive mask, back in place. He turned. In the mouth-hole, a smile.

"Okay. I am a reasonable man," the leader said. One eye winked. "I believe your sorrow. You make your point and earn another chance."

FORTY-ONE

"WHAT'S WITH THE Buddha routine?"

To help steady herself, Kate's new tactic was to fly circuits in her head. Sitting cross-legged, in line with the runway boards, she would shut her eyes and run through the whole sequence, from pretakeoff checks to touchdown. Each time she flew, the exercise became more real, alive with lovingly remembered details. Now she imagined herself releasing her harness after parking up, felt the frayed edge of strap where it passed through the buckle, heard the catch clatter against the door frame as she cast it aside.

"Seriously, it's disturbing." Clay's hand gripped her arm. She looked up. "I can take incoherent muttering from George, but not you. What's going on?"

"I'm flying."

"Sure you are." Clay smiled nervously.

"No. I am. I'm remembering how to fly."

He took a deep breath, squeezed her arm again. "Come on, Kate, don't you fry on me."

She tried to smile back, touched by his concern. "It's just an exercise."

"We're better off practicing staying sane. Coming undone doesn't look like much of a challenge. It seems anyone can do that."

"Exactly. That's why I'm flying. I'm practicing, to keep from going mad. It's just circuits, round and round the airfield. A drill. Takeoff to landing. The repetition is helpful; it stops the thinking about . . . anything else."

"You're a pilot?"

"Yes. I learned to fly. When we get out of here, I'm going to train again."

"For real?"

"I have a license. But I have to keep it current. I have to fly so many hours to keep from having to start again. Which is why I'm practicing."

He breathed out, relieved. "I didn't think of you having that sort of money in the real world."

"I don't."

"Come on. Only rich kids get to fly planes. Kids with loaded dads."

Kate shrugged. "Mum wouldn't take his maintenance money, so he put it aside for me and Rachel. She won't touch it either."

"Your sister?"

"Right. We fight. When I think of her, pretty much all I remember is pointless fighting."

"Why?"

Kate paused, then muttered, "No good reasons at all."

"Now, maybe. But there must have been at the time."

"Sure there were. But they seem irrelevant from here. For a start, we both hate what our father did to my mother, but why'd I let Rachel's decision not to see him get between the two of *us* so badly? It's daft. He hurt us enough; why use him as an excuse to hurt ourselves? How pointless is that?"

Clay shook his head. Kate's laughter was flat. "Anyway, he persuaded me to spend my share on something I really wanted."

"But why flying? What's wrong with a horse? All the rich girls I knew—"

"I never wanted a horse. My father encouraged the flying. At first I thought I wanted to skydive, like he does, to help find out what he's about. But he convinced me otherwise. He said I could do better than fall out of a plane, thought I'd get more out of learning to pilot one."

"Right."

"And I'm sitting here now remembering."

He nodded with her.

"Except that at times it feels almost real."

Clay's eyes were bright in his face now. He laughed under his breath. "Whole thing feels fake to me. I keep having this sensation that it's all made up. Like we're on some *Survivor*-type show, with the public watching. There's probably a greasy host cruising the wings, one eye on the ratings, getting ready to organize a vote. Which one of us the guards is going to bump off next."

Kate smiled with him. He went on. "I have to fight to remember it's real. That's what it is with the songs. If I can remember how the song goes, that's proof of some sort of reality. It's protection from being just . . . here. Here doesn't make sense on its own; it's getting less and less real." He lowered his voice. "Take Diane."

"What about her?"

"The more I look at her the less like *Diane* she seems to be. The girl I fell for had this flirty sense of humor, but it's gone. Or it's twisted into something unrecognizable. There's just venom in place of her attitude; she's turning vampish; she's going *mean*."

Kate whispered, "No," but wished she hadn't, since the protestation sounded weak.

"It's true. And the change is making it hard to remember exactly how she used to be. I look at her, I see her now, but the Diane I knew won't come back to me. The songs are different, though. They come back word for word. The same now as they were before; they form a sort of bridge, allowing me back home. Just for moments at a time, but still, it means I'm not stuck here, and that's crucial, because I'm scared being stuck here means going crazy. It's a constant fight against that."

He began to laugh. While Kate watched, the laughter turned silent and took him over. It bent him forward, made him clutch at his sides, shook his shoulders noiselessly.

"What's so funny?"

"I mean, what isn't?" He fought for breath. "The whole thing is hilarious. I just *refuse* to take it seriously. The floorboards are deadpan, the bars are a scream, the guards are fucking clowns. I hate myself for laughing, but I can't help it, it's a joke a fucking minute."

His shoulders kept shaking. Kate's smile back was equally desperate.

"Hate them for it, not yourself."

"Them. Why? I can't. I've tried, but it's too much effort. I truly can't be bothered with hating them. Beyond 'Kashmir' we don't even know why they're doing this to us. You can bet, somewhere down the line, it's my fault. Or, more properly," he paused, "yours." Kate shifted on the planks, unable to speak. Clay went on. "America or Britain. Always is. Your guys carved up India, we've failed to solve its problems. Or we're probably exploiting them. Makes it our fault, almost certainly. There'll be people out there saying as much already. I'd be reading their columns back home, agreeing. I'm American. So it's my fault. I asked for it, me, me! Which in turn makes it that much easier to hate *myself* for what's happening." He spoke in staccato bursts. Kate still didn't know how to respond, so stayed silent. His eyes refocused on her. He gathered himself apologetically. "Don't mind me. Like I say, it's a constant fight. . . ." He trailed off.

Kate looked around the room, at George whispering his prayers, at Ethan, feet to the skirting board, doing sit-ups, at Diane braiding Jan's hair. Her eyes returned to Clay. "Madness is relative."

"Thanks for the vote of confidence." His voice was light-hearted, his own again. "Must count for something. I'll forget it comes from a hostage who thinks she has wings."

FORTY-TWO

KATE'S NOTEBOOK WAS as soft as cloth now, concave in the hollow of her waistband. Her tiny handwriting had advanced through the pages at the front and back, crinkled borders encroaching upon the virgin territory in the middle. What would happen when the invasion was complete? They'd be free by then. There could be nothing beyond the last page. Her hand moved tenderly down the front of her gray sweatshirt.

"Another round?" Clay asked the room at large.

Ethan's eyes stayed shut. Diane rolled onto her side and sat up. She yawned, while poking one long fingernail into the mat of her hair. Jan propped himself up against the buttress, blinking.

"Yes. I have one," he said. "If you want it."

"Definitely." Clay smiled. "Anything to keep the excitement at bay."

Kate stood and stamped her feet, shook the stiffness from her arms, and settled back down. Since the guards were still refusing to give them anything to read, Clay had begun a daily round of storytelling to help speed up the glacially slow days. "Create enough hot air and we may forget the cold awhile."

Jan cleared his throat.

"I am sorry but this is about my father again. You see, we own a small yacht. She is moored in Ijmuiden. When I was thirteen years old my father and I were sailing her off the coast, near Holland. The sea was quite swollen, and the wind was big too. My father was thrown over the rail by a heavy wave. We have a man-overboard drill which my father has taught me. I should throw a life-belt float at him in the sea immediately and let the boat carry on sailing straight for about fifty meters. Then I am supposed to throw one more life belt into the sea. This gives two points in the water which provide a line to aim at when I am able to turn the boat around and come back. My father should be at the end of the line. Of course the technique is not perfect, but it is supposed to give a bigger chance of finding the man at sea."

Describing this maneuver Jan's pale hands first undulated with the waves and then became two buoys fixed in the floor.

"But I panicked. My first thinking was that my dad was hurt. I was very close—I nearly jumped in after him to help. Then I was unable to untie the life belt. The knots were similar to metal. Instead I undid things, pieces of rope, and threw those in instead. They sank like heavy chains. All this time the yacht was going forward in leaps, with nobody at the helm to keep it straight. She began to swing around into the wind. I could not see my father in the sea for minutes and minutes until I saw his white head way away, looking like foam in the top of a wave. I was yelling and throwing in life jackets and plastic containers and I even untied the fender floats. Finally I was so frightened I just released the anchor, in full, in full."

The room was dim in the late afternoon. Leaning back, Kate saw a bank of asphalt cloud through the barred window. Diane, pacing now, crossed the gloom. Jan coughed painfully. His eyes flicked left and right as he gathered himself to go on.

"After that the boat was not organized, turning and pulling at the sea, and I became lost. I was disorientated. I did not know whether my father was to the land side or farther out to sea. I did not know if the anchor cable was long enough or if we were dragging or what. I loosed off the big sail but this just helped it to crack backward and forward over the deck, with a noise going off like bombs."

He paused, wiping his face with an open palm. "I thought by then that maybe my father was drowned." Kate watched him shiver, looking to Clay for the encouragement to go on.

"I was sick in the cabin and could not think and took off my jacket, thinking again I should jump overboard to look. But instead I saw a little sense finally and took down the sails properly. And just as I was finishing doing this my father appeared at the stern end of our boat and pulled himself up the ladder onto deck."

Reliving this, Jan began to tremble. Opposite Kate, Ethan blew out through his mouth. The noise wasn't sympathetic.

"He was too tired to speak at first, he was exhausted, just held me until neither of us cried anymore. And then he started shouting and shouting about the drill, the man-overboard drill. He had jumped into the sea on purpose, taking hold of a fixed rope with him"—Jan held the imaginary rope-end high—"but I let it loose. I cast him adrift!"

Ethan laughed. Jan joined in silently.

"Jesus. That's one way to give a lesson," said Kate.

Another pause. Diane knelt next to Jan and stroked his upper arm, as if it were a cat.

"Yes. My father and I still sail the boat every summer. We will have the chance to do so again, yes?" He blinked again at Clay, who smiled weakly.

"Of course. What about you?" Clay now caught Diane's eye. He went on imploringly: "Do you have a tale for us today?"

"No." The stroking stopped. Her lips formed a pout as she sat back against the wall.

"Nothing?"

Diane shrugged her shoulders. As fast as the poor bloke tried to reel her in, Kate thought, she seemed to slip away. That he still bothered trying was testimony to something. She looked across at Ethan, who was staring fixedly at a patch of wall.

"Okay then. I do," she found herself saying. "You'll remember this, Ethan. That time you took me gambling."

Ethan's smile of recognition was a start. Kate looked to the rest of the room for their attention.

"Ethan wanted to go high-rolling. I thought you had to look the part for a casino, so I borrowed a proper dress and a pair of my sister's flashy shoes. Only I'd got the wrong end of the stick. Ethan met me in his jeans, and we wound up at Walthamstow dog track."

"Dog track?" repeated Jan.

"Greyhounds. Chasing a mechanical rabbit. Racing." As she explained, Kate heard herself from afar. The self-deprecating point in the anecdote up ahead wavered even as she pressed on.

"So I tottered around in the dirt after him, trying to fit in. But I was determined not to seem a complete fool. I studied the little book of statistics they give you and made strategic bets according to the length of the race and which dogs were supposed to be in form. And I just about broke even, which was good enough."

Clay agreed in silence. Diane had her eyes shut, could even have been asleep. Kate felt a peculiar rising panic.

"Meanwhile, Ethan was just putting money on at random. Two quid on any dog that took a leak before the race began; a fiver if it shat. He won about twenty quid by the time of the last race, and put it all on the red dog."

"Black," said Ethan.

"Whichever. Just picked a dog at random. And of course it came in first and that trebled his total winnings to more than fifty pounds."

Ethan was still smiling, but fixedly. Kate found herself lost, directing the remainder of the story at him, trying to get through.

"You were very generous and spent about half the winnings on lager in plastic glasses. I was legless by the time we stopped drinking, and we'd missed the last tube south. You remember what you did next?"

A brittle nod.

"We were by some taxi rank, waiting for a cab to the nearest bed for the night. You remember, I said we could stay at my sister's. You bet me the rest of the winnings that you could walk the length of the pavement on your hands. I was barely able to stand up straight so that seemed a safe gamble. The color of your face when you finished! But, of course, you did it, you won."

Kate could no longer hold Ethan's gaze. She tried to smile, but the result felt wooden. She pressed on. "But, like a gentleman, you refused the money."

"Not quite. I invited you to sleep at mine instead." His voice was mechanical, his attempt at a joke humiliating: "Twenty quid for a whole night. I thought that pretty cheap, considering."

This wasn't how it happened. They'd gone to his after Rachel refused Kate's request for somewhere to crash. She'd told the story against herself: the inappropriate dress, failure with the form sheet, underestimation of Ethan's talent. More than that, she'd told it to his credit. How could the reminiscence not warm him? She stared at the palms of her upturned hands.

For a while nobody spoke. In the distance a mule brayed. George rolled over in his corner, drawing Kate's attention away finally. The bandage, which he still wore, was now as gray as the floorboards. He was merging into them, his prayers fading to a whisper. The black lines between the planks were another set of bars. Ever since they'd moved to the Marriott she'd clung to the possibility of a way out beneath the wooden floor, allowing herself to hope in spite of Ethan, who remained dismissive of Clay's nightly finger-shredding battle with the nail heads. A few days ago Clay had finally managed to work one of the boards loose. Together they had looked beneath it while Ethan stood reluctant guard.

Clay's voice started up again; Kate tuned in: ". . . then Ethan? You got us another MGM production?"

He didn't answer immediately. She shuddered, thinking of her anticipation as the plank groaned upward. For nothing: honey-combed joists, a mere four-inch gap separating the boards from cement foundations. Ethan did not gloat. Yet it took Clay's laughter to stem her tears. No bigger than a hand-span, full of dust.

FORTY-THREE

A LAKE SPREAD OUT beneath their upturned umbrellas, despite the ornamental stand. They waited. Rachel watched water seep across the grid of checkered tiles. Beside her, on the bullet-hard leather Chesterfield, her mother sat stoically, hands folded into a plaid lap. Striped wallpaper rose up on all sides to a distant ceiling, bordered by cornicing at least two feet wide. A chandelier hung high above their heads, like a portcullis ready to drop. For all its gilt and grandeur the room felt wrong. The window was cut in half by one of the walls. They were in a segment, annexed, partitioned off.

Petition, partition. The words rolled idiotically inside Rachel's head. She glanced at her mother, who seemed small and fragile in this new context. Rachel took and patted a mottled hand, enveloped it in hers. The older women had been shrinking all morning, as the surroundings became less and less familiar. On the underground Rachel had taken over, organizing the tickets, shepherding her mum and Michelle through the crowd, as if in charge of the expedition, rather than the reluctant third party. In the tube carriage the strip-light stamped cruel bags beneath Michelle's eyes, and cut through her mother's foundation to the truth of her papery face, dry as a moth's wing.

An aide arrived noiselessly on the rug in front of them, offering coffee.

"Oh, thank you. Thank you." Rachel's mum squeaked forward on her seat. Was she about to help pour?

Rachel lit a cigarette and asked, "How long are we going to have to wait?"

"I'm afraid I don't know exactly. Somebody will be down shortly, I'm sure. But can I help you to this, or maybe a glass of water, in the meantime?"

"Parliamentary Under-Secretary Westerby," Michelle said loudly. "We expected to wait. He's a busy man, after all!" She laughed like a schoolgirl and hid behind her hand. Which was worse? Her mother's appalling meekness, or Michelle's embarrassment?

The aide nodded kindly. "I'm sure somebody will be with you before long," he reiterated. "The situation is in hand. In the meantime . . ."

Unknown to Rachel, Michelle had organized for a photographer to meet them in King Charles' Street, to document the handover. By the time they arrived he'd become an inevitable knot of journalists, bedraggled in the rain. Mercifully, the ensemble was turned away when the three women were greeted by another aide at the security desk. Yet Michelle's triumphant "He wants to meet us alone" did not necessarily follow. They'd been warned that the Parliamentary Under-Secretary would not be able to meet them in person: Michelle's optimism, in the face of this advice, was unhinged.

Now her mum was holding a cup up to the light, complimenting the fine china, as if this were an antiques fair. Rachel flicked ash into her saucer in retaliation. Across the rug Michelle touched the little crucifix she wore, for reassurance. Then she lifted her new vinyl briefcase to her lap and began to fiddle with the combination locks. All those names held fast inside. Rachel saw the shape of this endeavor plainly: the countless unconnected people whom these two women had, by will alone, woven together, stitching signatures across page after page, in a hopeless attempt to *do something*.

Her father had used the same phrase, when he last phoned. *Let me do something*. Rachel told him about the petition. If he wanted to join in with its pointlessness, so be it. "No," he had made himself clear, "I mean let me do something to help you." Rachel breathed, "It's a bit late for that," but inaudibly. When he said he hadn't heard her, she read out Michelle's number and hung up.

Both locks pinged open simultaneously now and Michelle, eyebrows furrowed, peeped inside the case. Her stonewashed knees bounced in anticipation. She held the lid ajar for a second, as if fearing the petition would escape given the chance, and then she shut the case again, spinning the locks emphatically. What must it be like for Kate, Ethan, and the rest, incarcerated? Rachel found she had to close her eyes to remember the detail of her sister's face; the impossibility of understanding what Kate and Ethan were enduring blotted the image out entirely. She couldn't even pretend to know how Michelle felt, clutching her plastic briefcase to her anorak in the chair opposite, or what her mother was thinking as she smoothed the creases from her skirt. The separateness was insulting, underlined by the incongruity of the three of them sitting in such an imposing room, waiting for a miracle.

Now Michelle was bouncing to her feet and her mother had risen too. A small man with gelled hair and a pink tie strode into their midst. The sheen of his suit rippled as he turned beneath the chandelier.

"So sorry to keep you waiting."

Michelle's mouth opened and closed. The man rattled out his name and title, but all Rachel heard, as she stubbed out her cigarette, was the word "Unit." Beside her, her mother took a little step forward. To prevent the disaster of a curtsy, Rachel found herself moving toward the man, with her hand outstretched. She became immediately conscious of her own business suit, shaking hands with this young man in his.

"As was made clear, the Parliamentary Under-Secretary is unable to receive you in person today, but I'm delighted to accept custody of your petition on his behalf, and of course to answer any questions you might wish to put to us." The salesman's smile he flashed was full of self-confidence, said that a reception with him was one up on anything they might have been expecting.

Rachel realized he was looking to her to hand the document over, and was surprised to find herself turning to Michelle and gesturing at the briefcase, as if summoning secretarial assistance.

"You realize of course that we're doing everything we can, in close cooperation with the Indian, Kashmiri, and Pakistani authorities, to negotiate an expedited end to your relatives' ordeal," the man was saying. "Everything we can."

Michelle was staring at her thumbs, rubbing the combination

dials—Rachel fought back a wave of impatience. Her mother's voice said, "Of course."

"While at the same time remaining mindful of the . . . wider context of the Kashmir . . . situation. There are obvious sensitivities . . . as you know . . . terrific difficulties to overcome . . . the balance . . . fragile . . . delicate." Rachel found herself unable to latch onto the precise sense of what the man was saying, heard only occasional up-jutting words as he slowed to negotiate them, and tumbling phrases as the flow of what he was saying sped up again. . . . "But you must rest assured that despite this . . . tricky context . . . we're exploring every avenue open to us . . . using our best efforts to resolve the crisis."

It being impossible to look at the man while he made this speech, Rachel remained fixated upon Michelle's stuttering fingers, which sprung the case finally, emptying its contents onto the rug. The document looked unfamiliar: Michelle had stapled its pages together and fixed them inside a manila wallet, on which she'd stenciled the letters PETITION in red felt-tip. Rachel saw this without taking it in as she stooped to pick the thing up, because beneath the lettering Michelle had also glued three photographs. George with a pint of beer. Kate graduating. Ethan sitting on the bonnet of a car. The front cover of a family album. Even here, in this tiny image, Ethan's smile looked seductively bombproof, beyond recrimination. She turned with the binder in her hand to see that the little man was making himself comfortable in the throne-sized armchair on the opposite side of the coffee table. The words *ordeal, tricky context, rest assured, every avenue, crisis* rung in her ears. She stumbled backward and sat down heavily on the Chesterfield, waving the petition at arm's length nevertheless.

"What are you on about?"

Rachel's mum whispered, "Rachel!" in her ear, but her complaint was already spilling out.

"Do you think we're fools? Nobody's lifted a finger in two months. Not since the kidnappers made contact again, after that botched army raid. *Doing all we can!* They executed the Israeli and escaped with the others. My sister! Ethan! And ever since then you've done nothing. Nothing at all!"

The aide didn't blink. He smiled calmly, allowing an ameliorating silence to descend. Michelle laughed nervously again as she retook the petition from Rachel and crabbed sideways to hand it over.

"That's my husband, George. Ethan and Kate are the young pair, there. We're beside ourselves," she explained.

Beside ourselves. Although slumped on the couch, Rachel could not feel the seat beneath the back of her legs. The room's staginess seemed accentuated; the enormous velvet curtains and oversized furniture reduced the four of them to actors in an amateur scene. She felt superimposed. Her suit, unused for months, no longer fitted properly; it sat too low on her hips. Never mind. She had no job to return to now, anyway. And no comeback either—though she'd sputtered "unfair dismissal" down the telephone, her boss had replied calmly, beginning at "If you want a passable reference" and finishing on "bad *habits*." She broke her phone, slamming it down on the kitchen work surface, but her fury petered out quickly in the aftermath of his call. Such a pathetic hardship, set against Kate and Ethan's plight, warranted no attention. Like the couch supporting her, she simply couldn't feel it. If she let her hands drop down beside her now they might equally stop at the plush armrest or continue through the sofa entirely. The man's nonresponse to her outburst further confirmed her ineffectuality. He had begun talking again now, reiterating his "condolences" to Michelle, his benign smile aimed at each of them in turn.

"I'll make sure that the petition is shown to the Foreign Secretary himself," he said. "This sort of statement has its effects."

"We're trying everything to keep the pressure on through the press. You know, making sure they're in the public eye, but it's not easy." Michelle wrung her hands.

"Everyone seems to have lost interest," Mum was agreeing.

"The newspapers aren't bothered anymore."

"No. Unless there are new angles, they don't see a story worth reporting." The young man glanced sympathetically at Rachel. He couldn't have been more than thirty, and yet his manner suggested that he, along with any number of his own family, had been held hostage at one time or another. Now he was continuing, "I can assure you that we aren't as fickle. Things may look to have quietened, but beneath the surface there's always a welter of activity. And this"—he rapped the petition with the back of his hand—"is an effective means of doing your bit."

Her mother nodded enthusiastically at this platitude and took hold of one of Rachel's hands, but although she watched fingers close round her own and squeeze, the appropriate sensation seemed to take forever to travel up her arm. She ached for a drink. How on earth would she ever begin to feel what *they* were going through? It would weld the pair of them together, for good. Repulsed by her own anger, Rachel slumped forward. Now the man had bounced to his feet. His polished toe caps were advancing across the rug. A crisp handkerchief snapped wide in surrender and pressed itself into her open palm.

FORTY-FOUR

"WHAT ABOUT YOU then, Ethan?" Clay was saying. "You got us another MGM production?"

"Yeah, another matinee!" Diane lit up.

Ethan didn't tell stories about himself, yet he knew he had little choice but to contribute to the entertainment. His tactic, therefore, was to describe plots. Films, television shows, novels—whatever came to him. Westerns and war movies mostly. How he'd built such a store of hardwired précis was a mystery. He'd watched enough afternoon television in the real world, but hadn't the point then been the *not* paying attention? He did not volunteer, but as now, when pushed, the next victory of right over wrong was always ready to play.

Diane had jittered into the space in front of him and sat down in one movement, fluent as a ballerina.

"Okay," Ethan sighed. The trick was to concede defeat without giving an inch. "*Rio Bravo* then. One of Howard Hawks's best, a real epic." He paused, gathering himself, then went on. "John Wayne's this sheriff, right, called John T. Chance. Pretty early on in the film he's involved in a three-way brawl with his drunken deputy, Dean Martin, and a local rancher."

Diane now edged closer to Ethan, sat staring at him, hugging her knees, a child in front of the TV. Only Clay's songs, which he whistled or sang to himself in the evenings, had the same enrapturing effect. Ethan looked over her head at the others, avoiding eye contact.

"The fight gets out of hand and the rancher ends up gunning down a bystander. The Iron Duke pulls himself together, tracks down the murderer, and slings him into the local jail."

Ethan continued looking around the room, but without really seeing it. The walls held frames from the film. Townscapes and interiors, a water trough and saloon doors. No big Western vistas at all. He heard himself talk for a while about the low lighting and the cramped camera angles and then the room was coming back into focus, with the real walls looming darker than before.

"But the rancher has a big-shot brother, who heads up this outlaw clan. They're set to ride into town and storm the jail. Old John Wayne needs to hold on to the prisoner until the state magistrate arrives to take him away, but he's way outnumbered and the help on offer from his comrades is pretty paltry."

He paused again here. It wasn't that he didn't know what came next, just that the sound of the word "paltry," left hanging there, felt right.

"Yeah, there's just Deputy Martin, who's a perpetual drunk; an old hanger-on with a gammy leg, called Stumpy (ha-ha); a child gunslinger whose name I forget; and a female gambler called Feathers, who doubles up as the love interest, as you'd guess."

"What is a girl named Feathers like?" asked Jan.

Ethan leaned back against the wall and took his time describing the way the woman and the rest of the characters looked and how the grouchy old jailer stole each of his scenes. He talked up Dean Martin's drunken self-loathing and hinted, as the film did, at the implications of Feathers's call-girl past. It felt good to hold the story at arm's length, assured as a critic, and as detached.

"To begin with, the Iron Duke tries to make do alone. His pride gets in the way of accepting help from a bunch of losers. But the losers shape up eventually and there's this famous exchange in the heart of the film: the bad rancher finds out who's helping John Wayne and asks, 'Is that all you got?' and Wayne deadpans back, 'That's *what* I got.'"

Ethan paused again, searched each puzzled face in turn. Exasperated, he spelled it out. "He's resourceful. He'll make do with what's available."

Jan chewed his lower lip, still perplexed. "So, what happens then? Do they manage to keep hold of the prisoner?"

"Jan, this is John Wayne we're talking about here."

"Right. These people help him and he succeeds. Despite his unhopeful friends."

"Hopeless friends," Ethan corrected him. "Yes," he continued, but distracted now, the words arriving more tentatively, the point of the story seeming to have snaked away from him. He felt a flicker of confusion play in his face and looked down to hide it. On his lap his broad fingers knitted themselves into a miniature rib cage, and he found himself inspecting each upturned nail in turn. Wrap the thing up. "John Wayne saves the day," he said. "The end."

Diane began to applaud. Looking up, Ethan saw Clay rolling his eyes at Kate over the top of Diane's head. Kate smiled conspiratorially back, then dropped her gaze, but too late: the applause had stopped. Ethan glanced at Diane to see her face aghast in a *caught you* stare. Outside the distant pock-pocking of gunfire came and went, accentuating the silence.

"Let me tell you about my sister," Clay said eventually.

Jan, quietly: "I didn't know you had one."

"Yeah. Clara." Clay carried on, talking to fill the gap. "She's a year older than me. But until recently I never really knew her. She was always so secretive and removed when we were growing up, the sort of kid that kept her bedroom padlocked and spoke Pig Latin with her best friend." He set down these words slowly, laying bricks in a wall. "She was real bright too. Won the interstate math championship at sixteen, but didn't bother to tell us. We found out about it in the town paper."

"You never told me about the paper." Diane still looked offended.

"Well, it's true," Clay said equably. Turning back to the others, he continued. "She went away to college on the east coast and wound up working out of New York, doing something nebulous called 'information management,' which I could never quite figure out. She didn't offer any detail. For years I hardly saw her. She'd turn up at family get-togethers from time to time and the two of us would try to talk but, to tell the truth, I never really knew where to begin. Our shared experience ended with the homemade pickle on the table. Every time we met up was like starting from scratch. I'd forget the name of her current boyfriend or, worse, mention an ex. She couldn't remember which school I taught at."

"Teach at," said Diane.

A pause. "Right. The school I teach at. We were strangers, brother and sister in name alone, talking to one another through inch-thick glass."

Here he paused again, pushed his fringe back from his face. His chin looked stronger now that his face had thinned.

"A couple of years ago, at Thanksgiving, I offered her a ride to San Francisco airport. We stopped for gas. She went to use the rest room. While she was gone I noticed her bag had tipped across the back seat and started gathering up the spilled stuff. Microfiche and papers, 'Confidential' stamped everywhere. I was curious, but didn't have time to find out more. She arrived back at the car with me halfway through the job and went totally ape. I didn't ask why. I drew my own conclusion, imagined she must be working for the government. But as it turned out I was wrong. She was an industrial spy."

"Sounds pretty glamorous."

"Dangerous too." He nodded at Kate. "The last case she worked on involved a crooked lawyer. She had to tail him and recover some stolen documents. The job went wrong. First she somehow fell for the lawyer, then he beat her up. Put her in a coma. For two days she was as much dead as alive."

"My God."

"She recovered alright in the end. And at first she agreed with the police, that she'd help them press charges against the guy. By then he'd turned himself in."

"Of course."

Ethan saw that the story had become a conversation; Clay was explaining what happened to Kate, rather than to the room at large. Something in the tilt of her head made it obvious, at that moment nobody else existed. He felt an odd sense of relief.

"Well, you'd think. But she changed her mind. We managed to persuade her to come back to the family home out west, to convalesce, and by the time she arrived she was adamant she wouldn't testify against the lawyer. Even though he'd confessed. She insisted she was as much to blame as him for the accident; said she'd provoked what happened."

Ethan held back from venturing that she probably knew, allowing Kate's "No way," to fill the pause instead.

Kate thought for a minute, resolution hardening in her eyes, and went on. "But it's strange, isn't it, the surprises that even those closest to you can spring. Like with my own sister. I know her, as in I think I know what she spends her time doing, for the most part, but I can't really understand what drives her. I can guess, but I'll never be certain, and she can't know for sure about me. Whether or not we want to keep secrets from one another, they happen. It's not about privacy, or openness. No matter how close two people think they are, there's always a hidden part. You see the whiteness of teeth in a smile, but not the roots, buried in bone. There's always an unknowable part, making it impossible to predict how a person will react in any given situation."

Ethan's face felt like a wooden mask.

"You're right," Clay continued. "Clara's refusal to press charges was just the beginning. She left her job in New York, and decided to stay on in San Francisco. Joined some not-for-profit IT think tank, does volunteer work at my school. Just before we decided to make this trip she leased an apartment in our block. Isn't that right, Diane?"

Ethan turned with Clay for Diane's reaction.

"That *is* right. A true story."

"Honey?"

"And what's more"—Diane's words were clipped—"I've finally remembered one of my own to tell." She yawned wide: pink tongue, blanched lips. "How about this for a tale? It's certificate X: My First Kiss."

Clay laughed, his eyes blinking double-time. "Ouch," he said, as Ethan again inspected the tips of his fingers. "Okay, slay me."

"I was eleven years old, pretty inexperienced."

"Pretty and inexperienced," Clay corrected. A lame compliment, and apparently defensive; it sounded as if by cutting in he was testing the brakes.

"Whatever." Diane pouted at everyone in turn, turning longest toward Ethan. Whichever way you looked in a room this size, imminent disaster threatened.

She went on. "Fourth of July. Mom and Dad were having this barbecue, with a ton of friends over. Everybody with watermelons ear to ear, like those enormous cartoon grins." Her demonstration was a grimace. "All the adults knocking back Buds, us kids sipping the dregs, all of us in and out of the pool. I was drying off in the garage when this guy Bruce came in and asked me for a kiss."

She stopped here for a long while. It seemed to Ethan that this fragment might, disappointingly, have been all she was going to offer. Clay let out a slow breath. But the sigh reinflated Diane.

"Yeah, he came swaying around the Ping-Pong table with this yellow towel around his waist and let it drop. The tops of his legs, above his shorts line, were thin as poles and an odd sort of putty color. Eugh." Another grimace. "'What do I have to do to get a kiss out of you, kiddo?' he asked, bold as brass. I remember looking up at him—"

"Up?" said Ethan, driving in the nail.

"Yeah, this guy was forty at—"

"Sure, sure," Clay cut in. "Some things are best . . . Why don't we leave this for now?"

"Because we're all friends here," beamed Diane, continuing. "I just stand there staring. I'd never seen one before, and this had—wait for it—gray hairs!" She giggled into the back of her hand with mock coyness.

"'We won't bite,' he said. 'And neither should you!' He took a step toward me, staggered really, flapping in my face, and steadied himself on the lawnmower. I didn't know what to say. Bruce got my dad a good deal on the sprinkler system and his wife coached tennis and he had a hand on my arm pulling me toward it so I couldn't go anywhere anyway."

"Please, Diane." Even in the gloom Clay's face was white, his voice papery.

"Sure," Diane went on, smiling cheerfully, "I knew what he was asking was wrong, but—"

"Please."

The smile broke into more laughter, but her words dried up. Ethan ran his tongue round the inside of his teeth and allowed himself to survey Diane's aftermath. Clay had his head in his hands. Kate and Jan were staring uncomfortably at different patches of wall. George rolled over again and lay still. A snowdrift of silence blotted out the room.

FORTY-FIVE

KATE BRUSHED THE HAIR from Jan's face, which lay upturned in her lap. A sliver of each eyeball, as yellow as old fingernail, flickered occasionally beneath half-shut lids. His forehead was waxy to the touch. Encased in blankets, huddled with her beside the radiator, he clutched at his sides and shivered and moaned, struggling against himself. As he'd weakened, and in flat contrast to George, Jan had become more dependent on the others. He seemed to have grown younger. Where beforehand he had been superstitious of talk about their release, he now asked Clay to describe how it would happen, and hung on to the detail of his imaginings like a child. As Kate looked down at him now a snatch of undecipherable speech escaped from his lips.

In the last fortnight the weather had worsened. Gusts of powdery snow blew through the window gap from time to time; ice formed on the black bars. Sounds filtering in from outside were muffled and flat. The gunfire no longer echoed. They asked for

more blankets, which were refused. Instead the single iron radiator—in the games corner at the rear of the room—gurgled itself
alive one morning. As unlikely as any other of Diane's comments
at first, her announcement that they'd switched the heating on
turned out to be true: the blackened pipes gradually, miraculously,
warmed. For an hour or so, while the radiator bubbled along at
blood temperature, they'd sat in a row with their backs pressed to
the iron, trying to convince one another that the heat was still rising. And later, when the metal was definitely cooling again, nobody would admit as much. Clay called Khalid to the door. The
guard proudly explained that the concession would be repeated for
an hour each morning *throughout cold,* which made Diane weep.
So feeble a privilege served purely to underline their discomfort.
Ethan, Kate noticed, let the others warm themselves, preferring to
keep up his routine of exercise during the morning instead, an act
of generosity that impressed and annoyed her at the same time.

Now, while Kate comforted Jan, curled with him against the
dying pipes, Ethan pushed out squat-thrusts at the other end of
the room. Clay still made his point of joining in every now and
then, though Kate suspected this was more for Ethan's benefit
than his own. Clay gasped in time, jerking awkwardly on the
boards, while Ethan moved fluently beside him. The muscles in
his shoulders showed through his T-shirt as his knees drove im-
placably forward; by contrast Clay looked bony, uncoordinated,
and ill-knit. She felt a confusing stab of tenderness watching
him. Ethan's set came to an end. He stood up. Clay flopped onto
his stomach mid thrust and lay spread-eagled for a moment,
playing dead.

"How is he today?"

"I haven't a clue. Worse, I think. We have to make them fetch him a doctor. He needs medicine."

Clay sat up stiffly, nodding agreement. "And they should bring somebody qualified to have another look at George too."

"They've made it clear that's not going to happen." Ethan began pacing his circuit beneath the window, width by width.

"Abu would refuse us permission to piss if he could." Clay followed the footsteps back and forward, which made it look as if he was slowly shaking his head. "Sadiq's not much better—he's incapable of thinking, just does what Abu says. The only hope is that Khalid sees sense, or, better still, that we get the chance to persuade the main man himself."

"They've said a doctor is out of the question," Ethan repeated.

"It's not just a doctor and medicine for those two." Diane sighed crossly. Her next sentence ramped in volume so that the final words made Jan shift in Kate's lap. "We're all going to freeze to death unless they sort out proper heating and give us something decent to eat."

"They've already refused that too." Ethan spoke calmly.

"Yeah," agreed Clay. "But they're not beyond having their opinions changed. We can apply pressure."

"What have we got to bargain with? You really are full of shit." Diane spread her fingers across her lowered face, disconsolate.

"Maybe, but . . ." Clay trailed off.

Ethan spun on his heel, shrugged his shoulders, paced out the fifteen feet to the opposite wall.

Kate shut her eyes to minimize the impending conflict. Yet even closed down, some extra awareness, sharpened by captivity, kept

her aware of what was going on. The steady beat of Ethan's foot-
falls, reassuring as a metronome; the grinding of sandy dirt upon
the boards as he turned before each wall. The pressure of Jan's
skull against her upper thigh; a ripple of discomfort that shivered
through him, prompting her to another futile stroke of his forehead. That was the sound of Diane drumming clawlike nails; Kate
did not have to see pouting lips to experience the weight of their
sulky effect. Even George's silence became a physical presence inside her head, a negative shape, persistent as hunger, around which
all else configured.

   In her diary Kate kept a tally of the days of their captivity, each
entry recorded with the precision she'd learned in flight training,
as a row of numbers: month, day, hour, minute. There was something irrefutable about such accuracy. Today's entry, which she'd
recorded just an hour earlier, was already safely stowed in the
space beneath the skirting board, each number lovingly illuminated: 11191028. It was if by nailing down the exact moment she
could somehow claim it for her own, stem the loss that each further minute represented. Yet the futility of trying made itself clear
with each of Ethan's continuing footsteps. They'd been held in the
Marriott for longer now than their stretch at the farmstead, and
no numerical symmetry, key date, or other imagined prediction
would mean the end of the ordeal. Soon four more digits would be
necessary, to mark the changing year. The darkness behind her
shut eyes deepened as Kate took this possibility to heart, truly, for
the first time. Time would just go on and on, for longer than they
could; the numbers would never run out; they would extend beyond the end of her notebook.

   Two thoughts joined in her head, coupling with the slow yet

inexorable momentum of rolling stock. The beat of Ethan's walking marked out one dimension; George's implacability confirmed another. His attack may have been futile, but the act of resisting wasn't. Ethan pivoted and carried on: endlessness. George loomed: persistence.

"You're right." Her eyes blinked open, fixed automatically upon Clay.

"About what?"

"There is something that we can do. Something we *have* to do, in fact."

"What's that then?"

"We're nothing to these men, and yet we're everything, right? It's like they keep saying: we're currency, we're a kind of investment. Individually, we're expendable, but they need to keep the majority of us healthy if their plan is to work. When one of us has tried to run away or fought back they've done their worst, but they just see that as stamping down hard to protect the rest of their investment. What we've got to do is show we can devalue that investment en masse. That way we threaten their whole plan." The idea came clear as she spoke, yet something made her shy away from explaining how, at the farmstead, she'd won ground through refusing to eat. The struggle then had been private and its reward, the notebook, was still a secret. Still reluctant to give that privacy up, she presented her suggestion as if considering it for the first time. "So say we refuse food. If *all* of us threaten not to eat, they'll have to take us seriously. If we're demanding improved conditions—a doctor for Jan, more heating, better food—and promising to starve ourselves worthless unless they give in, they'll soon start making concessions."

Ethan's pace slowed. On reaching the wall he stopped and leaned his forehead against a patch of plaster. Kate felt herself hanging on his response, and turned in irritation to Diane and Clay for theirs instead.

"You mean a hunger strike?" Diane made a double-take face, eyes agog. Next came a smile. "There must be an easier way than that?"

The rectangle of window slot lit up momentarily as the sun emerged from behind a cloud, making a pale parallelogram on the floor in the middle of the room. If Jan pulled through his delirium he would doubtless follow their lead, but would it be right to weaken him further by imposing such a decision? Would George have an opinion at all? Even if Diane agreed in principle, she would as likely as not change her mind tomorrow. Kate broke from the patch of fading sunlight to see Clay still gazing at the space where it had been. Surely he would see the logic in her argument; the triumph inherent in any act of will; above all, the worth in such a sacrifice, if it worked. Ethan was still leaning against his island of plaster when she checked, inscrutable as the wall itself. She sat mesmerized by the back of his neck angling forward into the curve at the base of his skull; the composure of his face in profile, nose touching the wall; the stillness of his hanging arm. Why, if she believed that the key was communal consent, had her breathing turned shallow waiting for him, in particular, to respond?

FORTY-SIX

Up this close it was impossible to focus immediately ahead; the cracked plasterwork remained a comforting blur. Ethan let the weight of his body press him forward into the wall, and tried to block the decision. No use. Kate needed his answer. He didn't have to turn and check; her gaze felt hot on his back. While it was still obvious that dissent could only provoke the guards, that obedience and loyalty would be rewarded eventually, an old dilemma confused matters: with his eyes shut he could hear his father explaining how strength of mind and body would always win respect. Perhaps she had a point despite herself.

At handover the day before, Abu had interrupted Ethan again, this time in the middle of his sit-ups. Clay, who was at least capable of effort, had long since fallen by the wayside, but Ethan finished his set. The guard was obviously impressed: when later he escorted Ethan to the toilet he clapped his hands upon Ethan's

shoulders in the corridor. No blow came. After the shock subsided, Ethan turned to see admiration written in the guard's face.
Within the bristling beard, Abu's lips were set in appreciation: he
puffed out his chest, made the denim bulge.

Important as physical prowess was, brute strength could only
go so far. The muscles in Ethan's back locked; he rose from his
heels to the balls of his feet, levering pain into the numb center
of his forehead. A demonstration of mental toughness, of
willpower, might raise him still further in the guards' eyes. Abstinence was part of a universal language. He dropped back down
to flat feet again and pushed off from the wall. Turning to agree
with Kate, he saw the transparent expectation in her face. Dauntless eyes fractionally wider than usual, lips parted as if about to
speak.

The hopefulness of her expression stopped him short. Shouldn't
mental toughness start closer to home? Wasn't honesty its cornerstone? He should explain his infidelity, how it meant nothing,
sprang from an ambivalence that no longer made sense, and now
caused him regret. Why not take the risk and explain further—
how he now understood what was going on? As in *understood.*
Obligation, bravery, honesty: of late he'd found himself dwelling
on these terms. They sat in his mouth, alien and yet remotely
familiar, as if his tongue were tracing the long-gone outline of
milk teeth.

Before he could speak, the lock rattled in its metal housing and
Ethan turned to face the door as it swung inward. Sadiq reversed
toward him through the empty frame, carrying his tray. Today he
wore a long gray shirt beneath his fatigues. Its tails hung down to
his knees, giving him the look of a waiter in an apron, or a priest.

The tray bore their daily helping of cold rice, served in an orange Tupperware bowl. A portion of vegetable slop, in a similar container, sat next to it, on top of a pile of greasy plastic plates. As usual, there was no cutlery, and no hard-boiled eggs this morning either. They all watched in silence as Sadiq lowered the tray to the floor and stood back.

"No, thanks."

Sadiq looked quizzically at Clay, who was advancing toward him.

"Not today," Clay reiterated.

Ethan glanced at Kate, still cradling Jan in her lap. Gratitude lit her from within. Her pale eyes shone, unable to conceal a sense of triumph as they followed Clay's progress forward. Ethan dropped to his haunches. He felt usurped and oddly disappointed.

"Not eat?" Sadiq asked.

"No." Clay waved his hands, palms down, back and forth at waist height. "We no eat. Nobody eating. Protest. Problems here. Tell the boss." His smile was as reassuring as it was patronizing. "This man"—he gestured at the black shape of George, walled inside his soiled bandage—"and this man"—he motioned at Jan—"both need a doctor. We won't eat until the doctor comes."

"And we need some heating. We're freezing to death." Diane spelled out the words slowly, rubbing her sides, a children's TV presenter.

"Something to read as well." Kate, continuing the act, made a book of her hands and turned its imaginary pages. His English wasn't good, but there was no need to humiliate Sadiq with this play-acting. Ethan therefore intervened, rephrasing their requests without the petulance.

"When you give us a doctor, more heat, food, and books, then we will eat."

The guard nodded in time—doctor, heat, food, books—and then, as if in clarification, repeated, "No eat today?" while gesturing vaguely at the tray.

"That's right, you're getting there," said Clay. He shrugged, as if to say the decision was out of their hands.

Sadiq scratched the bridge of his nose, resting his other hand on his hip, and returned Clay's shrug. Not his problem, the gesture said, do as you will. Ethan pulled his shoulders back and lifted his chin. Then, with deliberate care, he stepped forward, scooped up the tray, and handed it to the guard, bowing his head as he did so, as if presenting him with a ceremonial flag. It was vital to make their point without arrogance. Sadiq nodded once, in silence, and backed out of the room. He may not have been the brightest of the guards, but he understood about dignity.

FORTY-SEVEN

———◆———

"I THOUGHT A CARROT MIGHT HELP."

Kate sat in the precious solitude of the bathroom, notebook spread across her thighs, stub of pencil hovering over her Diane notes. The back of her hand was gray in the watery light; its freckles had long since faded. Her fingers trembled as she continued recording what Diane had said.

"You know, to go with the stick."

The phrases were difficult on their own, but what of the physical signs? Two raw wrists and a flame-red cheek meant nothing at first. She could easily have inflicted those harms upon herself. And her coy, self-satisfied smile was at odds with what she was saying. She may well have wanted to tell Kate, a woman, and not the others, but words whispered girlishly at the floor lacked weight. They evaporated as they were uttered, along with Diane's breath in the cold morning air.

Kate groaned and ran a hand through her hair. Loose strands came out between her fingers, reminding her of Rachel. Their bickering, from this distance, was unfathomable. It made her want to weep. She looked down at her nails, flecked and broken.

They'd not eaten for eight days now, and this time it was taking a worse toll. When she'd refused food before, the stand had been hers alone. It had been painful, but in a strangely abstract way. There was nobody to complain to, and somehow that had helped. Sharing the experience was much harder. Diane's whining strengthened Kate's resolve to continue with their protest, but at the same time it struck a chord. When Clay claimed the rules should allow them to "draw straws and cut jerky from the loser," she barely smiled.

Now this from Diane. She had spoken with the confiding air of a playground ally, murmuring conspiracy from behind her hand. Kate's instinct, never mind the fact that it was Diane making an overture, would always have been to take a step away. She did not go in for best friends of that sort, considering such relationships one of her sister's weaknesses. There was always something combustible and short-lived about Rachel's pacts; one minute she and another girl were an infatuated tangle of secrets, the next they were enemies. Betrayal seemed par for the course. The point, even before the alliance stalled, seemed as much about excluding others as about friendship.

She had seen enough of Diane to be wary. One kind word could equally be followed with another or a cruel stare. Yet the confines of the Marriott necessitated a relationship of sorts. They tore rags from the same sheet, after all, sharing some hardships the men did not. Her tone this morning had suggested something of a similarly personal nature, but what she was saying made no sense.

Diane goes on. She says, "Thought it would be a worthwhile swap." Her eyes gleam, deep in their sockets, above those cheekbone shards. "My little sacrifice for all of our benefit."

She's just returned from a twenty-two-minute stint in the washroom. I'm waiting my turn, hoping for as generous an allowance. A slender hand grips my forearm, another cups further whisperings into my ear, even as I try to pull away. Then the smile threatens to become a pout.

"Might as well use it before it starves away." Bizarrely, she follows this with a dance step.

My normal voice sounds weirdly loud. "Use what?"

Diane taps her nose. This breezy indifference suddenly plays across her face as she glances in Ethan's direction, like she's checking for his uninterrupted disinterest. When she turns back to me though, her bottom lip's all shivery.

"But he took advantage," she whispers. "Check this out."

She offers up her palms, cocked forward to expose red wrists. The soft skin of her left forearm is raised in this painful welt.

"And . . ." She turns the red stripe of her jaw up to me, rolling her eyes as she does so. "Animal. But hey." She tries another smile. "That's to be expected. It doesn't alter our deal."

"Who did this to you, Diane?" Poor girl's hand is light and hot in mine. It twists away out of sight, hides with the other behind her slim back.

"It's a fair price to pay." Her face is ashen, yet she musters one blithe wink back at me. "You wait. Fuck not eating. We'll see some proper progress round here now."

Now, calm in the washroom, Kate made herself write those words down, quote by quote. Despite the stubby pencil her handwriting was minute. With her head on one side the page looked beautiful and abstract, precise as code and somehow ancient. Faintness overtook her. She turned to watch one viscous drop of water follow another from the tap, each taking an eon to form and fall, then looked back down for the sense of what she'd written. The description allowed room for ambiguity. That was the thing about the diary: no matter how bad things were in reality, the written account of them allowed more hope. Hunger helped too; it made even the smallest doubt elastic. The cramped fist of her stomach and lightness in her head somehow muddied what Diane had been explaining. Kate balanced the notebook on the porcelain cistern and steadied herself with the ceremony of her scrupulous washing. She splashed a handful of water into her face, hoping for a shock of clarity, but the icy water was simply numbing. It ran down her chin bent forward over the basin, fusing both: a stalactite.

She picked up the pencil to continue.

"It's like I say. There's always an easier way." Diane now has her hands on her hips. She looks arch. In profile the flame of her cheek is blusher.

None of the guards had ever harassed Kate with anything more than a corralling prod in the back. The likelihood of such . . . interference . . . had preyed upon her for the first few days of their captivity, but since then, and particularly since their transfer to the Marriott, it seemed to have grown more and more remote. There had been no lasciviousness on the part of the guards. No innuendo even. Khalid was too polite. Sadiq's disinterest was compounded by his lack of English. Only in Abu's rolling, predatory gait did Kate sense any kind of threat, and even that was just the echo of his physical hostility toward the men. He'd never so much as raised his hand against her.

Is she making it up to curry sympathy? A diversionary tactic, to distract us from the fast? She stands before me, chewing a fleshy lip, which seems to have grown bigger still in her pinched face. As I stare at it the lip crumples, and suddenly Diane is sniffing back teary snot.

"But I never said he could have a trophy. A photo! He took a fucking—" *The whispered sentence breaks into a full-blooded sob. Ethan veers from the trodden path of his floorboard, toward us.*

"What's up?"

I look at him over the top of Diane's head and manage a shrug: who knows? Her shoulders begin to shudder. Those beautiful fingers cover her downturned face. In the background George's muttering starts up:

"I am Alpha and Omega, the beginning and the ending . . . which is, and which was, and which is to come . . ."

This seems to tip Diane off balance. Ethan puts out an arm to steady her, then stands firm as she presses herself extravagantly into his chest. A matinee swoon. I can't help narrowing my eyes at this, but Ethan doesn't catch the expression; he's staring at the crown of Diane's head.

She's skeletal and clinging to Ethan for support, yet her embrace somehow manages to be voluptuous all the same. There's this familiarity, this ownership in the way she tilts the blusher-bruised cheek into Ethan's throat, both hands clasping the back of his neck, one long leg raised against his thigh.

He could have pushed her away more definitely.

This touching embrace is cut short when the metal bottom of the door scrapes open behind us. Diane's sobbing cuts out. When she looks up it's hard to say whether her expression is distraught or ecstatic. Is the whole episode a deliberate ploy for Ethan's attention? I'm standing there rigid as Clay breaks into the circle and says quietly: "Your turn."

Her turn. Kate carried the shield of her skepticism high when led by Khalid down the yellow corridor. He seemed intent on keeping his head bowed even lower than normal, cloyingly pious. The patchwork of rectangles running the length of the corridor made the blanked-out feeling worse; there was no knowing what long-gone messages had once adorned the ratty corkboard. Yet those hard-edged shades of brown confirmed a fact. There had, once, been posters. As Kate continued past this evidence, Diane's flimsy tale grew a similar backbone. The door to the guards' room stood ajar. She instinctively slowed to glance inside. In the pause before Khalid nudged her forward, she caught sight of Abu, with his back to the door, laughing at Sadiq. Long shirttails flapped down beneath his denim jacket. With an upstretched hand he was waving something at the fat man, whose grin was unmistakably nervous. Khalid stepped around her to obstruct the view with his own face.

She'd misread his piety. It had morphed to shame. She held her ground for a moment longer, craning round him to see what was going on.

Abu was a referee, issuing the red card. The card was glossy, and waved in triumph. In the bathroom Kate's handwriting wobbled describing how the Polaroid had flashed yellow as it caught the electric light.

FORTY-EIGHT

THE WINDOW BARS were useful for pull-ups. Ethan looked up at them, contemplating his last set of the day. Raising his chin above the cement lip grew exponentially harder with each missed meal. Only a miracle of will would push him to his paltry target of five. On tiptoes he reached for the bottom of his two preferred bars, shoulder-width apart, braced himself for the effort. The cold sucked his palms to the metalwork. He took a deep breath, held it, and drew himself up the wall. *One.*

He held himself square in the window frame for a second, then relaxed back down and tuned in to Clay, who was singing to himself.

"Seen a man standin' over a dead dog, lyin' by the highway in a ditch
Lookin' down kinda puzzled, pokin' that dog with a stick

Got his car door flung open, he's standin' out on Highway
  Thirty-one
Like if he stood there long enough—that dog'd get up and
  run
Struck me kinda funny, seem kinda funny sir, to me
Still the end of every hard-earned day people find some
  reason to believe."

The head shots were like that—a reason to believe. Ethan prepared to pull himself up the wall again, remembering how one by
one they'd been escorted to the guards' room the day before and
made to stand against a blank wall while Abu took photos. There
was something inherently lighthearted about a Polaroid camera
despite the big man's furrowed brow: Ethan associated the instantaneous results with childhood parties. He made sure to lift
his chin and, looking directly into the lens, smile determinedly.
An after-flash persisted though he looked away, blurring Freddie
Ljungberg among the wall of Arsenal faces over Abu's shoulder.
The ramifications of being photographed began to sink in, out-
weighing the fear that had pressed down as Sadiq steered him
out of the familiar corridor. Why else but to prove that they were
staying the course?

"Go the Gunners," Ethan said.

Sadiq, who had been standing to one side, roared with laughter. "Gunners!"

"You like football?"

"Football. Yes." The fat guard pretended to kick a ball.

"I am a football fan too," Ethan explained, speaking slowly.
"My team is Aston Villa."

"Villa Park. Football man! Villa Park!" Sadiq, still beaming, said something to Khalid. The youngster trotted from the room. Abu, Ethan noticed, remained unimpressed, fixed on his point-and-shoot with a professional's concentration. Sadiq babbled on, pointing at the posters.

"Highbury best. David Seaman. FA Cup. Double double. Premium League."

Chin over the lip again: *two*.

Khalid reappeared, dribbling a plastic ball through the doorway and around imaginary opposition before passing it across the rug to Sadiq. The fat man gathered the ball inexpertly, took a step backward, aimed his coast-to-coast grin at Ethan, and skewed a pass in his direction. Ethan squared the ball deferentially, with one touch, back to Khalid. The youngster trapped it and once again began dribbling around the room, pride and glee mixed in his face, any pretence of authority long gone. He pirouetted immediately in front of Ethan, taunting him with a schoolyard drag-back. The maneuver was so signposted Ethan had to check an impulse to ruin it with a tackle. Instead he nodded appreciatively, toes flexing in grimy socks. After a further one-two with Sadiq, whose inane grin persisted, Khalid chipped the ball into the air and tried to keep it up. He managed to bounce it on his knee twice, then lost control, clipping a ricochet toward Ethan, who let it roll onto the bridge of his right foot. Lighter than a proper football, but completely predictable nevertheless, effortlessly his, and quite suddenly the most important football ever, bouncing from his toe to his knee to his left instep, back to the knee, again, again, up to the forehead, dropping to the knee, again, again, again.

Khalid moved in. Sadiq was laughing. Even Abu smiled as

Ethan trapped the ball, offered it to Khalid, then spun away from him with it at the last minute. Khalid came at him again. Ethan played a give-and-go off the wall, collecting the ball behind the guard. Now Sadiq lumbered forward to check him and Ethan stopped dead, man and ball, to let the guard drift past. Despite the confines of the room there was all the space in the world to jink left and right and leave everyone rooted, and it felt right because Abu was laughing now, joining in, shouldering Ethan out of the way, but forgetting to take the ball, which Ethan had already back-heeled to safety. All three of the guards now came at him and it was as simple as breathing to lift the ball over the couch and fall through the gap between it and Khalid, whose laughter was breathless and infectious, and buoyed Ethan on again to stub the ball through Sadiq's planted legs, re-collect and spin past Abu and finally to drag the ball up onto the heel of his flicking left foot with the toe of his running right, lifting it over all three of the guards as they came, line abreast, to stop him. The trajectory was perfect and the defense wooden, woefully slow. They were children in a park and Ethan was an uncle or elder brother, turning to receive his own pass, trapping the ball once again, halting only because laughter had combined with weakness to rob him of his breath entirely. Abu clattered into the couch. Ethan kicked the ball away and leaned forward, hands on knees. Everybody stopped.

Three.

A palpable confusion registered. Ethan kept his eyes fixed on his feet as they slowly stopped swimming. The big toe of his left foot was poking through its threadbare sock. His fingers pinched the wool and dragged the hole sideways, tucking the toe back inside. When he looked up, Abu's face was unreadable once again. The big man turned away and ambled past the fireplace to the table in the corner. Sadiq's smile had yet to fade. And little Khalid, bouncing on the balls of his feet, was still abandoned.

"You are a fine footballing man!" he laughed. "A very good player, yes!"

"No."

"Yes! David Beckham!"

A strange sensation flooded Ethan's limbs, acute as pain, intoxicating as laughter. His heart was beating wildly. The wall was full of pointless heroes and yet these three men and the hierarchy above them and its absolute, unfathomable cause gave everything a relevance, even the now inert plastic ball and the cruelty of an endless gray bandage and the horror of a corpse hung up by the feet, and even the stupid hole in his gray sock, just there; imbuing them and him and everybody not too blind to see, with a point.

"Patrick Viera," said Sadiq, and thumped his chest.

Four.

Abu had turned back to face him and was giving him a plastic carrier bag, with something heavy inside. Ethan took the bag in silence, opened its mouth, made out a pair of army-issue boots.

"Try these," said Abu. The granite composure of his face looked suddenly forced, threatened by his own generosity. "For the cold," he added, in explanation.

With exaggerated care Ethan loosened the laces of each boot. He stepped into the left first, and rethreaded its eyelets one after another until they reached the top. The others looked on as he repeated the process with the right. Once the boots were done up, he flexed forward, rocked backward, and announced, "Perfect fit. Thank you. Thank you very much."

He tried to pull himself up to the window again now, hanging flat against the wall. His back and shoulders were dead, his biceps and forearms burned, his stomach felt as though it had been torn in two. Yet what threatened the last pull-up entirely was his tongue, so swollen through thirst that it filled his throat, big as a fist and dry as dirt. Never mind swallowing, it was a fight to breathe. The wall loomed. He fought the temptation to scrabble upward with his toe caps, and hauled.

The boots were a kindness, which Ethan appreciated. Yet you had to respect the balaclava's masterstroke more. It confirmed the old adage: to defend, attack. The first sign was Khalid's appearance in the doorway that morning, without the customary tray.

"You will eat again today? I should bring breakfast?"

Weary yet patient, Clay explained not.

Khalid eyed them each in turn, hoping perhaps for dissent. He nodded in the direction of George. "He is suffering enough. Please?"

"Is that a fact?" Clay raised his eyebrows. "We're all suffering."

"But—"

"No buts, pal. We've explained what we want."

"This is very regrettable."

"Fetch us a doctor if you're so concerned," Kate suggested bitterly.

Khalid's exasperation shriveled. He turned to go. When he reappeared a few moments later he carried a pistol and accompanied the balaclava, who leaned in the open doorway to ask his question.

"Who is in charge here?"

Ethan's lips parted, but a hint of something rhetorical in the man's voice stopped him from speaking up.

His suspicion was confirmed as the balaclava continued.

"Me. I told you before. I am making rules for you. Your special task is obeying." He came forward into their midst and looked around. An outstretched finger pointed at George. "Already we see what happens if you make problems. Hurtful things. I am keeping control like this, not the other way around. If you are needing something, you can ask. It may be possible to help. But"—he paused—"if you make unreasonable demands, if you are giving more difficulty, I must show again how I am in charge."

The man's tone was unequivocal, his words clear and hard. Ethan felt admonished. He lowered his eyes and followed the balaclava's boots as they crossed the room to where their plastic water jugs stood side by side against the wall. Two hands reached down. Ethan understood the man's thinking in that moment with a gratifying completeness, even before the balaclava had lifted the first jug clear. He sat in awe as the water uncoiled from first one spout and then the next, forming a stream fast enough to snake across and between the boards, toward the buttress and under George, who sat impassive as a boulder in its path.

"If you will not eat you are not needing drink to wash it down. Without food and water there is no need for toilet. Everyone will be very comfortable here in this room only, I am sure."

A parental smile formed in the mouth-hole, underlining a logic that came from a higher vantage point. The protest was over. With any luck their stand may have fulfilled its objective of winning a little respect. Ethan had proven himself capable of abstinence, which would not have gone unnoticed. Either way, with one bold stoke, this man's will had now overcome theirs. Water pooled beneath George. In the quiet it was audible, trickling through gaps in the floorboards. A master class.

"When you have finished with threats and nonsense I will give you back food and water and toilet, but not before. You have the choice."

The balaclava made a start for the door. Khalid drew himself aside to let him past.

"It makes no difference."

The balaclava's khaki trouser leg flapped as his foot hit the floor and stopped. Kate had risen before him. Her pale face was ghostly. She swayed like seaweed underwater, but spoke firmly.

"We did make requests, but you ignored them. So we don't have a choice. If you won't give us water, the end will come faster. We need . . ."

Ethan gripped his forehead with interlocked hands, his thumbs stopping up his ears. Yet despite pressing hard he could only block out the precise sense of Kate's words; the tone of her voice would not go away entirely. There was almost something appealing again in her bolshy naïveté. Ethan had a sudden memory of her clutching the plastic beaker full of fruit rind in the quadrangle and felt an urge to reach out for her, to protect her from herself. But before he could, his chest constricted with a burst of suppressed laughter which came from nowhere and wound up in a cough. The balaclava was smiling again when he looked; he too could see the funny side of Kate's front, puny as a baby's fist. On she went, turning for support to Jan, Clay, Diane, and finally Ethan himself. Though she was just there in front of him, she seemed impossibly distant.

Now Ethan struggled to pull himself up the last inches of wall. As the thought of making the target became a reality his body grew numb. He was beyond himself. One of the others would crack first. Diane complained constantly and Clay, too, was clearly having his doubts. The tip of Ethan's nose was over the lip now. The bristles on his chin made a satisfying sound as they brushed the cement edge. Outside, in the half-light, the river was as dull as a sweep of tarmac at the bottom of the slope.

Five.

He held himself there, as rigid as the bars he clung to, the toe caps of his new boots nudging at the plasterwork, with the picture outside swimming in and out of focus. Beyond hunger, beyond thirst, stronger than ever.

FORTY-NINE

❧

THERE WAS NO HORIZON. Instead, a dark visor curved down in front of her face. The visor, she recognized, was for instrument training; it blotted out the canopy glass, leaving only a crescent of cockpit interior visible, a slice of dials set in familiar rows. For a moment the six main instruments were obvious, and then they were an unreadable assortment of needles, numbers, and letters once again.

"So what heading are you going to hold for takeoff?"

Kate heard her instructor's voice but he wasn't in the cockpit with her. When she turned to check, she found herself staring at a familiar peeling wall.

"It's not a trick question."

She knew the answer, but could not speak.

"I'll give you a clue. We're on runway two zero, right. . . ."

She turned beneath the visor again, to check, and this time saw the seat empty. Even given the answer, she was unwilling to repeat the words to nobody. Unwilling or unable. He wasn't there, and anyway, she wasn't qualified.

"You're having me on. Two hundred should do it. Relax. Let go of that lottery ticket. I've put us on the centerline. All you have to do is hold the course and pull back when the airspeed reaches sixty, just like normal. Okay?"

The front of the visor bobbed once. Infuriating! She tried to pull it off, but the thing was clamped too tightly on her head.

"Right then. Power up."

The dials reconfigured briefly, requiring concentration: there was the heading indicator in the middle of the bottom row, pointing just past due south. And above it, to the left, the airspeed indicator read zero. Her mouth was dry, struggling for the word "No," because this wasn't happening. She wasn't instrument-rated, which meant she wasn't in control. Ahead of deciding not to push the power lever in, though, she had already done so; the propeller tone rose and they were bouncing blindly forward down the hard runway floorboards. The airspeed needle climbed through twenty, thirty, forty knots. Her throat was swollen and plugged with dust. Forty-five, fifty. They were definitely rushing forward now, yet there wasn't space in the room. There was nothing she could do; all her influence had dried up. All she had to go on were the instrument readings, which were suspect: the gyro could be out of kilter or the dial uncalibrated, she might be veering to the left or right, was undoubtedly about to leave the runway and plow into a fuel truck or hangar or the guards' quarters. A yell formed, but her tongue had died, swollen and split. The direction needle threatened to wobble toward one ninety and Kate over-corrected with the right rudder.

"Steady."

Clay's voice sounded in her headset, cool as water. He had eyes she could fall into, but something always held her back. Since he wasn't in the cockpit either his voice was just another distraction. All she wanted was to cut the power and call a halt, but she was beyond speech, accelerating. With each passing second she knew she was drifting farther off course, the probability of a collision becoming a certainty, her ineffectuality more and more terrifying.

As the airspeed nudged sixty knots she sensed the nosewheel lifting clear of the strip. If she forced the stick forward, she might yet keep the plane on the ground. But by now the perimeter fence at the end of the runway would be rushing to meet her, with the hawthorn scrub beyond it yawning, and that left her no choice but to pull up. She hurtled at the window bars, her lips cracking as they stretched wide to accommodate the panic.

"Attagirl."

Now the other dials jumped: the artificial horizon bobbed and the vertical speed indicator showed a climb. Her eyes skipped from them to the airspeed to the altimeter, as its dial cranked through two hundred and fifty feet. For a second she managed to hold the picture in her head, saw the plane situated in all dimensions, even thought to check the oil pressure and the fuel gauge, but immediately regretted doing so. Empty! No fuel. No oil. Everything about to grind to a halt. Though she mouthed the word "Help," it only tore her lips further.

"You're okay, you're okay." His voice was soothing. He cared for her, you could tell. Yet she could not reach for him. "Don't panic," he whispered.

Exactly. Clay was nothing if not pragmatic. She forced the circles back into their rows by clamping her mouth shut, and found that her teeth were furry, coated with something metallic, iron filings. She was caught in a magnetic field, and the dials were a rack of little mirrors, flashing on and off as she turned through the sun. Out of nowhere a sequence of instructions sounded.

First, scan the instruments to glean the necessary information: attitude, altitude, heading, speed.

Second, visualize the desired new flight path.

Third, select the new attitude and power.

Fourth, hold them.

Finally, trim.

She started to follow orders and once again the readout made a certain sort of sense. But the picture didn't tally—it was at odds with what her body *knew* was happening. An untrained pilot attempting instrument flight will mistrust the readout, fatally, within minutes. And she *wasn't* qualified for this, because *nobody* was. Nevertheless she scanned the dials again, determined not to give in to her instincts, but the taste of blood in her mouth was overwhelming, and although she could visualize the plane at a thousand two hundred feet, still climbing gently, banked to the left and turning through one hundred and thirty-eight degrees, she was light in her straps, suspended in a corkscrew dive, upside down and inside out and pulling back on the hand in hers.

Her pulse hammered in time with the propeller. The dials became meaningless again and then began to fade entirely. Which made no difference really because she could do nothing anyway, because she was utterly impotent. No amount of hauling or pushing on the control column mattered, there was just the sensation of a bunch of hot fingers squeezing back, and she was definitely falling, tail first, down a bottomless hole. The cockpit air boiled, searing her nose, throat, and lungs. Or else she was breathing flames. She tried to tear the visor off again, but found that it was no longer there. And then there was no visor at all, and no dials, just blackness. It didn't matter whether her eyes were open or shut, there was nothing to see. Only darkness, closing in.

FIFTY

R ACHEL RATTLED THE cocktail stirrer among ice cubes and wiped a smear of lip gloss from her straw. She'd chosen the restaurant for its scale and pace, but now found the din over-whelming. Looking back down the bar she watched the revolving door until a figure coming through it looked likely. She stubbed out her cigarette. Shorter than the head shot suggested, younger, but definitely her, and looking confusedly about.

"Julia Fulford?" Rachel sounded eager despite herself. A hostess.

The woman's face lit up. "Jules," she exclaimed. "Please!" She disentangled her arm from the loops of a woolly bag and offered her hand up to Rachel. Next to her by-line she wore her dark hair scraped back behind her head; before Rachel it stuck out in country-girl ringlets. She pushed her glasses back up her nose and peered over Rachel's shoulder at the cavernous restaurant interior. "Cosy!"

A waiter arrived, intent upon showing them to a table. Rachel feigned reserve by ignoring him, but Jules scuttled off in his tracks, fighting free of her cardigan as she went, all elbows. Rachel's kitten-heels felt suddenly wrong. She dismantled the te-pee of her serviette as they sat down, and surreptitiously dabbed the makeup from her lips.

When she looked back up, she found Jules openmouthed, about to speak. But the waiter cut her off, thrusting two menus across the table with a matador's flourish, defying them not to order a drink. The noise of a thousand diners rose like surf. Out of the corner of her eye, she was aware of other white shirts weaving back and forth between the tables, trays held high. They seemed choreographed. Rachel ordered another vodka and tonic to slow the place down, heard her choice echo back conspiratori-ally across the table.

"Can I just say, on behalf of all of us at the paper, how sorry we are that your sister is in this . . . situation. I was vaguely aware of the story, but not the details. Since you called, though, I've gone back over the archived articles and . . ." The ringlets shook from side to side. "I have a sister myself. You must be going spare."

"Of course." Rachel shrugged. "But everyone seems to have lost interest."

The table next to theirs erupted with laughter. When Rachel looked, it took a few seconds for the paper hats to register. An of-fice Christmas party, the tablecloth thick with spent bottles and plates. One bald man stood out, laughing himself purple, strug-gling to speak. "So she's bent over, and the post-boy's . . . going at her. . . ." He dissolved again; the rest of the room surged louder.

"Well, I'm here." Jules smiled and shrugged and looked from side to side to emphasize the fact.

"I haven't wanted to talk to journalists until now," Rachel tried to explain, but competing smells rose up to overpower her: aftershave, duck, cigarette smoke. She fought on. "It goes back to my father. You made a spectacle of his private life when I was a girl, and he took off for good."

"Okay." Jules now looked nonplussed. "But I'm pretty sure that wasn't me."

On the next table voices rose with competing puns. "Special delivery!" "Registered male!" Somebody knocked a bottle over and waiters descended. Rachel continued.

"The point was they got the details of the story wrong. They said he got the girl pregnant, which wasn't true. And she was seventeen, not sixteen." The woman before her nodded vacantly, apparently unable to keep up. She tried to spell it out. "But the damage was done. It killed our family. You print lies, they stick. So my instinct was to say 'no' when the reporters came asking for background. Whatever I said would just wind up distorted and do no good. Leave it for the diplomats was what I thought."

A different waiter arrived to prompt their order. He pulled a pad from his belt, suave as a conjurer, and hovered while Jules read the menu with her forefinger. When finally she made her choice he scribbled shorthand pointedly and took off at pace.

"But they're doing nothing. Since the petition, nothing at all. And before that, Ethan's father—Colonel Hughes—was coming out with lies. Virtually saying it was Kate's fault. I mean, what's that got to do with anything at all?"

Jules shrugged. "People always want to find out *why*. It's only natural to want someone to blame."

"Yeah, well." Rachel curled strands from her fringe around a finger and pulled, continuing quietly: "I want to tell her side of the story, and raise awareness again. There's nothing else I can think of to do."

Again the other table: "Rowe walked right in on them. The personnel director getting personal. Pants down for the postie. Brilliant! She'll never live it down."

"Well, . . . I'm honored. That you chose to speak to me, of all people. I'm sure you know—but I'm not really news. It's more opinion in my column." She dug in her bag, as if searching for an example, but pulled a handkerchief free instead.

"Yes, but your column has heart."

Jules smiled, then blew her nose loudly, in the direction of the office party. "You said you had an angle, a way of breathing new life into the story?"

The restaurant noise surged loud again. Why did they pack the tables so tight? The waiters had to sidestep between chairbacks. That was what gave the impression of dancing. Left two three, right two three. Rachel's hand trembled picking up her glass.

"I take it you meant a more personal account. Something along the lines of what the last six months have been like for the family, for you."

"Something like that."

A team of waiters converged upon their table, as if to make an arrest. Plates landed. A stack of sausage and mash sat opposite, seared mullet swam on a bed of bok choy down below. The fussy presentation sparked a different sort of nervousness. Now that she'd committed to giving this woman a story she began to doubt whether what she had to say would be sufficiently interesting. It was only background, after all. Which somehow needled. A countercurrent of envy gripped Rachel, absurd, yet tangible all the same. The restaurant spun around the table. She shuddered, took a long pull on her straw.

"Anything ever happen to you to make everything that went before it meaningless?"

Jules looked quizzical.

"You know, say you're involved with a person, or people, on one level, and you're fine with it, and then something happens, and suddenly what went on before makes no sense anymore. No sense at all. You're just sorry backwards, for everything that . . . happened."

"You mean you regret something you did?"

Rachel drained the rest of her glass. "Yes, because you can't undo it, and you can't apologize for it either."

"Because you missed your chance?"

"Even worse than that. There never was a chance. You didn't even know you wanted to apologize until it was too late. Like hearing about some fantastic event that's already over. The regret lands right after the opportunity to express it has gone."

Jules thought a moment and then said, "Are you saying you want to apologize to Kate for something you did before she was taken hostage?"

Rachel nodded, but her mouth started talking, intent on a change of subject. "You know, Kate wants to be a journalist," she began. "Always has."

Jules raised an eyebrow. "Common affliction, but . . ."

"She'd want me to speak with you."

"I'm glad to hear that. I'm sure she'll thank you when she gets back." The reporter leaned forward and laid her fingers across

Rachel's. "And I'm sure the two of you will have a chance to clear up past differences then, too."

The woman's optimism rolled forward with the drink, opening Rachel up. A picture of Kate spilled out. Unpretentious and organized and principled. Hardworking and loyal and adventurous. The stubbornness and gullibility and moralizing were nowhere to be seen: all Rachel had to do was hold the gate wide and allow the positives to pile past. Jules didn't even need to take notes. She just sat opposite, framed by that big hair, chomping through her sausages in a workmanlike way, one eye fixed on the food and the other on Rachel, who felt she could talk more freely the more freely she talked. Pointless anecdotes helped. Having explained Kate's vegetarianism, she found herself recounting a story about a hedgehog, a baby hedgehog, which her sister had "rescued" and fed for a month with a stolen science-block pipette. Even then, at age twelve, Rachel had known the exercise was futile. She told Kate so, and indeed, she'd been right—the thing died eventually. But that wasn't the point now, so she left it out. Instead she chose to take a replenishing gulp of wine, and was immediately in the middle of a description of patio doors. Her mother's. It was relevant to describe how the poor woman now kept them dangerously clean, insisting on soaping them down *daily* as part of the maniacal routine of housework which she employed to keep the real world at bay.

"It's not like they were ever dirty before," Rachel explained. "I mean, that last day, with the pigeon. Wham!" She jabbed her glass forward to illustrate, never mind the spillage. "Stupid thing flew bang into them. I thought it was dead. But Kate went out to it and brought it back to life."

Julia leaned back from the table again. Gently, she explained, "I feel for you. I really do. If I'm to make an article of this, though, there has to be a point to it. Something revelatory, something new."

"Yes, but the pigeon. That impressed everyone. Healing hands, Ethan said, healing hands."

"Ethan's the boyfriend, right?"

Rachel nodded and bit the inside of her bottom lip.

The reporter's eyes narrowed. "And the . . . disagreement . . . between you and Kate, did that have to do with him? Did that happen then?"

The wineglass was an ally. A final slug from it helped. "Sort of, but it goes back way before then. The root of it starts with our father."

"And was he there with this pigeon? Did he come back to see them off?"

Words were stones rattling around Rachel's head, and each sentence spoken meant less to carry. This woman, Jules, was alright. She showed her teeth when she smiled. Rachel's head was light; she looked up to the ceiling and saw a million panes of glass suspended, end on, above the dining space. An instillation, or a modern chandelier. Hundreds of guillotine blades, poised to drop. Looking back down, Jules's mouth was shiny and mesmerizing and her crooked smile was reassuring. Rachel found herself nodding back at the reporter, agreeing with her. Of course she'd make contact with him, if it would help. A reunion, repentance, forgiveness—she'd do whatever was necessary now.

FIFTY-ONE

JAN WAS BREATHING too fast. The sound broke in upon Kate's stupor as she sat staring at the grain of the floorboards, contours on a hatefully familiar map. She stood stiffly and moved to his side, knelt down, and asked, "What's wrong?"

"Nothing," he said. His eyes were rapid-blinking and wet. It looked as if he'd been crying but as she studied his face it split into a false smile. Still panting shallow breaths, he began to laugh. She put a hand on his forearm and squeezed. There was nothing soft beneath his shirtsleeve, just the sharpness of bone.

"He asks me every day, on our way to the bathroom. Khalid. How are you? he says. Fine, I tell him. I am fine." He shook his head, still laughing. "That is the only answer for the question. What more can I say in this circumstance? We are all of us fine, thank you very much."

Kate looked over her shoulder, at George sitting alone, Ethan stretched out on his back sleeping, Diane hugging her knees. She caught Clay's eye and he rose to join them.

"But I am not okay," Jan whispered. "I am anything except."

Kate still had hold of the arm. Jan looked down at her hand. "Ever since the first day I have not tasted food," he said. "Something went wrong in my mouth. My tongue does not work. I can see an egg, I can see rice, I can feel them in my fingers, but they do not taste. Even when we eat curry I taste nothing at all."

Now Clay tried to calm him, whispering reassurances. Jan looked up at them in turn, apparently amazed. "I am too afraid for any more of this," he said simply.

"I know," Clay agreed. "But don't you see that they're afraid too? They've locked us in here, but in doing so they've locked themselves in too. Without us they're nothing. They have to look after us and that's what they're doing."

Jan shook his head. "George was talking last night. He said he would make a way out."

"In which case he was dreaming."

"He said he would fight."

Clay turned to look at George. "Think about it, Jan. George can't fight. And if he could, it wouldn't do any good. He'd make matters worse, if anything."

"But something has to finish it," Jan said. "It can't just go on."

Clay opened his mouth, then shut it without speaking.

"This morning I had a chance for an end," Jan went on. "Somebody left help in the bathroom. A bag made out of plastic, in the sink. In our circumstances it was a weapon. I wanted to use it. I got as far as putting the bag over my head. It went inside my lips when I breathed in. In and out, in and out it went, the bag without air against my teeth, against my tongue. Still I did not taste anything. I tried to breathe up all the air. I wanted to, I honestly did, but I failed. I lost my nerve."

"No, you didn't," said Clay. "You *held* your nerve."

"I bit a hole in the bag. I ruined the chance because I was weak."

Kate saw Jan's eyes close, deep in their sockets. His Adam's apple threatened to poke through the skin of his throat. She stared at his face, which looked suddenly old. And yet in recent weeks he had become more and more childlike, asking Clay to sing his songs at night, laughing himself weak at the American's lamest jokes. When the guards issued new clothes he was inconsolable for days, convinced that it meant their captivity would never end. And now this panic breathing, contagious in so confined a space. As Kate again squeezed Jan's arm the shape of her selfishness became clear. She wanted to steady him for her own sake.

She looked to Clay. He was still reasoning with Jan, trying to convince him that patience was their best tactic, that the balaclava would surely trade them soon. Kate stopped hearing the words, concentrated instead on the music of his voice, on his apparently limitless calm. How he had wound up with Diane in the first place? Like Clay said—the past was harder and harder to dig back to. Looking back, she could no longer recall what Diane had been like before they were taken. Or any of the others. It was even hard to remember the old Ethan clearly. There were memories, yes, but they were abstract; she could no longer feel them. A shocking thought came to her, that she couldn't recall the sensation of her old self. When she tried she suffered emptiness instead. The present had obliterated the past, and now stretched into an impossible future. Just as there was no *before*, there could be no *after* this.

But Clay was still murmuring the opposite, urging Jan to think about home, of how he'd soon get the chance to keelhaul his dad again. He traced the shape of a boat on the floor, made Jan shut his eyes and think of the light in a yacht's wake. Once he'd started on this picture, he asked the boy to help fill in the details, and kept him talking.

Keeping up their morale like this was Clay's way of enduring the crucifying impotence, his form of resistance. He used laughter to unnerve the guards. Abu in particular hated to see evidence of a joke he could not understand; the senselessness of their finding anything funny at all, given the situation, made him bristle. When the big guard checked in on them before handover Clay would blow him a kiss good night, then face down Abu's indignation with a vapid grin.

Jan blinked more slowly now. His breathing had quietened; his smile was no longer at odds with the rest of his face. In place of his whispered reassurances Clay had begun, quietly, to whistle. Low, growling laughter came from the far corner of the room.

"For sure. It'll all turn out right in the end. Ha ha ha." George sat up. A grin split the gray stubble below his bandages. Since he so seldom spoke, except to mutter his incoherent prayers, everyone turned to look at him. "It'll all end happily ever after if we can just hang on. Roger fucking Whittaker there will save us, Jan. It's a certainty."

Kate's heartbeat quickened. She sneered, "No, your God is bound to beat him to it, George. We should pin our hopes on that."

George laughed again, shook his head, and lay back down. Kate felt Clay's hand brush her knee. As the color in her cheeks subsided she glanced at Ethan, to find that he was watching her. Or at least his head was propped up on his hands, and he was looking their way. In the dirty half-light it was impossible to make out the expression on his face.

FIFTY-TWO

ETHAN SAT STARING AT another set of contours, the whorls of his fingertips, stained with ink. Raised voices filtered into the room from down the corridor. The guards debating strategy, no doubt. He began to turn back through the pamphlet's pages once again. Though he'd had the booklet less than a day, words and phrases, when whispered, already sounded familiar.

"We are with vision of state with no divisions, only itself, free from long struggle against the prejudicial approach inherent in occupied Kashmir and in others."

Khalid's face, when he handed the typed pages over! Proud as a schoolboy, showing off cult comics. "Now everyone is eating," he said, "I have discovered the solution for your reading request! This will help with long hours. In the English language!" He bounced on the balls of his feet, buoyed with initiative, and sidestepped round the room dropping a booklet into each lap.

"Conditions are better now. You have two hours of morning heat. Sadiq and Abu are agreeing with that."

"Imprisonment of our leaders and comrades is anti the point of view, not expressing the general will of our people, who are above all forgiving."

They'd sat in silence for an hour or so after he left. George never even raised his head. But Clay, Kate, and Diane, still pressed against the dying radiator, were each intent on their copy, commuters on the evening train, with Jan, too weak to take any notice, the drunk slumped in their midst. Ethan read while pacing the floorboards, until giddiness lowered him back to his dark patch against the window wall.

"Belief in the one way of going will prevail as History shows that in both past and future the rights of people here are not in alignment with the leadership currently in provision."

Diane tossed her copy aside with an uncomprehending sneer. Over her head. Predictably, Kate spoke first, excited indignation in her voice. "Christ. It's completely incoherent."

"Yup. Ikea flat-pack manual meets undergrad ethnic-studies tract," said Clay.

Diane muttered something then, but Ethan was back among the words on the page, swimming through them stroke by stroke, in time with the pulse in his neck. It was depressing, but no real surprise to see that nobody else had a clue.

"1947 is gone but still it speaks. The situation from India since then is unattained and contrary to all our will."

Then, as now, Ethan felt flushed. Since they'd begun eating again—in the end Clay cracked first, convincing Kate with re-markably ease that "even Gandhi has a weakness for water"—his insides had liquefied. All of them fell to the same sickness. But the guards were doing their best to help. They'd seen fit to provide more water, and emptied the necrotic bucket in the corner of the room at more frequent intervals through the day. Now these further concessions. An extra hour of heat. And not just any reading material—a glimpse of something relevant, something heartfelt. Though it took concentration to keep the newsprint still—those voices in the corridor now threatened to prick through the page—the effort paid off.

"This young group has new blood flowing with righteous pace for freedom and we will prevail. We have belief in the exact boundary laid down by authority. There is no bigger purpose, just the arm around our land for its true people."

Love letters. Hard to stomach if you're not the intended recipient. Mawkish and overblown, incoherent even, at times. But these words made sense despite themselves. He'd read of "passion defying eloquence" at school; this was proof of what it meant. The more intense a feeling the harder it is to put into words. As Ethan's stained fingertips continued to turn the pages he felt again the enormity of such a compliment: that Khalid had seen fit to allow them this privilege was the surest sign yet.

"Our fists speak louder than the mouth in certain situations and this makes for regrettable actions necessary at some time."

In a way the mistakes were charming. Sloppy expression could be tidied up. What mattered was that you spoke the truth, unequivocally. That was to be admired. The phrases tasted potent as Ethan sat repeating them below his breath.

"Ethan?" Kate's face bounced on a level with his. She looked hopeful.

"Government of India let loose a reign of terror and showered bullets on innocents whereby thousands of thousands have been killed or worse. In such circumstances the arm must be iron with will as every person involved will see."

"Sure. Daft, isn't it? But how about giving it a rest. You must have had enough of reading that shite now?"

Skin as pale as egg white, lips yolk-gray. Her resistance was a fragile shell. He could see through it, now, and felt suddenly sorry. Her hand, stroking his knee, was brittle to the touch. If the point was being truthful, no matter how difficult the words were to speak, he had a duty to try. Lying no longer made sense; the inconsistencies had begun, in his dreams, to show their teeth. She was still smiling at him. Yet he held back: it was too hard to know where to begin. She'd resist, think him mad. Perhaps he could start with the booklet first, explain that she must look beneath the surface to appreciate what its pages meant. Even that seemed too hard. In the end it was as much as he could do to nod reassuringly back. He stared down at the paper again for guidance, letting the words sound noiselessly in his head.

Only through struggle with sacrifice can our rewards be expected. Without that strength there is nothing. So peaceful meanings are the best, which is our absolute aim, but in order to overcome and army defeated there are sometimes contradictions.

"You're still burning up."

"No, I'm fine."

"A brave face is one thing, but you can admit you're sick to me."

"This—" He wagged the booklet like a fan. "—means more—"

"With any luck, you're right. Maybe they'll give in on the medic too. Though if that"—now she gripped the other end of the pamphlet—"is anything to go by, the best we can expect is some sort of witch doctor."

"No. It means more, in itself." He eased her fingers free of the booklet and smoothed it flat. "I'll share it with you. I'll help you understand."

She grinned at him nervously, warily almost, opening an unbridgeable gap. He felt the threat of tears prick his own eyes and, since such weakness was unthinkable, simply smiled back. He didn't have to see the page to recall what it said.

Suppression through the drama of state-held elections is not the way. State terrorism also is killing innocents throughout this region and is ultimately responsible. With one true way it shall finally be possible to overcome difficulties for all individuals and parties involved, but there must be this pressure.

Necessary pressure. Though he shut his eyes the obligation would not go away. The sooner she too knew the truth of their role, their place in the bigger scheme, the sooner they would both be safe. Yet with her face gone for just a second the voices in the corridor grew louder. They weren't speaking English, but it didn't matter; the gist was obvious, admonishment, not debate. Discipline in action, a dressing-down. Another random gobbet of text sprang, word for word, to mind.

Mother is a Mir Hamdani Kashmiri presently living in Lahore, Pakistan. She has never been to Kashmir, but perhaps feels unexplainably hurt and helpless every time I come across Kashmiri news, and the terrible doings.

An unexplainable hurt was the problem. Truth was indeed a

terrible doing. But the voices had grown louder still. The door shot inward with a final barked expletive, and Abu thrust Khalid into the room. The balaclava stormed in behind them. He took a moment to compose himself, then spoke again in Khalid's direction, through clenched teeth. The young guard shook his head furiously, intent on making amends.

"I have made a bad mistake. The literature is not necessary. It is not authorized, not allowed. I am not permitted to give it away to you." He looked distraught, a failure before the boss, neutered before his captives, unable to meet anybody's eye. More quietly, he continued, "You must give back every copy to me now."

"Man," sighed Clay. "And I was so *into* it, too. You're talented, Khalid, know that?"

"Definitely," Kate agreed.

Ethan found the contradictions too knotted to unpick. On the one hand he felt for Khalid. Such insults were enraging. On the other his ultimate allegiance was up the chain of command, to the balaclava. There had to be a reason for his intervention, yet none would come. It was easiest to stare back at the pamphlet and drink in more of the incantation.

There is ample literature in the public domain about Israeli-Indian collaboration in many areas for everyone to see that they are swine. Against such a force we are in struggle to overcome without the same might. We rely instead on the bigger heart.

Khalid was scuttling about the room now, retrieving copies. George's lay unopened beside him, where it had fallen. Clay handed his back with a weary smile. Picking up the others, the young guard became a prefect, collecting tests. Shame colored his cheeks above the line of his thin beard, and Ethan recognized this as humility. Kate inevitably made matters worse. She looked away in disdain, refusing to help by offering her copy up. Khalid had to pull it out from under her calf. Pearls before . . . That was the point, Ethan saw. They'd been offered a glimpse through the curtain, a chance, and collectively they'd blown it. Why else would the balaclava have ordered this retraction? He felt torn; handing his own thumbed copy back was like giving up his passport all over again, and yet, since he was among the undeserving he could expect no different treatment.

If not our supporter, then the person is an enemy. They are committing ineffable crimes against all of humanity. Everybody is a part. We have no choice except the fight.

Taking the bundle of booklets back from Khalid, the balaclava's stare seemed to bore straight through him. He clipped the boy across the top of the head and shoved him through the open door, then turned to glare at each of them in turn. Ethan could not be sure whether or not his nod of understanding was answered in the leader's narrowed eyes.

FIFTY-THREE

⸻

"Rip it, if you have to. Pull it out!"

That made no sense. Though he had more than his fair share, they'd never get him to give up any of his blankets. At least they had each other's warmth. Kate and Diane lay on either side of Jan; Ethan and Clay framed the triumvirate. Only George stayed apart, shut inside his blackened head-cloths. Coming to, Kate felt vaguely resentful. The bitterness latched on to those bandages as she awoke. Why did he refuse to take them off, even now? Though she tried, she could not picture the outline of his face.

"Get it out of me!"

Kate opened an eye and fought her hands free to roll up a sleeve. There was just enough gray light to check Clay's watch— 6:12. Movement along the row distracted her from its face. She sat up to see Diane—the spat words were hers—struggling with a nightmare beneath the sheet.

"Cut! Cut!"

There wasn't much point in waking her—wherever she was, here wasn't better. Rubbing the sleep from her eyes, Kate looked down at the slab of Ethan's turned back. Though he'd conceded that it made sense to sleep close, away from his perverse daytime position beneath the window, he remained a rigid bookend throughout each night. On her other side, Jan lay curled as tight as a fist. Despite the flat dawn light and his wispy beard, shadows hollowed the planes of his face. In the last few days his delirium had become more constant, and he'd begun to breathe through the permanent O of an open mouth. Each new in and out seemed a shallower sip than the last.

"The head's stuck! Cut! Tear it out!"

Now the disturbance was annoying, but since Diane lay beyond Kate's reach, she could not shake her awake. Or preferred not to. Lately the girl had grown yet harder to read, liable to outbursts—aiming her animosity at Clay mostly—through sharpened teeth. Kate feared their bite. Sensing her own cowardice now, she rebelled against it, and made herself say "Shh!"

Diane threw back her blanket and sprang to her feet. The whites of her eyes flashed around the full circumference of dilated pupils. Her shrunken chest heaved. "Shut the fuck up yourself. I'm the one it happened to. I'm the one that needs the knife."

Kate flinched, startled to see Diane awake.

"The head needs cutting off. Stuck up, where that bastard—"

"Calm down, Diane. It's okay." The sleep was thick in Clay's voice. He reached a hand in her vague direction.

"Nothing's okay. You know nothing anymore! *They* know. They have the picture." Her voice was at a shriek now, wavering madly. Ethan stirred behind Kate as Diane kicked Clay's hand away. "You!" She glowered at Kate. "You of all people should understand. For all anybody knows there's a bearded head needs cutting out of you, too!"

Kate saw Clay's expression as he woke to take in this outburst. The affable front had yet to form. Instead a slackness in his mouth combined with something beyond dismay in his eyes, a torpor aimed at Diane which said: *I give up.* Broken free. The sight was as gratifying as dawn—a brief warmth flooded Kate. She felt the shape of Jan slump sideways like tipped ballast as Clay, a mask of composure configuring, rose stiffly to his knees.

"Come on, calm down." Again he reached out to take Diane's hand. She wrenched away from his grip.

"Fuck—off!"

Beside Kate, Jan summoned enough breath to groan. Diane thrashed harder against Clay's weight, all elbows and wiry limbs. He lurched woodenly after her. Both of them passed before the window and gained the middle of the floor, ballroom dancing. Kate felt the blankets shift behind her: Ethan turning. Though Clay tried to placate Diane she was possessed. The mat of her hair stuck out from either side of her face, as rigid as a hat brim, accentuating the brittle jerking of her head.

"All of you. Cut them out! Cut—"

Clay shouted over her, patience shot: "Cut? Cut? What are you talking about? You're out of your mind. Hear me? Out of your mind. Cut it *out,* yourself!"

At this Diane strained backward, dragging him across the room, her neck and head whipping with each frantic stride. He fell toward her. They collided and stuck together, he clutching her for support and she pushing against him with her nose pressed into his right ear. Clay yowled, and then Ethan was upon them, trying to separate the pair, twisting and yanking, and it was obvious as they spun again through the light that Diane was fixed to Clay, locked to his neck with clenched teeth. Kate yelled "Stop!" but panic made her unable to get up, let alone help. Clay let fists fly and kicked out and stumbled again with Diane and then without her, Ethan the referee now embroiled in the fight, the three of them falling in all directions. Ethan tripped backward to stamp, heavy booted, into Jan's hollow stomach.

Kate saw: the twin horseshoes of Diane's raw bite-mark below Clay's ear as his hand rose to meet the shape; Diane on all fours, head down mid pant; Ethan, still off balance, trampling Jan and beginning to fall; Jan's eyes full of fright as he folded further to clutch at his groin through Ethan's legs; and lastly the impossible sight of George's bandaged face following Ethan's course as he tripped backward and slammed into the boards like a felled tree.

"Boots," gasped Jan.

Diane hissed. "Your fault, Clay. It was done to me because of you."

Kate was still staring at George. Blank once more. He rolled slowly to face the wall again, a whale disappearing back into the deep. She turned back to Clay, saw him lift his hand gingerly away from his neck to inspect the blood at his fingertips. He caught her eye and shook his head, bewildered. "It's okay. But Jesus. The bitch bit me!" His wince faded into silent, hopeless laughter. "As in *chewed* me, with her teeth!"

Stretched out, felled timber, Ethan groaned, lifted his head, let it drop to the boards again with a wooden thump. "Fucking unbelievable," he whispered. The outthrust V of his boot soles wagged once, just inches from Jan's face.

"Rafi. Kicking. Why Ethan? On me." Jan rambled, found the thread, and, as the lock rattled in the metal door, sewed a sentence. Barely audible, but it sounded like a question. "Why is he wearing Rafi's old boots?"

FIFTY-FOUR

As Ethan suspected, all he had to do was watch Kate closely before her turn. Though it felt cruel, the cruelty was mitigated because it had a point. Everyone would benefit from his vigilance and firmness in the long run. Loyalty is its own reward. And anyway, indulging Kate's weakness wasn't a serious option. So he sat close to the spot and kept his eyes fixed and unblinking on her face, rising above her frustration, until eventually she gave up and time ran out and she had to set off to the bathroom empty-handed.

Funny how you could learn a lesson at such a long distance. But, looking back, his mistake at the doctor's seemed obvious now. The GP was bald and the skin on his head was blotchy beneath the strip-light, giving him the look of a diseased apple, yet he had a kind smile. He made Ethan's mother sit in the waiting room behind her dark glasses, saying, "You're a big enough boy; let's have you in on your own, shall we?"

The little gloved fists and shields and bayonets said you should be brave and they were right there when Ethan, seeing his mother stiffen as he stepped past her with the doctor, shut his eyes. "Okay," he said in a firm voice, yet wilting inside.

Happily, he'd not fallen to the temptation of a confrontation on the spot the day before when, suspicions confirmed, he'd spied Kate slipping the exercise book out from under her sweatshirt. Furtive as a pickpocket, she stooped to slide it in one practiced movement into the gap beneath the skirting board. Indignation swamped Ethan immediately, but the idiocy of Kate taking such a risk stunned him silent. How the hell had she got hold of a note-book in the first place? Now, though the anger was gone, there was still the question of what to do with the evidence. The next step should have been obvious, but Ethan found it hard to cross the room and act. He sat mesmerized by a song Clay was whistling, which somehow held him back.

The doctor had been like the balaclava, in charge. He told Ethan to take off his shirt for the injection and then turned his bare arm between moist fingers. The bruises were a map—yellow desert, purple sea, brown earth. "Hmm," he'd said. "What have we here?"

Here, we had a simple decision to make. If he left the pad in its hiding place he'd have to stop Kate from taking it again the next day. Though he could probably manage that, she might retrieve it in the night, or when he was next gone from the room. And if that happened one of the guards may catch her red-handed. An untenable risk. He could try to take her aside and talk her round, but what if she refused to give the thing up? There'd be another scene. Best to act now, take the evidence with him during his trip to the washroom, flush it page by page down the toilet, and head the problem off entirely. That was leadership, after all, being decisive. Taking responsibility in a crisis, making the covering tackle, being the safe pair of hands. What was his problem then? Why not do it now?

"Looks like somebody's been in the wars." The doctor's glasses went blank, reflecting his angle-poise lamp, and then his cheerful eyes were back again. "You've not much shoulder left for me to aim at."

"Dead arms—at school," Ethan had explained.

"Really? A big lad like you?"

"Uh-huh."

"Want to give me the other arm then?"

Ethan complied. He looked down too, saw more of the same, heard the doctor breathe in through his teeth.

That the notebook meant something truly significant to Kate, Ethan did not doubt. But he had to overcome that hurdle. It was just further evidence of her dangerous insistence on living in the old world. Different rules applied there. Later he'd explain. You could want to be a journalist, and keep a notebook, and fill it with little observations in a time before the balaclava, but to do so now was unhinged. This new world wouldn't fit on the pages. The propaganda had been proof of that. Poor old Khalid! If you taunted the boss with written words, anything might happen. Which made Ethan's decision yet more obvious: in destroying the evidence he'd be doing Kate a favor, a cruel kindness. One day, she'd see, and thank him. Yet *still* he found himself hanging back.

The doctor fiddled with his wrappers on the little tray of capsules, wipes, and medical instruments. His hands looked too big.

Ethan stared at the ensemble and saw an in-flight meal. A fork instead of a syringe, a carton of UHT milk instead of the vial of drugs. This was probably a test. The doctor would report back. It was therefore very important not to flinch. Ethan puffed his white chest out and sat up as straight as a soldier, yet the plastic seat cover stuck to the backs of his legs.

"My dad's a doctor too," he said.

"Oh, yes?"

"In the forces. He's a colonel."

"That sounds grand."

Now there was a new problem: Clay's tune was over, which meant the minutes were slipping by. How long had he sat prevaricating? Unless he retrieved the notebook now, the opportunity may be lost. Propelled by this fear Ethan marched Rafi's unlaced boots across the room, left right left, steeling himself with the thought that, sometimes, you have to hurt those you love to protect them. Those were the doctor's orders after all.

"I think we better try a leg."

Obediently, Ethan dropped his boxer shorts to reveal a chunky white thigh.

The doctor said, "That's better," then started an unconvincing conversation about football while he twisted off caps, drew the syringe full, and flicked the needle. He needn't have bothered with the diversion, Ethan was determined to be brave regardless, and barely registered the scratch when it came. The swab afterward was hot then immediately cold. "Done." The doctor smiled. "But before you go, why don't we have a chat about those arms with your mum?"

"No!"

The big man sat back down in his swivel chair, his piebald head dropping to Ethan's level. Man to man. "Okay, okay. But maybe you can help *her* by telling me about what's going on behind those sunglasses?"

On his haunches, Ethan rocked forward to inspect the crack, made out the gray spine of the notebook shadowed in the recess. His blunt forefinger was too big. Fearing he might prod the book farther back, out of reach, he lowered himself to his chest and stomach for a better look, poked a pinkie into the crevice, and pressed down.

"What are you up to?"

With the gap at eye level it was straightforward enough to drag the notebook forward an inch, until a corner of its cardboard cover stuck out into the room. Pulling the book out all the way was easy after that. Having made his mind up to intervene, the practical act felt less like a violation. It was simply necessary.

"Jesus, Ethan. What are you playing at?"

Rocking back up onto one knee, Ethan turned to see Clay standing above him. "Nothing. It's not important."

"To you, maybe." A cartoonlike look of concern—wide eyes, mouth open—had taken hold of Clay's face. "But have a heart. Put the thing back."

Ethan was computing. So this guy *knew*. He understood what the notebook was, despite Ethan's cramming it, bent double, down the front of his shin, into the top of Rafi's army boot. Which put Clay in Kate's league of stupidity and signaled a faltering of the last likely ally. George gone, Diane mad, Jan sinking. Kate . . . Kate. Clay was still reasonable, except that now he clearly wasn't. He didn't have a clue. This wasn't about rights, for

God's sake. The American's jaw was working furiously, the scraggy blond beard around his mouth bristling in apparent consternation, yet whatever he was saying was just so much noise. No, it wasn't about rights, not rights at all: obligation was the thing.

The doctor had been trying to explain something similar. He unhooked his glasses from one ear, then another, revealing tired little grooves on either side of his nose, and wiped each lens on his tie. His eyes, naked, were bigger and softer still.

"You really should speak up if you know something, son. Otherwise it'll just get worse. Really, you *should*."

Though the memory had pained him ever since, it was pleasing to look back now and know his instinctive loyalty had been right, he'd done a good thing.

"I'm not your son," was all he said.

Now Clay knelt too. The thin line of his lips was almost blue with cold, though the blood crept back into them with his attempt at a reassuring smile. He took a long time to speak.

"Think about this, Ethan. You don't need to take that away from her." He pointed at the edge of notebook sticking out of Ethan's boot. "You're not playing fair."

Clay's teacherly tone was infuriating in its condescension, but the balance remained tipped in favor of pity. The poor guy didn't understand. Playing fair! Sometimes you had to forfeit a point in the interest of the wider championship. Ethan folded his arms across his chest, resting thick wrists on his raised knee and, as if to underline the implacability of his position, said nothing. Later he was ashamed of his complacency, which allowed Clay to make such an audacious play, but at the time he was simply astonished by Clay's sleight of hand: one minute he was smiling calmly, the next his fingers whipped out for the notebook, grabbing the cover and, luckily for Ethan, landing a fistful of military leather tongue, too. He pulled hard enough to drag Ethan's foot a few inches across the floor and then Ethan had hold of his forearm with one hand and a bunch of crumpling pages in the other. He shouted, "No!" and thought the follow-up—*Help . . . protect . . . herself* (the doctor, glasses slotted back into position, had explained such a concept long ago)—but it was too late. The staples popped and a flock of double spreads, dense with feathery scrawl, fell limply to the floor.

"Jesus, Ethan!" Clay scrabbled for the pages. "What the fuck did you do that for?"

"Me? Me!"

Then, the worst of all possible worlds. One of Sadiq's gray trainers landed out of nowhere with a soft but emphatic thud on a sheaf of splayed paper.

"Give."

Diane burst out laughing. "Got you! Ha, ha."

The guard seemed to be trying to contain himself in his triumph. He puffed himself up and demanded: "Who is this?"

The question was of course *whose* and Ethan understood precisely that Sadiq had to ask it and, now that he'd done so, must receive an answer. Nobody said anything, but no answer would not do. The trainer tapped out an impatient beat and Ethan's anger at Clay ground into the wall of a new dilemma. For Kate had stepped into the room and was sinking to her knees, tilting further forward now onto two splayed palms, each planted on its separate dirty floorboard. Turning back, Clay's face was short-circuiting inches from his own, and once again the train of allegiance and loyalty and leadership and bravery had skipped the tracks and was jackknifing in his chest. This wasn't his notebook or his fault. Yet the chain of command made him responsible all the same. He'd been blind to the crime for too long and once he'd discovered it he'd not dealt with the problem adequately, which made him to blame. Clay let go of his half of the notebook. Ethan gathered up the pages and stood to hand them over.

"Me," he said, tapping his chest. "Mine."

FIFTY-FIVE

———◆———

KATE DIDN'T NOTICE Sadiq lead Ethan from the room. One minute he was there, picking up the pages of her journal, and then the floor was empty. Her head was cold. She regretted having tried to wash her hair in the basin. Shutting her eyes, she saw the water uncurling from the tap again, oily as iced vodka. While she sat, not looking, not taking in the fact of what she'd witnessed, a dribble leaked from the root of her improvised ponytail, ran down the back of her neck, and drew a frozen line between her shoulder blades.

Deep down, a part of her had always suspected they would catch her out with the journal eventually. Yet to have it happen was crushing. When she turned toward Clay she found him shaking Diane by the shoulders. Her blond hair was flicking back and forth on either side of her upturned chin, lips apart, giggling in his face. It almost looked as if he was rattling the laughter into existence until he raised an open hand and abruptly the noise stopped.

The same hand was on Kate's shoulder now, drawing her close. "Come on. In the scheme of things . . . ," Clay was saying.

It was strange to have her head stroked and to hear such soothing words, but to begin with they had no effect. She felt numb. The hunger and cold, weakness and fear were suddenly overwhelming, too much to take in. Now the journal was gone there was no evidence to refer to, no scale to measure the misery against. And yet to be held this way—a hand on the back of the neck, lips pressed to the forehead—was old and new at once, and comforting. More words broke in.

"It was an accident," Clay pleaded. "He didn't mean it."

Which was sweet, really, and ironic, because until that moment the loss had been more than enough to concentrate on. She hadn't got around to apportioning blame. In trying to excuse Ethan, though, Clay in fact helped her to the opposite conclusion. Ethan had handed her journal to Sadiq. In doing so he had willfully betrayed her. That much was plain.

Down the corridor somebody switched on a radio and ran the volume up until the song began to fragment. Still, the tune was recognizable, a snatch of something sickly, by Andrew Lloyd Webber, from *Cats*. Clay's face, inches from her own, saying, "Fuck, real torture," made her laugh, which was entirely inappropriate, and yet irrelevant all the same, because a shout of pain broke through the din.

She recoiled, appalled by her own reaction, for the yell made sense. Ethan deserved to suffer and she felt better for hearing him in pain. He owed her, not just for the journal, but for having walled himself in behind the plane of his turned back, night after night. The scream was the sound of those debts being repaid.

As soon as this malevolence registered, however, she was engulfed in guilt and sought a way to disown herself. Since Clay's face hovering before hers represented a betrayal as wrong as the thought itself, she jerked back from its lips. Jumping to her feet, she ran at the metal door and began hammering upon it with clenched fists.

"It's not his! Stop! The report is mine!"

Reaching the song's finale, the speakers gave up. The corridor became a cacophony of snare drums, drowning out Kate's accompaniment entirely as Clay hauled her back from the door.

FIFTY-SIX

Ethan allowed Sadiq to march him the length of the corridor. He'd taken an irreversible step; there would be time enough later to reconsider why. For now there were more immediate questions to consider, like how square to hold his shoulders as he walked ahead of the guard, while keeping his eyes respectfully low.

Throwing open the door to the guards' quarters, Sadiq revealed Khalid, belly down on the rug, and Abu, sprawled in his socks on the couch, both of them watching TV. A cheerful fire glowed in the grate. The scene looked very Sunday afternoon. As Abu rose in annoyance to shut the screen off Ethan felt guilty of some social blunder. He tried to take a step backward to acknowledge the interruption, but Sadiq stiff-armed him onward, gabbling excitedly all the while. On reaching the middle of the room he forced Ethan to kneel down, then waved the pages of manuscript in his face before handing them triumphantly to Abu. A pace or two in front of Ethan, the guards conversed. Since they were not speaking English, he focused on faces. Abu, stroking his beard, scrutinized one page and then another, yet holding them upside down. Clearly he could not read Kate's scrawl. Khalid was initially keen to inspect a few pages but, having turned up the cover of the exercise book, handed the lot back to Abu, as if fearful that their contents might be infectious. His sad face said Ethan's failing was a personal slight; Ethan wished he could tell him the truth.

"Where are you getting this from?" Abu rolled the exercise book into a baton and slapped Ethan across the face with it.

The question was a good one. Ethan had no convincing answer and found himself shrugging.

Abu repeated both the question and the slap.

"I don't know." Nothing else came to mind. Abu laughed and smacked him left and right again. Though his face stung, the real hurt was in having to lie like this to the guards. They'd never been anything other than straight with him, and this was how he repaid their leadership. The paradox came startlingly clear in the gap between the next two blows: past wrongs meant that Ethan owed it to Kate to take the blame, yet until these men had shown him the meaning of loyalty, sacrifice, *love*, he'd never have bothered. More blows rained down, and all clear thought evaporated, leaving simple shame. The indignity was crushing, and it was Kate's fault. Abu tossed the battered roll of paper aside and, warming to the task, delivered a series of harder slaps with the flat of his open hand. Though the repeated question kept coming,

Ethan couldn't think of a better response. In a way it was the truth. Jarred left and right, his wits clouding, it was as much as he could do to stick to the original answer. "I. . . . Don't. . . . Know."

There was a pause, in which the room stopped spinning.

"I am sorry," Ethan said. "Honestly, I apologize."

"Too late for that," replied Abu, turning to confer with Sadiq, who stood with his arms folded proudly across his belly. He'd done a good job. In the balaclava's absence the next step seemed to be his and Abu's decision. Before them, Khalid deferred. He bent to retrieve the journal from where Abu had thrown it. The two older guards boomed at one another in heated discussion, but Khalid, looking furtive, edged away. Ethan watched in astonishment as he sidled across the rug and, with an eye on Abu and Sadiq all the while, tossed the roll of paper into the fire. For the long seconds before the journal caught alight Ethan could do nothing but stare at the shape of it lying among the flames and then, when it was too late, he saw the facts plainly. The diary was proof of a crime that must be paid for and Khalid was destroying the evidence because he was implicated. Ethan shouted "No!" and, as the plume of smoke above the papers became flame, he found himself lunging past Abu toward the fireplace. It was the right thing to do. Yet the big guard was too quick for him. Ethan felt the shock of a proper punch across the side of his head and fell in a heap.

He was a long way from the action now. There was an argument, and he was in the middle of it, but somehow he'd become unimportant at the same time. The diary was ashes and smoke, and flames were coming out of Abu's ears, yet Khalid appeared to be holding his own. Not important, his shrugging shoulders seemed to say. Better for all of us if the thing is burned. And though Ethan knew beyond doubt that Khalid had given Kate the exercise book there seemed no point in saying so now; the failing was obviously disappointing and yet Khalid's youth made it inevitable that he'd commit the odd blunder. He was a kind, intelligent kid, learning the rules. Like a younger brother, really. Which made it up to Ethan to help show him the way. No point at all in making an enemy. The balaclava was a strict father, and would want Sadiq to place a paw under each of Ethan's arms and drag him upright and haul him through into the far room.

The bulge of the guard's stomach pressed comfortingly into the small of Ethan's back and then it wasn't there and Ethan was swaying in his boots which were a present.

Far room. Hammer.

The word made you want to flinch, but by staying stoical, in fact, you could enforce the special link. It was most important not to sit down. Khalid was nowhere to be seen and Abu was rolling up his sleeves and the silver teeth were still poking from the rafters in the mirror, there, but as the blows began they were just soft fists and more slapping. If only Kate could see his sacrifice now. The same question, over and over again. Which made it easier and easier to keep on repeating the same answer. Poor old Abu; his heart wasn't in it. One two three. His face was wet. A pause for breath. Four five six.

The youngster would know that Ethan was taking the rap for Kate. That had to be a good thing. Already he was trying to help. He'd started some music playing, to take Ethan's mind off the hardship. Between blows, Rachel sprang to mind, and that made a sense of sorts: was this his punishment, might it help with the guilt? The song was all wailing. It made it easier to cry out. Yes, there'd be time enough later to prove again his allegiance to the cause. Abu and Khalid and Sadiq under the balaclava's command—and Ethan, he was part of the squad too. As Abu worked him over, pummeling his chest, raining down blows on his head, neck, and shoulders, the connection grew stronger. Nobody wanted this, but for now it was everybody's job to knuckle down. Ethan doubled up, winded, and consequently more intimately involved. Enduring this would make him stronger. A bib of sweat stuck Abu's shirt to the barrel of his chest. In the mirror, drawing himself straight, Ethan's front was dark red. They'd forgive him for sinking to his knees now. All part of the display of rigor and self-sacrifice, which was necessary and bearable and over.

Sweat shone in the big man's beard. One thought blotted out all others, dwarfing pain. This was a let-off, a tacit kindness, and in not retaliating, Ethan had proven himself grateful; he had passed a test. With any luck the balaclava would hear of his bravery. The discussion now was probably about that.

Sadiq yanked Ethan to his feet once again and escorted him back through the guards' room and along the corridor. Patchwork corkboards scrolled by. For an odd moment, he was leading Ethan by the ear toward a school detention, which made sense, because the punishment was for a greater good, the rough hand twisting his ear was in fact loving and on his shoulder, helping him to a better version of himself. Approaching the threshold, Ethan swayed to one side to allow Sadiq to work the lock, dimly aware of an impending hero's welcome. It had all turned out for the best. He'd shown courage to Abu, obedience to Sadiq, self-sacrifice to Khalid. Threads in a tapestry of love. And to his fellow captives, he'd demonstrated leadership and a willingness to take responsibility. The bloody nose and swollen eyes would look good. He drew himself to attention as the door came open and was preparing to march when Sadiq grabbed him by the arm and slung him roughly forward, too fast for his feet, to crash head-long across the boards. That was surprising and uncalled for and then obviously all part of the bigger picture, a dramatic entrance to drive the point home. It was important to overcome the indignity swiftly, but daft that a single press-up, from the knees, could be so unfeasibly hard.

"You," a voice was saying. "All of you."

Ethan managed to twist round and saw that Abu had followed them into the room. Despite the gray half-light, his eyes gleamed. He was still breathing hard. An outstretched finger swept round the four walls, taking them all in, returning to Ethan last. It was a convincing portrayal of unhinged menace, which, for reasons momentarily beyond Ethan, the big guard seemed determined to prolong.

"This man tells lies. He did a crime. Means *everybody* must have a punishment."

He strode across to George, who, as usual, was lying with his face to the wall, and kicked him hard in the small of the back.

"Up, Mr. George," he panted. "Starting with you."

FIFTY-SEVEN

KATE WAS KNEELING BEFORE HIM. Her voice started up. He tried to listen, but the pain drowned everything else out. Shards of wet black hair fell forward to frame her anger, and her beautiful soft mouth was working to express it, yet he couldn't understand her. He smiled anyway but that was not what she wanted.

"Why did you do it? Why, why?"

He managed to stand, let her corral him beyond the buttress. She was still going on: "What could my diary possibly matter to you?"

Where should he begin? It was about the balaclava, not her. Obedience and rank, loyalty and leadership. He steadied himself, holding her by the wrists. An overwhelming urge to speak plainly pressed in on him. It would be a relief, frankly, finally to have done with the charade. And yet the old laws still stood.

Think of the doctor with his blotchy head. It was *necessary* to keep things from people, even if you wanted to let them know.

Rachel had tried to break the rule. A glass in one hand, naked but for the towel around her chest, she'd weaved back into the bedroom after answering the buzzer.

"Never guess who it is. Your boring little girlfriend. Unannounced, on a Sunday afternoon. Surely she should still be in church?"

He crossed the hall to stare at the intercom screen. Then, as now, Kate was right there, and so far away. A black-and-white astronaut, seen from ground control.

"Get back here and tell her you'll call her later. You're not up yet. Put her off."

"Really, you think I should?"

"If you don't, I'm gone. It'll be the last you see of me."

"My, my. A threat. Maybe I'm bored of you. I bet she will be too, when she finds out."

He took the glass from her hand and put it down. Forcing a smile in spite of himself, he whispered, "You're not going to do that."

"Do what? I didn't say I was going to do anything."

"We had an . . . understanding."

"Ha! Is that what you call it? Suddenly so formal, and I thought we were just messing around."

He kept his voice flat with feigned boredom. "You know what I mean."

"Do I? You're sure about that?"

"You said you could cope with this. If it turns out you can't . . ."

"No. That was *your* boast. I was high and willing. I just agreed to spread my legs."

"And now you really want to tell her that?"

Rachel rolled her eyes and shrugged. "She'll find out sooner or later. Bound to, somehow."

Though he doubted it was real, her voice rang with a metallic conviction, and the sound of it made everything suddenly clear. The perverse thrill of encompassing both Kate and Rachel dried up inside him as she spoke. Although, at the time, he felt no guilt at having deceived Kate with her sister, he realized that, of the two of them, only she mattered. Rachel pirouetting in her towel became irrelevant again: the act had always been transparent but now it was tiresome, not titillating. Still, he had to force himself to keep calm. He sighed and said, "We both agreed she didn't have to know."

Rachel fell toward him, her breath hot and sharp. "Did we, Ethan? Well, everything changes." She righted herself and spun away toward the buzzer, stretching theatrically.

"Don't you fucking—"

"A dare! That settles it." She pressed the switch.

The building had just one set of stairs. In the time it took Kate to climb them, Ethan made a decision. He threw himself and his clothes into the wardrobe. That he'd so abase himself for this farcical, last hope, was a revelation, and in this way Rachel's stunt proved something he'd never otherwise have known.

He waited, crushed among designer suits, while Rachel, suddenly sober, strung the agony out, pretending her way through two telephone conversations, and engineering a pointless argument with Kate. At one point it sounded as if the pair of them were entering the bedroom. When her sister left, Rachel flung back the wardrobe door, dropped the towel to the floor, and fell laughing onto the bed.

"Your face!"

Kate's anger had burned out. He gathered himself, reaching for the utter calmness with which he'd dressed before Rachel that day. Back then it had spoken for him. Rachel raised herself on one elbow, her laughter fading. She pulled the duvet across her bare chest with a defensiveness echoed by Kate now, slumped on the boards behind folded arms. He stared down at her, righteousness and truth singing in his ears, making it so tempting to explain how the old duplicity had begun to fade even before he discovered this new regime. But that was the thing about Kate, her charm almost. Though she thought otherwise, she couldn't bear much reality. You had to dull its edges for her. She was repeating Rachel now, but crying, not laughing.

"Your face, Ethan. Your face."

FIFTY-EIGHT

SOMETIME DURING THE NIGHT Kate woke to feel Jan cold beside her. When she tried to move his arm, the rest of him turned too, pressing his stone cheek into her neck. She was unable to break the silence, and instead lay as still as he was until dawn. Only then, when Clay stirred at the other end of the line, could she find the courage to speak. And when she did it turned out that Diane was awake and listening and immediately became hysterical: the band saw began again and did not stop until Khalid poked his head around the door to ask, "What?"

After the day of the beatings, Jan's death was inevitable. He never regained consciousness to eat. What rice she and Clay pushed into his mouth either fell out immediately or was coughed clear later. Most of the water seemed to dribble back out too. The thin shape of his hand, pressed between hers, felt as brittle as slate.

Sadiq and Khalid were back in the room, unfolding a new pink sheet. Ethan stopped his pacing to watch—looking almost as if he'd like to help. Clay had his head in his hands. He was moaning "No, no, no," which was understandable and annoying at the same time. What did he expect to happen? Jan was eager and harmless and petrified and therefore dead. They'd killed him. His eyes weren't quite shut, yet the delicate rim of their parted lids was blue. Kate felt her own eyes brim with tears as she tried to think of something, *anything*, reassuring to say. In a way, he was lucky, wasn't he? No longer here, no longer battling this. But he was dead and she couldn't bring herself to speak, and was instead distracted by the young guard spreading his end of the cloth out on the floor. His fingers shook hard enough to send ripples back along its edge. He knelt beside Kate and began trying to ease Jan's hand out of her own.

"Fuck you," she whispered.

Now Khalid would not meet her eye at all, but when, finally, it had been her turn to face the guards about the notebook, he'd ridden blithely over her accusation.

"Khalid knows," she pleaded. "He gave it to me."

"Not true. Another story," was all the young guard had said.

"First Mr. Ethan, then Mr. Clay, now you! Everybody lying," Abu laughed at her.

"No," she had tried to explain. "Him. He knows the truth."

Though Khalid tried to look nonchalant, even attempting a yawn, his eyes flicking left and right and up and down would have given him away, if only anybody had been interested. As it was, they were either tired out by the exertion of beating the men or else squeamish about assaulting her, and intent on getting the punishment over with. She had spent the previous two hours spellbound with fear, trying to block the memory of Diane's Polaroid, and saw sense now in not provoking a change in the guards' outlook. The notebook was her anchor and now it was gone and she must try to carry on untethered. The first slap across the face stung. By the sixth, Abu was yawning too. And in under fifteen minutes she was back in the room with the others again.

Ethan's smashed face looked much worse on her return. One eye had swollen to a black slit, jammed tight beside the pulped bridge of his nose. A beard of dried blood hung beneath his split cheek. She offered to clean his face, said "Sorry" as he flinched from her first touch.

"I accept the apology."

"What?" She tipped more water onto a strip of sheet and paused with it an inch from his face.

"Perhaps now we can start again, with a clean slate."

"Clean slate?"

"You must see; they've kept their end of the bargain. If the punishments fit, so will the rewards. You'll start complying now, yes?"

The urgency in his tone made her bite down on the inside of her mouth. She dabbed again at the cut on Ethan's cheek, hoping to snap him out of it, but this time he didn't flinch.

"All I see is the mess they made of your face, Ethan. I'm sorry it was because of my journal, but they have to take the blame." This was only part of what she felt. It wasn't, after all, as if she'd been caught—he'd betrayed *her* and must therefore shoulder at least some of the responsibility for the hurt he'd brought upon them all. She dabbed again at the cut, but it did no good; it didn't shift the bitterness behind her own clenched teeth.

"But, you see, they had no choice. Did they?" He sounded exasperated. "The rules say as much: a punishment to fit—"

She interrupted: "To fit what, Ethan? Nothing fits. That's the point. Please tell me you agree." It was as though she were whispering at him down an impossibly long corridor: she could see he hadn't heard. "What's the point of this?" She pressed the open cut hard, so that he had to draw away. He raised his fingers to his face, as if appreciating the wound for the first time.

"I deserved it. It's like I was trying to say. A punishment for past sins. It redresses the balance between us. It's my sentence for—"

"Sentence? Punishment? What are you talking about, Ethan? They beat everybody. They *beat you*, for nothing. You need stitches. This is going to scar."

He smiled to himself, thinking something through. "Well, exactly. Like a tattoo. A scar is all part of the uniform. To mark an occasion. Like a memory, or a vow. A scar is for life."

She shrank from him at that; the glow in his eyes belonged to someone else. In the days that followed, as Jan sank beneath his mask of bruises, it had increasingly to be Ethan's fault. He would show no sorrow for what he'd done; if anything he seemed almost to grow more proud of it. His only further comment, when confronted by Clay, was a slurred phrase that included the words "my initiative."

The sheet before her was an improbably neat square of pink penicillin, poured too late. It couldn't help him now. Khalid freed Jan's hands and Sadiq took his feet, or rather hooked the backs of his knees. With some effort they levered and lifted and sidestepped and placed the body squarely in the middle of the cloth. Ethan had paced off to the far end of the room and now stood in

the winter sunlight, with his hands on his hips, as the two guards
began folding. Kate looked up at his face with tears rolling down
her own and could be forgiven for thinking he was overseeing
the burial of a family pet. Only George cared less. Diane's head
remained bowed, but Kate could still make out the shape of her
lips, furious behind a waterfall of hair: "Get it out of here," she
mouthed, over and over again. Clay was kneeling down beside
Kate and drawing her to his side, which was fine because in this
moment nothing could be considered inappropriate.

Time passed. It seemed the guards were wrapping a present.
Their attempt to look respectful, folding the sheet in a neat corner around Jan's feet, came out comical though. Any minute now
Abu would appear with ribbon. Yes, they were wrapping up a
present, never mind that it was a week late.

Diane had been determined to celebrate Christmas; she was so
adamant that the guards would make some concessions in honor
of the day that Kate herself had almost been convinced. Of
course she knew the date was meaningless to them, yet each time
the door opened it promised anything from freedom to news from
home to a hot meal, and delivered nothing. That one day made
everything worse. The guards couldn't have crushed her expecta-
tions had Diane not raised them first. A season of ill will. Christmas brought memories of home crowding forward, yet in doing so
it managed to push the reality further away. The thought of lying
bloated on the couch in her mother's overheated little house, inoc-
ulated from the gray afternoon with its frozen, leafless trees waving at her through the double glass, made the hunger and the
floorboards and the pinprick-hard snow gusting through the bars
even less bearable. An odd thing happened: as the memory of nor-

mality made that normality recede, it so accentuated the stark coldness of where Kate was now that she grew numb. Christmas day turned into Christmas night and both the here and now and the there and then wavered, threatening to cancel one another out entirely. In the darkness, cradling Jan's head in her lap, with Ethan less than twenty feet but a million miles away, and Clay somehow out of bounds, she sat in a trance, doubting everything.

The journal had helped keep things real. It was like her instructor said: "You haven't flown the flight until it's written in your logbook. Unrecorded time doesn't count." Now that the logbook was gone there was no proof that she had the flying hours, no testament to what had passed, no space to record what was still to come. The feeling was suddenly claustrophobic. Bringing the room back into focus, she saw that there *was* a ribbon; Khalid had taken out a big needle and was sewing the length of folded sheet shut. His fingers were still shaking. Watching their progress, Sadiq clasped his hands beneath his belly and lowered his head piously. Rage burned in Kate's chest. Khalid's black thread somehow made it up to Jan's chin and Sadiq now stooped to fold the boyish face away.

Except that *they* should not be allowed to cover up Jan's face. She crawled forward on all fours to intervene and, surprisingly, Khalid stepped back. Holding her hair in place with one hand, she bent down over Jan like a mother. The skin beneath his eyes was purple, close up. She failed to stop the questions forming. Would his beard continue to grow? Might it prosper finally, now that he was dead? She pressed her lips against his forehead. Dry leaves against marble; the combination felt real. By the time she sat back up her own hands were already tucking him in.

FIFTY-NINE

THE WINDOW BARS stood gray against the black sky, like a set of shoulder stripes. Left, right, left, tramped the boots down below, marching him back and forth at the head of the column, before row upon row of floorboard troops. If only his own squad weren't such a shambles. Even after all this time and attention, they just got worse. No wonder headquarters appeared to be losing interest. They were an undisciplined riot. About turn: left, right, left.

No use blaming the others entirely, their failings had to reflect his leadership. After all, rot spreads. Hardly a day went by now when he didn't try to take her aside and explain how he felt, but somehow he always wound up giving a team-talk instead. She didn't make the confession easy, staring at him like that, as if he had two heads. There was a hint of accusation in her eyes, which froze the important truths before he had a chance to speak them, and yet until he confessed and made her see his new love he'd only have himself to blame.

The balaclava had made just one trip to see them in the last couple of weeks, but when he came, what a visit! Uproar in the corridor, a real setting-to. Ethan sat quietly to listen at the door crack, surmising that the leader was angry to have lost a man. "No!" his shouting said, he didn't like it, not one bit. And of course—"How the fuck had they let this happen?"—he held the contingent of guards responsible. You had to feel sorry for Abu and his men. Jan's weakness wasn't all their fault.

Godlike, the balaclava intervened, and summoned a doctor to give the rest a checkup. The little medic was so old the hairs on the back of his fingers were white, yet he had a leather bag, just like Dad, and prescribed injections confidently. It was tempting to tell the man about the anger of his broken teeth and the sharpness just beneath his ribs, but the balaclava and Sadiq were presiding so Ethan stripped to the waist instead and stood straight, left hand gripping right wrist behind his back. When asked how he felt he dropped his gaze down his chest and stomach. The subcutaneous camouflage had faded, but was still clearly visible, a precious uniform. He focused on his boots.

Since then conditions had improved, in the form of doubled rations, more clean water, extra blankets, and near constant heat. But although there was so much less to complain about, Kate's insubordinate streak grew wider day by day. Even Clay had his job cut out soothing her round the clock. The American had pared down well over time, a wiry tenacity emerging as the remnants of his complacency fell away; the diary incident and his girlish singing aside, he might make a competent officer yet. You had, after all, to look to a man's strengths. Clay was undoubtedly a calming influence upon Kate, and still did his best with what remained of Diane. In that way he was a foil. Though Ethan occasionally found his teeth grinding as he observed Clay pandering to Kate, the American's methods were reconcilable to the greater good if you thought about them in this way.

For there were more important matters to attend to, and Ethan had to tackle them alone. His liaison role was delicate. In view of the balaclava's concessions, it was up to him to express the group's thanks, and not just in platitudes: such generosity necessitated a similar act in return. After much thought, Ethan made his offer when escorted back from washroom detail, pausing in the corridor with Khalid.

"I've been meaning to ask," he began. "The literature you distributed—"

"Please, don't stop. Keep moving." The young guard looked nervous. He pointed down the corridor, as if Ethan might have forgotten the way.

"I understand." Ethan took a step forward, found himself pulling up again, despite the risk. "But if you'd give me just a minute of your time, I'd be grateful. I want to make you an offer. Think of it as a grassroots initiative. Listening to the ranks."

Now the youngster just looked confused. A knot moved in his throat and his fingers pecked at one another. He was equal parts authority and kid brother again, and Ethan's deference was suddenly shot through with tenderness. He simply had to demonstrate his goodwill.

"You see, I get it, Khalid. I appreciate what you were trying to do." Ethan reached out to clasp the guard's khaki shoulder, which stiffened.

"Please! Move!" The youngster spoke through bared white teeth. He looked unsettled, afraid almost, and his arm twitched beneath Ethan's hand, which withdrew, fingers spread to placate. A couple more steps onward were unavoidable, yet he would not allow himself to give up. That was the point about taking the initiative—it took courage. As Khalid yanked the key chain up from his belt and began jabbing at the lock, Ethan tried again.

"Sure, it was an early draft. A bit ragged at the edges. In need of attention. But I saw past that. Do you hear what I'm saying, Khalid? I know what it meant for you to hand those copies out. I *understood*."

The guard opened the door with apparent relief. Or perhaps his smile was an invitation to go on.

"In."

Ethan, emboldened, chose not to respond immediately. The poor guy was embarrassed by the reference to his generosity. There was something bashful in his downcast eyes, which made Ethan press on.

"I'm offering to help, Khalid. It was an easy mistake to make. The boss didn't want an early draft sent out, for obvious reasons. He was right about the others—they weren't ready for the material in such a raw state. I *get* all that. But think how pleased he'll be with the improved version! I'll go through the pamphlet for you. Or, if you like, we can tidy it up together. Between us we'll prepare the thing for redistribution."

The guard's hands paddled and pointed, directing traffic. Again the gesture suggested Ethan may not recognize the route home, which was amusing, so Ethan smiled. Khalid's bafflement in response was definitely a front, though. Ethan glanced right, through the door, and got the point straightaway. Kate and Clay were sitting directly opposite and, having paused mid stone game (how unbelievably embarrassing), were staring at him like a pair of gargoyles. Even George had rolled over to face the door, his mouth open below the bandages. Which made it impossible for the youngster to respond to the offer. Ethan kicked himself for having made himself clear too late. Khalid's understated *in you go* nod made sense—as did his demonstrative slamming of the door. They would have to continue the conversation in private, at a later date.

"Tell me I didn't hear that right." Kate's face was so pale with rage that it seemed almost green.

Clay, head in hands, began to laugh.

"I'm not sure what you heard. It was a private conversation."

"A what?"

"I was talking to Khalid."

"Yeah, I know. You were offering to help translate the crap he handed out. What in God's name do you think that will achieve?"

She couldn't be expected to understand why he'd made the offer, but this knee-jerk anger was disconcerting. To himself, George was growling: "And I stood upon the sand of the sea, and saw a beast rise up . . . and the beast which I saw was like unto the leopard . . ." Ethan opened his mouth to reply to Kate, then shut it again without saying anything.

"You're trying to drive a wedge between them, right?" offered Clay. "Get Khalid to dish up more of his dissertation and maybe the balaclava'll fire him or something."

He couldn't stop himself this time. "I'm doing no such thing."

Clay seemed not to have heard. His hopeless laughter started up again, then stopped abruptly. "All well and good, but you'd be better off getting rid of one of the other two. Khalid's harmless. He's their least offensive player."

George: ". . . and they worshipped the beast, saying who is like unto the beast? Who is able to make war with him?"

Kate cut in. "Were you, or weren't you, trying to trick him into something . . . advantageous, for all of us?"

"Exactly that."

"Then what was it?"

Ethan could feel his pulse in his neck hammering with excitement. Perhaps there was hope in explaining after all. He struggled to think of the right way forward.

Kate continued, "Because we ought to talk it through, first. You can't just start making unilateral decisions, taking action that might affect all of us."

"Yes, yes, yes. Every one of us. Khalid included—the whole unit. There's a chain of command, see. We have to work with . . ."

Ethan trailed off. George was still muttering his madness— "He that leadeth into captivity shall go into captivity: he that killeth with the sword must be killed with the sword. Here is the patience and the faith of saints . . ."—but Ethan's eyes were on Kate. Her head was in her hands, and she was groaning. Looking down at her sucked something out of his chest, so that for long moments he found it hard to breathe.

"You'll understand one day," he found himself saying. "One day, I promise, I'll get clearance to explain." But she was shaking, not listening, and a hot coal of sorrow burned in his stomach for fear she'd never see. It was dismaying, her lack of foresight, his inability to confide. Yet he could not risk a scene, and was instead forced to focus on the basics. He retreated to his post and, with a torn strip of shirttail (it didn't show, tucked in), sat spit-polishing the mirror he'd managed, over the weeks, to raise in the toe cap of each boot.

Remembering this now, Ethan stopped his pacing and undid his laces. Stars had risen. He sat beneath them listening for the sound of the evening patrol. Though the night watch had been reduced to just two guards (one of the three left at dusk these days, no doubt to report to the balaclava), discipline held. Somebody always poked a head around their door before extinguishing the corridor light. It was a comforting gesture, encouraging to know that they would be watched over through the small hours.

The only noise at the moment though was George whispering to himself as he sat cemented to the buttress. After the diary beatings, attending the doctor's surgery, he'd screamed bone-split loud, and returned with a new set of bandages for his trouble. Since he couldn't need them now, the episode was further evidence of the balaclava's tolerance, giving away medical supplies to comfort a deluded invalid.

When Ethan had considered the embarrassment of having George in his command he'd made one last effort to help the guy shape up. Braving the stench, he'd offered to accompany him wall to wall, on exercise. "I'll be accompanying you up that fucker's arsehole soon enough," was all the thanks he received for his efforts. The man was a casualty of the cause, awaiting evacuation. Best to let him rot until then.

The fist felt strong bunched inside its leather house. Ethan's other hand returned to work, drawing out his oily reflection.

SIXTY

———◆———

K ATE ' S   HAND   RAN across the stubble of a shorn head. She burrowed closer. Warm breath blew into her ear. She pressed her cheek against a smooth jaw, comforted to have such a dream of the old Ethan, clean-shaven and comprehensible, and then it wasn't a dream because the warmth came again and it was real. Pulling through the last layers of sleep she felt the exhilaration of their early days, when the tenderness he showed her was all the more intense for his apparent coolness beforehand. But there was a problem. The arm around her was slight and all wrong. She opened an eye, confused, too close to the face to make it out, and then the logic of its features overtook her. Unlike Ethan, Clay had accepted the recent offer of a haircut and a shave, and now looked the younger of the two. She drifted again, recalling how Clay had joked with Ethan.

"Like Samson, eh? Hanging on to it for strength."

"True to form," was Ethan's nonsensical, mumbled reply.

Kate ran the words together. Unshorn. Uniform. She brought the face into focus again. Chop logic. Not Ethan, therefore wrong; Clay, therefore not right.

Since Jan's death, the gap he'd left had shored itself up. Bracketed by Ethan and Diane, she and Clay slept close. Kate suffered a familiar contradiction of guilt and longing now, easing herself away from Clay, careful not to disturb his sleep. When she reached out for Ethan behind her, though, her cast hand just found space.

She levered herself upright stiffly, the landing strip of floorboards beneath her creaking in sympathy. At the far end of the runway Ethan sat cross-legged, fiddling with his boots. Nevertheless, Kate made out the fullness of his bearded face as it bobbed upon his chest. For a moment, as everything came clear, she was overcome with sorrow, and then the fact that he felt able to leave her in Clay's embrace pricked. Still in her socks, she padded through the gloom and dropped down on her haunches beside him.

"What are you up to, so early?" she whispered.

His hands stopped working. "Keeping . . . you know . . . in shape."

"Keeping *what* in shape for *what?*"

The whites of his eyes were ultraviolet. They narrowed.

"We're shafted, Ethan. They're going to keep us here until we die, like Jan. You realize that?"

He shook his head, whispering to himself, "Must take care of the gear."

"And you're pandering to the bastards. You've given in."

"No, no." He laughed softly. "There's a structure in place. A battle plan. The chief's got it all worked out. Have faith."

"What chief? What are you on about? Faith in *what*?"

Again his silhouetted head shook. His tone was almost patronizing. "You're not the pilot now, Kate. Not captain. Different ranks apply. Try to understand that."

"Nobody's a fucking pilot. These are terrorists, Ethan. They have an agenda, which is nothing to do with you, or me. We're incidental. We're hostages. We're *victims*, get it?"

Despite the gloom, she sensed that he was smiling, which was infuriating. It felt as if she were attempting to talk with him on the seabed: spoken words just bubbled upward out of reach. So she sat in silence for what seemed an age, and then changed tack.

"Is it Clay?" she whispered. "Because—"

"No, it's not. He's very able. Bags of potential. Yes, he's a decent soldier. And, in the circumstances. Given history. My broken ranks. You have every right. It's my duty, my *duty* to help you see." Pausing, the tip of his tongue worked invisibly to moisten his lower lip, which glistened wet. "The incident was regrettable. With the notebook. You were not entirely to blame. I understand. It was a lack of discipline, that's all. An infringement, an unfortunate slip. But only a momentary breach of the code. Going forward, there's a new M.O. I promise. I'll show you the way. Strategies are in place. . . ."

Phrases ran into one another like water. A stream of militaristic prattle. Kate's sadness was as heavy as chain mail. She became claustrophobic and found herself fighting back.

"Because Clay makes sense. Without him I could not bear this.

I'd have given up long ago. In adversity, you see what people are made of." She paused, reached for his hand, stroked its marble knuckles, let the hand drop. "What are you made of, Ethan? You're complicit. It feels like treachery, and it makes me sick."

At the word "treachery" Kate sensed Ethan stiffen. For a second, the thought of him looming rocklike beside her was frightening. Yet before she could change the subject he went on in earnest explanation.

"Treachery, disloyalty, you're absolutely right. But can't you see, I'm making amends?"

"Making amends for what?"

"I betrayed you. Stuck a knife in your back. I took advantage, and I don't know why now. It makes no sense, here. I can only think that I did it because . . . I could."

"Did what? What are you talking about?"

His eyes gleamed in the moonlight. "Rachel. I was with Rachel too, Rachel and you. It's all nonsense now, I know. But back then there was something . . . irresistible in having you both. Her all sassy and pointless, you so straight." He shook his head, continued jabbering. "She *hated* me at college. And I ignored her. We kept a mile clear. But as soon as I met you, boom! Everything changed. It started out as just funny, for me, that she should be so keen. I had no idea what was making her engage all of a sudden, except that I'd found you. But there you go, that was enough for her, that alone. She wanted covert action. Nothing mattered. She's attractive. I gave in to temptation. I mean, it had to do with wanting you both. If she could cope with it, I certainly could. Nothing echoed then. There were no repercussions. Keeping things that way amounted to a challenge. Laughable now, of course. She wanted to take *me* on, head to head. Shameful, pathetic. But I rolled with it."

He'd gone mad. He was making up this idiocy to torment her. But why? Her shoulders shook. This would pass. It was just turbulence. She wiped a sleeve across her face, yet the horizon didn't clear.

"But I was changing, you see, taking hits left and right, incurring casualties. You were helping me to change. My mercenary status was compromised: clandestine operations were decreasingly effective, so I suspended them. I started to feel for you and it led me to make a choice. I saw off your sister. She threatened to wreck my cover as I disengaged, but doing so would have wrecked hers too. I called her bluff."

Still no picture. She'd have to trust to instruments. "Sure, Ethan," she said, her voice echoing in the headset. "Whatever you say."

"And then I came with you on this trip, on exercise, so to speak. I see why now. The trip was a way of making up. It's worked so well! It's brought us to this point, here, now, where I'm able to give you the truth, straight. With the balaclava's help we'll go further still. There are no half measures. Now that I've let you in I just know you'll understand."

More static. "You're telling me you had an affair with my sister." Though she spoke the words, they meant nothing.

"I'm confessing that, yes." He waved the point aside, as if it were old news, and went on. "But in the past. Now we're here and I'm talking about the future. Now that it's all cleared up between us there's nothing to prevent you from coming with me, from grasping . . . higher certainties. Think of it!"

"I don't know what you're talking about. I can't believe you. I *refuse* to believe what you say."

"No!" He had hold of her wrist, handcuff tight. "You're making a mistake. I'm on the inside. Everything is under control now. I'm making up for all of us. I'm going to prove myself, I swear. . . ."

The rant continued but Kate didn't hear it because the pressure of his grip cut everything else out. In a way, the pain was a blessing. She felt the bones in her forearm flexing as he pulled her toward him, his fingers tightening all the time, and in the instant of her acquiescing, before his grip slackened, there was just the blissful possibility that he might snap her wrist entirely. A distance opened up. Though he still had hold of her and was whispering frantically in her ear, about loyalty and fidelity and truth, she didn't allow him inside her head.

Instead she heard Clay's reassurance, superimposed again: "No diary can make sense of this, Kate. We'll have to tackle that one together."

He was right. Losing the journal hurt, but without it everything just carried on. It was no less and no more real for not being written down. You didn't have to hold up a mirror in order to exist: no article she or anybody else might write would affect the truth of events. The guards were still guilty; Jan was no less dead. *And Ethan still made no sense.* Time ground forward, whether you kept a record of its passing or not. She could not visualize the notebook anymore, had forgotten its shade of gray, no longer felt for it in her waistband in the night. She used her bathroom time to think instead. What use were words she never shared, anyway, compared with those Clay offered?

"I'm bound to miss this place when we get out. I mean, I'll *definitely* want to relive it. Buy me a set of Dictaphone batteries then and you can have my memories, too."

His kindness was worth a thousand pages of notes, and the voice in her ear now had faded and stopped, leaving nothing but warm breath against her cheek. As when she had woken next to Clay, Ethan's proximity now was wrong, which left her stranded. She realized that he had let her hand go, and crossed her arms. The hot echo of his grip remained.

SIXTY-ONE

THE DOOR SWUNG INWARD and Rachel found herself staring at a woman with a child on her hip. Tracksuit bottoms, a bare midriff. Her father's girlfriend was still young. At first the woman was distracted, untangling her son's fingers from her hair.

"Yes?" she said.

When Rachel didn't answer the woman focused for the first time and her lips parted in apparent recognition. She set the child down.

"I'm sorry to come without warning," Rachel mumbled. "Is he here?"

"He'll be back soon. Come in." The woman smiled. "He's out running."

Rachel followed her down a corridor into a cluttered room that smelled of stale incense. The woman swept children's books from a sofa covered with an ethnic throw and invited Rachel to sit. She sank into soft cushions, then perched forward to wait.

With his mother making tea, the boy approached to show Rachel a plastic harmonica. A half brother she had never met. Not knowing how to talk to him, she took the toy and blew into it. Six notes up, and then down again, at once a question, *What—am—I—do—ing—here?* and a call for help.

The door banged. Rachel handed the harmonica back and her father was in the room before her, the boy hugging his legs. Red knees turned to face her and stopped moving. Rachel looked up. "I've come to talk," she said.

"Apparently!" Her father smiled, ran a palm over the sheen of his forehead. "One moment while I fetch a towel. Jacob'll look after you."

The lack of ceremony was unsettling; this wasn't how it was supposed to start. Despite the double vodka she'd sunk en route her nerves sang. She stared at the boy, who backed away. He had Kate's full mouth. From down the hall Rachel heard voices and laughter. Although she knew of her father's situation, she hadn't imagined such domesticity, for his life to appear so complete.

"I signed the petition, as you suggested." He had returned, and now settled into a chair opposite. "And I got your message about the journalist. Of course I'll help. But what I really wanted was to talk with you. So I'm pleased you've come."

"Of course." This sounded presumptuous, but he appeared not to notice.

"It seemed even more important that we find a way to get along," he continued, "at a time like this."

Rachel gathered herself to say her piece, but her father's attention shifted to Jacob, who was pulling compact discs from a pile and posting them behind the radiator. She pressed on regardless.

"I realize I've been wrong. It's pointless holding this grudge. I've come to accept your apology."

He turned back to her, surprised. "Apology?"

"For what you did. To Mum, to me, to Kate."

"What I did." He repeated the phrase slowly, as if tasting the words.

"She always wanted me to take this step, to . . . to let you back in."

"And I'm grateful to her for that. But forgiveness, as you put it?" He paused, put his palms together, an oddly priestly gesture. "What happened was unfortunate, in that it hurt us all. The most lasting damage has been that you and I don't know one another as well as we should. I'm sorry for that, believe me, and yet I don't see it as a matter of apologies. Some things just happen. They are beyond blame."

Again he became distracted by Jacob, who was now pulling the laces from one of his trainers. Rachel remained silent. She looked around the room, at the tired furniture, at a map of Africa in a clip-frame, at an ancient, dusty computer poking from behind a beanbag. On one wall was a collage of skydiving photographs. She fixed upon the hexagon of falling bodies at its center, felt their weightlessness.

"And you say Kate *wanted* us to make up, but you're not quite right." He ruffled the boy's hair and retied his shoe, then looked back at her. "She still *wants* it. You have to believe in that, Rachel, you mustn't give up."

"I haven't."

"Yes, but I know you, better than you'd imagine. If you're not in control of a situation you panic. Just like Kate. Neither of you is much good at trusting to fate."

Rachel dug her fingers into the arm of the couch, but held her tongue.

"That's what I thought I'd be able to help with." He smiled. "Faith, and acceptance. I thought that together we'd stand a better chance of seeing this thing through."

Saucepans clattered down the hall. Jacob rolled on his back at the foot of his father's chair, offering his stomach up like a dog. Rachel felt herself sinking beneath this triteness. She wanted to stand up and go, yet continued gripping the sofa, forcing herself to stay still.

"You say Kate and I are the same," she said, "but we're not. We're quite different. If I lack hope, it's not because I can't control the situation, it's because I'm a realist."

"That's negative thinking, Rachel." He made another sanctimonious temple of his fingers and continued. "Denial is very destructive."

"Maybe. But there are other, worse character traits." She felt a flush of anger color her throat. "I seem to have inherited one of them from you."

He looked up from his son and, for a second, gave her his whole attention.

"Meaning?"

"I may not be like Kate, but that hasn't stopped me wanting what she has."

There was a pause, in which he wiped his face with the towel again, worrying an answer from it. "I know, I know. You feel guilty that it's her out there instead of you. That's natural, I've felt it myself. But you don't have to want to swap."

Rachel stifled an odd urge to laugh. Instead she ran a hand through her hair, turned a knot of strands around her index finger, and pulled as she went on.

"No, I'm talking about something less . . . worthy than that. I'm on about plain jealousy. Never mind that I could have had Ethan before Kate met him. It was only once they were together that I cared, only when I had to hurt her to get him."

Her father shook his head and opened his mouth to speak, but was diverted once again by the boy, who had wedged himself between the television and the wall. He said, "Watch the wires," matter-of-factly, before switching back to Rachel.

"Ethan? You're not serious. Kate's boyfriend."

Rachel bowed her head, felt the first follicle give.

"Well, that's . . . unfortunate, but . . . you can't always account for passion. At times it takes over and"—he paused, held his palms up, as if what he was talking about was evident on the walls—"at times you have to follow your heart."

Her mouth set, lips drawn back, she said, "No, it wasn't real passion. I may have confused it with that for a time, but I was fooling myself. I had to have Ethan because of Kate, not despite her."

"I'm sure that's not true. You're just beating yourself up."

"It *is* true. And what's more, it was because of *you*, too. She let you get away with cheating on us all, so why not really test her? Why not up the ante, show her what it was like for Mum, bring the thing closer to home? Let her forgive *that*. That's why I started it. I mean, to begin with I didn't even like the guy. Cute, but a complete waster. Couldn't see why all those girls in college queued up for him. It was only when Kate joined them that I bothered. And at first I just did it out of plain . . . spite."

"I still don't believe you. Jealousy, maybe, but not vindictiveness. You must have seen something in him."

"Only afterward. At first I was just going to leave it at one . . . night. Proof enough for Kate that betrayal hurts, that blind trust is pathetic, that she was an accident already happening." She paused, chewing her bottom lip.

"But . . . "

"Exactly, *but.* Somehow he found a way in. The fact that he could be so . . . *ambivalent* disarmed me. He just didn't care one way or another. He treated it as a game, and gradually that sucked me in. What started out as plain infuriating became necessary to me, and finally turned into a perverted sort of love. I wound up desperate for him to pick me. I was sure he would. Couldn't see how I could lose, really. After all, he and I were the same, we had the knowledge, we were capable of doing the cheating. All I had to do was tell Kate and, bang, they'd be over. I'd be the one coping, I'd be the sister doing the rising above."

"All's fair in—"

"Christ! Don't start! There was nothing *fair* about it at all. Can't you see? Something in me just wanted to pull them apart. I got *that* close to doing it, but in the end I couldn't. He called my bluff. He knew I wouldn't go through with it. And even if I had, he'd have left us both if he couldn't have Kate. *He preferred her.*

She won." Rachel paused, looking wildly about. "Why do you think they went to Kashmir in the first place?"

Again the priestly gesture with his hands, demonstrably accommodating, but finally he seemed at a loss for words.

"Because of me. When I heard Kate was going to India with Ethan, when I realized he meant what he said and had finished with me for good, I goaded her into it. Don't you see, I must have *wanted* this to happen. *Go find yourself a war zone.* That's what I said; that's what she's gone and done."

"Not true." There was no anger in his voice. "Kate sets her own course. Never mind what you said to her, she's been on about Kashmir for years." He was still nodding at her, crushingly understanding. If anything there was a hint of a smile in his eyes. "I'm sure that's what you feel now, but you mustn't. It's just another example of deferred guilt. You've got to realize that Kate's . . . situation . . . now, has nothing whatsoever to do with you."

She drew breath, determined to try again, to make him see the plain fact of her shame, and his own reflection in it, but Jacob had climbed up on the arm of his chair and now fell into his lap. Her father laughed with the boy and rolled his eyes at her.

She breathed out and looked away, saw the parachutists again, plummeting on the wall. Something changed; she felt herself giving in. She suffered the sudden vision of Kate's face, full of remorse, after their disastrous flight together. The smell of sick in the car returning to London, Kate's unspoken apology as she loaned Rachel her clean sweater; its disproportionate significance—hanging limp in her wardrobe—now.

She watched her father rolling Jacob on his lap and forced back her resentment. There was, perversely, something almost satisfying in his blitheness. She would make peace with him despite it.

She stood and heard herself say, "I'd like to come around again, to spend some time with you, if that's alright."

"Of course." He turned his palms upward and smiled serenely. "Our place is your place. Come and go as you please."

SIXTY-TWO

"You can't count on any warning."

"No." She tensed up.

"Because, wham!" He cut the power. "The engine can fail at any time."

Kate was daydreaming. In place of the darkening ceiling she'd substituted an infinite blue sky. With her eyes shut there was a cockpit and she could tilt the horizon left and right and pull the nose through each point of the compass, unreeling turns at will, free to head off in any direction. Shadows lay between the rolling hills and wind lines fanned out on the lake below, which flashed silver and gray as she turned through the early morning sun.

"And when it does you've got to be ready. The response has to be instantaneous. There's no time to think."

Already, Kate imagined, she'd responded, instinctively pushing the nose down to establish a glide. But her mind was racing to work out the next step. Should she look below for a suitable landing site? Or run through the checks to try to revive the engine? The gap between the alternatives yawned, mocking her inaction.

Meanwhile, the corridor light had definitely angled into the room. There stood Abu in silhouette, and now he was performing his pointless tour, pacing past each of them in turn, yawning with boredom. Another lights-out. Kate thought about the cockpit again. How could she have forgotten the drill? It was as much as she could do to remember that the optimum glide range was just two miles for every thousand feet of height lost. No distance at all. She steadied herself: this was, after all, only a simulated emergency. There was nothing wrong with the engine, and even if there had been, the instructor was in charge.

"Every wasted second counts."

That was true, and yet it didn't matter, for the sky had darkened again, revealing Abu as he turned past Ethan beneath the window slot and tracked back toward the door, passing the arras on the way. Kate's eyes followed him, absently willing the guard out of the room, and then she found that she'd fallen behind his footsteps, her gaze having snagged on George. In the gloom it took a second for the strangeness of his appearance to come clear. The bandages were now a scarf. Even as she understood this change, however, it was overtaken by a sequence of events that took place outside of time, at once in slow motion and on fast-forward, so that what happened appeared both unending and seeming to be over before it began.

One minute Abu was moving beyond George and heading for the door, inspection complete; the next, George had risen through the collapsing tepee of his blankets and begun to move after him. The covers fell noiselessly to the ground, revealing George's arms, one of which appeared longer than the other, because something was hanging down from that hand. Whatever it was glinted maliciously as George swung it at the back of Abu's head. The guard saw nothing coming. He staggered sideways with a grunt, passing through the wedge of corridor light at an odd angle, half falling, half dodging the next blow, which George silently hacked down from on high, as if to drive in a stake. The hammer glanced clumsily off the top of the guard's head. He sank deferentially to one knee.

Kate tried to shout. Yet when she opened her mouth to suck in air her lungs filled with fear instead.

George stepped back to admire his work in the imperceptible pause that followed. Then he advanced again, growling, *"The beast that thou sawest, was and is not . . ."* and around him the space came alive. Clay was on his feet beside Kate. She was dimly aware that Ethan had also sprung up at the far end of the room. George's voice rose, *". . . and shall ascend out of the bottomless pit, and go into perdition . . . ,"* and Kate found that she, too, was clawing her way upright, but once standing she did not know what to do. Time slowed down further. George yelled, *". . . they that dwell on the earth shall wonder! . . ."* as he closed in on Abu with the steel hammer raised again, his one eye black and enraged and fixed upon the guard's face. Kate heard everything distinctly—George's broken scream, *". . . for he is the Lord of lords . . . ,"* Abu's left hand scrabbling over the boards as he steadied himself from toppling further sideways, and the thump of Ethan's boots as he launched himself forward into the fray. Still down on one knee, Abu dug at the pocket of his combats, a prospective bridegroom fumbling for the ring. He looked confusedly down at his hands. The slick of blood on his forehead shone as it caught the light. Then George was above him again, lashing out. The hammer came down in a graceful arc to meet Abu's curls.

Time now stopped: a second nailed in place. As the steel teeth caught in the top of Abu's head, his lap exploded. A white flame lit George's chest. Ethan, who must have thrown himself in the half-beat before George struck, crashed headlong into him as the gun went off.

Kate screamed but heard nothing. The crunch of metal into bone, the horror of a gunshot at close quarters, the recklessness of Ethan's intervention; it all happened right there in front of her, but she was encased in glass. There were just confusing details. George's shirt was undone. The optimum glide speed was seventy knots. His chest and stomach were revolting, black with dirt despite the lightning. Of course you worked out where to land before fiddling with the engine. No part of Ethan touched the ground as he arrived, an all-star making his tackle. Look for a field without power cables, preferably away from roads or houses. Diane, crouched by the wall, had her hands over her ears and her eyes squeezed shut. George's face, by contrast, was split in two, closed half, open half; both jerked back with the flash, as if in consternation. No, there weren't parachutes in a mono-prop trainer. The gun knocked George backward and Ethan drove him sideways and Abu followed, dragged forward by the claw hammer, which was still embedded in his head.

Ethan rolled sideways and George struggled out from beneath him, his fist still white on the shaft. Abu was stretched forward, his arms flung out before him, prostrate in prayer. He appeared to nod in agreement as George yanked the hammerhead clear. Then the guard mumbled something, slumped sideways, and reached for his knees in an attempt to curl up. Kate realized she was standing over him, inspecting a flap of forehead that had torn forward. It made his fringe unnaturally long, obscuring his eyes. She would have liked to lift the flap clear so as to see his expression, but felt herself pulled roughly back by Clay before she had a chance.

"Traitor," Ethan hissed at George. He crouched over the guard's feet, on all fours.

George laughed. Or at least he tried to. The sound began dry and turned wet, becoming a shapeless gargle. With his free hand he clawed at the scarf of bandages, now black instead of gray, intent on scratching an itch. Then he held bloody fingers up to his eye and squinted. The sight seemed to distract him for a moment.

"Jesus fucking Christ." Clay's laughter was manic. "This hasn't happened, please, no, *no, please!*" He still had hold of Kate's arm and was her pulling toward Diane, further from the action.

Each breath George took sounded like the suck of an emptying sink. He continued to stare incredulously at his hand until his attention was caught by one of Abu's feet, which twitched. He was curled tight on his side now, and the twitching movement was not his own, but caused by Ethan, who had begun heaving the guard over by his fatigues, presumably to get at his gun.

George seemed to recognize that the moving foot had sinister implications. He advanced on rubber legs, shaking his head. Kate was no more than a couple of yards away, and yet the feeling of separation had worsened; she might as well have been watching actors on a screen. She was paralyzed by panic, her powerlessness now intoxicatingly complete. She felt no impulse to try to warn Ethan, or stop him digging for Abu's pistol, but watched dispassionately as George staggered forward and Ethan looked up and George swatted at him with the hammer, landing a single blow between his eyes.

Ethan keeled over, falling on top of Abu. George sat back on his haunches. His chest was sodden. Blood ran down his arm and hand and dripped from the hammerhead. He looked at it, wiped the silver shaft on his trousers, then tossed the tool away. His mouth fell open. He sank backward without saying anything and lay still.

SIXTY-THREE

A VOICE FOUGHT THE jackhammer heartbeat in Kate's head.

If the engine dies, what do you do first?

Laughable. She wasn't flying. She'd lost control.

So, the voice persisted, take it back. Keep flying—nobody else will.

"Oh, Christ. Oh, fuck." Clay's words were flat.

Each second of inaction eroded the likelihood of success. She struggled to steady herself, biting down on the inside of her mouth. As her teeth met through the skin of her lower lip a spark of pain illuminated the obvious: panic was part of the problem; she must work despite it. She must shake free of Clay, who was still gasping wildly, and make herself go forward to grab Ethan's collar. He was cement heavy. His shirt tore as she hauled, but he came with it, sliding off Abu. He rolled onto his back and didn't move.

"Check his pulse," she told Clay. "Quick."

Galvanized by Kate's tone, Clay hesitated forward, his laughter hollowing out. He bent over Ethan and put a hand to his neck, then started back when Ethan coughed. Diane was fluttering round Kate, looking from George to Abu, treading barefoot in the pool of blood that now connected them. She began to moan, turning Kate's head.

"Don't you fucking start!"

Clay seemed to have caught on. He worked in silence with Kate to lever Abu onto his back. The bit of skull flapped into place as the guard rolled over, which was better, but now the light revealed that one side of his face had been hollowed by the hammer. She forced herself to lean over his mouth, listening. Nothing.

Point the nose down and level the wings.

The gun was still tight in Abu's grip. She unclasped his fingers, one by one, and then the thing was in her hand and astonishingly heavy. Clay had returned to Ethan and began shaking him, urging him to open his eyes. Then he was hissing at Diane, whose moaning had ramped up again to a low wail.

"Shut up. You'll fetch the other one."

That made no difference, the scream just got louder, so Kate turned to help. She waved Diane up out of the puddle and steered her tenderly to the door, amazed at how compliant and quiet the girl instantly became, until she realized she was still holding the gun and directing her with its barrel. Diane's face was white as bone. Kate raised both hands, palms forward, so that the gun barrel waved at the ceiling. Now she found herself in the film too, the good cop reassuring a victim she meant no harm. The sensation was ridiculous; adrenaline made her want to laugh. She dropped her arms and held them behind her back, with the gun out of sight.

"Come on, look at me," Clay urged. "Open your eyes. Open your eyes!"

Ethan sighed in apparent response. Kate turned to see Clay slap him roughly about the face. Ethan's eyelids flickered for a second and then shut.

"No! Wake up! We've got to get out of here."

The eyes blinked open again and Ethan rolled to his side, planted a hand, pushed himself up. He came to. As he took in the scene a look of anguish overran his expression. He seemed to want to say something, but although his lips were moving no words came out. While Kate watched, a line of blood ran from his forehead down the side of his nose and into the darkness of his beard. He was staring at her, and then he was staring past her. His consternation melted into apparent relief. The arm supporting him gave at the elbow, and he sank sideways. From the floor, his contented gaze drifted from Kate's face to the space over her shoulder again. He nodded and smiled, this time managing a whisper. The words were barely intelligible, but sounded like "Kate . . . too Kate." She mouthed his name back.

Once you've set up the glide, find a safe way down.

She broke from staring at Ethan and turned to Clay for help, but found that he too was looking past her in the direction of the door. She swiveled further to follow his gaze, and there was Khalid, holding Diane by the hair, a pistol pressed against her temple. Both of them had their mouths open in shared panic. Khalid's voice cracked when he spoke.

"Stop now."

There was no decision, no words with which to make one, no pictures spelling out consequences. Just a split second, and one route out. Kate felt an extraordinary pulse of fear shoot from the soles of her feet to her scalp. She brought the gun up and fired without aiming. As she did so, Khalid pulled his own trigger. Kate's hand kicked upward with the recoil. She was a conductor, whipping with her baton, and Khalid was a dancer, in step. He pirouetted, flinging Diane away. In unison the pair fell apart and crashed to the floor.

SIXTY-FOUR

THE SAME ORDER, over and over again: "Open . . .
your . . . eyes."

He tried to obey, but couldn't do so for long. Open or shut, it
made no difference anyway. There was just the memory of a flat
hammerhead swinging to meet him. A single coin, flung in pay-
ment. When it hit, the pain had nothing to do with his forehead,
but came from everywhere else at once. It tasted of rust and
smelled of ammonia and split the air like a jet overhead. You had
to hand it to mad old George. For a cripple with one eye, he was
a good shot.

Then the smell was cordite and blood had run into his mouth
and the memory of a real sound registered, a gunshot. Abu had
managed to get off a round. That meant an emergency, a combat
situation. Ethan struggled again to comply with the order, and
found himself staring up at Clay, which was instantly reassuring.
The American could deputize until reinforcements arrived. He

let himself sink back beneath the surface and allowed Clay to deal with the specifics of who had shot whom. The art of delegation was, after all, the cornerstone of good leadership.

"No, wake up, we've got to get out of here."

Not real orders, just nagging. Yap yap yap. It took a while for the sense of Kate's words to catch up with her insistent tone. She was probably right, though; best if he fell in with the rest of the troops. All hands on deck, a full complement for the parade. Yet reengaging took real effort; he seemed to be pushing the building up off its foundations in levering himself upright, and once there had to struggle to stop the scene from pulsing in and out of focus.

The horror registered. One man down in a lake of blood. The hostile down too. Kate, standing straight, her hands behind her back. And behind her, Diane, edging toward the open door.

It seemed he would have to find the strength to intervene after all, but then he saw Khalid appear over Kate's shoulder. Though he was just a kid, he had the training. Ethan was fully confident of his abilities. And rightly: the lad was swift to understand their predicament, he devised a solution there and then, and he showed great foresight in having brought the proper hardware for the job. In two quick steps he was at Diane's side, a handful of her hair in one hand, his revolver pressed against her head with the other. His eyes were as wide as hers, but in acting decisively he had taken control.

Poor old Kate! Ethan felt sorry for her but could not help smiling as the hinge of his elbow began to give and he allowed himself to subside. "Late," he whispered. "Too late."

Khalid gave them the order to stop, his voice admirably calm. Considering the mess before him, he was coping well. The first half of a thought, involving Abu and George and wrongs and rights and retribution, began to form, and then there was more lightning and the room cracked in two.

Either he blacked out again in the firefight, or simply couldn't keep up. It seemed to take Ethan ages to work out what was happening, and as long again to infer why. Diane was on her side with an arm twisted up behind her back and Clay was kneeling beside her saying "No" between gulps of fearful laughter, and Kate was stepping over Abu toward Khalid, who was also stretched out on the floor. He clearly wasn't going anywhere, yet Kate was pointing at him as if he might disappear at any moment. Not pointing, Ethan realized, but aiming. She retreated a few steps, an eye fixed on Khalid all the time, and knelt down next to George. As Ethan clambered to his feet Kate pulled a sheet from the pile that George had discarded and began to tear it into strips. Quietly she pleaded: "Come on, Ethan, you have to help me."

He was already at her side, hovering over Khalid, staring down into the young guard's eyes, which relaxed. Or at least the pupils grew. "Please, mercy," Khalid whispered, and again, "mercy, please." To have seen the hurt done to Abu's face was bad enough. A fist rose in Ethan's throat as he swept the lad's fringe out of his eyes.

Clay's laughter subsided to sobs. Then it stopped entirely and he said, "Half her face is gone. The whole of one side of her head." There was a matter-of-fact, prerecorded ring to his voice.

Kate was working with a strip of bandage, sorting out a tourniquet for the young guard's legs, which, writhing down below, must also have been injured. Ethan cradled his head. The youngster's eyes looked lost and the insides of his lips were blue. He gasped, as if cold. Ethan loosened the boy's jacket at the throat to reveal a white T-shirt, now turning red. When he pulled the coat farther apart he saw a hole below the right shoulder, and then the intolerable redness welled through it again, bleeding across more white chest. Arsenal colors. Ethan pressed the jacket back down with his palm against the hole and ordered, "More bandages." Below, Kate's tourniquet had stilled Khalid's legs. Ethan felt an unexpected rush of gratitude toward her; ever practical, she knew what she was doing. She rolled Khalid over to stop him choking. As Ethan continued to stare down at the lad's furrowed brow, she was busy fastening strips of sheet behind his back. And after that she was off again, checking on Abu, before gliding over to Clay and Diane. The boy went slack, then frowned in confusion as tears fell from Ethan's nose into his face.

"Have mercy."

Clay's voice: "No, no. She can't end like this."

"It's okay, Khalid. You're going to be fine."

"Spare me."

"You're alright. Hang in there, son."

"She's gone, Clay."

"Forgive me," Khalid whispered.

"Dead."

"There's really nothing to forgive." Ethan smiled.

"Her beautiful face."

Ethan glanced across to Clay, who was still bent shivering over Diane. Beside him Kate was staring at that watch, insistently tapping its face. The sight was incredibly tiring, as was her voice saying: "We have to go now! We must get as far away as possible before the morning changeover. Clay. Ethan. Now. Now!"

Ethan looked back down at Khalid.

"Never meant for this harm."

"You've done very well. Leave the rest to me. Don't worry. I'll run things until Sadiq shows. We'll call in medics."

"Besides which, anybody might have heard the shots."

"They'll decorate you for this. Both of us."

"We've no idea how far away they are." Never mind her first-aid help, Kate's insistent voice was becoming maddening. "Every second counts," she was yelling now. *"Every second counts!"*

Clay's shivering turned into silent hysterics again, visible across the room. Then he stood, put one hand on his hip, and ran the other across his shaven head, staring down at Diane as if she were a hard problem he had to solve. Meanwhile Kate gathered up a blanket and began to swaddle the girl's corpse.

Ethan looked back at Khalid, laboring there in his lap. He stared down at him a long while, head bowed, overcome with feeling. Fearing that the boy's face was turning gray, he tried shifting him into a more comfortable position. The lad's arm would not come forward. It was tied behind his back. Aghast, Ethan saw that the bandages were shackles. The treachery dawned on him: Kate had bound his hands and feet.

Now Clay was trying to pry Ethan out from under the boy. He'd stuck his head under Ethan's arm and was straining upward in vain.

"Come on," Clay said. "She's right. We must go *now*."

He nodded at Kate in the doorway. The scale of her betrayal

suddenly loomed. Ethan laid Khalid's head gently on the boards. Feigning weakness, he allowed himself to be pulled up straight, an arm around Clay's wiry shoulders, his chin pressing heavily into the top of the smaller man's head, which smelled oddly clean in the instant before Ethan's forearm became a bar pinned across his throat. From there it was straightforward to rip Clay's other hand up behind his back into a half nelson, and a necessary demonstration of authority, strength and commitment to push that hand up until the shoulder cracked and the American made a noise, albeit muffled by the knot of his clamped windpipe.

"Nobody's going anywhere," Ethan explained.

Kate took a couple of steps toward them, then stopped short. Her mouth, twisting for words, was the only movement in a blank face. "What are you talking about?"

Clay sounded trapped inside himself. Since any noise was bad, Ethan tightened his grip. A speech about loyalty and fidelity would have been appropriate, but this wasn't the time for explanations, and anyway, the others had proven themselves incapable of comprehending the new world order. One man down, one badly wounded, two hostiles quelled. Clay, despite his childish struggling, under control. Only Kate remained. He'd soon have the situation in hand, and then it would just be a matter of waiting until the balaclava showed. Given time, he would understand. *He* was the medium through which to atone.

The back of Ethan's forearm was wet with drool. Clay seemed to have slackened. Ethan released his grip minutely, but long enough to allow Clay to cough a word.

"Gun."

Clay's foot stubbed the pistol from Khalid's side, sending it across the floor. A track faded in the wetness. Kate stared down at the gun, then demonstrated why she didn't need it, by raising both hands. One still held Abu's revolver; two clumps of keys hung on different lengths of chain from the other.

That presented a tactical problem, but not one that Ethan couldn't overcome. Kate's allegiance had shifted too, after all. That was a weakness he could exploit. Ethan had already tightened his hold on Clay again; now he crunched Clay's neck harder and lifted him, by the ripped arm, a few inches from the floor.

"No," Ethan repeated. "You can't leave now, Kate. Not alone."

Her soft lips hardened to a blue line. She leveled the pistol at Ethan, shut one eye—comical, really—and said, gently, "Ethan, you must let Clay go."

In response Ethan leaned farther back. There was nothing to Clay, just skin, hair, and bone, all jiggling to the rhythm of his feet. Ethan's right arm was rigid with veins, but, in the scheme of things, still relaxed. He might easily have dug for more strength and broken Clay's neck. Indeed, the barrel, waving in his direction, just feet away, so angered Ethan that he was tempted. If it had not been for Khalid's plaintive whimpering, there, at his feet, he would have risked the sacrifice. But the boy was vulnerable and in pain and Ethan felt the responsibility welling up. True valor meant taking that responsibility, by putting unit before self. And Kate seemed so placid, taking aim. Her one open eye was bottomless. She had drawn a bead on Ethan's forehead and, in the calm otherness of her expression, he saw that she was capable of pulling the trigger again. Who knew what she might go on to do after that? Khalid moaned again. All for one. Esprit de corps. There was no way Ethan could sacrifice a comrade. He stepped back from Clay, letting him fall. The American sank to his hands and knees.

Still, the accusatory finger of Kate's gun did not waver. Clay half crawled, half clambered to her side, picking up Khalid's pistol on his way. Four eyes held Ethan in place as the pair backed from the room, and then it was as much as he could do to stand to attention as they closed the door. After some fumbling, the lock chopped shut.

SIXTY-FIVE

ETHAN DRAGGED THE BOY clear of the lake. Then he untied him, tore fresh strips of sheet, and sat him up to bind his shoulder, over and under, round and round: a field dressing the old man would have been proud of. Working methodically, he made a bed of the cleanest remaining blankets, rolled one into a pillow. In time the boy's eyes closed and tear tracks dried across his cheeks, yet he stayed warm.

Though Ethan beat the drum of the door periodically, nobody answered. At first this was a terrible frustration, but, after a while, with Khalid mumbling reassurances from deep within his dream, he made a blessing of the delay and turned to address other tasks.

There was much to do.

First, he mopped the floor as best he could, using George's mound of blankets to soak up the spilled blood. His footprints dried in the smear. Never mind; they would see he had made an effort. Next, he drew the three bodies into an orderly line. That looked right to begin with, and even better when he afforded Abu a few feet of decorous privacy, drawing him away from the other two. As big as a bear, even in death. The poor man's forehead. Ethan pressed the torn scalp back into place and, after deliberating, pulled the cover from Diane (it was almost unstained) and laid it solemnly across Abu. Two bloody rags were enough to mask the dead hostages' faces.

A cowbell sounded in the distance, so Ethan pulled himself up to the window and shouted. Down below, the river ran black beneath the diamond sky. He called out again, but still nobody answered.

On watch he grew cold and, fearing Khalid would feel the same, drew the boy up onto his knees, hugged him close to his chest. The young guard breathed through cracked lips; his eyelashes were black against the gray halftone of his cheeks. Transfixed by the stillness of the boy's face, Ethan joined him in sleep.

Religious music. A coffin sitting on a conveyor belt. The vicar's voice intoning and the coffin starting forward in a shudder of pedals. His father's hand squeezing his own as two screens slid inward and a curtain began to drop. That's all, folks. Despite the incantation, the mechanics of all this rolling and sliding and lowering were dimly audible. Why could he not imagine where his mother had gone? Was he even trying? No. Because she could have chosen not to leave. Likewise, it was enough that Kate and Clay were elsewhere, and that he had chosen to stay behind. They no longer mattered. A decision had never felt so right. He'd proven himself through it, done something absolute for once, taken a stand. The screens ran into and past one another end-lessly, growing noisier, until the sound was that of an engine, recognizable as it shuddered to a halt.

The balaclava was already in the room, shouting. Ethan smiled up at him.

"They rushed us, sir. They gained the upper hand."

More shouting. A mist of spit in the early sun. Though un-derstandable, the boss's rage was unnerving.

"One of them had that hammer. From the rafters. You can't blame Mr. Abu. I apologize unreservedly. It was a terrible over-sight on my behalf."

Sadiq had arrived, too. At the balaclava's request, the fat guard uncovered each of the three bodies and bent to feel each for a pulse. Understandable but, as Ethan explained, futile. He tried to give a proper report of what had happened, then talked of the necessary improvements the operation should make for next time, but nobody seemed to listen. Instead Sadiq began trying to wrest Khalid from Ethan's grasp, with such brutality that Ethan objected.

"No! Sir. Tell him. Gently!"

The balaclava drew a revolver from inside his jacket and fired it once, aiming at Ethan's knee. At first Ethan did not know for sure that he had been hit. He felt only a tremendous shock, a jolt-ing of every fiber, which, since there was no pain, could equally have been caused by the impact of a bullet or the revelation that the leader was prepared to fire one at him. Next he was buried, chest deep, in a weakness as thick as snow. His hands lost the power to grip. Sadiq yanked poor Khalid from his heavy, useless arms and dragged him clear. And then the numbness retreated, from everywhere but his injured leg. He seemed suddenly hot. Ethan looked down to see the dark edge of a wound, beneath singed trousers, black cloth livid with blood.

Sadiq began yelling at Khalid, evidently distraught. When he got no response, he started shaking the boy roughly by the shoulders, knocking his head against the boards. Ethan wished he could intervene, but found himself unable to get up. A shocking lassitude left him powerless. Mercifully, the balaclava stepped in to help. He muttered something at Sadiq, stopping him instantly, then watched him waddle from the room. Once alone with Ethan, the balaclava paused and his eyes turned glassy, deep in thought.

Ethan had a reassuring idea of his own, and said it out loud: "Kneecap, sir. Yes. The knee is my punishment."

"Eh?"

"I accept it."

"You accept what?"

Ethan didn't press the point, because the balaclava appeared distracted. He turned and went to the middle of the room and stood looking down at Khalid and across at Abu and in the direction of the other two bodies and finally back at Ethan, and then he scratched his head, as if unsure of who was missing.

The numbness retreated further, became a shrinking no-go zone around the wound itself. Imagine the scar! Ethan pushed himself back against the wall, so that he was at least sitting up straight. Of course the leader would need some time to take all this in.

"Where are they?"

"I'm sorry?"

"Where have your friends gone?"

"Oh, right. AWOL. They didn't say."

The balaclava snorted.

"I ask again. Where?"

"Really," Ethan explained, "I don't know. As I say, I tried to stop them. I'll take my share of the blame."

The balaclava dropped to his heels, so that he was at Ethan's level, which was kind. He looked suddenly Indian again, squatting there, head wobbling.

"I want to know when my hostages escaped and where they think they are going. You must tell me, now."

In earnest Ethan replied, "I'd say they set off at about nineteen hundred hours. Abu came in about then, sir, at the start of the night watch." Dishonor . . . "But as to their plans, I truly don't know where they're headed." Deserter . . . "I'm sure they can't have got far in one night. Both are weak, neither have any training." Indiscipline . . . "If I can help with the recovery exercise, you must let me. . . ." He paused, unsure of what he'd said or thought. "We did our best to detain them. Khalid in particular deserves praise." Betrayal . . . "Again, I'm sorry."

"I will count to three."

"Sir. Honestly."

"One."

The balaclava lifted his pistol and aimed it at Ethan's head. The simplicity of the gesture. Its power to teach. Of course Ethan's knee was not punishment enough. Look at the place. Captives lost. Men *dead*. The whole operation blown. And that cursed hammer! All of it was his fault. Way up behind the steady gun barrel two eyes blinked, then shone.

"Two."

If he'd had an answer, Ethan would so gladly have given it, but since he didn't have one, answering couldn't be the point. The point was accepting what those brown eyes meant. They were sure enough to encompass Ethan's failure, unequivocal enough to act upon it, deep enough to return his love.

The balaclava took a breath.

Was there anything more noble than martyrdom?

The gun barrel bobbed and the leader stood up and pressed it against Ethan's upturned forehead to deliver his blessing.

Anointment: an act of consecration.

The giving of a new life.

Ethan closed his eyes on "Three."

SIXTY-SIX

THEY BROKE THROUGH CLOUD well below a thousand feet, the fields and villages surrounding Lyneham abstract behind swathes of rain. She felt no sense of homecoming; this could have been anywhere. Though her mother sat beside her, Kate had never felt so alone. The RAF crew's attentiveness somehow made the separateness worse: she was the hole at the center of everyone's attention.

The publicity had begun ahead of their arrival in Delhi. She knew it had yet to peak. But the more words she read describing their escape, the less it seemed to be her and Clay the reporters were writing about. The reality came in little flurries; nothing was yet in perspective. The smell of polish in the hotel lobby was more astonishing than her first hot drink; the sight of clouds from above more transfixing than her mother's face. Of course it was a *miracle*, all the more piquant for the *tragic fate* of the others, and yet those words could not illuminate what had happened. Though *terror, hardship,* and *loss* painted a picture from afar, they conveyed nothing of a raised hammer, or the iron boards, or a boy going cold in your arms.

"Love, there'll be a crowd. Photographers. You might want to freshen up."

Her mother's makeup bag settled gently in her lap. Seeing that smile, she had no alternative but to beam back. Immediately, though, any outward happiness was again inappropriate. Since the news about Ethan had come through, grief was required. Resetting her expression in the pop-up mirror, Kate mollified her mother with mascara, as she would never have done before.

She and Clay had, separately and together, given the army officers and foreign ministry officials and embassy representatives numerous accounts of their flight. Though at the time there had only been fear, she'd since relived the detail of their route downstream, following the starlit river through the night. Wherever the stream went, they reasoned, it would eventually run through people. When dawn arrived they stopped in a culvert full of snow between the riverbank and the road, intending to hold out for nightfall again. Clay was certain the sporadic rumble of dark green trucks meant Indian military; Kate feared more militants: for all they knew the river ran through Pakistan. In the end they grew so numb with cold that the dilemma solved itself. The first truck, wary of vagrants, perhaps, spattered them with gritty slush. The next pulled over. Its albino driver startled Kate, and Clay had to hold her from running, yet the officer was courteous and believing; he made an immediate three-point turn and radioed ahead to Srinigar.

"Kate," her mother now began.

They were taxiing now, across slick tarmac. She handed the makeup bag back.

"Remember, Rachel will be here to meet you."

So much was strange she'd stopped trying to make sense of it. Captivity made a mockery of all the old tensions, anyway: Whatever the truth of the past, she had no alternative but to score a line beneath it and start again. Rachel was her sister, and Ethan was gone. The sight of him standing there, wooden-faced, his madness as frightening as it was pitiful, pinprick pupils resolute even as Clay shut the door. How could she explain to Rachel the steps that led Ethan there? The six months of captivity might equally be summarized in a column of text or remain untellable for a lifetime. She'd already been inundated with offers from newspapers wanting her exclusive account, yet right now could not imagine where she would begin. The journal would not have helped: if anything she now felt pleased to have left it behind. Her past ambitions seemed as insignificant as the bickering that had accompanied them. She had turned all the reporters down. It was all that she and Clay could do to convince people of the circumstances surrounding the end, and even then, no matter how she tried to explain it, their having left him dwarfed Ethan's own betrayals.

But every second counted. There had been no turning back.

Following their instructions, the army had found the village, and the deserted compound, but too late.

One, two, three . . . four bodies.

From the cursory description there had been the hope, for a morning, that he'd come to his senses and somehow followed.

The "youth" could have been Khalid. By the time of the first Delhi interviews, though, photographic evidence confirmed otherwise.

"You say *you* locked him in the cell?" The consular official clicked his pen nervously, not wanting to commit the fact to paper. "Why?"

"Otherwise"—she spread the photographs out—"there would have been six."

The plane had stopped. Crew members busied themselves by the door. Through her window, Kate saw men in uniform struggling with a triangle of metal steps, trying to maneuver it into place. An expectant semicircle of people stood a little way off beneath the shifting roof of their umbrellas. The captain, all epaulets, had come back down the plane to wish her well in person, and her mother was thanking him for that. In the brief pause that followed, she took Kate's hand and continued speaking.

"The waiting turned Rachel inside out. It changed her." Here she trailed off, before picking up another thread. "We have to stick together. You understand what I'm saying?"

"Of course."

Her mother's eyes were watery behind her glasses as Kate helped her up. She took them off and dabbed her face with a handkerchief, suddenly very old. Their roles over the last few days had inverted briefly: Kate paused to let her mother collect herself, led her mother to the door.

At the top of the steps, she faltered. Her right hand went to her left elbow for the reassurance of Clay's watch, still high on her forearm. She had tried to give it back to him when they parted in Delhi for the final time, but he insisted she keep it. There followed an awkward moment, in which his kindness threatened to spill over into something more. Despite herself, she had turned away. Seated in the finery of Kate's hotel lobby, the new clothes and frosted glass coffee table with its marble chess set and matching ashtray made her feel overwhelmingly present in a place and time where, above all, Ethan was not. He belonged to a past that would always overshadow her and Clay.

The hand cupping her face had fallen to her shoulder. Clay's laughter was already wry again. "Just keep the watch, to remember me by," he said.

Flashbulbs popped pathetically as she descended, swamped by the falling rain. The semicircle broke apart to meet their advance, but nobody seemed to be speaking, which gave the scene a mimed quality, making her descent down the metal steps stagier still. Apart from her sister, Kate recognized nobody to begin with. Then the umbrella above Rachel wavered and the man holding it was her father. He had his arm around Rachel's shoulders. The red and white triangles of the umbrella revolved as the pair advanced beneath it, squeezing past the reporters. At the sight of the two of them Kate stopped, opened her arms wide.

EPILOGUE

One circuit of the airfield. Less than five minutes from takeoff to landing. She'd flown the same pattern countless times before, and yet the intervening time made everything unfamiliar. The stretch upwind seemed to take an eternity. She banked a little early, staring back down the glassy wing in a climbing turn, and wobbled level at an odd angle to the runway. Now she was heading straight at the sun.

She corrected her course, yelling instructions like a novice: "Power, altitude, trim." These words readied the plane for the easy, downwind leg. She called out the prelanding checks and all of a sudden there, before her, stood thirty seconds of doing, well, nothing.

She tried to take in the silver lake, the pale green of the hills below, darker dots of trees, their long shadows cast by the morning glare. But the incredible sense of space dwarfed all detail: before the view had really registered she was calling out more checks, watching the landing point track backward down to her distant left, thinking about the penultimate, descending turn.

"Uniform Golf Whiskey turning base."

The end of the runway inched up the side window. She forced herself to relax the stranglehold of her hand on the control column, banked to thirty degrees, leaning forward to see the runway come into view ahead of the propeller. As the knots dropped, and the tree line flashed below, and the little black shadow racing and hopping in the dirt grew, she felt her heartbeat quicken. Low sun flashed off a car windscreen as it turned in the car park, down to her left. Distracted, she caught a glimpse of her sister leaning on the railings, a mug of tea in her hand.

Since Rachel's confession they had come a long way. Her contrition was shot through with its own grief for Ethan, which cut to Kate's heart. She had time for just one thought as the plane descended: how unexpected it was of Rachel to have risen so early in this show of support.

Every minute detail of the scene was alive and scrolling up to meet her. It was vital to keep the nose inched into wind until the last instant, and then to kick it right with the rudder as she rounded out to hold the plane steady for the last foot or two before it sank, to settle gently, on the strip.

Yet she was rusty, over eager. Perhaps too keen to impress. She stamped right and pulled the nose up early, with the plane still a fraction too fast, and felt it balloon and drift. Overcompensating, she dropped the nose, knowing as she did so that she'd missed the aiming point and would thump ignominiously into the blacktop a hundred yards too late. The airframe shuddered with the first bounce. Sinking back down seemed to take an age: it was as if she were landing in a hole. Finally, though, her seat was thrumming to the asphalt again: she was driving, not flying, taxiing along the gravel track to park up before the club house.

Undoing the harness, her reflection swam in the perspex. No longer alone. Through the cockpit side-window she watched Rachel wave once, push off the rail and walk towards her, an outline against the sun.